COURT

OF

HONOR

Books by William P. Wood

Rampage
Gangland
Fugitive City
*Court of Honor**

* Published by POCKET BOOKS

COURT
OF
HONOR

William P. Wood

POCKET BOOKS

New York   London   Toronto   Sydney   Tokyo   Singapore

POCKET BOOKS, a division of Simon & Schuster Inc.
1230 Avenue of the Americas, New York, NY 10020

Copyright © 1991 by William Wood

All rights reserved, including the right to reproduce
this book or portions thereof in any form whatsoever.
For information address Pocket Books, 1230 Avenue
of the Americas, New York, NY 10020

Wood, William P.
    Court of honor / William P. Wood.
        p.   cm.
    ISBN 0-671-73176-9 : $20.00
    I. Title.
    PS3573.0599C6   1991
    813'.54—dc20   91-4211
                                                                             CIP

First Pocket Books hardcover printing November 1991

10 9 8 7 6 5 4 3 2 1

POCKET and colophon are registered trademarks of
Simon & Schuster Inc.

Printed in the U.S.A.

For Jane and Jack,
and the others who make justice seem inevitable

"And since no Crime could be e're Lawes were fram'd;
  Lawes dearly taught us how to know offence;
Had Lawes not been, we never had been blam'd;
  For not to know we sin, is innocence."
                          —SIR WILLIAM DEVANANT

COURT
OF
HONOR

1

J UST AFTER IT OPENED IN THE MORNING, EVAN SOIKA WALKED INTO the Best Buy gas station's small store.

The owner was behind the cash-register counter pouring a large beaker of water into the coffee machine.

"I'll have some fresh in a couple of minutes," Prentice said.

"I don't want any coffee."

Prentice turned on the big coffee machine, which immediately began gurgling. "I always like the first cup in the morning the best."

"I just need some gas."

"What pump you at?"

"How should I know?"

"They all have numbers over them."

"You look. You tell me."

Prentice peered past Evan Soika. Parked in the center pump island was a green compact car, older model. "You're at number eight. You really want premium?"

"That's where I parked?"

"Yeah. Unleaded premium."

"That's what I want."

It was hard to talk because Evan Soika had walked from the cash-register counter, down the small store's narrow aisles. He glanced at the cans of beans and ravioli, chocolate pudding. He fingered the

1

displays of beef jerky and bags of potato chips, anything people could buy on the run.

Prentice took off his coat and hung it behind the men's room door, just to the side of the cash-register counter. He kept an eye on Evan Soika wandering the aisles. Soika wore a long gray overcoat, because the March early morning was chill, the sun only a red-hued ball in Santa Maria's gray sky. One sleeve of the coat was badly torn. Soika kept his right arm at his side stiffly. His hair was uncombed and he chewed his gum aggressively, unpleasantly. He looked flushed in the store's fluorescent lights.

"How much?" Prentice asked, pushing a stack of newspapers against the cash register. The coffee machine gurgled.

Soika paused, holding a tiny can of pork and beans. "How much what?"

"Gas. How much do you want?"

"I don't know."

"Fill up?"

"Sure."

"Well, how much do you want then?"

Soika put down the can. "I ain't put anything in yet."

"You pay here before you pump any gas."

"You get the money before I get any gas? That's great."

"That's way the company set it up. People drive away without paying."

"Tough shit."

"Can't stay in business that way."

Soika grinned. "I don't know how much gas I want." He looked into the frozen food section, the piles of TV dinners, then at the bottles of inexpensive wine and soft drinks. "You're the only place open around here." He walked back to Prentice at the cash register.

"I'm an early bird."

"No customers so early."

"They come. All the time."

"Nobody here now."

"It gets busy pretty quick."

"Yeah?"

"I'm not the only one gets up early."

Soika nodded. "I'm here."

Prentice stood close to the cash register. Just below it, on a tight shelf, was the .45 pistol the company said he could keep for emergencies. "People come in here all the time, all day," he said.

2

"I been up all night," Soika said, his stiff right arm locked as if splinted.

"Work late?"

"Do I look like I been up all night?"

"No. You look pretty good."

"You sure?"

"Get some coffee in you. Starts the day off right for me."

"Yeah?" Soika said, glancing around the store once more, outside at the pumps and his lone car.

"Brighten you up."

"Okay. I changed my mind. Give me some coffee."

Prentice turned, trying to smile because he was nervous now. "It isn't quite ready. It's a big machine, gives out forty-eight cups before I change it again."

"Okay. I want some chips, something to chew on, couple of beers." Soika one-handedly reached around and brought the cans and bags in front of Prentice at the cash register.

"Going on a trip?"

"What?"

"You taking a trip?"

"No."

"Never mind. Look like things you eat on the road," he said, charging up the food. No one else had driven into the gas station at five-thirty, and the North Wilmont Avenue neighborhood of small stores was deserted.

"It's none of your business," Soika said, coming beside the counter, almost at Prentice's side.

"I just asked. I don't care."

"I know you don't care. You just asked because you're a fucker."

Prentice's head jerked up. He said calmly, "You got eight dollars here. How much gas do you want outside?"

"You hear me?"

"Sure I did."

"You don't care I called you a fucker?"

"All I want to do is take care of your gas and food."

Soika grinned again. "Give me some coffee now. It's ready."

Prentice turned to check. "It's not. I hear it when it's done."

Soika pointed a sawed-off shotgun at him when he turned back. "Give me your fucking money." He shouted it.

Prentice stepped back from the cash register. "I don't care. It's not mine."

3

Outside the streetlights automatically went off in the gray dawn.

"Give me the fucking money," Soika shouted, holding the short-barreled shotgun with both hands, pressing it against Prentice's jaw.

Prentice tapped the cash register's electronic keys, jamming his hand into the bills, pushing them up and out hurriedly toward Soika. Soika used one hand to wad the bills into his overcoat pocket.

Outside, approaching rapidly, Prentice heard sirens. Their sound was clean in the empty morning.

"They better not be coming here," Soika yelled, head twisting around, looking, staring back at Prentice.

"They can't be. They got to be going someplace else."

Two Santa Maria city police squad cars angled abruptly to a stop alongside the Best Buy's pumps and cops jumped out, guns drawn.

Soika stopped chewing his gum. The shotgun pressed brutally into Prentice's clenched jaw.

IN AUGUST, LATER THAT YEAR, ON A HOT, DRIZZLING DAY, TWO men sat arguing in a large conference room in the Department of Justice in Washington, D.C.

"You want me to go easy on them because they're judges," Neil Roemer said belligerently.

"I did not say that," Paul Cleary answered. He was Roemer's superior, the Assistant Attorney-General.

"It's the only explanation. You want to tie my hands." Roemer extended his wrists as if seeking the rope.

Breathing deeply, Cleary said, "All I've done is raise a question about your ways and means." He felt dulled. The damp weather probably. Also remember to take the low blood pressure medicine on the hour.

Roemer snorted in anger, got up, and paced the otherwise empty conference room. Cleary studied him. He saw a middle-aged man with a square pink face and tightly groomed graying hair and mustache. Broad shouldered from his years as a boxer, with a paradoxical double chin and black eyes. Dressed in simple creased slacks and a blue blazer and his trademark blue suspenders.

We laughed at him, Cleary thought. We imagined we were so much smarter than him.

Roemer turned to face Cleary combatively. What does he see? Cleary wondered. I'm older, nearly sixty, third in the nation's law enforcement hierarchy. Cleary was slouched in a high-backed leather chair at the long table, dressed for a Southern summer in a pale-green and white seersucker suit and diffidently knotted bow tie. His thatch of white hair drooped down his forehead. I still probably look like a law school dean, he thought.

Every so often during the brawling meeting, Cleary sipped from a porcelain cup of steaming tea and regretted not bringing an umbrella on a rainy day.

Roemer had his hands on his hips. "Paul, we've staffed out this operation, we've gotten reviews, we staffed it again. Now we've got the Special Projects Committee to sign off on it, and you're trying to tie me up with last-minute objections. I know how it's done and I sure as hell resent it."

Of course you know how it's done, Cleary thought. You survived three presidents and you've worked with U.S. Attorneys from Seattle to Orlando. You're a seasoned infighter in these marble corridors, and I'm only the former dean of Boston University Law School. All I ever did was teach antitrust law to classes of prospective lawyers until the new administration in Washington decided I was the man to lend a distinguished name to the Justice Department.

They didn't tell me how to put a leash on you, Neil. He sipped the tea, thinking how to answer Roemer. He thought of sitting in the faculty lounge, watching Roemer on TV announcing some investigation for bribery, some high-level prosecution for betrayal of public trust. You were so pompous, so absurd in a plain white shirt, rolled-up sleeves, those blue suspenders. I made jokes that you looked like a Southern demagogue. What a fool. What an underestimation.

I taught antitrust law, Cleary thought, but compared to you, Neil, I'm a wide-eyed child. I can't match the Byzantine turn of your mind, the serpentine twists you build into every investigation.

But you get results. You're a legend around here.

You're untouchable.

Cleary struggled to his feet, swept by a brief spasm of vertigo. He balanced on the dark wood of the table, palms down, white flesh on the nearly black mirrored polish.

"I agree with your targets." He resorted to a brisk, classroom tone, his defense when challenged. "What I find lacking in your proposal is some concrete way to make it happen."

"You're joking." Roemer was temporarily startled.

"You want to target dishonest judges. You don't want to use the standard tools. How do you get into the targeted judicial community?"

Roemer paced beneath oil paintings of former attorneys general, patriots and rogues, a few fools, and at least one waistcoated dreamer, mutely hung on the dark-paneled walls. The late-August afternoon was gray through the high-curtained, rain-dotted windows.

"I can simplify," Roemer said. "You're fairly new here."

"Humor me."

"All right. Like a lot of people here, you think we should conduct every undercover operation by the same rules. Set up a dummy corporation to provide cover. Rent offices. Hire a few front people. Get the Bureau's guys in as operators and bidders. Make the approaches to the targets slowly, gingerly. The kind of standard undercover operation that takes months to get on its feet and months to deliver."

"You want to move faster?"

"I say cut through all of that. Forget the setups. Go right for the target."

Cleary squinted. "That's my point. How do we get close?"

"The best way," Roemer said, his voice heavy with long experience. "When you can get it, you get one of their own."

"You intend to turn a judge?"

"Absolutely." Roemer nodded.

Instantly, Cleary understood Roemer's success over the years. He was a man with an idea, a simple and powerful one, and his conviction about it was inescapable. You can find corruption anywhere, Roemer insisted, all you have to do is look hard enough for it.

Cleary's one scruple about undercover operations was Roemer's relentlessly pushing people to the limits of their moral tolerance.

How far would I go before I took money? Cleary wondered. Or lied to a grand jury? Or voted the way someone paid me to? That was Roemer's tactic. No one knew the limits of tolerance.

Roemer's official title was the Department's chief Public Integrity

6

Officer. Deceptive name for what he sets out to do, Cleary thought. He's in the temptation business.

"It's a risky approach," Cleary said aloud. "These people really aren't criminals." He finished his tea.

Roemer said, "So you want me to go easy."

"No. Judges aren't like bad cops or dope dealers or crooked politicians."

"They're worse. I'm going to take down any corrupt judge I catch. No deals. We go to trial."

"Let them resign."

"It's not good enough. I tried it," Roemer said. "People have to see everything in the open. No plea bargains."

Cleary strained forward. "Judges are like us. They took the same oath to dispense justice. They won't respond to your approach like criminals do."

"A judge is only a lawyer who knows somebody." Roemer came toward Cleary, hands in his pockets. "They act the same way as a hooker when you show your money."

Which means you can burn anybody around here, too, Cleary thought. Nobody is safe. He wondered again about the rumors that Roemer had collected unsavory details about his Department superiors over the years to use in a tight situation.

"I'm not persuaded you can twist a judge to work for you, Neil."

Roemer said, "He might do it for reasons of conscience."

"If he didn't?"

"I'd find something to make him work for us."

Roemer took out a small finger guard and began picking lint off his blazer. He looks so immaculate, Cleary marveled. How do you stay so clean? Not every Roemer sting had gone well. There was the Griffin thing in Cincinnati four years ago; targets had been tipped off, a nervous breakdown. They were cops selling stolen VCRs. Then in Yonkers, a city councilman tried suicide after being photographed and recorded taking a bribe for voting to raze an apartment building.

Roemer escaped blame, and Cleary recalled seeing him on TV, adroitly explaining both failures. People and their hopes and fears always got mixed into a sting, and Roemer didn't quite get the full human dimension when he went after targets. He was light sensitive, though, his critics said. Find a TV camera crew and you'll find Roemer.

Get hold of Roemer, the men of the new administration told Cleary. They just didn't tell me how, he thought.

7

He wondered again, as he did with greater frequence, about the wisdom of leaving the law school and going into government. The choices he made now were more ambiguous, the consequences more devastating.

"I think northern California is off the beaten path for a major sting," Cleary said sharply. He was still braced on the table, feeling his blood dully push its way to his brain.

"Santa Maria County is the right size. It's central. There will be a lot of noise pulling rotten judges out of a place like that," Roemer said. "Everybody's cynical about big cities, New York, Chicago. They don't expect big-city corruption in a place like Santa Maria."

He put away the finger guard, stretched to loosen his collar, and stared impatiently at Cleary. You're in my way, he seemed to say. You could get flattened.

"I don't know if publicity is the goal of a sting," Cleary said.

"It alerts people to look around their own community. It tells them it can happen to them."

Roemer, Cleary saw, was determined, and he had secured the support of many of the senior department heads.

Cleary tried to maintain his position. "I want appropriate notification to the offices in any district you go into, Neil."

"Sure. I'll be checking other sites once I get Santa Maria set up. But no leaks to the FBI, okay? I'll bring the agents I want, when I want them."

"And regular updates to Special Projects, all right? I want regular reports, Neil."

"That's understood."

"It's a damn sensitive operation. These are judges."

"I watch my step, Paul. You won't have any complaints."

He knows we're locked in a duel, Cleary thought, sinking down again into the creaking embrace of the leather chair. How many others have sat here and tried to leash him?

Roemer tapped his fingers on the table. "Are we done? You'll sign off, too?"

"You've got my approval. You've thought it all out." Cleary managed a grin in defeat. "You have a judge in mind for your way in?"

Roemer turned to the conference room doors. "I've got a name."

"Who is it?"

"Let's wait until I hook him."

"Is he dirty?"

Roemer shrugged and opened the doors. "Could be."

Cleary did not envy the anonymous judge, unaware and unpro-

8

tected, who was about to be visited by the great and incorruptible Neil Roemer and the weight of the Department of Justice. He felt for his blood pressure pills in the seersucker coat. "Bring some heads back," he said as Roemer walked down the corridor. Bloodthirsty imagery was expected around here, Cleary thought distastefully. Some department meetings sound savage.

You and I will settle our scores, he thought of Roemer.

He saw heavier raindrops through the windows and thought of Boston's gray and red brick during a summer storm, the blue flower garden outside the law school dean's office, and wondered again if coming to Washington was the worst mistake he had ever made.

3

THE SAME LATE-AUGUST DAY WAS HOT IN SANTA MARIA, CALI-fornia. A blue sky gleamed metallically above the city, cloudless, windless, endless. Those who could huddled in climate-controlled skyscrapers or air-conditioned bars or put their heads beside open refrigerator doors. Those who could not drank a lot of ice water and cold tea or cold beer and waited and sweated.

Timothy Nash sat on the bench in Department 14 of the Santa Maria County Courthouse. It was cool in his courtroom. He looked down at the jury. It was midafternoon and early in the prosecution's case against Evan Soika.

"Do you have much more, Mr. Benisek?" Nash asked the deputy district attorney.

"Not very much, Your Honor," answered Craig Benisek, one of the younger Major Crime deputies. He had leathery skin and a persistent squint.

Nash nodded. To the right of the bench in the witness stand was a slender city police officer, his uniform a little too big. "Go ahead then," Nash directed.

Benisek sat at the counsel table and methodically went on with

9

his direct examination. Nash glanced over at the jury. It had seven men, five women, a mix of retired electricians, old Army men, an insurance salesman, two grocery store managers, a fireman, a farmer. Mrs. Spirlock patted her new hairdo. Archie Marleau, paunch hanging over his belt, arms folded, listened to the testimony blankly.

Over the two months of jury selection in this trial, Nash had gotten to know each of the jurors. Mrs. Anderson had trouble staying awake after lunch. Mr. Slipe coughed whenever he crossed his legs.

Nash had seen a lot of juries as a prosecutor and a judge. He never learned to read one of them. Each was different and unpredictable.

But one thing he had learned was that jurors didn't care much about what went on in a judge's mind, unless it was about the case on trial. We're cardboard men and women sitting on the bench, he thought. Living monuments.

Just below the bench, so he could not see her, was his clerk, Violet Yopp, evidence from the trial on her desk.

In front of Nash sat Evan Soika and his two defense lawyers. Nash had watched Soika's appearance get better as the trial approached. He was now clean-shaven, hair stylishly thick, dressed in plain black slacks and a white shirt, the long sleeves concealing the decorative tattoos on his arms. Two deputy marshals sat behind Soika, ready to grab him.

As Benisek questioned the cop on the stand, Soika's lead defense attorney, Vincent Escobar, yawned and covered his mouth. Nash watched Escobar and Soika with equal attention. Either one was capable of wrecking the trial, Soika physically, Escobar by something he did in front of the jury.

I've got to watch them every second, Nash thought. Escobar would love to get a mistrial and start over again.

Cindy Duryea, Escobar's assistant, patted Soika's arm.

Nash wiggled his toes under the bench, trying to get his circulation going. Benisek was, with his usual complacency in this trial, taking the cop through the location of various events. The cop stood and pointed at a large blowup of the Best Buy gas station mounted on a board beside the jury box.

He thinks because he's got a great case, he doesn't have to work, Nash thought coldly. He thinks the jury will vote for the death penalty if he bores them enough.

"And where were you when you first arrived at the gas station, Officer Ross?" Benisek asked.

Ross, standing to one side of the witness stand, pointed to the upper edge of the blowup picture. "Just outside here. It's a Denny's restaurant. The other officers, fire department, and some men from the SWAT team were in the parking lot."

"So that's about fifty feet from the station's store?"

"Maybe sixty."

"You agree with that, Mr. Escobar?" Nash asked.

"Of course, Your Honor," Escobar said with a little smile. "I measured it at sixty-three feet."

"Then we'll accept sixty-three feet," Nash said. Soika shook his head and Duryea patted his arm again. Escobar was intently trying to raise the point on a mechanical pencil. He stared at it, fiddled, all in silent, distracting concentration. Nash knew the jury was watching Escobar, not listening to the witness.

"Please don't do that, Mr. Escobar," Nash said.

"Your Honor?"

"We're following the testimony."

"I am, too."

"All right."

"Is the court making an order?"

Nash pressed his feet harder into the carpet under the bench, unseen, angry. "No, Mr. Escobar. Just please give your attention to the witness."

"I am doing that, Your Honor." Escobar grinned at the jury. "Very much."

So had the whole trial gone until this moment. Nash felt tired from riding herd on the posturing and preening, sometimes from Benisek, always from Escobar. The threat of letting the trial slip away from him weighed on Nash.

Ross, the cop, clasped his hands in front of him. He looked at Soika, then at the judge.

Benisek, who hadn't even detected Escobar's attempt to distract the jury, went on calmly. "Could you see the defendant or the victim when you arrived?"

"I could see them both," Ross answered.

"You can resume your seat, Officer," Nash said.

Ross sat down. He looked like a small-town veterinarian.

"Where were they both?" Benisek asked.

Ross twisted in his seat, pointing at a photo lower on the same board. It showed the interior of the gas station's store. "Mr. Soika was in front of the closest window here. Mr. Prentice was right beside him."

"Could you see the shotgun?"

"I sure could." Ross smoothed down one side of his hair. "The defendant had the shotgun right up against the victim's head."

"And that's when you started your negotiations with the defendant to release his hostage?"

"Yes, sir. I got on the phone we had set up in the parking lot. This whole area was clear of cars, no pedestrians, nobody. So I had a pretty good view of the gas station."

"Was this a special phone?" Benisek flipped a page on his legal pad.

"Regular handset. We got the phone company to dedicate a line to the gas station, you know, clear it for us. So only me and Soika could use that line."

"How long again was it after the first call that you arrived?"

Ross closed his eyes briefly. "Maybe thirty minutes."

"Describe the call again?"

Ross cleared his throat. "As I said this morning, sir, somebody put in a call reporting the gas station was being robbed."

"A crime in progress?"

Ross shook his head. "It was vague. The call was that somebody saw a suspicious car, suspicious subject go into the gas station. And the gas station was being robbed."

Escobar was on his feet. "Who put in that call?"

"Sit down, Mr. Escobar. You can ask that on cross." Nash leaned forward tensely. He knew Escobar was trying to create another disturbance.

"I should be allowed to ask while it's fresh," Escobar said to the jury.

"Sit down," Nash repeated, calm he did not feel in his voice. "This is still direct examination. You know that."

Escobar nodded without concern and sat down. Nash sat back. It would be a miracle if this case went to the jury at this rate.

Benisek rapidly finished his questioning. "How long again did you talk with the defendant?"

"About eight hours."

"And you stopped?"

Ross sighed, crossed his arms. "I stopped when the shotgun went off."

* * *

12

They adjourned for a fifteen-minute break, the court reporter stretching and chatting with Scotty Shea, Nash's bailiff. Soika and his lawyers remained in the courtroom. He was handcuffed.

Nash went into his chambers and closed the door. He sat thinking. He had a great deal to think about that day.

When he called court back to order, the jury settled quickly.

"Go ahead with your cross-examination, Mr. Escobar," Nash said.

Nash watched Escobar walk to Ross, the attorney shorter and fatter. Nash had the impression Escobar liked running the risk of a contempt citation in this trial, liked trying to insult the judge or come close to it. Escobar was an old courthouse regular, appointed to this case. He seemed to be taking special pleasure in it.

Escobar stood by Ross, who sat on the witness stand.

"When you started negotiating with Mr. Soika, you told him you were a detective, didn't you?" Escobar asked briskly.

"Yes."

"That was a lie?"

"I wanted him to think I was really senior, that I was more than a hostage negotiator."

Escobar interrupted without raising his leaden voice. "Officer Ross, you lied, didn't you?"

"Yes, sir, as I said."

Escobar broke in again. "The judge will tell you to answer the question I ask, Officer, not what you want to answer."

"Objection," Benisek finally said.

"Sustained. Answer the question, Officer, and don't lecture the witness, Mr. Escobar," Nash said.

Escobar rubbed the fingers of one hand as if they were greasy. "Officer, you told Mr. Soika you'd bring a car for him, didn't you?"

"He asked for one."

"And you had no intention of bringing a car, did you?"

"No, sir."

"So you lied again."

"Yes, I did."

Escobar let his hand drop to his side. "You also told Mr. Soika you would make sure he would serve no more than five years in prison if he gave up, didn't you?"

"I thought he'd believe that."

"So you lied again?"

"Yes, I did."

"And when you told him you'd have his girlfriend at the police department, that was a lie, too, wasn't it?"

13

"I didn't know if she'd be there." Ross's voice stayed as cool as Escobar's. He folded his arms.

"You told Mr. Soika that the mayor and chief of police were unavailable, didn't you?"

"We decided we would not bring either the mayor or chief of police to him as he demanded."

"So you lied once more, didn't you?"

"I suppose so."

"No 'suppose' about it. A lie?"

"Yes, sir."

"When you told Mr. Soika no attempt would be made to take him by force, that was also a lie, wasn't it?" Escobar glanced back at Soika, then up to Nash, his expression disdainful.

"It was up to him."

"But then your department did rush the gas station," Escobar said harshly, "and caused the accidental discharge of the shotgun, killing Mr. Prentice."

Nash didn't wait for Benisek's tardy objection. "Don't answer, Officer Ross. It's objectionable and you know it, Mr. Escobar."

Escobar pivoted on his small feet. He smiled. "I'm sorry, Your Honor. It's late."

"Anything else for the witness?"

"One more question." Escobar turned back to the cop. "During the entire eight hours you talked to Mr. Soika, you lied time after time, didn't you, Officer Ross?"

Ross stared at Escobar. "You bet I did."

The jurors shifted in their seats, watching the two men. Mrs. Spirlock patted her stiff hairdo again; several people cleared their throats loudly. Nash asked Benisek if he had anything more.

Just ask the right questions and you can take that lousy impression away, Nash silently implored Benisek. He hoped Benisek would take the most vigorous line.

Benisek did. He asked, "Officer Ross, you've been a narcotics officer and hostage negotiator for years?"

"Yes, I have."

"During that time, have you had much success either buying illegal drugs or enticing armed hostage takers by saying, 'I'm a Santa Maria police officer. I would like to take you into custody'?"

"No." Ross grinned as the jury chuckled gaily.

Nash sighed quietly. They were the questions he would have asked, if he'd been able, and not sitting up on the bench, remote

14

from the struggle in the courtroom and intimately involved in it at the same time.

He said to the jurors, "I'm going to send you home for the day, ladies and gentlemen. You may be tempted to talk about what we did today," he said solemnly, "but you are not to discuss this case until it is given to you. This is a serious case. The defendant and the People are entitled to your full attention and best judgment."

As he talked, one or two of the jurors nodded. Always pause before you send them out, always let the jury know who is in control, like a captain on his ship, his father said. It was one of the frequent pieces of advice he offered on the craft of judgeship.

"So have a good afternoon, ladies and gentlemen. Remember to be back tomorrow at ten A.M. for the continuation of the trial," he said. Shea opened the courtroom doors and let the jurors file out quietly, like churchgoers after a service, into the noisy corridor.

Nash left the bench, pausing as Soika was shackled, belly chain on, handcuffs, held by his two marshals, and taken back into the holding cell beside the courtroom. Nash had heard the same speech he'd just given made by his father twenty, thirty years ago, in the old courthouse with fans stuck on the walls on little stands, the air hot and languid in summer and everyone sweating all day. "We dance around it most of the time," his father told him when they sneaked ice cream sodas on the way home later, "but the rest of it—the whole turkey dance from parking tickets to robbery, embezzlement—it's all window dressing. Life and death count and it's in our hands, Timmy." His father had sentenced six men to the gas chamber over the years. "Nothing else matters," he said.

Shea, looser now without the jury around to keep him looking stern and cold, joked with the court reporter as she packed up her machine. The courtroom's doors were locked, the lights would be shut off next.

Nash picked up several files off the bench as he turned to go back into his chambers. Everything I need, he thought, looking at the scattered paper on the bench. A list of approved psychiatrists to summon into court, alternative sentencing facilities, a large blotter with the latest sentencing guidelines, how much for a robbery today, a possession of heroin, holding a loaded gun, raping a child. A bail schedule on yellow copy paper for easy reference, a list of lawyers, such as Escobar, on the indigent-criminal defense panel, notebooks and books stuffed with scripts for reciting canned speeches on terms and conditions of probation, increasing a defendant's prison term, how to hold bail hearings, hearings to relieve counsel, hearings to judge sanity, hearings to exclude evidence. A black-bound copy of the latest California Penal Code rested on the day's calendar of cases, his own notepads of comments on the Soika trial. He kept tissues and a carafe of water handy, too. Just underneath the bench was the "goody" button for emergencies. Push the button and bells went off throughout the courthouse and marshals came running.

Nash said to Shea, "Make sure all the evidence gets locked up, Scotty."

Shea, hands on his hips, gave a mock salute. "Sure thing. Hey, you like that about the sawed-off going off accidentally?"

"I don't know what happened." Nash grinned. "Except if Escobar says it happened that way, it probably didn't."

"Gun doesn't go off that way," Shea said.

Nash thought Shea was trying to impress the reporter. He turned to his chambers, looking once more at the papers and notebooks on the bench.

I've got scripts and buttons for everything in my life here except what matters most, he thought. My divorce. My marriage.

Roemer and the lanky FBI agent named Adams sat in the plane's rear, alone, near the small galley. Roemer sighed, stretched his legs out, and listened to the engine's dulling rumble.

"Okay, let me have it," he said to Adams.

The agent reached into a thick black briefcase and handed Roemer a heavy tan file with green tabs. Roemer took it with a smirk. "This is all new stuff?"

"Everything we had at the Bureau on the guy."

"I don't want to fool around with material I've already seen," Roemer said.

"No, this is fresh. It didn't come over with the other files you saw."

Roemer sighed again. "Weighs a ton."

Adams agreed. Ahead of them, the seats in the plane were filled, an attendant slowly pushing along a cart of drinks. "I'm going to need a couple of those before we get to California," the agent said, sliding down a little in his seat, looking out the window at the gaseous banks of clouds around them.

"Don't talk. I've got to read," Roemer said, opening the file. "Maybe you guys have something on Nash I don't know about."

4

TWO MEN IN BIKER COLORS, BEARDED AND WEARING SUNGLASSES, their clothes stained and rumpled, sat in Nash's outer office. Nash sniffed as he walked by them. No stink. They weren't real bikers. Undercover narcs, he guessed.

"Can you get me a cup of coffee, Vi?" he asked his clerk. He took off his robe, breathing wearily. The self-confidence he had sitting on the bench, out with the jury, collapsed when he was alone. It had been a long day. It would be, he knew, a longer evening. One of the longest of his life. Jesus, he thought with disgust. I can't even avoid self-pity about losing my wife.

"You should have a soft drink instead of coffee," Violet Yopp said. "Or some juice."

"I need the coffee."

"On a hot day, it's not good for you."

"Vi. Please. Just let me have it," and she caught his rare impatience with her. Violet bustled to the coffeemaker in the all-purpose closet just outside her office.

She was only five feet tall, sixty, a diminutive, carefully dressed Asian woman who had been assigned to him when he first became a municipal court judge four years ago and then volunteered to follow him up to Superior Court. She said little, but was very loyal. Her improbable last name, Yopp, came from a husband dead thirty years before. She remembered his father. They all did, all the older clerks and secretaries and bailiffs around the courthouse. Jack Nash was a great judge to work for. A great father, too, Nash thought automatically.

He went into the small green-tiled bathroom in his chambers. One of the minor luxuries of being a judge was never having to pee or wash your hands in public anymore. Or at least while you were in the courthouse and the whole apparatus worked diligently to insulate you from the million little bruises and shocks of daily living. Everybody was polite to a judge. Everybody gave way, smiled, offered things.

Everybody wanted the judge to like them.

Nash washed his hands, then his face, rubbing cold water on his bare arms, sleeves rolled up. He heard Vi come in.

What is this? he wondered. The day of your divorce? Thirteen years and it's gone and he couldn't make out why. Kim's leaving was a terrible, uninsulated blow. Nothing around the courthouse could cushion it for him.

For the first time, at the age of forty-four, he suddenly and absolutely knew he was going to grow old, grow infirm, lose his wife and child and he would die. Not immediately, but certainly.

I used to think I was immune. He dried his hands, combed his thinning blond hair, pleased he was still lean. Other guys had divorces and families torn up. Other cops and lawyers got gray and flabby and slowed down. But I know it's happening to me now. Kim proved it with this divorce.

I'm not immune, Nash thought, snapping off the light. There are no exemptions.

Vi stood patiently beside his large brown oak desk. Muster some cheer for her benefit anyway, he thought.

She gestured at the coffee cup set decorously amid the papers and piled reports.

"Who are those two?" Nash sat down, pointing at the bikers who waited just beyond his door.

"Two men from Narcotics with a warrant request."

"They can wait. Anything else of interest?"

She began reading through his phone messages and notes. "The Asian-American Law Society has you scheduled for a lunch speech two weeks from Tuesday."

His sipped her perfect coffee. "Speech? About what?"

"The role of Asian-American lawyers. Whatever you want, I suppose." She smiled conspiratorially.

"You accepted on my behalf?"

"I knew you'd want to attend."

"Thanks, Violet." He smiled back at her. "Maybe they'll contribute to my next campaign."

"You don't have to run for three years."

"It's never too early to start collecting." He pushed his hands through the magazines scattered on his desk. Skiing at Aspen, scuba diving off Jamaica, a list of lovely dreams he'd ordered in panic when Kim's leaving was final, and he had nothing to hang on to. Go somewhere, play in the snow or sun, just get away and pretend it wasn't happening.

"And Judge Atchley called three times," Vi said tiredly.

"About his fund-raiser at the Turf Club?"

"He didn't say. He wanted to see you badly." Vi was the epitome of discretion. Atchley was running for reelection, and he consistently came out last in every county judicial poll. He had been hidden in traffic court for nine years. Nash groaned slightly. The other judges would close ranks, a rule his father drummed in. We stick together, no matter who the asshole is or how dumb he is. Nobody can knock off an incumbent judge. So far Nash had avoided Atchley's entreaties to make a campaign contribution. He disliked Atchley very much.

"I better take care of it." He headed for the back door of his chambers.

"And Master Calendar called," Vi said after him. "How long will this trial go?"

"DA is still in his case. Who knows."

"I'll tell them we don't know so we don't get any short cause insurance trials."

"Good. Tell the narcs to wait. I'll be right back."

They would sit patiently. Everybody waited for the judge.

Except the ones who matter, he thought.

FROM THE OUTSIDE THE NEW COURTHOUSE LOOKED BLEAKLY modern, white concrete with rectangular windows, eight stories high, like the embassy in Kuala Lumpur or some exotic frontier. It was supposed to persuade the natives that progress was clean, stark, big, and unstoppable.

Behind every courtroom in the vast white block ran a bright, windowed corridor. Nash walked down it, past other courts, high boxes of trial transcripts stored there because room had run out everywhere else. Through the wall of windows that was the court-house's blank ice face to the world, he saw the orange and white box of the county jail and the hurried downtown of Santa Maria, all gleaming and hot.

Another judge leaned against the window, smoking a cigarette because his clerk wouldn't let him do it in chambers. Nash had known Judge Frank Wisot for years. He was the senior judge in the county, as respected as Nash's father. He taught junior Bible classes at Valley Methodist Church and played piano at parties.

"In a hurry, Tim?" Judge Wisot asked jovially, smoking hard.

"Going to see Harold. He wants money."

"Jesus. I got hit twice. I bought a goddamn table at his goddamn fund-raiser."

"He can say he'd do the same for you, Frank."

"I don't need a goddamn table. I don't have goddamn fund-raisers," Judge Wisot snorted. He had spent exactly eight dollars and forty-two cents for his last election campaign, all of it for postage.

"Maybe I can get him to take an IOU." Nash walked on. Judge Wisot chuckled and stared thoughtfully out the window.

Atchley's courtroom was only two floors below Nash's, yet they usually saw each other only at the weekly judges' meeting. Nash's father hadn't really warned him of the isolation or loneliness of being a judge. Like lobsters in our own little crevices, he thought now, we don't like to come out.

He swung into Atchley's courtroom. Bach on violins lightly filled the air. There was no one in the clerk's office. Even the bailiff, who generally liked to sit and read the newspaper or tinker with his landscaping business, had left. Atchley didn't inspire much loyalty.

Nash walked in without knocking. "What's the problem, Harold?"

Judge Atchley was on his hands and knees beside the sofa, his head bobbing up and down. He was in his shirtsleeves, and his shiny, moist face was red. He grunted at Nash's voice, looking up in confusion.

"Oh. Tim. My pen, my special fountain pen rolled under the sofa here. I can't reach it." He looked for help.

Nash didn't move. "Is that what you wanted?"

Atchley grunted again, getting to his feet. He wiped his hands. He was a little over fifty, overweight, and generally slow in manner and speech. But he was not stupid. He read Spanish literature and German philosophy. He played the violin and had a large framed picture in his chambers of the Santa Maria Dixieland Jamboree six years ago when his band won first prize. Atchley wore a red-and-white-striped shirt and pants in the picture; he was sweating and playing the trombone.

"Of course it's something else." He huffed toward his desk. He had a stack of diet-soda cans in front of his shelves of law books. "You want a drink? It's warm. I can't take ice, you know. Makes me sick."

"No thanks, Harold. Just tell me what you want." Nash couldn't keep the annoyance from his voice.

Atchley plucked a can, popped it open, drank long, and burped in surprise like a child. He was, he had told Nash at their first meeting, allergic to nearly everything. He did not use any deodorant or strong soap. He was ripe in the warm room.

"I need help with the fund-raising dinner in two days. My treasurer says things are slow." Atchley burped again.

"I can't give you much," Nash said truthfully. "This is a bad time." He left out how much Kim was going to drain from his paycheck in child support and alimony.

"I hate this," Atchley said fiercely. "I hate running around asking for money. Don't you? We're judges. We're not politicians."

"It's only every six years."

"What I was really hoping," Atchley went on slowly, "is an endorsement. Maybe even a radio spot."

"I'm in the middle of a death-penalty trial. I shouldn't do that," Nash answered. He wanted to leave. He would drop off a check tomorrow.

"Just your name, Tim. You can just say I've done a good job and you think I'll do a good job for another term."

"I can buy a ticket. That's the best for now."

Atchley's face hardened and he burped gently. "What about your father? Would you ask him to give me an endorsement?"

"You should ask him. It's better if you do it."

"He doesn't like me. I'm not a good judge, according to him."

"Then he won't do it. I can't ask him."

Atchley drank again, his face in a scowl. He fell back into his leather chair limply, watching Nash with undisguised bitterness.

"We're not all lucky like you, Tim. I couldn't count on my father smoothing the way for my appointment. I couldn't sit back and let him arrange a step up to Superior Court."

"Don't make an asshole of yourself." Nash turned to go. "I'll leave a check with your clerk."

"But you won't come to the fund-raiser."

"I don't know if I can."

"If it wasn't my fund-raiser, you'd show up. It's at the Turf Club. That's doing pretty good."

"I said I'd give you a contribution," Nash answered.

Atchley burst out, "I have to work, work, work all the time to stay here." He swept his hand around the room. He shook the soda can. "I have to get down on my knees for money."

"You're not making any friends around here by complaining," Nash said, glancing back.

"I wouldn't need friends, Tim, if I had your family behind me. Just one good word from the great Nashes."

It would do no good to get mad at Atchley. He was probably a permanent courthouse fixture. He had, Nash recalled, said one profound thing from the bench. A defense attorney claimed his client was an innocent man. Atchley shouted back, "He's not innocent. He may be not guilty, but nobody's innocent."

The volume on the Bach violins went up suddenly behind Nash.

"Sorry to keep you hanging around, guys." Nash waved the two bikers into chambers with him. "What have you brought over?"

One of the bearded narcs, cocky, brusque, a manner familiar to Nash after his years as a prosecutor, fiddled with a stack of papers. "We got this old hubba whore, Judge. Name's Maizie, and she's giving us diddly shit for a couple of weeks and now she's ready to turn. She's got a couple of things going at Vice, and I said, hey, man, let's work this gal."

The other narc, his black beard stubbly, poked at a fern beside the sofa. "What's this, Judge?"

"Ask my clerk. She bought it." Vi had done all of the thoughtful dressing of his chambers, plants with bright blooms, embroidered pillows on the sofa.

"Hey, Rog, we got to get one of these things for the office," the black-bearded narc said. "We could tell the pukes it's some kind of exotic weed. Get them excited."

Nash grinned, reassured by the old routine of reading a warrant request and the casually brutal atmosphere of narcs. He didn't recognize these two guys. They were new, at least since he had been in charge of Major Narcotics for the DA's office.

"Is Maizie your snitch for the warrant?" he asked.

"She could be."

"No kidding. Is she your snitch here?"

The bearded narc asked, "Between us? That's it?"

"Stays in here," Nash promised.

"Okay, she is. Does it matter?"

"If somebody wants to tear this apart later and maybe say I didn't read it carefully," Nash said. "All you got here is that this information about drug sales at the house came from a confidential reliable informant."

"That's old Maiz. Really reliable." They both chuckled.

Nash felt a short rush of sadness. The narcs had given up Maizie's name too easily. She counted, obviously, for little in their scheme of things. Snitches were always at the mercy of everyone, their protectors and enemies alike. He imagined her, a prostitute who had sex for cocaine, a hubba whore. Desperate enough to turn for the cops and work for them.

If Maizie worked around Sunrise Avenue, down by the car lots, she was probably black. If she roamed East Ninth, she was white. Skinny, dressed too poorly no matter what the season, shorts and a thin blouse in summer, the same blouse and jeans in winter. Her teeth were bad. Her hair was dry and she was anxious all the time. She couldn't read very much or write or even think clearly. Nash had met her and talked with her again and again when he worked informants with the narcs. There was nothing sorrier, more disgusting, or pitiable than a junkie hooker.

Nash put his feet up on the corner of his desk as he worked on the warrant. One of the narcs yawned.

"Say, Judge, you miss doing all this shit like when you were a DA?"

"Like you guys calling me at two in the morning for a warrant to break down some door? Like trying to get you to talk normally in court?"

"Yeah. All that shit." He grinned back at Nash.

"Sometimes I do," Nash admitted. Most piercingly today, he thought, when I'd give anything to go back six years in time.

He worked with the narcs on the search warrant for a half hour, and the longer he delayed, the less he thought about where he would be at five P.M. He did not want to struggle with the knowledge it would be the last time he walked through the doors of his home.

He made corrections on the warrant request. "I get the feeling you guys in Narcotics are bringing over most of these things to me. Is that right?"

"You have the background." The black-bearded narc fidgeted with his battered wallet, hanging on a chain from his pocket. "Some of these other judges, they don't get it. They don't know what's going on outside."

"You think I'll sign anything you bring over?" He was annoyed the newer narcs thought he was so compliant.

"We know you read them. If you say it's good, hey, we know it ain't getting shit-canned in court when the defense puke screams Fourth Amendment violation."

"Don't fool yourself," Nash said. "Nobody gets away with anything." He meant more than the search warrant on his desk. Vi was typing, stopping frequently to answer the phone. They all want to talk to you, his father warned him. Everybody's got a cause or wants a favor.

Nash reluctantly signed the warrant request. There was nothing to keep him in the courthouse, and he did not want to leave. If he drew out the final act, he half-persuaded himself it wouldn't happen, like a magic spell rendered useless because some essential ingredient is omitted. If I don't go home, Kim can't leave. She can't take Ben. He handed the warrant to the stubble-bearded narc.

Nash walked them out. The narc said, "Maiz says she knows another place, they got an indoor-cultivation deal going. Maiz says the whole house, and it's a new place on Grandview, got these solar units, got the sprouts in the best dirt, and irrigation, the whole nine yards. You walk on the street, you don't see diddly, and they got maybe two hundred grand worth of sensemilla growing in there."

"Maybe I could do that with my house," Nash said. "Everybody's moving out today."

The narcs laughed, taking it as a joke. One said, "Hey, yeah, you break out all the interior walls, you got space for a couple hundred plants."

Vi glanced up disapprovingly at them. They were too coarse and unclean for her judge or chambers.

"Maybe I need some excitement," Nash said as they shambled out, more like bikers than any gang in the city except that they didn't smell right.

He stood, hands in his pockets, looking back in his chambers. Vi was typing again. Nearly four P.M. Time rushed away from him. On the walls hung diplomas and letters of appointment to the bench

24

from the governor, photos of being sworn in by his father, the two Nashes grinning at each other in secret gloating at having come so far. There were fading newspaper pictures of cases he'd tried when he was a deputy district attorney. A high-school basketball trophy was set on top of the high bookshelves, between California Supreme Court Reports and law books in green- and gold-bound volumes, yellowing dead pages.

On the far wall, he could see the framed portrait of the three judges in the family, his father with a mass of white hair, standing taller than either of his two sons, Tim and Richard. Richard was a federal magistrate in Philadelphia. The three Nash men, posed in their black robes against a shimmering studio background, were solemn. As the camera clicked, Jack Nash had hugged each son hard. "I'm very proud," he had whispered heavily.

The empty space next to the portrait had belonged to a candid picture of Kim, Ben, and him taken on a rainy September five years ago, Kim in her long red coat holding Ben by his small hand. Nash was smiling, gray rain glistening on his face. When Kim said she was leaving, he put the photo away in his bottom desk drawer. Only a formal picture of Ben remained, somber and bemused, like a nineteenth-century child study in lifeless monochrome.

Seeing it now, Nash was frightened by his own loneliness.

Vi said as she typed, "I'm almost finished with the changes you wanted on the jury instructions."

Nash nodded indifferently. The stack of instructions Escobar and Benisek had submitted was half an inch thick. Words and rules. Three local TV stations had submitted petitions to have cameras in the courtroom when the verdict was announced. Reporters sat watching the testimony, but Nash felt very far from the trial at that moment.

The relentless afternoon died away outside. "I'll be up in the cafeteria."

"Don't forget you have dinner with your parents at seven."

"I don't forget anything," he said coldly. It was Jack and Hilary Nash's way of supporting their flagging son. Let him put away thirteen years of marriage and a child and invite him to a comforting dinner. Cocktails first, perhaps.

6

THE CAFETERIA WAS A WAY STATION FOR PEOPLE FORCED TO REMAIN in the courthouse. Nash got a cup of coffee from Len, the blind cashier who trusted people far more than he should, and found an empty table. In his wrinkled shirt, downcast over the hot coffee, he looked part of the late afternoon. The large room, smelling faintly of bacon grease, old custard, and cleanser, was partly filled. Tables of families talking low, lawyers telling loud stories, lone people staring out into the Santa Maria skyline through the wide windows, thinking about what had happened to them, what was going to happen.

Nash mechanically waved to two other judges sitting down the room, Pedrotti and Arevola. He used to run at Northside Park at noon with them. He might do it again.

A tall man strolled to him.

"The wheels of justice grind more quickly these days if you can take time off in the afternoon," the man said with a smile.

Nash looked up, gaped briefly. "My God, Mr. Terhune. There has to be some crisis to get you over here." He shook hands warmly and pointed at a chair. Seeing Dennis Terhune again was a little like shifting the world right once more. Childhood heroes have the dazzle of invincibility about them.

"I came down to see you, Your Honor. They told me you were off the bench." Terhune sat down gracefully.

"Sent the jury home for the day. I gave them the usual little pep talk. I like to hear the words even if they don't get my juices going much anymore." Nash grimaced.

"Routine kills every ideal."

"You have something before me? A motion? Case? Something I can do?"

Terhune put his hand up a little. He was a man Nash had admired

26

since childhood. Only a few years younger than his father, Terhune wore urbanity as easily as his tailored charcoal pinstripe and custom-made shoes. His face had the sharp sculpted look of an ascetic even though Terhune and his wife were frequently pictured at charity dinners. He had wit, manners—qualities Nash rarely saw in his court and missed.

Even more, he missed those early days when Terhune and his father were friends and law partners and he visited their deep-carpeted offices in the fine old Lexington Building. The tall building had ornamental knights and angels and stood like a steady monument on Jackson Avenue, the main boulevard through downtown Santa Maria. It was Dennis Terhune who always gave him a gum-drop or chocolate mint during those office visits.

When the partnership broke up, as acrimonious and grudging as any divorce, Nash's father picked up the habit of small bribes with candy during his son's visits. He had never done so before Terhune.

"I don't have anything formal," Terhune answered. "No business on the plate for me. I'm footloose. Like you." He glanced idly around the room, as if it were the El Dorado Club and he might know someone.

Nash saw that Terhune, as always, sat with crossed legs, coat buttoned. Even years ago, Terhune practiced law in the old style, formal and precise. He never took his coat off, even on summer days like this, when no machine kept pace with the enervating heat.

"I didn't see you at the County Bar lunch in February." Terhune sounded casual. "And I didn't see you at the State Bar Convention in April. I thought I'd better check in for our yearly meeting." Nash, despite his father's barely concealed contempt, had kept in touch with Terhune over the years.

"I've been busy," Nash said. The two legal events had coincided with Kim's upheaval and the dissolution of his domestic life.

"And then you picked a jury for months, I hear. This Soika hostage case. But the hostage is dead. Unbelievable that this goes on in this city. Really."

Nash thought Terhune, whose extensive and lucrative practice was entirely business law and real estate, would hardly understand the cruder, elemental aspects of life or what went on in a criminal court trial.

"It's a tough case, but the DA's coasting because he thinks it isn't. The jury may hate the idea that everybody lied to Soika, and they might believe his story that the shotgun went off accidentally when the cops stormed in."

27

"No. They couldn't."

"They do sometimes. You can't tell."

"I wouldn't have any trouble with a verdict," Terhune said, as if he and Nash lived in the same legal world.

"That's why neither side would let you on a jury. If this one comes back with a first-degree verdict, it'll be my first death sentence."

"Sobering thought."

Nash immensely enjoyed seeing Terhune, but time still grew short on his own immovable obligation. And he had the odd feeling that Terhune, the elegant and unperturbable lawyer to the richest people in the city, was uneasy with him.

He's got something on his mind and he doesn't want to tell me what it is, Nash thought.

Terhune took out a slim cigarette and lit it. "I don't feel like a social outcast smoking here." He grinned.

"Did you want to see me about some business your firm has on my calendar?" Nash asked. "A client's kid got busted for drunk driving?"

Terhune shook his head. "No, no, Timothy. Your mother is well?"

"Charging ahead. She wants to open a restaurant."

Terhune nodded vacantly. This surprised Nash. He had always assumed, based on the mutual silence from his mother and father, that Terhune's infatuation with Hilary Nash had been one of the reasons for the law partnership's fiery collapse thirty years ago.

"How about Jack? In good health? I hear he's handling a lot of private matters these days."

"He likes private judging. It keeps him happy. He's making a lot more money than he did on the bench."

Nash drank his coffee. Terhune nodded again without interest. The silence lingered. Terhune looked at his gleaming shoes, gazed abstractedly at the grayish linoleum on the floor, the pairs of people walking slowly with trays of food.

He probably hasn't been in a courthouse for years, Nash thought.

Nash wasn't going to say anything about his dying marriage. He didn't know if Terhune had heard about it. It was a private pain he laid out openly only for brother and parents. He finished his coffee. Almost time. Almost five P.M.

"I've got to get back." He started to stand up.

"Are you busy this evening, Timothy?" Terhune almost blurted out.

Nash began, "Tonight's impossible for me—" and was interrupted.

"Because there's someone I'd like you to meet." Terhune spoke without looking up, making a show of indifference.

"I've got other plans."

"We could work around them. How about before dinner? A few drinks?"

"Not tonight. Can't be done."

"Later? After you've taken care of everything else?" Terhune now looked up, and Nash was startled to see something akin to pleading on the well-shaved, cologned, and massaged face.

"Who is it?" Nash asked curiously.

"It can wait until we're together, Timothy. It's all friendly and you'll find it worthwhile."

"Is it business? I don't have any spare cash now." He thought of Atchley's sour recriminations. "Nothing at all."

"No business. I promise I won't ask for a donation for even a worthy cause," Terhune scoffed, stubbing out the expensive cigarette in the cracked plastic ashtray. "It's simply someone I want you to meet."

"That's about the vaguest invitation I've ever gotten." Nash loosened his tie, his neck cooler. "Maybe I could help out on one of your committees some other time. No possible way tonight for me."

Terhune stood up, twisting his slender, wrinkled neck as if to unlock a hidden spring of tension. "I wish you'd trust my judgment, Timothy. This is very much more important than anything you've planned."

"We'll have to do it some other time." Nash stood up.

"He won't be in Santa Maria very long." Then Terhune paused. He followed Nash toward the side door and the bins of dirty plates and cups. "I'll arrange another time for you."

"Any other time. If you think it's important." Nash dropped his cup in a bin.

"It might decisively influence your life."

And that, Nash silently thought, is exactly what I don't need dumped on me now. They walked out to the elevators. "It's good seeing you again," Nash said, and shook hands with Terhune and watched him step into a crowded elevator.

"I'll be in touch soon." Terhune nodded curtly, and the doors closed.

On the way back to his courtroom, Nash was stopped by three insurance defense lawyers. They wanted to tell him how good the fishing was on Merriwether Slough. Their true backslapping purpose was to find out how he intended to rule on a motion for summary judgment they had filed before him.

After he finished with them, Nash, as he did every evening, gathered up the probation reports from the open metal file cabinet by his desk where Vi meticulously put them. It was a stack six inches high, all the people he would have to sentence tomorrow before starting the Soika murder trial.

He said good-night to Vi. She was rubbing lotion into her dry little hands. She said Atchley had called again. Nash swore.

As he passed the holding tank in the courtroom, the heavy metal door cracked open and Scotty Shea stuck himself partway out. His muscular bulk held the door open.

"You up for anything, Tim?" Shea wiggled his hands as if drinking. Over the last months, he and Shea had visited bars in the southern end of the county, finding one-night pickups among the small-town women drinking hopefully, eagerly, on weeknights.

Nash shook his head. "I've got some other things tonight, Scotty. Tell me if you get lucky, okay?"

"Over and out." Shea slipped back into the security cells where Soika and the other prisoners were brought up from the basement lockup after their daily bus ride from the main jail.

Nash thought of Terhune and Shea. He would, for that one night, like to trade places with either of them.

The heavy reports under his arm tugged him awkwardly as he left the darkened courtroom.

7

OUTSIDE OF THE CONTROLLED AND CONFINED COOLNESS OF THE new courthouse, the lowering late-summer heat pressed down with exhausting fury as Nash drove onto the freeway, and the path he had taken for five years.

The sky above Santa Maria was washed blue with russet near the horizon, the fading sunlight acid yellow through thin clouds. To his right was the commercial center of the city, dominated recently by glass and green-stone office buildings and an enormous new hotel with a pink-marble facade. This hotel, like the others in the city, specialized in conventions that seemed to sweep in and out again like tides. Nash took pride in the growth of the city. He liked the construction and the bustle. He drove now with the windows down, the hot air rushing over him, making him sweat even in the light suit.

The summer air smelled of dried grass and dust, a bitter mix. He passed beside the Tuolumne River, brown and slow and glassy, cutting through the middle of Santa Maria. He glanced around at the other cars crowding the freeway. All going to homes they could count on.

Nash had been especially proud when he and Kim bought their two-story house on Avila Avenue, in the middle of stable old homes with flower-covered walls and thick old trees along the street. He had been supervisor of Major Narcotics for a while, with a certain salary increase to come. His parents helped with the mortgage payments.

Now he hadn't been home for close to a month and braced himself for the inevitable changes.

He parked and found the front door open. It was eerie inside the living room. Most of the furniture had been sold or moved out. He didn't want it. He didn't want anything from the house on Avila Avenue anymore. All that was left in the room were a couch Kim had bought and a sagging upholstered chair. The room was hollow and bare, the wood floor glistening as if wet. The few remaining pieces of furniture were like debris left after an oceanic disaster, washed ashore.

He heard movement upstairs and followed the sound, trying to be passionless as he went up the carpeted stairs. Close your eyes and you can pretend it's any evening, he thought. Nothing's changed at all.

Kim was in their bedroom, or what was left of it. She had two large, open boxes on the naked floor, and she came out of the walk-in closet with an armload of winter coats she dropped carelessly into one box.

"Taking everything?" he asked, knowing it was petty.

"Come on, Tim. You said you didn't want any of this stuff. It's mine and I don't want to give it away." She had on a print shirt

31

and skirt, her legs supple and long from years of biking. Now she wanted to go back to school for her master's in counseling. The marriage had begun as a joke and he just hadn't noticed it.

"I don't want any of it." He glanced at the dusty bureau where she'd kept her makeup, the drawers where his clothes had been, partway open, like drab mouths.

"It's silly for you not to live here." She went on cleaning out the few clothes left from earlier raids. "You've got the whole house. You don't need to rent an apartment."

He didn't bother to answer. Kim often talked to him without expecting a reply. She was a few years younger than him and had varied during their marriage from being too heavy to too thin. At the end she finally achieved some equilibrium, her figure taut and attractive. Her auburn hair was tied in the back with a small piece of yarn.

Where their bed had been was a large square of heavy dust, as if it had settled through them while they slept or made love, each of them obviously dreaming of different things over those nights.

"What time's your flight?" he asked, standing motionless as she worked, hating every moment.

"Eight forty-five. I brought Ben with me so we could go right from here."

Nash was surprised. "I didn't hear him. Where is he?"

"Someplace around. I think his room," she said, waving vaguely.

"I'm going to keep fighting, Kim," he said. "You know I'm going to fight you every step."

She sighed, making that dismissive, too patient sound when an argument struck her as undignified or pointless. "Don't threaten me. Not again and again. The court order's final. The support payments are settled. We've agreed about the property."

Suddenly, Nash found himself shouting. "I did not agree you could take my son. I do not agree that you can just leave for Los Angeles and keep him there."

"You had a chance to fight it. You lost," she said, folding the tops down on the boxes. They obstinately stuck up.

"It's an asinine ruling and I'm going to get it reversed," he said, then dug at her weakest point. "You're going to be back in court anyway. You can't live on the budget the judge saw. You never had to live on a budget when we were married."

"Well, I'm going to try. I'm trying a lot of things I didn't think I'd ever get a chance to do." She faced him defiantly, and Nash, standing in the barren, dusty ruin of their bedroom, had never contemplated hating Kim so intensely. He had, with perfect contrariness, a desire to make love to her.

"It's all bullshit about finding yourself," he swore, pacing the room. "Who do you think you are? We've got our lives, our son. You don't give that up. You cannot do it."

"I don't have the same devotion to perfect families you do." She dabbed at a sweat bead near her eye. She had distrusted the Nash clan from the start.

"You've got fair warning," he said savagely. "It's not over. I'm going to fight you and I'm going to get Ben."

"Your father can pull all the strings he wants to, but we're leaving Santa Maria tonight," she said. "Do you want to say good-bye to Ben?"

He swore at her again and turned, afraid he might show how deeply he was hurt. He stumbled down the hallway, bare walls where bright-flowered pictures had hung, down to Ben's room.

His son sat on the uncovered mattress in the center of the room. Small for his age, but energetic, Ben had Nash's light hair and exuberance, a lineal gift from his grandfather. And he had Kim's toughness, her blunt features. Nash stood in the doorway, too hesitant to intrude. Ben faced away from him, toward the blank walls that had blazed with posters of the world, wild animals, Batman. The closet, which normally seemed burst open with too many toys and clothes idly stuffed into it, was white, empty.

Nash's anger at Kim spent itself, leaving behind sorrow. "You sure cleaned this room. Look at it. I don't think I've seen it so good." He strolled in.

Ben looked up, then stood up. He was dressed for travel in neat jeans and sneakers and a sturdy coat. The airless room was hot and Ben was sweating. "I don't want to go," he said.

"I don't want you to go."

"So I don't have to?"

Always the bargains with imperious power, Nash thought. Please God, give me a little less pain and I'll pray every day. Give me enough money for the car payment or the next hit of speed or smack or whatever or let me keep my family together. I swear I'll be good. Ben was only learning too early that the bargains were one-sided, offers made into silence.

Nash put his arm around Ben. "No, you have to go, bear. You're flying to L.A. You like flying, right?"

"I don't want to go. I don't want to leave our house."

"Bear, things don't ever stay the same. Things always change, and sometimes you don't like what happens, sometimes you hate it, but you have to do it."

"I could come live with you."

Nash looked into the puzzled, terrified face. "I'm going to see you again in about a month. And we'll be together for a while and I'll see you a lot. Maybe more than we think right now."

Ben half-nodded, half-pushed away from Nash, wandering to the large, curtainless window and the shadowed backyard abandoned below him. "I got to leave the tree house we made." He pointed.

Nash looked. The dark bulk, sheltered in the massed branches of the large oak that dominated the yard, was barely visible. He and Ben had worked on the flimsy, uncertain boards hidden in the tree. It was filled with toys and a small pillow, crayons, a refuge from the world that never managed to be just.

Great for me to think like that. Nash held his son again. The judge denies justice.

"It'll stay here for the kid who comes to live next, bear. Like we stay here, too. Something we built together."

"I don't want to go." Ben was unable to get beyond that barrier.

Nash heard Kim calling from their bedroom. She must be finished. It was time to go, time to end. "I'm going to call you later tonight, soon as you get to L.A., okay?"

He led Ben by the shoulder back to the bedroom, found that Kim had gone downstairs and was checking through the kitchen a last time. We had so many plans for this house, expand the kitchen if we had another child, redo the redwood patio so you could sit out in the summer without worrying about mosquitoes.

The three of them were out of place in the stuffy kitchen. Kim closed a cabinet door. "I've got the car loaded and I can't think of anything else." She looked at Nash.

"Remember what I said," he spoke harshly, releasing Ben with reluctance. Kim took him possessively.

"Don't get into anything now, Tim. Let's make this simple and easy for everyone." She looked down at the inconsolable, confused face of their son.

Nash said nothing. The sunset streamed into the kitchen, falsely brightening the derelict. Their footsteps as they walked to the front door were hollow, echoing, and intolerable. Kim and he paused. She had packed the station wagon in the driveway. Maybe she was right. There was nothing to be gained by raging now, with Ben to listen and be hurt. Pretend instead she was only going away for one of those weekends that had actually been heralds of the end.

34

Only a couple of days and she'd return and they would stumble on a little longer, both acting.

"The listing will start showing up tomorrow," Nash said, low and tight. "The price we agreed for the house, two hundred seventy-five, assumable mortgage. Agent says the place shouldn't stay on the market for more than a couple of weeks. Everybody wants a place like this now."

Kim's eyes roved over the contours of the house, then settled on him. She held Ben by the hand. She wants to slow it down, stop it, too, he thought. She doesn't feel as sure it's as right as she's been telling me.

She jingled a key ring, put it in Nash's hand. "That's the house, the two sets for the garage door and the backyard lock. I called the utilities so they should shut off. You're sure you don't want to move in?"

Nash shook his head. "I like it where I am." Then, "I promised Ben I'd call tonight when you got in." He touched his son's hair.

"We'll be pretty tired."

"For Christ sake," he snapped.

Ben said, "I don't mind if I'm tired," and Nash wondered what Kim was saying to Ben when they were alone, explaining the inexplicable and inexcusable destruction of the family to him. I'd like to know the kind of lies, he thought furiously.

She said, "All right, call if you want. Don't make it too late." She sighed uncomfortably. "I know you've got the Soika trial tomorrow. I know it's difficult."

"I'm handling it."

"I just meant—" she said, then gently, "hell. We have to go. You've got my sister's address and number."

"I said I was going to call."

"Right. Right. Say good-bye to Dad, Ben," she ordered.

Ben waved silently, head down a little, the heat pressing down. Nash seized him quickly, held him, and then Kim and his son walked down the brick front path he'd built and got into the station wagon. Against the fading sun, in the dry, heated air, they were black cutouts punched in the light. He stood slightly back in the doorway and saw the car slowly turn the corner, disappearing.

He left the door open. He knew everyone up and down Avila Avenue. On Saturdays they joked as they cut the lawn or struggled to save dying bushes, commented on new paint, a baseball game on TV, endless mundane details that made life comfortable and bearable.

35

I don't have it anymore, he realized finally. He'd fight to get the visitation order modified so he could see Ben longer, even keep him in Santa Maria over school vacations. Kim would be before a judge sooner or later asking for more support payments, and that would be the ideal time to demand more time with his son.

But the moment-to-moment perception of unbridgeable loss was hard.

Nash went back to Ben's room, looking down from the window onto the backyard. The stone barbecue was never lit this last summer. The complex of cardboard-box forts Ben and the neighbor boys had made was gone. He and Ben had been reading *Treasure Island* lately, reaching the first instance when Long John Silver fools young Jim with his kindness. It was a lesson worth learning, this fraud of goodwill and happiness.

He stayed at the window for a very long time thinking of the story and its unfinished nightly readings.

8

NO LAUNDRY LIST TONIGHT, ED. JUST ONE CUSTOMER I HAVE TO see," Vincent Escobar said to the chunky deputy sheriff who perfunctorily moved him and his briefcase through the metal detector in the main jail's lobby. At the dinner hour the high-ceilinged big room was filled with people trying to see relatives in custody. They didn't like Escobar getting preferential treatment.

"Soika, I bet." The deputy sheriff grinned.

"Sure. He wants me to hold his hand."

The deputy sheriff handed Escobar his briefcase. "Man, I was looking at sniffing the pill, I'd like someone there, too."

"You know me." Escobar winked. "That's not likely."

"Shit. I know you, Vince. He ain't going anyplace."

"That's why I get these terrific fees from the county." At that they both laughed. As county employees, even on opposite sides, they appreciated the irony.

"Hey, you getting any more Dodgers' tickets? My wife, she's gotten hooked on that."

"I'll get you some tickets for the next game," Escobar said.

"The last ones were great. Primo seats."

"How about some tickets to the playoffs?"

"Shit. The Dodgers ain't getting in the playoffs."

Escobar shrugged.

"You know something about it?" the deputy asked. "Maybe you better put me down for two. No. Three. I can sell one."

"Sell a couple. I get you a half dozen," Escobar said. Nobody ever cared where he got the tickets. He knew enough clients and ex-clients to have a supply. It was enough that he spread them around liberally to clerks and sheriffs and bailiffs at the jail and courthouse.

"Thanks, Vince."

The line of people behind Escobar had lengthened, and the deputy sheriff barked at them to back up as Escobar sauntered down the corridor.

He had changed clothes since the trial that afternoon. It was still hot, so he wore knee-length tan shorts and a white sports shirt. His hand holding the briefcase slipped and he wiped sweat off his neck.

Escobar saved no tickets for himself. He had no interest in public events, either sporting or cultural. He preferred spending nights with his wife of twenty-six years and their four children and very large Newfoundland dog. They lived in a small one-story house on the north side of Santa Maria, near enough to the river that he could justify the medium-sized sailboat filling his garage.

If he was not at home with his wife and children, rather than sit in a stadium or theater, Escobar liked the excitement of a Korean reflexology expert. For one hundred fifty dollars an hour he enjoyed exotic and strenuous pleasures. He even represented one of his nighttime partners on a prostitution charge. It was hard for him not to laugh at her pathetic attempts to arouse his vigor on her behalf in court when she ran a tiny, pointed red tongue over her lips, staring at him.

He walked down a flight of stairs, hewn, it seemed, from marble, into a floor lit by fluorescent, humming lights where heavy doors rattled as they opened and closed. Every so often, he heard a voice in anger, but that was rare. It was often so quiet on the attorneys' visiting side of the jail, it was like a library.

"Escobar to see Soika," he said to the young deputy perched in the control booth.

"In number six. He's up now," said the deputy. "You want him restrained?"

"Is he ballistic tonight?"

"Yeah. Bouncing off the walls. He's burned about something."

"He's always burned," Escobar said. He cursed. "No. Leave him loose. Somebody nearby if I yell?"

"Keep someone in there with you, if you want."

"Just come running if I start yelling," Escobar said. "You want a Hershey bar? My secretary stuck one in the briefcase and I'm on a diet."

"I'll take it."

Escobar reached in, making sure he didn't show the other candy bars or cigarettes he usually brought to the jail. Not for clients, that was forbidden. But the deputies appreciated a little thoughtfulness and returned the favors.

He closed the briefcase after taking out a legal pad. "I'll pick it up on my way out."

"Sure. I'll watch it," the young deputy promised. He stuck the candy bar into his uniform shirt pocket. Three other lawyers, sweaty and red-faced, came in, murmuring about clients to see.

Whistling, Escobar walked down the line of attorney visiting rooms, each with a small window in the door. Most were occupied, two men intently debating how and where one of them would likely spend the next few years of his life. There was usually little high emotion, only resignation or incomprehension. A nickel for every guy I had to tell over and over what would happen to him when the store clerk pointed him out in court and I'd be rich. Richer, Escobar thought. He didn't believe in displaying what he had.

He went into room number six. He disliked being with Evan Edward Soika when his client was unencumbered by leg and belly chains and handcuffs.

"Ev. How's it going tonight?" he said.

"Shitty, Vince. Plain one-hundred-percent shitty and it's your fault."

Escobar sat down slowly and easily. Soika stood, trembled, paced, on the other side of a Plexiglas screen. There was a flat surface for them to write on or pass notes, but nothing thicker than a piece of paper.

Soika had journeyed from the California Youth Authority to state prison. Escobar had kept the jury from learning that Soika's prison time had been for another gas station robbery. It was a manslaughter conviction, though. The shotgun he had used in that earlier robbery had also gone off accidentally, Soika claimed, while pressed against the gas station attendant's skull.

"My fault?" Escobar said calmly.

"Yeah. You. Yours. How come you let that cop get away with lying about me? How come?"

"I did a good job for the jury. The judge's being a hard ass so it's not easy."

"So you're going to let the judge bang me into the fucking gas chamber?"

"No. I won't. You see how I'm working. I've got the jury seriously wondering if the shotgun did go off accidentally."

"Sure as hell did, man. I was ready to give up when the fucking cops charged on me."

Escobar smiled, nodding. It was like reassuring a skittish animal. At this point in a murder trial, even the toughest ones started to hear their own heartbeats.

Soika paused, sitting down, hands tapping in front of him. Escobar really wished there was something more than this flimsy Plexiglas between them. It was better in court with Soika. He was bolted to his chair, able to move only a little to the right or left. All the jury could see was an admirably quiet young man.

"Look, Ev," he said, "I'll keep the cop on the stand tomorrow. I'll work on him lying to you. I promise." Escobar wiped sweat off his neck. He very much wanted to go home to a barbecued steak. He might even have a water fight with the kids. Or he could waste a little time on the way home, stop at the East-West Massage Studio on south Sixteenth Street and really relax.

"Okay, okay." Soika was agreeable momentarily. "I don't get my phone calls either."

"No?"

"I missed them twice, Vince, when they take me to the courthouse."

"Well, I'll work on it."

"Shit. You get them. I'm supposed to get them."

"Ev, you've got to calm down. We've got a while to go on this trial, and the calmer you are, the more the jury thinks you got a bad deal."

"I got fucked."

"Well, I'm making that clear."

"So when I'm taking the stand?" Soika stared at him.

"I don't know."

"Fuck. You're my lawyer. You're supposed to know."

"I haven't decided if you're going to testify."

Soika bounced up again and Escobar gingerly pushed his own chair closer to the door. If he was quick, and shouted loudly enough, the deputies could be here in fifteen seconds. Not good. In that time, Soika could pummel him quite a bit, and Escobar had no illusions about his own ability to fight back. He wondered again why they never went after the DAs, the bailiffs, or the judge. Why do they always beat up or stab their own lawyers?

"I want to tell my story, Vince. I'm going to tell them every way the cops jacked me around. They got that guy killed. It wasn't me. It was their fault. Shit, I was all ready to come out, I put the shotgun down, and the guy picks it up, the cops start shooting, and that gun goes off in the guy's hands."

"If you testify, you expose yourself to cross-examination." Escobar was firm and direct. "The DA gets to go after you. Then Nash, the judge, he'll do it, too."

Soika snorted, slapping his hands on the table. It had a faintly muffled sound coming through the Plexiglas. "I can take care of myself up there."

Escobar had come to that moment when he needed to assert control over his client. The moment came to different people at different times as they were digested by the jails and courts, as they sat and listened to evidence rising against them and saw the faces in the jury box icily watching them. Soika had never been very tractable. His urgent whisperings and jigglings during this trial upset Escobar.

"You can't protect yourself from a guy like Nash," Escobar said sternly. "You might get away with it with the DA, but Nash's the judge. He's God in there to the jury."

"I won't roll over."

"You know what else happens if you hit the witness stand, Ev? I've told you five times already."

"You think I never took care of myself before you came along?"

"For the last time I'll tell you," Escobar said. "On the witness stand, all that stuff I've worked so hard to keep away from the jury will come out."

"It was an accident."

"Two accidents? Twice you killed a man with a shotgun when a robbery went sour?"

40

Soika frowned deeply. He stared at Escobar. "The cops killed the guy this time."

"I'm your lawyer. I'm pretty good at my job."

"Yeah?"

"I'm not in jail."

"Shit, Vince. You take care of me when I testify."

Escobar shook his head. "I can't. The judge will tear you up."

"So what're you doing? What's so great about what you're doing for me?"

"I'm going to keep you out of the gas chamber."

"I don't testify, I don't see how."

Escobar wiped away nervous sweat from his neck. His wife hated his work and the time he devoted to it, weekends and nights. He vainly tried to show her how his long hours, the ugly people and things he had to deal with routinely, were helping to provide for their retirement. A retirement that looked more attractive every year. He had done favors, both legitimate and not, for various people around the city and collected favors in return. Much of that was gathering interest in several bank accounts around northern California under the names of his wife's four nieces in Pittsburgh.

But over and above the financial rewards, Escobar liked being in court. He enjoyed besting men like Benisek, manipulating a pillar of the community like Judge Nash. It made life dramatic, gave it zest.

"So far the jury has the idea the cops should've lived up to their part of the bargain," Escobar said.

"I can tell them how I was bullshitted."

"So no matter what happened later, the jury can decide you were cheated. They don't convict guys they think were cheated, Ev."

"Yeah, but—" Soika wanted to go on and on with his complaints and demands. It had been this way ever since Escobar picked up the case. He would have gotten out of it, too, but for the fact that the desire to thumb his nose at the cops and the DA was great.

"So what I'm building for you is jury sympathy, Ev. And what that means, are you listening?"

"I'm here."

"What I'm setting up is a thing where the jury does what it wants, not what the judge tells them to do."

"So how you going to get this sympathy when the judge's pulling his shit?"

Escobar stood up. His legs had stuck a little to the plastic chair.

The sweat was not entirely from being hot. It was fear of Soika. Escobar had long ago admitted he liked the fear and excitement.

"Besides trying to get specific performance of your bargain with the cops, I've got some plans for Nash."

"Like?"

"I'm going to work on him. Rattle him. Upset him. He's just the kind of arrogant jackass who could blow up in front of the jury."

Soika sat down, hands flat in front of him, dark eyes on Escobar. "What good that do me?"

"The trial doesn't go to the jury."

"What happens?"

"Mistrial. We start all over. I may even convince Benisek he won't get a good result and you never go to trial at all."

A smile finally broke on Soika's face. "I like that, Vince. I want to walk out of here."

"So let me work on the judge. Okay?"

Soika stood up. He grinned widely. He was wearing jail sweats with a number in white stenciled on the pants and COUNTY JAIL on the shirt. "Hey, Vince. Okay."

Escobar picked up his legal pad. He had written nothing on it. These hand-holding sessions were not taught in law school or in the private practice of most attorneys. They were, he had found, an indispensable part of criminal defense work. He had five clients on death row at San Quentin. That was embarrassing. He had saved sixteen others.

"So I'll see you tomorrow. Don't give the guys here any crap about your clothes, Ev. Just put on what I left for you."

"I look like a dip."

"You look sincere."

Soika nodded, balled up a fist. "Hey, Vince. You want to know about the two guys in Redding? You want to know if I killed them?"

Escobar shook his head vigorously. "I don't want to talk about it. The cops haven't charged you. The DA up there says there's no case."

"I mean, between me and you. Just us. You want to know?"

Soika stared at Escobar. There was no question about these unsolved, still-open attacks on transients sleeping in alleys in Redding.

"No, Ev," Escobar said deliberately. "I don't want to know."

9

THE FIRST INSTINCT IS FLIGHT. TO PUT AS MUCH DISTANCE AS POS-sible between the cataclysm and yourself. So Nash locked the empty house on Avila Avenue and got into his car and started driving.

He followed Constellation Boulevard, an overbuilt slice of Laun-dromats and burger joints, used boat and car lots that cut through the older center of Santa Maria. In the oncoming night, the rings of lights around the car lots sparkled and the pennants dipped sadly in the windless air.

He drove westward and ended up, after the glowing office towers and neon signs downtown, at the embarcadero on the slow river. It was a place of warehouses and weathered wood and steel, ice cream stores and T-shirt tourist dives. He took his coat off to get any slight breath of a breeze. He walked among strangers, past places he and his brother played, dived into the river. He thought of how far he and Dick could walk along the slender beach until it grew so narrow the land and river merged.

A shuffling man in a stiff, old Army jacket wanted him to buy a winning lottery ticket.

He missed Kim and Ben. He anticipated the emptiness of Sunday mornings without Kim, in bed, lazily watching the day begin, eating toast and coffee. They had not done this for months and now would never again.

He felt separate already when he got up in the morning in his apartment without the pleasant sense of her body pressed against his.

He got back in his car. He was hot, tired, and lonely. He drove toward the north end of Santa Maria where his parents lived.

* * *

Jack and Hilary Nash owned a grand three-story, pink-plastered monstrosity they'd bought eight years before. His father explained that it was the showiest, most gaudy home the city had to offer, and now that he was going to make some real money after years of public service, he wanted to advertise his success grossly.

The neighborhood was dark, a few kids on bikes shouting as they rode by. Nash heard piano music as he walked to the house, and the overhanging elms and tall palms along the street shivered at their tops in the faint wind. His mother was practicing for her Thursday lesson. She was very good, a little shy about playing, but sweetly elegiac in style.

He went into the house by the side door, into the dark pantry. His father was speaking.

"I wasn't going to say anything," Jack Nash complained.

"Sometimes you don't hear yourself," Hilary Nash said a little distantly from the piano. "I don't want to push him about it at all."

"I wasn't going to push him, dammit, Hills. I won't upset him. You always think I run my mouth."

"You like to hear yourself."

"All I'd say is it's better for Timmy and Ben, and everybody, that Kim's running out. If Timmy wants to know, that's how I feel."

"Keep it to yourself," Hilary Nash said.

Nash came into the dining room. His father was at the pewter dry sink busily mixing drinks. He had a Camel cigarette stuck in the side of his face so he squinted like a scientist at the liquors in the clear-glass pitcher he held. The air-conditioning was on high and Nash's skin was suddenly cold.

"You have enough there for a couple for me?" Nash asked, pointing at the pitcher.

Jack Nash looked up, smoke curling around him. "Timmy. I didn't hear you sneak in. Drop your coat."

The piano stopped and Nash hugged his mother when she came in and took his hand.

"Is everything all right?" Hilary Nash still spoke with enough of a Midwestern twang to stand out against the neutral speech of Santa Maria. She was near seventy, but trim, white haired, and graceful. She had looked nearly the same, Nash thought, for twenty years.

"House's all locked up." Nash put his coat in a chair, took off his tie. "Kim and Ben are on their way to the airport. I'm on my own."

Hilary Nash led him to the living room. "I'd like to take some of your pain away. I wish there were a way for me to do that."

"There isn't," Nash said curtly. "I'm sorry. I'm tired and I kind of don't know what I'm going to do next."

His father marched in and handed him a martini. Hilary Nash had her usual ginger ale on the mahogany coffee table. The room was very high and in contrast to the Mediterranean exterior, tricked out inside as a Tudor mansion with beams and rough nails.

"To better times, Son." Jack Nash lifted his glass in a toast. Nash drank.

"Jesus Christ, that's strong, Dad." He coughed slightly. "This is what you have every night?"

"I don't have to stay sober for court in the morning." His father grinned. "It makes life a mite more enjoyable."

Nash sat down in one of the cushioned chairs. He smelled the rich odor of pork ribs and apple pie cooling. Heavy food to dull the senses.

"We talked it over"—Hilary Nash sat straight on the sofa—"and you can stay here if you'd like. It wouldn't be a problem for us. If it would help you."

"Move in tonight," Jack Nash said. "Stay as long as you want to."

Nash tightly held his icy drink. "No. Thanks a lot. I don't think it would be a good idea." He would not stay because seeing the two of them reminded him of growing up and then of how long they had been married. It was a digging reminder of his failure.

His mother said, "Dick called yesterday. He said he hasn't been able to talk to you."

"I haven't had time."

"He's thinking of you."

"I'll call him soon."

"He says he'd like to help."

Nash drank quickly. "I don't need everybody's help."

Hilary Nash stopped. She had never pursued raw emotions in the family. When they appeared, she retreated.

They ate dinner shortly afterward. Jack Nash, as always, ate like a lion, a full plate twice. Dinner was on his schedule, always at six sharp and wrath if there was any delay. It was a real sacrifice for him to eat so late tonight, Nash thought, picking at the food his mother had thought would please him.

He watched his father as they talked. Jack Nash was six feet tall when he stood, growing fleshy finally, with a curled mass of white hair and gray-rimmed glasses, the lined and hard features of a commander. Unlike almost any other man Nash had ever met, he

45

looked like a stern and wise judge. He was a fearful example to follow. Nash recalled sitting in his father's courtroom, listening to that resonant, careful voice from the bench. The defendants and lawyers were respectful as his father divined the truth of auto crashes and shootings, bad leases and insurance-fraud cases.

Sons for some time think of their fathers as being infallible and right. It was awesome when almost everyone else thought the same thing.

Nash remembered days playing with his father's bailiffs and clerks, cheating at puzzles with them, a childhood spent in a courtroom. At parties and receptions for his father, Hilary at his side, he and his brother ran, when they were young, carelessly among the well-dressed people. Sometimes his father, in a tuxedo, would chase them.

He's got a whole street named after him, Nash thought, the spontaneous gift of grateful homeowners for his ruling in a zoning case that kept a shopping center off their doorstep. Jack Nash was elected presiding judge of the Superior Court more times than anyone else because the other judges thought he was fair.

Jesus, if I started tonight, I'd never catch up. Never catch up as a judge or a husband or a father, Nash thought. He pushed his plate away. He loathed the petty bitterness that colored his feelings tonight.

His mother was talking until she noticed his distraction.

"Tim? Thinking?" she asked.

"Some rough spots in the trial tomorrow. I've got a cop testifying now," he said, trying to be conversational.

"Who's the DA?" Jack Nash finished eating and lit another Camel.

"Craig Benisek. I knew him in Misdemeanors. He's thorough. He takes it a little too easy."

"Who's the defense?"

"Vince Escobar's lead. Cindy Duryea's along if we get to a penalty-phase trial," Nash said. She would put on the last-ditch appeal to the jury to spare Soika, if it came to that.

His mother had her hands pyramided on the linen tablecloth. "I see him on TV every day. He likes to talk a lot."

"Should've issued a gag order," his father said, reaching for his wineglass again. "Keep all the chatter in court."

"I've warned Escobar." Nash felt compelled to defend himself.

"Hold him in contempt. That'll keep him quiet."

"I want to avoid a mistrial."

"Well, Timmy, you've got a high-visibility trial. Don't let it get away from you."

Nash finished his own glass of wine, saw his father quickly drink another glass, conscious of his mother's worried expression. She was always interceding between father and sons, especially during meals, when Jack Nash tried to stay the judge on the bench and lecture to a captive and passive audience. The heavy ticking of the hall grandfather clock carried in the silence.

"I've had to ask too many questions," Nash said. "The DA doesn't seem to see that the jury could get annoyed with the cops."

"You just better watch out for Escobar."

"I am keeping an eye on him."

"I know him. I know his stunts. He'll try to run the trial every chance. Objections without foundations. Talking objections to the jury. You order him to stop and he'll argue with you in front of the jury. He'll argue with the DA, something personal. You'll have to hold him in contempt sooner or later."

"I'll decide when."

"I know how these ladies and gentlemen work," Jack Nash went on relentlessly. "They want to make the judge so damned pissed off—excuse me, Hills—he says something dumb on the record."

"I don't allow anybody to do that to me," Nash said.

Hilary Nash was puzzled. "I can't see that any tricks will work. It doesn't sound like a difficult case."

Before his father could supply the answer, Nash said, "It's not a legal problem. Soika used a gun in the robbery. Someone got killed. Technically he's responsible no matter how it happened."

"I thought it was simple," his mother said.

"But Escobar's making it a case of cops lying, tricking Soika, jumping the gun, causing the death themselves."

"Put everybody else on trial when you're guilty," Jack Nash said.

"I've got to walk a fine line of making sure the jury hears the truth and yet I can't take sides."

"Of course not," his mother said with a little irony.

"Absolutely," Nash said.

Jack Nash ground out his cigarette. "Don't let Escobar run your trial, Timmy. Don't let the DA either."

"I'm in control of my own courtroom. I don't think anybody doubts that," Nash said coolly. The meal, what little he'd eaten, lay cold and heavy in his stomach with the liquor. He was far less sure of himself than he sounded.

"I think the police were justified in lying to save that hostage," Hilary Nash said quietly.

"We're hypocrites about how much truth gets told anyway," Nash said. "Juries miss a lot. We hide a lot of truth in court."

Jack Nash snorted. "Stay on the bench for a few years. Tell me if you've heard any truth. From anybody."

His father's cynicism had always been there, but only at home, away from his public duties. It was hard as a child to reconcile those caustic remarks at home with the deference and reverence the black-robed judge Jack Nash displayed at banquets or Boy Scout ceremonies or countless other civic functions. The court, he used to intone, was the temple of truth. Justice was only possible in an American courtroom.

Maybe he sat up there all those years, or too many of them, thinking just the opposite, Nash realized.

He changed the subject, sorry he and his father had even sparred lightly as they had too often in the past. "Dennis Terhune came by after court." Nash smiled. "In the cafeteria. He looked like a fish out of water there."

"If you shook hands with that bastard, I hope you counted your fingers afterward," his father growled.

"It was a social call."

"What did he want?" Nash's mother asked. Perhaps the old rumors around the courthouse, never spoken aloud while he was nearby but part of the folklore of a fading generation, were true. The two senior partners of Terhune, Marks, Heifitz and Nash had broken up because they loved the same woman: his mother. She was already married to Jack Nash as he strove to build one of the largest and most productive law firms in the city.

"I don't know what he wanted," Nash answered. "He was mysterious. He wanted me to meet someone tonight."

"Terhune and his deals," his father scoffed roughly. "He's always got some deal over here, and he's got to tie it up with some other deal over there," he said, gesturing broadly across the table. "I don't know why you talk to that crooked son of a bitch, Timmy. Jesus, I don't."

And so the hatred had gone all these years, the two former partners prospering alone, and in his own way, each established a reputation for honesty, fairness, and decency. Except when his father spoke of him, Nash would have assumed Terhune was a good man.

They finished dinner quickly, no one wanting to linger at the table. For a while they sat in the living room, Nash relieved to be around familiar things again, the thick, blue-upholstered chairs, the flowered sofa he and his brother had romped on as kids.

When his mother went into the kitchen to get a glass of ginger ale, he followed her.

At the refrigerator, out of earshot of his father, who had turned on a TV baseball game, she said suddenly, "Nothing you've ever heard about Dennis Terhune and me is true. None of it about him and your father."

"I never thought it was true."

"But you started wondering again when you saw him today."

"I thought about it," he admitted. "He was nervous and that was odd." Nash felt as if he were being chastised.

"Whatever your father and Dennis split up about was totally separate from me. We've had a good life. You should never doubt it's been exactly what it looked like."

He rarely saw his mother's resoluteness. It was unsettling, as if another person were revealed, lending credence to the inchoate courthouse rumors.

Nash folded his arms as she filled her glass and stood by the sink. "Why did they break up? I've heard everything from a bad romance to embezzlement. Dad never told me directly," he asked her pointedly.

"I don't know for certain. Honestly. It was a long time ago. Your father came home one afternoon, in the middle of the afternoon"— she chuckled at the shock of that lapse—"and he was furious." She sipped slowly. "He went on and on for hours about Dennis. Personal things generally."

"Like what?"

"Unpleasant personal things. I haven't thought about it in a long time," she said to end it.

"That was the reason for the split? Dad didn't like Terhune's after-shave? It was a good practice. They were taking in a lot of money, everybody says."

"We did very well those years. I think it must have been some basic argument about how they were going to run the firm. Your father never liked sharing decisions with Dennis. He never liked having a rival partner."

"Did you ask him?"

She smiled. "You know your father. He didn't want to tell me. No more said."

"Some of the guys at the courthouse, the ones getting very old, they're talking more, Mom. They say it was a case. Some case they had together went bad or something." Nash knew he was interrogating as he had when he was a prosecutor, but these questions had shaped his own life.

"It could have been like that." She set her glass on the blue-tiled counter. "All that mattered was that we picked up and moved on. Where your father went, that's where I went."

"Things have changed," Nash said, drawn back to a few hours before with Kim.

His mother realized what he meant. "You shouldn't blame Kim for everything that's happened to both of you," she said carefully. "I'm not excusing her. I only want you to know it's very hard being the wife of a judge, Tim. Some women muddle along with it, some can't stand it."

"You and Dad managed."

"Your father and I have worked very hard at staying together. There were a lot of things that worked to pull us apart."

Agitatedly, Nash walked around the large, gleaming kitchen. "I worked. I tried hard with her. I told her tonight I won't let her take Ben. He's my son."

Hilary Nash put a hand on his arm. "Go ahead and fight. I want you to know I've been luckier than a lot of judges' wives. I know wives who drink, who are hard, who simply gave up. Nobody wants to talk to you, Tim," she said, touching her chest. "It's always the judge everybody wants to meet, to be with, to flatter. Anywhere you go. You become part of his furniture."

"Kim never minded the brownnosing when we were out. She thought it was funny, at parties, dinner, people going out of the way to talk to us."

"To you. Not her."

"You didn't run away," he said harshly.

"I was lucky. Kim's a different person. You need to accept that." She kissed his cheek gently. The gesture confused and disarmed him.

"I better go," he said, her arm falling from him. She stayed in the kitchen while he went back to the living room and got his coat. His father looked up from the TV. He was in an easy chair, legs propped up on a hassock. His buttoned, tangerine-colored sweater gave him the jauntiness of a salesman.

"Taking off?" Jack Nash asked with studied calm.

"Long day tomorrow. I've got the trial. Got a heavy morning calendar first."

"Do all the twelve-oh-three referrals to probation first, take their damn guilty pleas last," his father advised. "I'll walk you out."

He lumbered from the chair with a groan. He strolled out the front door with Nash, onto the lawn and into the still, warm night. The massed camellias around the house looked clotted in the dark, the air heavy with sharp lemon.

"No pep talks, Dad," Nash said abruptly.

"I wouldn't know what to say."

Nash looked into the dark, across the street to the other big houses fired with lights. "I don't know what I did wrong."

His father was silent. Then, "Maybe you didn't do anything."

"Look at you and Mom. You made it work. So I wonder where I made a mistake."

Jack Nash lit a Camel, exhaling. His resonant voice sounded as it had when Nash listened raptly to it from the back of the courtroom years ago. "Your mother's a very smart woman. She made one mistake in her life. Marrying me." Jack Nash chuckled slightly. Nash had heard this deprecatory line many times. Now it finally had the ring of authenticity. "We don't choose them, Timmy. They choose us."

"I can't make sense of anything tonight," Nash conceded, inhaling the dark night. "Thanks for the advice. I'm sorry if I sounded off."

"You're entitled to it," his father said, stumbling uneasily into the strained intimacy he had with both his sons. "You let me know if I can do anything for you."

"I will."

"You call me. Anytime, you call. You want to go somewhere for a drink, go anyplace, you call me, Timmy."

Nash was moved by the offer. He had seen sides of his mother and father tonight they seldom exposed. "I'll talk to you soon, Dad." Ahead lay the long night.

"Last piece of advice tonight. Don't worry about the trial, keep those bastards in line," Jack Nash said. "If that bastard Terhune comes poking around, tell him to go to hell. From me."

10

I DON'T MIND HAVING A BUST HANDED TO ME," SGT. JERRY WITWER said.

"Christ, who does?" Sgt. Roger Valles, his partner, replied heatedly. "I just get pissed when it's handed to me on my fucking time."

The two undercover cops sat in a dented red Fairlane in the crowded parking lot of La Cabana Club on Meredith Avenue. It was close to nine at night, and couples walked or swaggered into the brick club. Salsa music floated out over the parking lot, the densely moving street. The club's sign, in pink and white and blue neon, flickered against the sky. It was partly hidden by high palm trees. The two cops passed a vodka bottle of water back and forth. They were parked at a right angle to the building's busy entrance. They could see whoever came in or went out. They watched warily to make sure no one was coming up behind them in the welter of cars and motorcycles passing through the parking lot with loud rumbling.

Every so often, drunks singly or in pairs would dance up to the car windows, press their faces to the glass, and shout obscenely. Witwer, for laughs, had put rubber bands in his beard. He would jiggle the phony vodka bottle and the drunks would laugh and stagger off.

Since getting the search warrant earlier in the day from Judge Nash, the two men had changed from bikers to simply construction workers out for the night, in sweatshirts and jeans. The sleeves on the sweatshirts were cut raggedly short.

Valles belched. "All I'm saying is, we work fucking Maiz for days to get her to put out, and when she does and we're ready to go today, fucking Shiffley takes it away and gives us this shit."

"You have to roll with it, guy. That's the job."

"But Christ, Jerry. You think it's okay to just come in, we're all ready to roll on Nash's search warrant, and just take it away? Give it to fucking Chavez and Enfante? Who don't know Maiz? Who don't know anything about the house?"

"I'm not going to fight it," Witwer said calmly. He held the vodka bottle in the crotch of his legs. "Shiffley said this was a big bust, so here we are."

Valles snorted. He looked at the ragged assortment of people parading into La Cabana. The club attracted a variety of customers. Well-dressed couples, pairs of young men with predatory eyes, a loner smoking something, snapping it into the darkness before going inside. "A big coke dealer at this drop-dead joint? Shiffley's crazy."

"Oh, man," Witwer groaned. "I'm so pooped."

"Another thing. I tell Shiffley, hey, Lieutenant, this search warrant deal was my last item, okay? I worked weekends, nights, I put in fucking twenty-nine overtime hours on Maiz and this crack-house bust. So I got twenty-nine hours of CTO coming, starting tonight, and my wife's got dinner reservations and we got a sitter. So don't tell me I've got to hang out at some drop-dead joint on some bust I know nothing about. I got compensatory time off coming tonight."

"You put in for twenty-nine hours CTO?" Witwer asked curiously. He sipped from the vodka bottle. Three men, shaking their shoulders, staggered, whooping and hollering, from the club.

"Damn right. I earned my time off. I shouldn't be sitting here, Jerry. You neither. This is bullshit."

"I only put in eighteen hours," Witwer said.

"I worked that extra weekend. Remember? You went to Fresno?"

Witwer nodded glumly. "Oh. Yeah. Maybe you did do twenty-nine hours."

Valles stretched. At his feet was a red light for mounting on the car's roof. They also had a siren in the unmarked car. "So I'm sick of this bullshit. Where's the fucking big dealer Shiffley's got us waiting for?"

Witwer studied La Cabana's building. "I ain't seen him."

"I'm going to look inside. Maybe he's a no-show."

"Maybe he ain't here yet."

"Shiffley says his snitch says the dealer's inside," Valles said. "You want to come?"

"I ain't sitting here," Witwer said. They had been waiting in the parking lot for close to two hours.

The two undercover cops got out and walked casually into La

Cabana. A mural of two gold peacocks, palms, blue sky, and sea had been painted crudely on the club's facade. Security lights blazed on the garish murals, making the colors shimmer biliously.

Valles led into the dim, loud club. He and Witwer had been with the joint city and county Narcotic Impact Project for a year undercover. They had good records and worked well together. Witwer was reasonable and calm, Valles brash and impetuous during investigations.

Valles looked down the bar, which vanished into blackness at the far end of the club. The music was deafening, piercing guitars and piano and drums. The voices were incomprehensible. A dance floor was so filled with people, couples only undulated without doing any steps. Baby spots, red, blue, yellow, and green, spun over the dancers slashing light and shadow.

He pushed slowly down the bar. Laughter, hands slapping the wood, two sweating bartenders spraying, pouring, shoving glasses out. From the corner of his eye, Valles saw Witwer at his flank, in a protective position.

It took a moment, but he spotted a small, olive-skinned man in a black shirt, a well-cared-for fedora with a feather in it, standing at the midpoint of the bar. He was talking and gesturing grandly to two young women who smirked.

Valles made a high sign and started out of the bar. He got out, took a refreshing breath of the warm night air. It was like syrup. The horizon was purple piped, transparent. Witwer was briefly held up when a middle-aged woman pinched and fumbled playfully with his rubber-banded beard.

"He's in there. Little fucker's having a great time," Valles said, slipping behind the wheel of the Fairlane.

"I ain't trying anything in there," Witwer said emphatically.

"Shit. See what I mean? We got to sit here until the puke wants to go home," Valles said disgustedly.

"I don't mind waiting until he's outside," Witwer said. "Remember Rudy Bustamonte? He got shanked here. We got two shootings here, man. Let's get him out in the open." He scrunched down in his seat.

They waited another forty-five minutes. Valles was more impatient. He became animated when the small man came out, dusting something off his fedora and putting it slowly on his oiled hair.

"Shithead's leaving. He's moving." Valles nudged Witwer, who was dozing, sharply in the side.

"What's he doing?"

Valles stared. "Fuck if I know."

The little man had walked into the parking lot. He stopped. He looked around very slowly. He put his hands on his hips and seemed to be cursing. He walked a few more steps. He cursed again. He appeared to be looking for someone or something. His head moved up and down, snakelike. He cursed again and got into a low, slim sports car.

"The plan's I let him get a couple of blocks, enough so I can say I saw some bad driving when I pull him over." Valles started the Fairlane and pulled into Meredith Avenue a few cars behind the sports car.

"You want to let the uniforms grab the guy?"

"Shiffley said he's ours. We get him. That's how it's supposed to go."

"I'll call for a backup unit." Witwer spoke into the radio's microphone, "Unit nine, westbound on Meredith, crossing Lux. We've got a late-model, black Austin-Healy, California license QAZ three five oh. We're going to make a DUI stop and request assistance." He waited for dispatch to acknowledge.

Waiting, he said, "I kind of miss the old days doing the Highway Patrol routine, 'Twenty-one fifty to headquarters.' It's not as much fun just saying it."

Valles wasn't listening. "Fuck it. It's clear here. Shiffley said the guy's a wuss. I'm going to nail him here."

He put the whirling red light on the Fairlane's roof and switched on the siren. Witwer told dispatch where they were.

· The sports car ahead slowed, pulled over to the side of the street. A hilly, weed-filled lot spread off to one side, several billboards dotting it. Cars brushed along indifferently as Valles pulled up behind the sports car. High streetlights burned overhead.

He got out, pinned a Santa Maria Police Department gold badge to the collar of his sweatshirt, and went over to the sports car.

Witwer waited in the Fairlane.

"Hot night," said the little man in the sports car.

"Could I see your license and registration, sir?" Valles asked politely. "I saw you weaving a bit back there. I think you may be having some trouble."

The little man stared at Valles. "Shiffley?"

"What?"

"You Shiffley?"

"No. I'm Sergeant Valles. Would you step out of the car?" Valles's voice had an edge and he felt for his gun, under the right side of

55

his sweatshirt. He did not like the fact that the little man, sitting nervously, hands on the steering wheel, knew the name of his superior in the Narcotic Impact Project.

"Where's Shiffley?"

"I said, out of the car. Move it. Now." Valles pulled his gun and pointed it at the little man. The face was small, pinched, a tiny black mustache thrust under his fleshy lips.

"Okay. Okay. It's okay," the little man said. "I'm here. I say to Shiffley, 'I'm here, I do just like you say.' Okay. You don't need no gun."

Valles was genuinely worried. Although the little man stank of cigarette smoke and sweat, he had no alcohol smell at all. He hadn't been drinking at La Cabana.

He closely watched the little man get out of the sports car, hands up, shaking slightly. He did not stop talking. "Everything looks great, looks real good. Anybody says it's good, you got me. No questions. Looks good. I should know. This is good stuff."

He shakily held out a brown calfskin wallet to Valles, who took it, flipped it open. Louis Vismara, Jr., read the name. A local address. Vismara carefully took off his fedora and put it on the hood of his car.

"How about this? How about I run, you chase me? You catch me easy, okay? Make it look really good?"

"Shut up, Louis. You wait here. You don't move at all," and Valles walked slowly back to the Fairlane five feet behind the sports car. He pushed the wallet to Witwer.

"Something's funny, Jerry," he said tightly. "Run this mope quick. When's backup coming?"

"Any second." Witwer took the wallet, looked at little Vismara, headlights skimming off him as cars rushed by. "What is it?"

"Fuck if I know."

Then Valles heard Witwer say, "Oh-oh," in that resigned tone, and when he glanced up, Vismara had started a sprint toward the on-ramp of I-5 running to the left of the street.

Valles started after him, shouting. He heard the squeak and crunch of the backup squad car behind him. Every so often Vismara would turn his sleek little head, put on a burst of speed. He never, though, seemed to run as if he really meant it. Valles caught him, pushed him easily down to the ground.

"Tell Shiffley, Louie made it good. Okay?" he husked as he was quick-stepped back to the squad car, Valles holding on to him tightly. He was handcuffed. He smiled fiercely. "Tell him I made it perfect, okay? Running and everything."

"I don't know what the hell you're talking about," Valles said.

"Pleasure working with you," Vismara said merrily as he was pushed into the back of the squad car. He asked a cop to retrieve his fedora before they left.

Valles and Witwer then did a thorough inventory of the sports car. Another squad car rolled up, lights whirling, and the roadside was congested with uniformed cops wandering around. Shiffley had promised that coke would be found on this man, and Valles quickly located four gram bags in the glove compartment and two more under the front seat. Witwer pried open the compact trunk and found a five-ounce package in the rim of the spare tire. It was enough for a substantial haul for the night.

They tagged the coke and brought it down to the police department to be booked into evidence. Shiffley had gone home hours before.

"I got a couple of questions for him," Valles said, pouring coffee so he and Witwer could write up the report on Vismara's arrest.

"I want to go home," Witwer said. He smoothed out the computer sheet of Vismara's lengthy arrest record.

Chavez and Enfante were also working on their reports. Maiz's information had been good, and the raid had closed a profitable crack house. Valles swore under his breath.

"That was our fucking case."

"So we got this one instead," Witwer said. He wasn't bothered by the sometimes capricious substitutions of police work.

"Right," Valles agreed, rolling paper into the typewriter. He lowered his voice so Chavez and Enfante wouldn't hear. "I don't know why, I don't know how, I don't know for who, but I tell you, partner, I think we just got set up."

11

Nash had rented a large apartment on Serrano Drive, a fenced-in maze of white-cupolaed buildings with a security guard, pools, and tennis courts. Driving in, it had all the sincerity of a whorehouse at night for him, blue and red lit, with laughter and music wafting throughout from parties that went on night after night.

He walked into the apartment, shedding his coat, tie, then shoes. He dropped the stack of court papers on the glass coffee table and got a beer. A woman shrieked just outside his back door, from the turquoise pool, and there was a lot of splashing.

The apartment was Spartan: empty shelves, two chairs, a stiff-haired couch. He sat down, flipped open the first probation report, and drank his beer. The final recommendation was five years, eight months in state prison for a residential burglary. Nash circled it. That would be his sentence tomorrow. He didn't look at the crime or what the defendant or victims had to say. Nash paused. He did not know how he could pass judgment in the morning.

He picked up the phone and tried Shea's home across town. No answer. Then he tried a law school classmate, a woman who practiced personal-injury defense. He talked aimlessly to her, heard her wait for his invitation, grow cool when it didn't come. He called other people, searching and reaching out for some word or hope. Every conversation was forced and pointless, some of the people puzzled at his call. No one would tell a judge he was boring them.

I just want to hear their voices, he thought, hanging up, ready to dial again. Not my own head all night.

The probation reports and motions for the morning lay piled up on the couch, their neglected bulk against his thigh. It was after ten already.

The phone rang and he answered it immediately.

"Timothy? Your line has been busy for the last hour."

"I'm popular tonight, Mr. Terhune."

"Can you spare a little time now?"

"For what?"

Terhune paused. "I can still arrange the meeting I told you about."

"You want to tell me who this is now?"

"He can speak for himself, Timothy. He's very good at it." Nash wondered about Terhune's sour laugh. "I'll pick you up and bring you back."

Nash frowned. "You're my chauffeur? Do I have to dress up for this meeting?"

"No, no, strictly informal. Come as you are," Terhune said with too much haste. "Twenty minutes enough for you?"

"Sure. More than enough," Nash said. He hung up and finished his beer, thinking about whoever wanted to meet him so much and why Terhune, who used others for the purpose, would shepherd the meeting himself.

Nash didn't care who it was or what it was about. It would occupy his time tonight.

"Where are we going?" Nash asked as soon as Terhune pulled away and drove the long, sleek Mercedes into the thinning traffic toward downtown Santa Maria.

"The Hilton," he answered. Terhune drove with concentration, eyes forward. He was still dressed impeccably at that hour, as if he could step from a board meeting to a dinner party.

"Do I need to know anything?" Nash asked. "Why this meeting?"

Terhune shook his head. "It's all self-explanatory, Timothy. They'll be impressed."

"Plural?"

"I assume there will be several present."

Nash breathed in the climate-controlled air, gently cooled and humidified. The interior of Terhune's car was leather lined, soft and expensive. He looked out the window at the glittering summer night, the city glowing faintly. "I don't want another job, if this is some kind of interview. I don't want to join a firm."

Terhune laughed briefly. His carefully maintained ascetic's features contracted. "I worked too hard to get you on the bench to help take you off it."

"This isn't a job proposition? Some offer I can't refuse, six figures the first year, big car allowance, gold circle partner kind of thing?"

"No. Nothing like that." Terhune's eyes stayed straight ahead.

A few minutes later, Terhune drove the big car into the semicircular driveway at the Hilton. It was one of the newest hotels, soaring up pale blue and sharp edged. Terhune waited for him and they walked together into the lobby. Nash had just thrown his coat on again so he was tieless, his short-sleeved white shirt wrinkled and worn from the long day.

Two large fountains sputtered and splashed in the marbled immensity. Men and women, flushed and jolly from the bars and restaurants off the lobby, wobbled to elevators or sat on long green couches around a grand piano. Nash listened to the spry, vapid rhythms in the vast room, sounding so lifeless compared to his mother's playing.

Standing at an elevator, he felt a surge of anger again, as he had with Kim earlier. A man in an incongruous mohair coat, sweating heavily, had his arm around a tall young woman in a tight black dress. They wouldn't look at each other.

"You're going to a lot of trouble," Nash said to Terhune. He wanted a rise from someone—Kim, his father, Terhune.

"No, I'm not."

"I'll just forget it. I said I don't want another job." He started to turn, but Terhune clung to his arm.

"We're here now, Timothy. It won't take long."

"What's the deal? Who am I seeing?"

Terhune smiled, without ease, his poise gone. "I can't say."

Suddenly Nash recognized the nervousness, the faintly hidden anxiety, even if it was being displayed by Terhune. "Are you being squeezed?" he asked slowly.

Terhune had out a silk handkerchief, dabbing at his upper lip and eyebrows. "I don't understand," he said. The man and woman looked at him.

"You're working for somebody." Nash lapsed into the old jargon from his days in Narcotics. Like Maizie working for the undercover guys this afternoon. Working was a way of clearing a debt, a threat. It astounded him to apply the term to Dennis Terhune.

"I still don't understand," Terhune said, the elevator doors opening, stepping inside. Nash and the couple followed.

"Sure you do. You know what I'm saying," Nash said. The elevator rose with abrupt speed, the woman gasping in surprise. Terhune cleared his throat.

"We're going to the twentieth floor, Timothy. I'm doing this on my own and entirely for your benefit." He stared up at the green ascending numerals.

Nash shoved his hands in his pockets. The man and the woman stood close together, still avoiding each other's eyes.

On the twentieth floor they walked briskly, wordlessly, down a carpeted hallway. Terhune checked the room numbers. Nash's up-surge of anger had given way to perplexity. He had been a prosecutor using snitches and halfway uncooperative witnesses for too long not to know the signs when he saw them.

Or think I see them, he thought. Tonight I might think anyone's bent.

Terhune stopped at a room at the end of the hallway, knocked, and the door opened. He stood aside to let Nash go in first.

The man who held the door for Nash was young, in a bland and shapeless blue suit. He did not look to Nash much like a junior associate in any law firm. Too compact, too professionally inquisitive as he looked over Terhune and Nash. He's got a shoulder holster, Nash realized when he briefly glimpsed the straps. He's some kind of cop, Nash guessed.

"I'm Dennis Terhune," Nash heard. "I'm late for a ten-o'clock appointment and I have a guest."

The man nodded. "This way, sir."

Nash led and Terhune followed into a large suite. The open curtains spanned the cityscape all the way west to the harbor, a night scene of silhouetted towers shimmering with ruby aircraft warning lights and streetlights below in long, sinuous lines. King of the mountain up here, Nash thought.

A man in suspenders, holding a large white mug and talking enthusiastically with two other men in bone-gray suits, looked up. A young woman, blond-haired, holding a legal pad, also looked at him.

The man with the mug instantly walked over, hand out.

"Dennis. Thanks for coming."

"This is Tim Nash," Terhune said without warmth to the other man. The suited men observed. Nash noticed the woman jot down something on her legal pad.

He felt his hand grabbed energetically. "It's a great pleasure, Judge. A great, great pleasure for me. I've been looking forward to meeting you. I'm Neil Roemer."

"I thought I recognized you. It's a pleasure for me, too," Nash said sincerely. Roemer's face was a little ruddier, hair thinner, the features blunter, than on TV. He was impressed with Roemer's reputation as a tough prosecutor.

"Judge, this is my assistant, Janice Dillon. She's one of the brighter lights in the U.S. Attorney's Eastern District office. Have you met before?"

Nash shook his head. He felt gawkish because she was attractive and Roemer a celebrity. He took her hand hastily. "No. We haven't met."

"I know your record, Your Honor," Janice Dillon said. "This is a privilege for me."

Roemer said, "Judge, before we go any further, I have to warn you that we will be discussing some very sensitive, confidential matters. I'm very anxious to have your thoughts, your input, because these matters affect your community. But if we talk about them, if you stay"—Roemer grinned sheepishly—"you've agreed to be bound by strict rules of confidentiality."

"I can't tell anybody what we've talked about?"

"You can't even say we've met. You can't say you've been here."

"You're not making me sign anything?" Nash asked jokingly. He glanced at Janice Dillon, but she didn't smile.

"Your word's good enough. There will be reliable witnesses." Roemer nodded at the other men. Cops of some kind, Nash thought, but not locals. A local cop would know who Judge Nash was and show some deference. The name carried the promise of reward or punishment in Santa Maria. These cops looked at him coldly, blankly, like a motorist pulled over on a traffic stop, with caution and obvious suspicion.

"I'll stay," Nash said. "I'd like to hear whatever you've got on your mind, Mr. Roemer. I'm an admirer."

"Good. Great. Terrific." Roemer grinned at Terhune. "Dennis, thanks so much for coming and all your help getting us together." He didn't extend his hand.

"I said I'd drive the judge home when you were done," Terhune said stiffly.

"That's all right. I'll make sure he has safe passage back."

Terhune hesitated, then said, "Good night, Timothy. Good luck to you," and he left. Nash thought Terhune's dignity had been affronted in some way he couldn't perceive.

Nash walked with Roemer and Janice Dillon into the suite. There was a wide-screen TV with a stack of VCRs beside it and a wet bar with a buffet of sandwiches.

"Have you known him long?" Nash said.

Roemer smiled. "Who?"

"Dennis Terhune."

"Awhile."

"The two of you don't move in exactly the same circles."

"You'd be surprised."

"Okay," Nash said. "Tell me what's going on."

"You want anything first? Beer? Something else? Janice, for you?" Roemer pointed at the bar. "I'm having coffee if you like that."

"Coffee's fine."

Janice said, "Nothing for me, Neil."

Roemer nodded and one of the plainclothes cops fetched a silver carafe and poured another mug. He gave it to Nash. Roemer waited as the cops went into the bedroom at the other end of the suite and closed the door.

"You know what I used to like?" Roemer's faintly beaten face creased with memory. "Ice-cold Kahlúa in a tall glass with cracked ice. Jesus, isn't that Joe Six-pack?" He looked to Janice.

"Your taste never got any better," she said. She sat on the sofa in front of the night-darkened window, pad ready. Nash sensed there was more between her and Roemer.

"But that's me," Roemer said. "I am simple. I like simple things. You know where I came from, Judge?"

"No."

"I grew up in the Mission District in San Francisco. Tough, tough neighborhood. It's where I learned to fight. I came home from school, and Jesus, I must have had a fight every day. I lost some. But I won most of them."

"You ever fight pro?"

"For about a year. I wasn't good enough for that. I was going to law school."

"Your stats are a lot better as a prosecutor."

Roemer nodded. "I still lose a few. But I win a hell of a lot more."

Nash glanced at the long table to his left. A chart was being prepared on it. He saw the names of the municipal and Superior Court judges on the Santa Maria bench. He saw his own name and his father's, too. "My dad's retired," he said, pointing at the chart. "He isn't on the active judges' list anymore."

"We put him there for reference. Because you're on it."

Nash walked toward the sofa, closer to Janice. He liked her quiet attitude. He stood near the window, looking over Santa Maria.

"So tell me why the Justice Department wants to talk to me," he said.

"You must miss it. A little, sometimes," Roemer began.

"Trying a case?"

"Putting it on, making it work. Making the right thing happen."

"I liked being a prosecutor," Nash admitted. "But I like being a judge more."

"What if you had the chance to do both?"

"I can't. A judge doesn't put on a case and rule, too. That's called a conflict." He grinned at Janice and she smiled back slightly.

Roemer didn't smile. "Do you know what my job is, Judge?"

"Corruption. Malfeasance. Cops who take payoffs, politicians taking it in brown bags."

"No." Roemer shook his head. "I deal strictly in honesty. I find the honest people in our system."

"That's not the way it looks from the outside." Nash grinned again. "I've seen a lot of your press conferences and a lot of guys with coats thrown over their heads going to jail."

"They're only the other side of it, the ones who don't measure up. But, I'm truly not looking for them. I want to find the honest men and women."

"I'm here because you want my help?"

"I know you want to help," Roemer said. He paced, tugging at the waistband fastenings of his suspenders. Janice flipped a page over.

"Doing what?" Nash sat down.

"Let's assume that I have predicate information that certain individuals have a predisposition to commit illegal acts." Roemer stood near the table of papers, the chart with judges' names in black felt pen. "I could create an undercover operation in such a way that we could test to find out who the criminal individuals are and who the clean ones are."

"A sting?"

"I could construct a scenario that would give each person a choice. Then we'd know who was crooked."

Nash sat forward. "Do you have information on judges in this county? Is that who you're going after?"

"I do have information."

"From where?" Nash glanced at Janice. She remained impassive.

64

It was as though she and Roemer had the performance choreographed, who spoke and who listened.

"I have sources," Roemer said.

"Who?"

"It's better you don't know who they are. If and when any cases are developed and we go to trial, we may want to withhold the names of these sources or claim a privilege. If I told you the names, you might have to give them up."

"I wouldn't have told you either," Nash said. He was pleased that Roemer protected his snitches. "I don't think anybody should give up an informant unless you put a gun to his head."

"That sounds like a prosecutor."

"When I'm on the bench, sometimes I do put a gun to their heads."

"You're right. Right, Janice? Good guys do not betray friends."

She raised her head a little. She had fine features. "It's bad practice," she said.

The possibility Roemer held out excited Nash. It wasn't like a trial where he sat, ruling when called to do so, unless the lawyer's conduct was so outrageous he had to act on his own. Escobar was like that. The whole Soika trial, in fact, demanded more of Nash's intervention than most cases.

I have to be fair, he thought, watch a DA fumble when he questions witnesses or poorly introduces some evidence. Or worse, when a defense attorney bumbles and I have to step in and save him so that justice to the defendant isn't sacrificed.

But Roemer offered a chance to participate again, cleanly and directly. Nash could decide what was right and wrong without the strain of neutrality.

"You're going after judges I know, right?" Nash asked. He was troubled by the thought.

"A corrupt judge is the worst thing possible," Roemer said firmly. "Worse than a bad cop, a bad lawyer, a crooked officeholder. A corrupt judge brings down the whole temple of justice."

"Yes. He does," Nash answered. "What are you looking for? Specifically?" He got up and picked out a sandwich. He wondered if the cops in the next room were listening. Roemer, he had read, always took precautions and planned carefully.

Janice Dillon answered him. "We're targeting very specific violations, Your Honor," she said. "We will find violations of 18 United States Code, sub c," she rattled off. "Conducting the affairs of an enterprise through a pattern of racketeering."

"Against judges?"

"We've used it against bankers, lawyers, investment brokers, anybody. It's wide open. Judges fall in, too," Roemer said.

"We will be looking mainly at bribery," she said. "Payoffs for rulings or favors."

"What else?"

"USC 1951, extortion under color of official right. That amounts to prostituting his office. USC 1956, money laundering because the bastards always try to hide the payments somehow. They go into real estate, they buy cars or houses or electronic toys." She smiled ruefully. "I've done this before."

"There's nothing new," Roemer added.

"And we'll look at bribery in a federally funded organization. Your county bench has a few government checks coming its way. I might be able to charge a crooked judge through that."

"The IRS's got to be involved," Nash said to her. He had largely forgotten the day's despair and weariness.

Roemer broke in, "Absolutely. I haven't gone after one of these assholes yet who puts a bribe or payoff down on his income tax. So, yeah, we'll have the IRS with us, and I'll be calling on your Franchise Tax Board when we get some solid activity going."

"I can't believe there are many judges here to go after," Nash said.

"I won't tell you the number or names of any potential targets tonight. Obviously you aren't one of them."

"I know all the judges on the bench. Some are old family friends. I grew up playing in their chambers, they were visitors at my house, I ate with them. They worked with my father," Nash said soberly.

"I know." Roemer folded his arms.

"It might limit my ability to help you."

Roemer stared at him and Nash grew uncomfortable. "Let me ask you something, Judge. What if you could stop a dishonest judge from screwing up a criminal case? What if you could nail someone who's selling his office? Would you walk away?"

Nash thought deeply, then said, "I don't know if I could turn in anybody I'd known for a long time. I don't know if I could cause the arrest of an old friend."

"Who does? When it comes to it, nobody can say until it happens," Roemer said. He looked at Janice.

"Have you done it?" Nash asked him.

"When I had to. Yes."

"Was it hard?"

"I won't lie. Yes. It was damn hard."

"I don't know if I can," Nash answered. He looked within himself without finding any definitive answer. In his life, and the inter-woven lives of the men and women he knew in Santa Maria, the connections were old and complicated. He did not know if he could betray one of those people for the higher needs of justice.

Roemer had seen this ambivalence before. He was a seasoned advocate for his cause. "If it helps, you won't be alone. The decision to proceed with a criminal investigation is mine. In consultation with the U.S. Attorney. I'll never ask you to undertake anything you find personally or morally repugnant, Judge."

Nash walked past the sofa, holding his half-eaten sandwich. Janice was sympathetic, he thought. She had covered pages of the legal pad with notes.

I won't be alone, he thought. I'll be doing something decent and honorable for everyone.

Roemer's method comported with his own when he ran Major Narcotics. The cops or informants never made the real decisions. They were his. He bore the full responsibility. Just as Roemer would bear it here. He felt the rush of cold air over his face from the vents by the window. He gazed across the dark, glittering speckled city he'd been born in, raised in, and now served. He decided.

"What do you want me to do?" he asked Roemer and Janice.

"We're going to set up a situation to test these judges. You'll be working for the Task Force on Organized Corruption."

Nash expelled a nervous breath. In Narcotics, he had never done the ground-level work. He would tell the cops what he needed and they'd bring it back or they wouldn't. But they did the hard human effort of persuading a person to deceive another. All in a good cause. Like Ross's lying to Soika to save a hostage.

He put down the sandwich and wiped his sweating hands. "I've never been undercover. I can't act very well."

Roemer chuckled. "You won't act. You'll be yourself, a judge talking to other judges. Offering them bribes to dump a drug case."

"What case?"

"It's a case we'll construct as part of the scenario. Just before you came, I got word the wheels are in motion. We've got a drug case in the works. One we control. When you were prosecuting, you ever come across a dealer named Vismara?"

"No," Nash said.

"You'll be hearing about him now. He'll work fine. We'll have you say you've got a court clerk working with you."

"To move the case into any court we want?"

Roemer nodded. "No names, you won't give up your coconspirators. This kind of story's worked for us in the past. A clerk can send our drug case wherever we want, to whichever judge we target. And you'll have a DA who's in on it."

"What if my target wants some proof, some name?" Nash asked.

"Judge, have you ever done an official-corruption undercover operation?"

"No," Nash said. "I did stolen property, drugs, things like that. Some were fairly complicated."

Roemer glanced at Janice. "Well, I can tell you that official corruption is different. The cover story matters more. The front man matters much, much more. The targets accept the front more completely."

"If we've picked a good one correctly," Janice said.

"You're perfect," Roemer said. "We're being very selective in our targets. These are judges we believe are already corrupt."

"I was wondering what happens if an honest judge turns me in, you know, turns me down and then reports me to the cops or the presiding judge," Nash said.

"It could happen," Roemer said with a nod. "In a dozen operations of this kind, it hasn't."

"Never?"

"No. If it did, we might have to bring that honest judge in on the deal, tell him what's really happening," Roemer said. "But barring the rare chance we stumble on a mistaken target, this operation's got to stay watertight. Nobody, no cops, no friends, no family, no one outside of us can be informed about it."

"I don't know if that much secrecy's necessary," Nash said, mostly to Janice.

She answered before Roemer, "It really is, Judge. In a city this size, more people involved in the operation means trouble."

"Trouble? Maybe some readjustments," Nash said.

"We get blown, we shut down," Roemer said directly. "Our targets run for cover, we have no usable cases, and you're left in a very awkward position publicly. Privately, too."

Nash thought they were trying to scare him.

"A lot of people won't trust you again," Roemer said, shaking his head. "If we don't go all the way through a trial, using you, you're always going to be suspect."

"Like I was really a crook myself." Nash nodded. "I know."

"Okay, so we're clear on that. Tight operation. That's got to be the rule." Roemer grinned. "I don't want you going through the rest of your life in this city with people thinking you were a thief and we turned you."

Nash thought of Maizie and the narcs again. In an undercover operation that ended too soon, the lingering suspicion always remained that the operator had been coerced into cooperation by the police. The taint of dishonesty was poisonous.

The Justice Department can say I was working freely until they were blue, Nash thought. I might have to resign from the bench. Who'd appear in front of a judge with that kind of reputation?

The only solution was for this sting to stay as secret as Roemer insisted.

"Do I have to wear a wire?" Nash asked.

Roemer laughed. Janice smiled, to Nash's embarrassment. "Did you ever wear one when you were a DA?"

"Never."

"We'll try to avoid it. You probably had shitty equipment at the local level. Old Fargos? Lousy recorders."

Nash recalled the gurgling, faint, unintelligible tapes cops brought in from undercover buys and stakeouts. "You could go crazy trying to listen to that junk," he said.

Roemer came to the window. Janice sat a few feet away, as if the circle were now complete. The cops behind the door were holding their breaths, he thought.

"What we'll do"—Roemer shaped the air with his hands—"is manipulate the situation so that you and the target are in some place we've prepared already. Maybe a restaurant. Maybe a hotel room. Maybe a car. But in each instance, I'm going to be capable of putting your transaction on video and audio tape."

"I won't push it," Nash said. "If they won't go for what I'm selling, I'll walk away."

"Absolutely," Roemer said with force. "Absolutely. I'm not here to make anyone do anything he didn't want to do in the first place."

Nash had made his final commitment as Roemer spoke. He wouldn't compromise friends or the reluctant ones. He would vigorously go after the others, the dirty ones Roemer said were on the bench. He was disgusted at the idea that a judge he saw at the weekly meeting, ran into in the courthouse corridors, or drank with at the endless judges' colleges and conferences was selling his office.

That's the old prosecutor, Nash thought. The prospect of nailing a bad guy still gets my juices going.

"What's your opinion, Janice?" Nash asked.

She paused in her writing. "You made the right decision. I never regretted making it."

He wondered what choices she had faced. He wanted to ask her.

Roemer clenched his fist, aimed it toward Nash. "We will run one of the most successful undercover operations ever, Tim. Believe me."

"We've named it, too," Janice said.

"What is it?"

"The whole thing's running under the name Operation Broken Trust. I picked it," Roemer said.

Nash liked it. He felt a flood of goodwill. "Why me? There must be other judges in this county to use."

Janice closed her pad and stood up. She came next to him. She wore a light, spicy perfume. Her eyes were gray-black. "My view is that you're fair. I know your record. I studied it."

"There was other stuff," Roemer broke in. "You're a former DA. You've been a judge for five years. You know everybody in this city and they know you. They think you've got integrity. Jesus, your father's almost a saint around here."

"So you want my name," Nash said. "You think the judges I contact will accept a story I tell them?"

"I sure do."

He frowned. He was disquieted by the seamless logic, Roemer's cold calculation. "Why should I be after that kind of money? I mean, why should these guys think I'm greedy?"

Janice folded her arms. "They won't think you're greedy, Your Honor. It's common knowledge you've just gone through a tough divorce. You could plausibly need money to pay for it."

Nash, oddly, was not offended by this dispassionate combing through his life. Perhaps it was because Janice delivered the intimate justification. He also accepted the necessity for the buyers to believe in the salesman before they would bite.

Roemer drew the curtains across the cityscape, closing in the suite. Isolating this little world. Us against them, Nash thought. He walked over and looked again at the chart of judges' names on the table. "Do you have something on Dennis Terhune?" he asked abruptly.

Roemer looked at him in puzzlement, then at Janice. "Not a thing. He's an interested party. He has some contacts back at Justice and he was the easiest trustworthy way to you."

"That's all?"

Janice picked at a sandwich, then chewed slowly. "Withholding information is a bad way to begin, Your Honor."

70

"I had to ask. He was acting strangely."

"We're like the tax men," Roemer said. "Everybody gets nervous when we show up."

Nash nodded. Roemer had a reputation of aggressively going after stock swindlers and bad cops, but without vindictiveness. He was a straight shooter and that suited Nash exactly.

"I do have one condition," Nash said.

"Go ahead."

"I'm in a major capital case. I'm about half through the trial. This sting can't screw it up. I won't let anything I'm going to do for you interfere with the trial."

"No, the trial's off-limits," Roemer promised. "I know how tough they make it in California."

"How do we start?" Nash looked at them. The bedroom door opened and the plainclothes cops strolled out, one tugging on his coat. They were all armed.

"We've got a number of things to do in the next couple of days." Roemer went to the table, cleared a space, and began scribbling in a crabbed hand on a legal pad. "So what I'm giving you now is an address and telephone number if you have any questions or something comes up."

"You're not staying in town?"

"Just tonight. I'm back in Washington tomorrow, and then I'll be here day after next. I've got a couple of other operations to look in on every so often." He tore off the page and handed it to Nash. "Those are secure numbers. They're not listed or tied to Justice in any way."

"Nobody's going to answer the phone and say, 'Operation Broken Trust'?"

"Not if we're lucky. Not working for me," Roemer said.

Nash said to Janice, "Are you going to Sacramento?"

"I'll be back tomorrow," she said. "You can call me at the U.S. Attorney's office."

Roemer walked Nash to the door. "I should have mentioned that Janice will be your liaison with me. My face's a little too well-known. You'll report to her most of the time. We'll only meet in emergencies."

"I did a sting once," Nash said, "that took three months to set up. We had a storefront, about four miles from here. City cops bought stolen property, taped and photographed whoever brought stuff in. It went on for close to ten months. We got everything. TVs, stereos, lawn mowers, bikes, somebody tried to sell us a dog. I told

71

a guy over at BNE about it. Bureau of Narcotic Enforcement? Took me about fifteen minutes to tell him what took us close to a year to gather."

"That's the way they go. All of the interesting stings make about one good war story," Roemer said.

"This one isn't going to take a year, is it? You're going to move fast?"

Roemer nodded, so did Janice, her legal pad at her side. "They're not even going to know what hit them."

12

NASH WAS DRIVEN BACK TO HIS APARTMENT. ALL HE FOUND OUT from his quiet driver was that the man was an FBI agent, normally stationed in the Brooklyn office. He had been specially detailed to accompany Roemer on this California trip. He was looking forward to going back to the dark, noisy streets of Brooklyn. "It's always daylight here," he said to Nash. "You can't get away from it. Like the sun's on you all the time."

He did not tell Nash his name. Nash realized that Roemer had never used any of the agents' names. He was favorably impressed with that attention to fine points and security.

His FBI driver left him at the apartment complex gate. Nash was weary but enthused, and he felt better than he had for months. He walked to his apartment, past the splashing pools, turbulent figures giggling in them.

He missed some familiar sight or sound in his apartment when he turned on the lights. Kim's bath oil, Ben's excited talk about school. All day he'd been in transitory rooms or courts.

He stripped down to his underwear, sat down, and dialed the number Kim had given him. He very much wanted to tell her about Operation Broken Trust, just as they had shared activities in the past. But that was impossible now.

He kept the slip by the phone. The stiff fabric of the couch stuck itchingly in his back.

Kim answered breathlessly, an impossible distance from him. "We just got in."

"Flight was okay? You're okay?"

She sounded bored and breathless. "The flight was miserable and I'm sick with something, Tim. Ben was a brat all the way down, and he's giving my sister a heart attack."

Nash gripped the phone tightly. "I miss you."

There was silence.

"I said I miss you," he repeated. "I could come down to L.A. after court tomorrow. We could have dinner or do something. I don't like being away from you."

"It's not so different from the last couple of months."

"It's different for me."

More silence. Kim said slowly, "Don't come down."

"I want to see you and Ben. You're still my family. I'd be back on a flight to Santa Maria tomorrow night."

"Why? What's the point? What's going to happen? Do we have something to gain, Tim? Really? You think so?" she asked harshly.

"I'm not talking about a major deal. Just a couple of hours with you two. I could see if you need anything."

"We don't need anything."

He let the phone loosen in his grip. "No. Maybe you don't."

"That's the way things are. We've both known it."

"Let me talk to Ben, Kim. I want to say good night."

"I'll get him." She paused. "I can't change things. I can't make myself different. I can't make you different."

"I won't ask you to."

Kim was suddenly angry. The phone at her end thumped down and he was afraid they'd been cut off. He waited and Ben came on.

"You take it easy there, bear," Nash said gently. "Remember you're a guest in somebody's house, okay?"

"Yeah, okay." His son was resigned, without spirit, and that disturbed Nash. He hated the fact that he would miss so much of Ben's growing up from now on, the day-to-day triumphs and discouragements. I won't be there when he comes home from school or when he gets a good grade or gets in a fight. I won't be there.

"You take care of your mother. You do that for me, bear?"

"I don't want to be here."

"I know. I'll see you soon. It won't be so long. Okay? You sleep well."

"Yeah, okay." Ben sighed loudly, longingly, and hung up. Nash held on to the phone, unwilling to relinquish the link.

Afterward he worked until past midnight on the probation reports, circling facts to recite at sentencing, adding up the years he would take from the men and women who would stand before him in a few hours. At two A.M., the total was eighty-five years and seven months, and Nash stopped counting.

Roemer squeezed his eyes shut, yawned, arched his back, and groaned. "That's it for the night."

"Can you settle things tomorrow?" Janice asked, pushing away from the table. Two FBI agents yawned widely opposite her.

"Sure. I've got our snitch and I've got our judge," Roemer said. "Cleary won't stop me."

"We could have trouble with Nash," she said, adjusting her skirt.

"Kind of a stiff," one of the FBI agents said.

"But he's our stiff," Roemer replied.

"I don't think he's going to bend very much if he has to." She poked at one of the full ashtrays on the table. "The next meeting has got to be no smoking." The FBI agents grumbled. A thin bluish haze lay over the room.

"He was a DA. He used snitches. He ran stings. The judge's got to know the way these things go."

"I just wanted to register my thought for the record."

Roemer nodded, looking at her. "I'd forgotten how great you look after midnight."

"Give it a rest, Neil," she said without irritation. "What you saw is all you're going to see."

The other FBI agent reached down and picked up a couple of dropped pencils. "Hey, I'm a married man. I don't want to hear this kind of talk."

Janice went to the wide-screen TV and turned it on. The bits of partly eaten sandwiches were left around the room, the yellow-shaded lights burned high and hard. Roemer, brisk and hard-edged again, adjusted the VCRs.

"Last item before we all go our separate ways tonight," he said. "Let's see how the judge looks on TV."

Nash's face, from the meeting earlier that night, filled the great space of the TV screen.

13

ROGER VALLES DID NOT SLEEP WELL, AND AT DAWN HE WAS awake, sitting up in bed, holding the phone. He did not bother to lower his voice. His wife, Arlene, lay beside him, wrapped in the blue blankets they had draped over themselves as the warm night became cool and an early mist rolled over the city.

"Jerry?" Valles said into the phone.

On the other end, his partner's sleepy voice answered, "Man. What're you doing to me, man?"

"You want to meet me at the Forty-Niner in a couple of minutes?"

"No."

"Just do it, Jerry, okay? I can't sleep. I got to talk to you about it."

"Man. Talk to Arlene. No. Talk to Maggie. Hey, Mag, Rog wants to say something," and Valles heard Witwer trying to awaken his own wife.

"No," Valles said roughly. "I mean it. Meet me at the diner about six-thirty. We got a problem. We got to do something."

"We got to sleep," and Witwer hung up.

Valles put the phone down. Arlene rolled over. They had been married fifteen years, and she now sold real estate from an office in a shopping mall across the river. Her hair was tangled when she looked up.

"Time to go already?" Arlene asked.

"I'm leaving early."

"It's only six. We don't have to get up for an hour, hon."

"I do."

"What's going on?" she asked. She blinked rapidly, rubbing an eye slowly.

Valles pulled on jeans and a light workshirt. "Same old shit."

"You won't tell me."

"I said, same old shit. Nothing else to tell."

"Don't get crabby. I don't want to know." She rolled away from him. He tied his heavy work shoes quickly.

"Just business. The same business. Nothing changes." The room was pale blue, a yellow streak of sunlight coming through the window, hitting the framed photos of the family on the far wall.

"When you getting out of undercover?" Arlene asked, her voice softened by the pillow.

"Why?"

"The beard still scratches me. All night, you're against me, the beard's scratching me. Like having a dog in bed."

"Yeah, hey, it ain't my favorite thing either. It's part of the job, looking like a puke." He scraped change into his pocket and pulled his Harley-Davidson jacket from the closet.

She mumbled into the pillow.

"What?" he said.

"If you make any coffee, leave some for me." Arlene had a full figure under the covers. Valles reached over and gently touched her back. He thought, for a moment, of getting to his appointment with Witwer late. But Arlene had been unpredictable in bed lately, sometimes enthusiastic, others annoyed, and he didn't have the interest to battle through her snappishness. Too many days had started with their going to work angry.

"I'll leave some," he promised.

She said something softly into the pillow and he left the bedroom. They lived in a single-story house, in a three-block-square development of identical homes. The only things different about their house, bought and heavily mortgaged three years before, were the choice of a driveway on the right side of the house and the sets of ceramic and glass wind chimes Arlene had hung outside the back door. Valles heard them, aimlessly tinkling in the faint morning breezes that came off the river delta.

In the living room he found his son, Harry, on the couch. He was snoring, his shirt pulled up to his chin, a beer bottle overturned on the floor. A small puddle of beer had seeped around the head of a girl, Harry's age, fifteen. She had thick features and black hair. The TV was still on, soundless, a black-and-white agriculture show flickering tractors and silos over the sleeping kids.

So who's this one, Valles thought, walking by. He kicked another beer bottle out of the way into the kitchen. Harry had more or less stopped going to Valley Central High. Valles had not heard him come in, but then Harry, like many thieves and burglars, had perfected the art of getting into a house at night without making any noise.

Valles heard one of them, either Harry or the girl, groan. He breathed harshly, slammed the drawers, and made coffee quickly. He watched the coffee spurt into the percolator's glass bubble. He and Arlene used to joke with other cops about how fast they'd made it to the altar before Harry was born. Beat it by four weeks exactly, Valles thought. You didn't think it would be like this later. He remembered kissing Arlene right after they were officially married, feeling the heavy weight in her middle against him.

They had a daughter, Karen, thirteen and away at school in Marin. She was slender, serious, and showed the only hope in the family of having any brains. I sure don't, Valles thought. I'm still here. So's Arlene. So's the rocket scientist, which was his epithet for his only son.

He braced himself against the counter. The dishes from yesterday were still in the sink, but he and Arlene kept things generally clean. Someone had taken a loaf of bread, meats, and left them open all night on the counter, and they had dried, gone stale.

The only problem with having Karen at a boarding school was her growing snobbishness. She thought his job was undignified, his disguises boorish. Alone in the family, her disapproval had the power to make Valles ashamed.

He turned to the sound in the kitchen door. Harry stood, bent partly, one arm over the girl. She ducked her head up and down and stared at Valles.

"Morning," Harry said, rubbing his belly.

Valles said nothing, poured the coffee into a cup, taking it with him. Harry and the girl brushed by him, holding each other up like wounded veterans. Harry emptied the coffeepot.

"Leave some for your mother," Valles said.

"There's more."

"Leave some for your mother," Valles repeated. He reached into the top shelf of the cupboard, above the china and glasses, and found his gun and waist holster. He brought them down.

"She can make her own," Harry said, holding a cup out for the girl.

Valles steadied himself. "Who's she?" he asked.

"Melissa," the girl said almost shyly, her darkly outlined eyelashes lowered. She and Karen were only separated by a few years.

"Get out of here," Valles said. Melissa stared at his gun.

"We're leaving," Harry said calmly. He went on drinking his own cup of coffee.

Valles put his gun and holster down and with a quick swipe of his hand, knocked the cup from his son's hand. The cup hit the floor, shattered, and splashed against the mock brick.

Harry didn't move. He sighed and took Melissa's cup and sipped from it.

Valles picked up his gun and holster again. "You both get out of here." He walked out, leaving them standing in the alien-seeming kitchen. He got into his car, on the right-side driveway, the wind chimes endlessly snickering, and screeched out into the empty street.

"You always have hopes for your kids, right?" Valles said to Witwer in a side booth in the crowded Forty-Niner. "When they're born, you look at them, you think, he's going to Harvard. Then they go to school. You look at them, their grades, you think, okay, not Harvard, maybe UCLA. Then they're in high school. You listen to them, you look at them. Maybe now for the first time really look. You think basically, okay, forget Harvard, forget UCLA. Maybe a community college. Then you stop. Forget community college. Please, God, just keep him out of CYA." He sighed loudly.

"Your kid's not going to the Youth Authority." Witwer yawned again and again.

"You didn't see him this morning. It's getting like that every day. I can't make him stay in school. I can't get him to do anything."

"Well, Rog, I'm real interested in your family troubles, but I'm not real interested in them right this second."

Valles frowned, waving a waitress over. The Forty-Niner was astride the converging north-south interstate and the main highway into Santa Maria. It was filled with men, a few women, talking very loudly, drinking coffee and eating eggs and bacon, the air thick with frying smells and too many bodies together. All of the waitresses, in faded pink uniforms, had sweat stains under the arms. Valles ordered breakfast and Witwer shook his head. A cloud of steam boiled from the kitchen.

"Okay, forget it," Valles said. "It's my problem. You and me, we've got a problem together."

"So you said."

"It's that bust, Jerry. I been thinking about it all night."

"Shit, no. It's just a stupid coke deal. It's nothing. It's something Shiffley's got going." Witwer leaned against the worn red Leatherette of the booth, folding his arms.

"I know it's Shiffley's deal, but it's screwy. We're the arresting officers." Valles's beard itched and he rubbed it. "Something goes sour, we eat it."

"We're just bodies. We ain't heavy into this one."

"So all I want to do is see Shiffley and ask him."

Witwer looked at Valles's food when it was brought over. "Ask him what?"

"What's going on. Why the setup. Who's Vismara. How come he's got Shiffley's name and he's acting so weird." Valles shook salt and pepper on everything and began eating with large mouthfuls.

"Shiffley won't tell you. It's some deep deal for him."

"So don't you want to know?"

"Not much. I wanted to sleep a little late this morning."

"How about we go to Shiffley and ask him?" Valles paused, fork upraised, fried egg hanging on it.

"I thought it was you. You go."

"We're partners, Jerry. We made the bust together."

"So did a couple other guys."

Valles drank coffee, eyes flicking around the large, smoky diner, the darting waitresses and people hefting themselves out of booths or from the counter, checks in hand. "I signed out for the coke, Jerry. My name's on the evidence sheet. I tagged it. Your name's on the arrest report."

"My name's on nine million arrest reports and I don't worry about something coming back on me." Witwer unfolded his arms and tapped the plastic tabletop in annoyance. "I did my job. I went home."

"You're crapping out on me?" Valles asked seriously. He wiped his mouth, dabbed at his beard. Experience had indicated that food often fell into the whiskers.

"It's nothing to get all shitfaced about. It's not our deal. So we don't need to worry about it."

Valles pushed his plate away. He tucked a few paper napkins into his pocket in case he started sneezing during the day. Humid summer weather often made him sneeze.

"I always help you out, Jerry," Valles said. "I'm looking out for us both on this. You know I am."

"I think you're all tight about something you don't need to get tight about. I don't want to get in Shiffley's face."

Valles took a toothpick from the small plastic holder on the table, chewed the end, then poked it into his teeth slowly. "I got to do what's best for us both," he said. "I'm going to Shiffley."

14

NASH SPRINTED UP THE STONE STEPS TO THE NEW COURTHOUSE. HE was late for the weekly morning judges' meeting. His briefcase, heavy with the probation reports for his own calendar that morning, banged sharply into his leg.

The morning tangle of people crowded the broad stone plaza around the courthouse. Nash had discovered he seldom saw individuals anymore. Even from the bench lately people blended together, and this muddle of men and women, kids in ragged clothes, stiff suits, one or two with books, was simply part of his furniture.

He glanced at the cornerstone of the new Santa Maria County courthouse. It had come from the ruins of the old courthouse. The cornerstone was chipped gray marble while the building on top of it now was of some glittering white stone. Nash had seen this cornerstone all his life, as a boy and a DA. He saw it whenever he came into the courthouse as a judge now. In blocky Gothic letters it said:

My Sword Is Truth
1924

The workmanship, as well as the sentiments, were identical to those inscribed on monuments and tombs in the city's oldest cemetery.

Nash wasn't cynical about the idea. When he first became a DA, his supervisor took him aside. "Our job's simple," he was told. "All we have to do, all you do, is make sure at the end of the day, the truth got told."

Nash excused himself hurriedly, pushing by a family in thick conversation in front of the courthouse doors, blocking them. *Tell the truth.* He walked past the three bailiffs working the metal detectors, waving to them. He was uncertain, but optimistic about today. Things would change and Kim's leaving wouldn't be so bad. He was anxious to get busy on the sting, to talk to Janice again. He tried to think of an excuse to call her as he rode the elevator to Department 14, got off in the empty corridor, and left his briefcase in the darkened courtroom with its silent, huge photos of a bullet-pocked gas station.

I want to get moving, he thought. He wanted to make things happen.

The twelve judges of the Santa Maria Superior Court met in the large chambers of the presiding judge on the eighth floor of the courthouse.

Nash picked up a sweet roll and a cup of orange juice from the conference table and sat down. The PJ's chambers were near the cafeteria and the court reporters' office. The noise was constant, the air always filled with the odor of scalded coffee and french fries.

Terry Kalbacher was that year's PJ, a squat man in shirtsleeves with graying hair and a perpetual tan. He stood behind his desk, as always, to run the meeting.

The rest of the judges stood or sat around the room, gossiping and whispering. Harold Atchley was in profound conversation with old Fred Miyazumi. Atchley nodded at Nash. The weekly meetings were informal, as though they all worried that any structure would tread on a fellow judge's prerogatives. Everybody was equal here.

Nash was at ease among them. It was the most exclusive club in the county, one he had been brought up in.

He couldn't stop checking his watch, though, trying to see when he could get away and call Janice in Sacramento. He was going to invite her to Atchley's fund-raiser, a way for her to see his colleagues as he did. There would be no suspicion if Nash brought her as a guest. He liked the idea.

At his side, Susanna Jardine, her napkin heavy with two wrapped sweet rolls, laughed with Dwight Peatling, the newest judge. He was young, a former tax lawyer considered brilliant. His shirts looked too starched and he often coughed nervously.

Nash glanced up. Kalbacher read off a tiny piece of paper. "I talked with Mike Sinclair yesterday. He says he likes getting cards."

"What's the room number at the hospital again?" Frank Wisot asked, legs crossed, head down.

"He's in number forty-six at Santa Maria Community."

"Thought I might drop over tomorrow if anybody wants to join me." Wisot looked up and no one said anything. He lowered his head again.

"Mike says he feels one hundred percent better. The quacks are saying they got all the cancer, so it all looks good."

"He won't be back," Ruth Frenkel whispered to Nash. She was heavy, wearing a bright red bow today.

"How's the guy from the Judicial Council doing in Mike's court?" Nash whispered back. Ruth's courtroom was next door to Department 8 where Sinclair usually sat.

"He's got a glass eye," she said. "He brings his lunch in a file folder, one of those accordion files."

"Sorry."

"He gave a rapist ten months in jail, ten months in county jail, and ten months community service in a city of his choice."

"Nobody's going to let him do that kind of baloney," Nash whispered.

Ruth Frenkel sighed. "They recalled the case, transferred it to my department, and I gave the bastard eighteen years in the joint."

Nash, however, listened and looked at Ruth with new interest. Was she one of Roemer's targets? Was Kalbacher? Who was on the list in this room? Or on the municipal court bench with its eight judges?

Nash felt like the ultimate insider and the greatest outsider. This might be the last meeting he had with these people before things changed forever. He knew that the county bench would be altered, no matter what happened in Operation Broken Trust. This meeting was the last of the old regime. And he was the only one there who knew it.

"Are you going to talk about the short cause delays?" Fred Miyazumi called to Kalbacher, breaking away from Atchley.

"Are you still having trouble?" Kalbacher asked. He noticed the nodding heads around the room.

"Every time I get a half-day divorce or a half-day contract matter, I end up staying in session until after six," Miyazumi said. Nash liked little Fred, a tough older judge who sometimes carried a gun outside of court. He had metal-framed glasses and drove lawyers and juries wild with his droning voice and obsessive comments on the record. "Will you stipulate that all parties are present?" he asked three times a day. Then, "Will you ratify that stipulation?" It took him almost twenty minutes simply to start a trial after every agreement had been announced, repeated, ratified, and noted again.

Fred's boast was that he had been reversed by the Court of Appeal only twice in sixteen years, and on both of those cases he had been ill. His specialty was long cases, multiple-injury trials, a fire engine crashing into a schoolyard and hurting twenty children.

"I can't get them out, either," complained Allen Burgess, licking his fingers from a sweet roll. "You've got to get the files down to us faster, Terry. Assign the matters and get us the file."

"It's the clerk's office," Kalbacher said. "I've been moving thirty short cause matters every day without any trouble."

"Into our laps," said Susanna Jardine.

Nash listened as the debate went on. Kalbacher would tell the clerks, again, to make sure court files were delivered to the proper courtrooms within fifteen minutes of a case's being assigned for trial. They talked about pension rights and how the issue would be presented at the Judges' Conference at the State Bar Convention. Paul Henshaw argued vociferously, in his high-pitched voice, for a tighter hand on jury questioning. "I don't want to sit up there for two weeks listening to a group of egomaniacal, lecturing lawyers asking the same questions over and over and over to the jurors."

"You're talking to a roomful of lawyers," Wisot said with a smile.

"Not me. Not anymore."

Nash got a cup of coffee from the conference table supplies while the meeting turned to electing a new traffic-court referee. Kalbacher called for a show of hands when the candidates were named. Nobody was shy about voting publicly. We're all among friends, all together in this, Nash thought.

Except me now. I'm different. I look around and wonder who may go to jail and whom I'll help send there. He sat down. It was a disquieting realization.

"And now," Kalbacher said, "the moment you've all been waiting for."

"You're not going to run again for PJ," Burgess said.

"That's right. I'm not."

"I was kidding, Terry," Burgess said. He stood by the room's curtained windows, like the hotel last night, filled with the cloud-laden blue sky and the dusty gray-black and shimmering tops of Santa Maria's crowded downtown business district.

"I'm not running. I'm hanging it up. Two terms was enough for me." Kalbacher seemed pleased. He grinned. "Ruth has mentioned she'd like to run."

At Nash's side, Ruth Frenkel nodded. "I want it. I think I'll do a good job."

"Anybody else?"

Susanna Jardine nudged Nash. "You could have it, Tim," she said, low.

He shook his head, leaning over to whisper, "One presiding judge in the family's enough."

Kalbacher gazed around the room. "No one else? Well, we'll take a vote at the next meeting. I think you've pretty much got it, Ruth," he said.

She smiled graciously, a little self-mocking. Ruth Frenkel was unmarried, plain, with a tendency toward heavy makeup. She told dirty stories at the bar luncheons and social functions the county put on all year.

Nash didn't think he could be PJ and be undercover at the same time, even if he wanted the job. PJ meant endless organization and bureaucratic dilemmas, meetings with the Board of Supervisors, every union in the courthouse, and every problem under the sun. He often wondered why his father had held on to it for so long.

"I need some advice on a petition," Susanna Jardine said, bending to him. Peatling had huddled with another young judge, Douglas Croncota, for the duration of the meeting.

"If I've got any," Nash said. He got up and stood close to her. Susanna was unaffectedly kind. She had come from being general counsel for a consortium of hospitals—Santa Maria Community, Our Lady of Mercy, Cameron-Pacific General, and some smaller ones. She had three children and her husband worked in the city planning department, doing studies of growth as Santa Maria rolled restlessly to the north over farmland and older houses.

"It's a riparian-rights question," she said. "I don't remember anything about who gets what part of the water on a riverway."

"Don't ask me," he said, laughing quietly.

"I've got one farmer saying he owns the left side of the river channel because of silting, and another one who says he gets it." She shook her head.

"I'll take a look at it."

"I've got to rule this afternoon."

"I thought it was urgent," he joked. "You'll sound like you know it by then."

84

He realized that Harold Atchley was speaking.

"I want to thank everyone for their support. Even poor Mike Sinclair has contributed to my campaign. I hope you can all come to the Turf Club tomorrow. It'll be fun," he said with forced delight.

"Any numbers on the race yet, Harold?" Miyazumi asked.

"I managed to piggyback onto a survey the Republicans are doing for their candidates," he said, sniffing at the humor. "I should have some idea after Labor Day."

"You've got a couple of Republicans here," Wisot said, holding an unlit cigarette.

"And some Democrats," Dwight Peatling added, speaking for the first time.

"Well, party labels don't matter," Kalbacher said, wiping a few crumbs from his sweet roll off his desk blotter into his hand. "We're all behind you, Harold. I hope you have a fine turnout. I'll try to make it."

Heads nodded, people muttered agreement. Politics did not really matter among these people. Waves of appointments by Democratic and Republican governors had thoroughly mixed the sentiments on both the municipal and Superior Court benches. What mattered was staying on the bench. Being a judge meant more to everyone here than anything else. It flew past politics, personal differences, folly.

The meeting broke up. Nash had a morning calendar to start, like most of the others. Looking at Harold Atchley's red face, thinking of his incompetent years on the bench, Nash hoped his name was on Roemer's list. He wanted to help take Atchley off the bench. It would be a service to the county.

Several judges chatted with Atchley, others laughed, left, dropping their napkins and cups in the garbage. Kalbacher went to his bathroom.

Nash said to Atchley, "I'll buy two tickets, Harold. Can I pick them up at the door?"

Atchley broke off chatting with Wisot and Burgess. "Sure, Tim. Thank you. I thought you couldn't come."

"I'll be there."

"Two tickets. Are you and Kim coming? A reconciliation?"

Nash shook his head. "You don't know her. She's from the U.S. Attorney's office."

Wisot winked and Burgess chuckled. "He always bounces back," Wisot said, poking good-naturedly at Nash.

"Is anything tough for you?" Burgess asked, partly joking.

"Some things. Not many," Nash said truthfully.

15

A<small>T THAT HOUR OF THE MORNING</small>, V<small>ALLES THOUGHT HIS BOSS</small> would not be at his desk yet. He drove from the Forty-Niner east, heading toward the river, then cut down a long street that used to be lined with factories and two canneries. In the summer, Valles recalled the purple stench of rotting, stewing tomatoes from the soup factory, the leaden, dull stink of fish from the cannery beside it.

He parked at the old Miyazumi Fish Cannery, red brick now buffed so it almost sparkled, a wide newly asphalted parking lot filled with expensive cars. No hint of its past lingered in the air. Men and women in stylish exercise outfits, some carrying tennis rackets or elaborate workout shoes, came and went from the white-washed entrance. It was now a health club called The Cannery.

Valles did not recognize anything here at all. He felt as though he were losing his grip on his life and the world. He recognized Arlene's features and his own on Harry's face. But Harry was a stranger.

He walked around the brightly lit, purposeful din of the health club. Men and women rode stationary bicycles or sweated on tread-mills or contorted themselves in the metal embrace of silver weight machines.

Valles found Lieutenant Shiffley grunting on a machine that mimicked climbing stairs without going any higher than a foot off the ground.

"There's about a hundred people here." Valles marveled at the determined, soulful multitude around him. It didn't even smell like a gym. The police academy basketball court and gym were real, sweat blessed and dark. This was a dream. People running after dreams.

"So what?" Shiffley answered with difficulty.

"It's kind of impressive."

"So what."

"You keep going up and down on that thing"—Valles watched his boss labor, legs white, corded, blue veined, and stringy—"and you still ain't getting anyplace."

"I'm getting a heart attack."

"Don't do it."

Shiffley was older by a decade than Valles. He had deep worry lines, black crew-cut hair, and no shoulders. He could run for hours. Dark sweat outlined his flimsy sleeveless shirt.

"What do you weigh, Valles?"

"Depends. Maybe one seventy-five, seventy. Something like that."

"You got a gut. You got to drop about twenty pounds."

"I keep it soft so there's more of me between anything that hits me," Valles said. The other men and women beside Shiffley were watching him. Nobody else had a beard in the whole place. A couple of tiny, sculpted mustaches here and there, and in his street clothes, a not very large gut riding comfortably on his belt, he looked as bizarre as a visitor from another world in this health emporium.

Shiffley let out a long, mournful sigh, and Valles feared he was hurt. But his boss only stepped off the stair machine, wiped his streaming face and neck with a towel, slung it around his neck, and put his arm on Valles.

"You and Witwer, the biggest bullshit artists on the whole Project. I tell people that."

"Thanks, boss." It was a compliment working undercover.

"So what's up, Valles? What brings you into my presence?"

"It's the bust last night."

Shiffley took his arm off Valles, wiped more sweat. They were at a small counter, and Shiffley got a bottle of cold apple juice. "I saw your report. Looks good. Looks really good."

"That's what this guy says to me. He goes, 'Looks good, looks really good,' first thing. He knows your name." Valles leaned against one of the stools. The clank of metal weights and the electronic whirring from radios, contraptions, TVs, people grunting, got on his nerves.

"So what?"

"I'd like to know who Louis Vismara is. How come he's so special Jerry and I get yanked to pick him up?"

"You got yanked because I ordered you." Shiffley steadily drank the apple juice and flapped his lips like a horse after a trot.

"It's a setup, right, boss? That's all I can see."

"Of course it's a setup."

"So who is he?"

"He's a dealer." Shiffley sighed again and started away from Valles, heading for the locker room and showers. They passed various men, some younger than Valles and in worse shape, and he felt a pang of annoyance Shiffley picked on him.

"Do we have to play?" Valles asked.

"I'm not playing. I'm taking a quick one and heading down to the barn." Shiffley stripped off his wet shirt and shorts, put a fresh towel around his neck. Valles sat on a polished wood bench. Mist from the sparkling showers curled into the carpeted, lemon-scented locker room.

"The guy worries me, boss. I told Jerry. I want to make sure nothing's going to come back and hit me in the face."

Shiffley flapped his lips again. He held on to the towel ends. "I wouldn't hang you or Jerry out. Not you guys."

"Okay," Valles said reluctantly. Other men, dressing or undressing, sauntered around the room. A few joked.

"Here's what I'll let out. It's for you. Don't pass it around yet." Shiffley leaned down a little toward Valles. "This guy's a snitch for me. He's going to give up some major deals for us."

"He didn't sound like a snitch last night. He sounded like he knew you already."

"That was bush for him to use my name. Look, it's supposed to be real." Shiffley's voice was hard to hear he spoke so low. "His buddies have to think we want him."

"It was kind of a favor to let Jerry and me make the bust?" Valles said helpfully.

"I said, you guys are my stars. I like you." Shiffley nodded. "I got to get a shower."

"Someone didn't snitch Vismara off? That was bullshit?"

"Sure someone snitched him off. So we had to nail him."

"Who snitched him?"

Shiffley shook his head. "Ask for my wife, ask for my first kid, ask for my boat. Don't ask for my snitches, Valles."

Valles nodded, stood up. He noticed the mechanical shoeshine brushes, bottles of after-shave, combs, razors, set out for club members on the tiled row of sinks. "Okay. I was kind of worried."

"See, that's why I like you. You pay attention." Shiffley gave him a mock punch on the arm. "Hey. I checked with the fourth floor.

They got a space for your kid as a student police intern this fall. I asked a couple of days ago for you."

Valles started to feel clammy in the steamy locker room, not completely from the hot shower nearby. "Thanks, boss. I'll have to take a pass."

"You said Harry should hang around the department."

"Forget it," Valles said, thinking of that morning's encounter and the others that had come before it.

Shiffley shrugged. He let go of the towel. He was white from head to toe. He had been Project supervisor for two years and had made several spectacular drug arrests. He had a photo, on his office door, of himself sitting atop eighteen burlap-covered bales of marijuana, his arms thrown open, a smile on his face.

"We're doing a little Sunday barbecue. About four-thirty. Tell Arlene, tell Witwer."

"Yeah, okay. We can be there." Valles definitely felt uneasy after their conversation, and he wanted to leave the cloying health club.

"Invite a couple of others, if you can think of anybody else who doesn't smoke or drink."

"I don't know anybody who doesn't smoke or drink," Valles said.

"I don't," Shiffley said, a little wounded.

It was taken for granted that undercover narcotic operations sometimes required a degree of secrecy and compartmentalization that was unheard of in any other area of police work. Valles accepted the premise that his superior would not tell him much about Louis Vismara. If he had been in Shiffley's position, he might not even have said as much as he did. Sources were protected like gold, even from other cops.

Valles drove downtown, thinking, his stomach gurgling from eating his breakfast too fast and the upset of his son and this odd arrest. He had to verify one more detail before putting the whole matter aside, as Jerry and Shiffley seemed to agree he should.

He would like to get a handle on his life, on even some small facet of it. He was only in his midthirties and so much seemed to be fleeing from him already.

He parked outside a long, low, tan-colored building that was sloped on a hilly street heavily covered by oaks and elms. It was made of painted cinder blocks and ugly. It was like a smudge beside the relatively graceful lime-green Santa Maria Electric Generation

Station Number 4, built in 1909, and frivolously filigreed with ivy and false columns. At the other end of the street, on the hilltop, was the police department, set a little away from the busiest and most crowded center of the city's downtown.

Valles went in a side door, reserved for authorized personnel, and ended up in a coldly lit, dusty-smelling room with a barred counter, a humming cop behind it. The public entrance, with seats made deliberately uncomfortable for the inevitable wait, was around the corner.

"Oscar," Valles said genially.

"Good morning, good morning," said the cop behind the bars, very fat in his blue uniform, tieless, a bush of gray hair popping out at his neck.

"I need to check some evidence I booked in last night."

"We got it."

"I know you got it."

Oscar hummed all the time. He presided over a warehouse of police department property, evidence seized in arrests and by warrant, some used in trials, some waiting to be used, some forgotten, some lost. There was no order or sense to the rows of steel shelves and tagged property beyond the artificial imposition of human numbering. Everything else was random. Valles saw TVs alongside rifles, huge brown bags stuffed with bloody clothes beside old chairs, footlockers stacked with a profusion of handguns and knives. There were baseball bats and radios, a stuffed toy horse, and a small chandelier, wilted as though it hadn't had water on the shelf.

"Drugs or money?" Oscar asked, humming.

"Dope. Coke, I think."

"A lot?"

"Hell if I know. I don't use it." Valles laughed and Oscar laughed, too.

"It went into the safe, I guess," Oscar said, "if it's only one of them little hauls."

"No kilos this time."

"Okay, come on back. You better take a look yourself." He buzzed Valles through the security door. The fluorescent lights made the long building look indistinct, the edges blurred on the dark, dust-covered collection.

Valles followed Oscar's swaying bulk down a straight ceiling-to-floor shelf-lined path.

"When'd you bring it in?" Oscar called over his shoulder.

"About midnight. There was a lot of shit to do first."

"Was the kid on? Salazar?"

"Yeah. He was on duty."

Oscar shook his big head sorrowfully. "He is so dumb. I hope he didn't book it wrong."

"No. I was right there. He got it right."

"He is so dumb," Oscar repeated.

They stopped at a wire-grilled enclosure, Oscar using a key fastened to his belt to open the gate. All of the evidence seized by the Narcotic Impact Project was brought to this specially designated place. A large moss-green safe was against the wall. Oscar began opening it.

"Here's Morales. That still hasn't gone to trial." Valles fingered an evidence-tagged leather jacket with a fur collar. He and Witwer had arrested the Morales twins eight months ago for selling kilo amounts of tar heroin.

"That's the bitch of it." Oscar swung open the thick safe door. "I hardly lose stuff here. It all keeps coming back; they get cut loose, they plead, they get sent to the joint, they die, all their crap stays right here. I should have a fucking yard sale."

"Do it a little bit at a time. Nobody'd notice." Valles read the Vismara case number off a card to Oscar. The fat man was on one knee, breathing hard, rummaging through the drugs in the safe, each in a signed manila envelope bearing the words SANTA MARIA POLICE. The big envelopes had spaces for a multitude of sign-outs as the evidence was taken from property to court and back again. There was also a space for the chemical analysis done at the county Crime Lab.

"Here's yours." Oscar handed Valles an envelope, frowning at its thinness. "You sure didn't grab much."

Valles took the envelope. There was his name signing in the four-gram bags, two-gram bags, and five-ounce package of suspected cocaine, his badge number, the time. It was countersigned by Salazar, the property clerk on duty. He felt his heart pounding as he unclasped the envelope. "Oh, Jesus," he said, his hand fumbling in the envelope.

"I told you Salazar'd screw up. It's nothing new. He booked in five cases wrong last week. Let's see if I got the case number there."

Valles shook his head, closing the envelope, the dusty, immense room pressing around him. "No, it's the right case. Salazar did it okay."

"So what's the problem?"

Valles shook the envelope in Oscar's dim face. "No dope. The drugs are gone."

16

NEITHER ROEMER NOR CLEARY HAD SPOKEN TO EACH OTHER FOR several minutes, their umbrellas up against the steady, light summer rain. As the Attorney General's helicopter lowered down to the convention center's barricaded rear parking lot, it was impossible to be heard over the engine anyway.

As soon as the helicopter's door opened, the AG jumped out, head ducked low, two aides beside him, one holding a black umbrella over him. Two Secret Service men went ahead.

"You don't have to stand out in the rain," the AG said to Roemer and Cleary. He had a big face, with a smile that looked as if it had been hammered out. Rain spattered them, whipped by the helicopter.

They all started walking, Roemer next to the AG, the greetings done. Cleary hung a little back, having trouble keeping up.

"Thanks for seeing me so quickly," Roemer said. A Secret Service agent held open the door and they went into a kitchen, the chefs bustling around large steel pots and frying food on stoves. The AG sniffed.

"Looks like a decent lunch. Are you staying?" he asked Cleary.

"No. I can't, Wayne."

"Too bad. It's a good speech. It's got a nice edge to it," the AG said happily. He hadn't slowed down, and now Roemer took his arm.

"What's the problem?" the AG asked.

"Let's go in here." Roemer pulled the AG—and Cleary followed—

into a large, wood-doored storage room. Gallon cans of peas and potatoes, beans, coleslaw, butter, were around them.

The AG shook some of the rainwater off his coat. "We have to talk here?"

Cleary said, "Wayne, I've found out," and Roemer cut him off.

"He's blocked authorization for the FBI agents and equipment I need. He's stopped Operation Broken Trust."

"Which one?"

"Judges. Corrupt judges in California," Roemer said. "I can't move suddenly."

"Sure. Okay. I got it." The AG stared at his watch. "I'm speaking in five minutes."

"Wayne"—Cleary worked on his old contact with the AG when they had been active in the President's primary campaign—"I've reviewed the whole operation and it is far too tentative. It could cause a great deal of trouble. And embarrassment."

"It could?"

Roemer broke in again. "Bullshit. I have a cooperative judge and an operative. I have information on dishonest judges. I need the agents and the equipment to start work. Cleary here says he won't release the money. Special Projects already gave its go-ahead."

"Pending my review," Cleary said. "We could be hurting people who haven't done anything."

"Not the way I set it up. Nobody gets hurt except the rotten ones," Roemer snapped.

The AG glanced around at a fifty-gallon drum of french-cut green beans. The kitchen sounds were loud outside the storage room, and he faintly heard the applause from the banquet room. He wistfully wondered how he could get past these two. Paul he could simply put aside with a friendly nod, some good words, but this Roemer would follow him into the banquet room, up onto the dais, maybe even stand beside him when he got ready to give his speech. It was a good speech, too. He had even written two paragraphs of it himself during the helicopter ride across the river to Alexandria.

"He's been against the operation from the beginning," Roemer said.

"I was never against it," Cleary snapped.

"He was never against it," the AG said.

"I want the agents and I want the equipment. You can't jerk an undercover operation in the middle. I've got an informant facing serious exposure."

Cleary's white hair was rain damp and he smoothed it down. He slowly shook his head. "I do not want to see the department embarrassed by ill-considered endeavors."

Roemer swore and stared at the AG. "It's your decision."

The AG detected a threatening note. Roemer had a fighter's loose-limbed stance, hands at his side, slightly beaten face set and implacable. The AG had a brief fear Roemer might slug him if he said no. This sort of sensitivity had come early to the AG. He had been lieutenant governor of Idaho when his predecessor dropped dead during a sack race at a campaign picnic. Suddenly he was governor and he had no friends. Yet he survived and prospered even when everyone around the capital snidely referred to him as "Your Accidency" behind his back.

These two were engaged in a contest, and the AG did not want to be part of it, not with Roemer's reputation, not to snub Paul. Best to let things develop and come down then.

"I think you should let him have his shot, Paul," the AG said. To Roemer, "You think there's a good chance for successful prosecutions?"

"Absolutely."

"Well. That's it. Go ahead." He smiled at Cleary. "Thanks for bringing me up to date."

He smiled again and shouldered by them. "You really can't stay at least for the speech?"

"Sorry, sir. I've got a lot to do and I'm going back to California this evening," Roemer said.

"Well. Good seeing you both again," and the AG left the storage room.

Roemer wore a slick raincoat, rumpled and plain. He said to Cleary, "You think you can pull stunts like that and stop me? I sent Joe Averback to prison and he made a million dollars every time he took a breath. I sent Rusty Majors to prison and I went to school with him. I prosecuted guys out of the department I used to have to my house for dinner. I liked them. I don't like you."

"I think you're under the impression you can threaten me," Cleary said. "I'm only doing what my conscience directs."

"I'm too rough for you, right? I'm not like you, your friends, your law school, everybody you ever knew," Roemer said quietly. "I've heard it before, Cleary."

The applause from the banquet hall rose abruptly, like a swell of wind-driven rain. The frosted bulbs in the room full of bulk-quantity cans gave Roemer a shadow from his head downward, like a mantle.

"This is not a personal matter for me," Cleary said, trying to leave, finding his path blocked by Roemer.

"It never is. I had a guy you could probably understand, back in Los Angeles, way back when I was pretty new."

"I don't need your war stories. We both have things to do."

"You'll like it." Roemer's eyes were cold. "We'd done a search warrant on a hooker and got these photos of a judge named Alcala, she and him doing everything, smoking everything, sniffing everything. He's got a big law firm defending him, these big Democratic Party guys, big fund-raisers. They figure me for some government drone, so I go in and play dumb bureaucrat. We're in their offices in downtown L.A., with the paneling and the gals with trays of mineral water and tea and cookies going into each office. You know the kind of office, big law firms with big letterheads?"

"I have known a few in my time."

"Sure you have. That's your world. I didn't believe it. And these two guys, they're shining me, treating me like I walked in with my head up my ass. They're talking about what should happen to Judge Alcala. They're talking about a letter of reprimand from the Judicial Council, maybe some unpaid leave for the judge. They're offering me herb tea and sandwiches. They're going to make the whole thing go away. So I start scratching my head and I take out my files. I start tossing pictures on their fucking mahogany desk, right onto the cookies."

Roemer made short, hard throwing motions.

" 'You guys have this one? You have this one?' I ask calmly, acting dumb, putting each photo down. Here's the judge eating the hooker, here's the hooker eating the judge, the judge with his coke on a mirror, we got it all. And these guys, these two big lawyers just go on, like these pictures aren't there, like they aren't listening to me."

Cleary thought that display of indifference must have burned into Roemer. He put more weight on his umbrella, using it like a cane to support himself.

Roemer went on roughly, "They start talking like I'm stupid, I'm so dense I don't get the whole thing. 'Don't you see?' they're saying. 'You donkey. We're powerful men. We have a whole political-party establishment behind us and we're behind His Honor, Judge Alcala. And we don't care shit if he's screwing, snorting, selling, or disgracing the whole courthouse. Now, do you honestly think, you stupid government shit, that you can make anything happen to him? We can make this all go away,' " and Roemer blew an imaginary speck of dust into the air.

The applause rose again, as if bidden. Roemer smiled. "It's the same guys out there. They love these speeches. They love hearing how great they run the world."

"I've got to leave," Cleary said firmly. He was annoyed and tired of Roemer's splenetic memories. He lifted the umbrella and Roemer didn't stop him. They walked out through the kitchen, the chefs still ceaselessly piling up plates of food. Roemer pushed his finger into one as they passed, licking it.

"It isn't bad," he said.

In the parking lot, the rain still fell. Up went the umbrellas. Men in dark suits loitered beside the helicopter, watching the two men who came from the convention hall.

Cleary said, "You lost Alcala? These men snatched it from you?" It was a neat explanation for Roemer's envy.

"No. I did not lose him. When those guys finished, when they'd gone through how it was all going to go, you know, a reprimand from the Council, a promise to be good from the judge, maybe even transferring him to some safe place like domestic relations and letting him do divorces and property settlements until he retired, then I stopped."

Cleary stopped. The summer rain flicked onto his umbrella, onto the black asphalt, the green trees beyond.

"Gentlemen, I said"—Roemer stood close to Cleary—"you aren't listening to me. I want the judge's resignation in my hand by the close of business today. I want his signed declaration he won't seek office again. I want a full statement regarding any contacts he's had with anybody about pending cases. And I want the names of any hookers or dope dealers he's friends with."

"Did you get them?"

"One of those gentlemen laughed at me. No. More a guffaw. I never heard one before. They went right back to talking about how they'd resolve this like they'd always done it. Back of the courtroom, before it gets to court, couple of phone calls to old pals and politicians. So I gathered up the pictures and my files. I got up. They were smiling. I said, 'Gentlemen, I wasn't going to give you a preview of my cross-examination of Judge Alcala when he takes the stand at the trial. But I will now.' " Roemer was vigorous and direct, looking at Cleary. It was a disquieting thing.

" 'All right, Judge,' " Roemer said, " 'when you bought the coke, what kind of deal did you make with the dealer? Did you have more than one? How long have you been using coke? Heroin? What other illegal drugs are you using? Do you use it when you're on the bench? Have you ever talked about trading dope for a favorable sentence? How about the hookers you know, have you made deals with them about lenient treatment if they're arrested? Have you ever been blackmailed by a hooker or dope dealer? How often have you used illegal drugs with hookers? Where do you keep your drugs? Under your robe? Under the bench? In your chambers?' "

Roemer grinned savagely. " 'Tell me, Judge, do you use cocaine in your chambers before court?' "

"I see the point," Cleary said, and meant it in many ways.

"So did they finally. They started stammering, 'You're not playing fair. We're not ready, we need a continuance. Let's talk. We need more time.' " He snorted. "I had the letter in my hand, his resignation in my hand, by four-thirty that day."

"Neil, I'm not your enemy. I want to work with you," Cleary said, aware that he sounded very much like Roemer's defeated lawyers.

"I don't care what you are." Roemer tightened his raincoat, lowering his umbrella, the rain falling on his face, reviving him. "I've gone after bad judges before. I've nailed them. I will this time."

"Remember you are still on my staff," Cleary said. "You work for me."

Roemer grinned at him, shaking his head as if to clear bad memories or the rain. "You don't even know what just happened. You took me to the big guy and you lost, Cleary. He isn't with you."

"I'm sure he'd support me about my own staff."

"You don't matter. It's my operation all the way," and Roemer left him, whistling to one of the men beside the helicopter. Cleary thought they might be old friends.

He had the awful sense that he had just lost control of Operation Broken Trust. He heard the derisive laughter from the men beside the helicopter, and one of them shielded a match for Roemer to light a cigarette.

17

THE SHIT DIDN'T GO TO THE CRIME LAB?" JERRY WITWER ASKED Valles.

"Nope."

"Man."

Valles nodded. "You ain't going to believe where it went."

They stood in a corner of a grassy backyard in the north part of Santa Maria, close by cornfields and large empty acres bounded by freeways and Cyclone fences. Scattered through the dry, dead grass were rusted axles and torn old tires, a whole engine sprouting nettles. Four people sprawled on a concrete patio. A young woman, in jean cutoffs and purple sunglasses, looked toward Witwer and said, "Elvis, you coming back?" She fell to her side a little, tipping over a plastic basin of reddish liquor and making the other three people squeal and scramble to avoid the spreading liquid.

"You told her your name's Elvis?" Valles asked.

Witwer shrugged. "It helped." To the woman he said loudly, "I got business, Erin. Don't give me any shit," and his gruffness made her whine. Motorcycles putted and sputtered in the front yard.

"You believe her name's Erin? How come these crankster broads have cutesy names all the time?" Valles asked in puzzlement.

"Now you got me worried," Witwer said low.

"Sure as shit, Elvis."

"Where'd the dope go? What's Shiffley doing?"

Valles shook his head and scratched his beard. "I don't know what he's holding, but he is. He gave me the biggest load of crap you ever heard."

"Man. The boss."

"He's holding out on us."

"So what about the dope?"

Valles turned so his back was to a weathered, high wood fence

and he could keep an eye on the sluggish, but sometimes ambu-
latory, people flopped on the small house's patio. "I checked the
evidence envelope. It's been signed out to a guy in the Sheriff's
Department. Note says he's transporting it to the Crime Lab for
analysis."

"Sheriffs' don't do our transportation. Give me a break." Witwer
bit his lip.

"And this guy ain't in the Project, either. He's some new narc
they got, name I don't know."

"So what's he doing with our shit?"

"I call Gus out at the Lab. I say, 'Gus, has the dope from my
Vismara bust shown up?' "

"And they never get that shit analyzed so fucking fast." Witwer
frowned. He waved when Erin began swaying her hips to an old
Beatles song scratching from a radio on the patio. "I get the DA
yelling at my ass all the time, where's the analysis on the dope,
how much do I have, like I can do it myself."

"Here comes your girlfriend," Valles said warningly.

Witwer groaned as Erin loped unsteadily up to him. "You want
to dance? Nobody wants to dance over there, all shitfaced."

"The sixties never die," Valles said sourly.

Witwer shook her hands from his waist, pushed her away. "I'm
doing some business here, you go back and you wait."

"You sing us a song, Elvis?"

"Yeah, I'll come over and sing. You figure out what you want, I
sing it."

"I don't care what you sing, long as it's nice," and she licked her
lip, trying to be provocative, succeeding only in making her tongue
hang loose for a moment.

"Go away. You go away, honey. You sit there." Witwer pushed
Erin firmly, sending her back toward the patio. He closed his eyes
in irritability. "I ain't going to get diddly from these morons."

"Elvis's going to sing," Erin announced when she sat down hard
on the patio. A grunting chorus of approvals followed.

"You listening to me?" Valles snapped.

"I'm not hearing anything else, swear to God, Rog."

"So, Gus comes back on the line, he's cracking jokes at me, and
he says, 'Hell, no, no Vismara dope's here.' So I say, 'Well, some
sheriff dropped it off. You check just to make sure?' So Gus swears
at me, you know he gets excited and he starts making that snorty
noise?"

"He's got a hole in his nose, he told me."

"Anyway, he says he checked. No dope. No sheriff brought it over, no cop brought it over, it never showed up, so what was I pulling? Was I trying to get his ass in trouble?"

"Man. Man," Witwer said, hands stuck in his pockets. He shook his head, making the wild tufts of hair he cultivated shiver.

"So I gave him the case number again and asked him very nicely to keep an eye if it showed up. Maybe it got misfiled or something."

"Bet he hated that."

"He just threw a shit fit at me."

"We got to talk to that sheriff, Rog. Like right now. We can't have our dope floating someplace we don't know where."

"That's what I told you this morning, didn't I? Wasn't that what I said, our butts get it if something goes bad?"

"Okay. You said it."

Valles kicked at a rusted power train, like a spine half-buried in the untended dead grass. "I checked."

"What's the guy say?"

"I didn't talk to him. He was signed out to the field. So I go to Ned Rose. I say, Ned, your guy's checked out our dope and it ain't at the Crime Lab."

"Okay. Good so far. Ned's a good guy."

"So, yeah, he says, that's shitty. That's wrong. So we go look through their logs. We go check their property inventory. You know what we find?"

"Our shit?"

Valles nodded, watching two of the patio floppers stand and hug each other fiercely. A motorcycle died loudly in the front yard. "Ned accounted for all the coke and all the crank they've grabbed in the last ninety days. All their guys on the Project, they add their seizures. So it's all there. All where it should be."

"I missed something. What's our dope doing in their stash?"

Quietly, Valles said, "It wasn't our dope."

"It's theirs?"

"This new guy, who Rose says is a real hot dog, he logs out the coke we found. Must have broken it up into those grams and the big piece himself. It came from a big haul Sheriffs made in January, the Fontana bust out on South Eighty-eight Street?"

"That's when I got my ass chewed by Shiffley for not telling him another agency had a big bust coming."

Valles kicked at the power train on the ground, squinted up into the untarnished blue sky. "So what it was last night, Jerry, the

100

Sheriffs let us borrow this dope from Vismara and then they took it back."

"Like a fucking library book."

"Rose didn't know about it, and he says he's going to get this new kid to burn whoever put him up to checking out the shit."

Witwer snorted contemptuously. "Rose's the one who'll get burned. Shiffley's in on it, Vismara's phony. Somebody's running something in town and they ain't telling us grunts."

"Who could that be?" Valles asked mockingly.

"Feds."

"And that could be anyone. Any agency," Valles said. It was a discouraging fact of undercover work that police agencies frequently did not inform each other of their separate operations, jealously guarding them. Most possessive of all, most secretive, were federal agencies, from the FBI to Alcohol, Narcotics, and Firearms. There was a great deal of backbiting, recrimination, and anger when local undercover cops stumbled across a federal sting. Valles knew two cops who had been reassigned to Auto Burglary when they fell onto a Drug Enforcement Administration marijuana sting. Valles did not want to go to a dead-end assignment. Nor did he wish to be blamed for any mistakes Shiffley or the feds made. He did not care very much if he jeopardized their operation. They had used him cavalierly and he resented it.

Witwer shook his head sadly. "It really gets me that Shiffley'd just lie to your face."

"I ain't taking it," Valles said.

Longingly, Witwer sighed. "What can we do? We just be getting somebody very big pissed off at us."

Valles leaned close to him. "Put aside that we're getting the short end"—but that was precisely what he refused to ignore—"and we're still sitting out in the breeze if something happens. We got to cover ourselves, Jerry."

"Yeah. I guess so."

"You got to mean it."

"No, no, you're right. I don't want to get stuck for Shiffley or any of these assholes."

"So we do this as partners? The whole way?"

"Yeah, Rog. All the way."

Valles took a breath. "First thing, we got to find this phony dealer Vismara. He's got to have the pieces. Maybe that's as far as we got to go."

"We run him through CII or DOJ again, somebody's going to know we're looking."

"We start with our own sources. We work our own snitches. Like Maiz," Valles said. "That's fair."

"Okay," Witwer agreed with growing enthusiasm. "Hey, you want to do some business with these assholes?" He looked toward the patio. Another man had joined the people squatting or sitting, passing a pipe back and forth.

"Sure. We're here," Valles said, the two of them walking toward the patio. Erin waved again and began jerking her shoulders to an invisible rhythm. Valles smiled at Witwer. "Besides, I want to hear you sing, Elvis."

Nash still wore his robe, but it was open, as he sat in his chair. Benisek and Escobar sat in front of his desk.

"I've got a jury standing in the hallway," Nash said to Escobar. "I'm not going to let a defendant manipulate this court."

"It's a gag, Your Honor," Benisek said. He had the day's Soika trial file on his lap. His after-shave was sharply peppermint, his face darkened with a faint shadow.

"It is not a gag, Judge," Escobar said again. "He refuses to wear the clothes I've brought for him."

"So he can sit at the counsel table in his jail blues," Nash said. "I'm not keeping the jury out there any longer." He swung around and called for Shea.

"Well, Judge, I'll have to go on the record and state that you're forcing my client to prejudice himself in the eyes of the jury."

"It's his choice, Vince. He could wear the clothes."

"He claims the jail kept the clothes where they got dirty."

"Oh, my God," Benisek snapped.

Nash stood up. "Have you seen the clothes yourself?"

"I brought Mr. Soika a clean pair of dark slacks and a white shirt and clean socks yesterday. It appears to me that the jail dropped them. They are soiled now."

"So he won't wear them?"

"That's correct, Judge."

Shea appeared in the doorway of the chambers. He gave Benisek and Escobar the shortest disdainful glance possible.

"Bring Soika up, keep the jury outside, Scotty," Nash said. "Tell them it will only be a few more minutes."

"He's giving us trouble, Judge," Shea said.

"Bring him up." To Escobar, Nash said, "I'll do this on the record, Vince. I know it's not you. You can't lead Soika by the nose."

"I only do what my client tells me." Escobar returned Nash's midget smile.

Nash led them into the empty courtroom. He had put cardboard slats into the high doors so that cameramen couldn't take pictures without his permission. It also kept people from peeking inside, a small thing that tended to unnerve jurors and anger him.

Nash sat down on the bench, took some water, and waited. He would not let Escobar stampede him into a rash or foolish action. He also wouldn't let Soika and Escobar lead the court around.

The courtroom was as bright as possible, though still immersed in a gloomy dimness from the bench backward. Only the judge was highly lit and visible, everything else, except for the counsel table, getting darker as the courtroom went back.

Soika came in, shackled, held between Shea and another bailiff, making irritated noises until he was dumped into his chair beside Escobar at the counsel table. Vince looks rested, Nash thought. Without a care in the world, the smooth, complex face serene.

Shea and the bailiff stood behind Soika.

Nash glanced around. Reporter was at her post, taking it all down, Vi seated beneath the bench in case he needed anything.

"All right," Nash said. "It's ten-twenty. We're convening outside the presence of the jury. The defendant, his attorney, and the People's representative are present."

"I want some clean clothes," Soika said loudly.

"Be quiet," Nash said.

"Your Honor"—Escobar was on his small feet instantly—"my client is upset that his clothing has been negligently handled by the county jail."

"Bring in the defendant's clothes," Nash said to Shea, who went to the closet off to the side of the bench.

"I'm a clean person and I don't like being kept in the hall there, you know, all tied up, next to these people, they're not clean." Soika rattled his belly chain and glared at Nash.

"Not yet, Mr. Soika. In a moment," and Shea put the box of clothes down on the floor beside Vi's desk. Nash came down off the bench and picked up the pants, shirt, and examined them. It was a ludicrous situation.

There were two moments when he realized that his career as a prosecutor was not limitless, that some sense of dignity or disgust would cut it short. The first time was hurrying down the courthouse corridor. He had been a deputy DA for a week. He was doing his first drunk-driving trial. The defendant had given a urine sample, and Nash was late bringing the bottle to court. As he hurried down the corridor, knowing the judge would be angry at his lateness, he noticed urine dripping from the leaking bottle. It dripped on his shined shoes, it left a trail down the corridor. Nash thought at the time, I went to college for four years, law school for three years, and I'm jogging down a hall with a bottle of piss leaking in my hand. Even the compromises taught in law school didn't take into account this aspect of humanity, the sheer messiness of people in trouble. Justice was measured in human terms, and although Nash accepted that fact, he couldn't accommodate the sloppy and coarse side of it, however hard he tried.

The other occasion came when he was handling an attempted escape from Folsom prison. It was the nearest major state prison to Santa Maria, and all of its cases were referred to the DA's office for prosecution. The defendant, a lifer who didn't even have a parole hearing set for three years or a release date, was rugged looking, hard. He said the guards were harassing him. They planted the knife found near him. He wasn't trying to break out.

Nash showed the jury the evidence seized by the guards, the defendant's soiled pants. He had hidden the knife, homemade with a three-inch rough blade, in his rectum wrapped in plastic. Nash showed the jury the plastic. He had a criminalist testify about the linkage of the knife and the plastic and the soiled pants. But the jury liked the defendant. He seemed to be a free spirit oppressed by the guards, and Nash hadn't been able to tell them about his earlier crimes. Too prejudicial, the judge ruled. The jury acquitted the prison inmate, the prison slapped him with administrative punishment close to what the court could have sentenced, and one of the women jurors started writing him love letters. The Folsom warden's office thought this development was humorous, so they sent Nash copies of the love letters.

I did everything I was supposed to, Nash thought, handling Soika's clothes to see if they had really gotten dirty. The whole case turned into a joke. Even with every piece of evidence, justice didn't come from what I did or what the jury did.

Not long afterward, he told his father he finally agreed he should be a judge. Jack Nash had been urging him for years to seek an appointment. His brother was already on the federal bench. With Jack Nash's backing, his appointment to the Santa Maria municipal court was never in doubt, and he got it a year later.

It wasn't enough, Nash realized, just to see that the truth got told. Sometimes hearing it wasn't enough for people, and often not enough for the justice system. Sometimes you've got to try to do some justice, too, he thought. That was the golden promise Roemer was offering.

He tossed the clothes back in the box.

"They look fine to me, Mr. Soika. I can't see anything."

"Look, they're out to mess me up," Soika said, rattling his chains like Marley's ghost. "They make me sit for hours there before they take me over here, they got me next to guys who don't shave, they smell, they don't take a shower. I'm a clean person."

Escobar stood up. "Your Honor, I believe there is a serious question that the county jail is interfering with my client's rights."

Nash shook his head and Vi sighed silently at him. They both had heard and seen this routine, like a wheezy burlesque act, too many times before. "What's the jail doing with Mr. Soika?" Nash asked Shea.

"Nothing special, Judge." Shea had on his officially bored expression, legs slightly spread. "He gets ready to be transported, he's chained with everyone else coming over here."

"They stink," Soika snapped, trying to rise from his chair. He couldn't get far because he was secured in back to the chair's seat. "It's harassment. It's a mind game because they know I take my showers, I keep myself decent."

"Your Honor can see how this treatment, this mistreatment, has adversely affected my client." Escobar held his hands out in dismay.

"He's making a mountain out of nothing," Nash broke in, taking the bench again, looking down on them all. "He's being treated like everyone else."

"And that's the problem. It's a constitutional violation of the rights of every inmate," and Nash saw that Escobar was winding up for a lengthy oration. He had, so far in this trial, expiated on the Declaration of Independence, several books of the Bible, and Macbeth. Nash didn't want to hear anything more.

"Are you going to take on the whole inmate population as clients?" Nash asked.

"I'm raising this constitutional breach, Your Honor. I have a right."

Nash had a pencil in his hand and he pointed it at Escobar. "We've talked this around and had our fun. The court finds that there is no violation of Mr. Soika's rights by bringing him over here chained up with other prisoners. That's for security, isn't it, Mr. Sheriff?" Nash formally addressed Shea.

"It is, Judge. That's all."

"The court hasn't addressed the foundational issue of fairness, subjecting my client to this cattlelike regimen," Escobar said, winding up again for a long talk.

"They stink. They made my clothes stink." Soika's mouth was hard as he snapped back at Nash, then Shea.

"Your clothes are perfectly clean. I examined them myself," Nash said.

"You're lying," Soika said.

"Mr. Escobar?"

"I can't endorse what my client says, Your Honor. I can only say there are larger issues here."

"You're a liar," Soika repeated.

Nash listened and watched. Vi would have her head down, the small, neatly pinned mass of dark hair on her head like a boil. She was furious, he knew. She hated anybody who attacked him in court. Shea leaned on the tank railing. He had the false nonchalance of a bar fighter ready to spring.

Nash knew if he got mad, obviously so, the record would show it, and Escobar and Soika would have their victory. Escobar could argue, he could even raise his voice, but he never stepped across the line. It would be the judge who looked intemperate.

"I don't care what you call me." Nash spoke to Soika, watching the dead eyes fix on him, the chains faintly clinking as if Soika's intense inner tension were running like electric current through them. "But I will not allow you to show disrespect for this court."

Benisek sat passively, hands on his files. All he wanted to do was get on with his witnesses. The vice of DAs, Nash thought, was their tunnel vision. But Benisek couldn't do much now anyway. It's my honor at issue.

Soika started to speak, but Nash spoke loudly over him. "You have a choice right now. Put on your clothes or stay the way you are."

"You can't force Mr. Soika to surrender his rights." Escobar was heated.

"What's it going to be?" Nash asked. "Make your decision now."

"I want my clean clothes." Soika pointed. "I don't want those stinking clothes."

"Bring the jury in." Nash looked up and ordered Shea.

106

"Your Honor," Escobar said hastily, patting Soika. "A moment to resolve this issue."

"We've wasted enough time. The jury's coming in."

Escobar bent swiftly to Soika, then said to Nash, "Give us a minute to change."

"Hold the jury for a second, Scotty," Nash said. Shea closed the high courtroom doors again, a glimpse of the milling jurors in the hallway, curiously craning their heads to see what the delay was this time.

"Thank you, Your Honor. I intend to keep this issue for further proceedings," Escobar said. The bailiff behind Soika was unfastening his chains to the chair, getting him to his feet.

"Take Mr. Soika to the corridor behind the courtroom. He can change there," Nash said.

"There's no privacy," Escobar protested.

Nash grinned at Soika, who was snapping curses at Escobar and Shea at his other arm, propelling him out of the courtroom. "There aren't any unclean people either, Mr. Escobar. He'll be safe. You have two minutes."

He sat down in his chambers, making sure the door was closed. He dialed the U.S. Attorney's office in Sacramento. Janice came on. Nash suddenly was nervous.

"I was about to call you," she said to him.

"We're thinking alike. I want to invite you to dinner tomorrow." He listened closely to her mellow sound. "There are some judges you should meet. I could tell you about them; you can read about them, but that's not the same as seeing them yourself."

It was a pale excuse, he realized. He wanted to see her. He hoped she would take it.

"Part of my job is to advise Neil about the targets," she said. "I focus information for him."

"This is a perfect opportunity."

"I don't think so tomorrow. You're not free, either."

"Why not?"

"Neil called from Washington. He'd like to get started with your briefing. He wants to begin making approaches to targets soon."

"You're going to give me my story?" Nash tried to think of some other enticement to get her to Atchley's dinner or dinner alone.

"I want to introduce you to your partner, too."

"This guy Vismara? Is he going to be at every meeting?"

"We think so. We need to coordinate things with you two."

"What time?"

"Louis is coming at five."

"Where? The Hilton?"

Janice laughed. "That was the one-night hospitality suite of the Gulf Coast Cotton Growers Association. We've got a new, permanent location at the Cypress Hotel."

"I know where it is. How about this: I'll come to the meeting if you go to dinner?"

"Does it have to be a deal?"

"I finished my morning calendar. I'm starting trial again. I've done nothing but make deals all morning."

Janice laughed again and he was pleased. "Can we go to dinner a little late?" she asked.

"No problem."

"I'd like to go. We can go from the hotel."

"Good," Nash said. He had been utterly cool, professionally perfect thus far. Then he added, "I want to go out with you even if we didn't have business."

It sounded juvenile, but it was the truth. He braced for a crack from her. But Janice said, "Well, I'm looking forward to it." They ended with banalities and Nash hung up. For an instant he felt guilty, as if somehow betraying Kim. The one-nighters were the result of desperation and loss. This was a choice made calmly, deliberately. He wondered what Janice looked like making love, how she would look at him.

He heard Soika's chains rattling again, being herded into the courtroom. As he got up, zipping his robe, Frank Wisot strolled in, smiling, beckoning Nash to him. He was smoking.

"I've got to hit the bench," Nash said. "I've got an in-custody defendant, Frank."

Wisot, in shirtsleeves, scratched his head. "I got a courtroom full of lawyers and yellers and I needed a little peace."

"Stay in here if you want." Nash smiled.

"I just ordered a new robe." Wisot glanced at Nash's father's photograph.

"The old one looked pretty beat up." Nash picked up his trial notebook, the record of what exhibits and witnesses had appeared in Soika's case.

"It's about four hundred bucks for a new robe," Wisot said, unwilling to let Nash go. "I paid eighty when I bought the first one, and you couldn't get them with zippers or snaps or Velcro. One size, the damn thing's hot all the time.''

Nash shook his head with a smile. ''Everything goes up.'' He heard Shea call court to order. The sound of people, rustling, shuffling in his courtroom was like wind blowing across a cornfield, sibilant, invisible, reassuring.

Wisot tapped his shoulder. ''Nothing left at the credit union. Put me right over the line.'' He wiggled his eyebrows and put out his cigarette. ''How about a little loan until our damn check comes Friday?''

''What do you need?''

''Couple hundred.''

Nash shifted the notebook. ''Maybe a hundred, Frank. I'm not too liquid right now.''

''I'll take it. I'll pester our new boy, Peatling. He won't refuse the senior judge.''

''What about the table you bought at Harold's fund-raiser?'' Nash thought Wisot was joking, a common thing for him.

''The check'll bounce all over the place. I'll make it good in a while.''

''Jesus. Harold'll go crazy.''

''What's he going to do? Turn in an old friend? The oldest trial judge in the county?''

''I didn't realize you lived such a risky life.''

''Everybody's got secrets, Tim.'' Wisot winked. ''Thanks for the loan.''

Nash's anticipation at seeing Janice chilled as he talked to Wisot. It struck him forcefully, for the first time, that he might have to hurt someone he liked. Perhaps it wouldn't be Wisot, but there were others: Frenkel, Croncota, Kalbacher, old Fred Miyazumi.

As he took the bench, Escobar and Duryea and Soika huddled closely below him at the counsel table, Benisek carefully stacking three legal pads, the jurors folding their newspapers and paperbacks, looking up at him, Nash realized there was going to be pain for him in Operation Broken Trust.

He'd thought so last night when Roemer sold him. Now he knew it.

18

THE NEXT DAY NASH ENDED COURT EARLY, TELLING THE JURY HE had an appointment. He changed quickly and left the courthouse with an odd mix of emotions, fear and anticipation and pleasure. His life had changed radically in the last few months, and he sensed it was about to change again.

He did not go to the Cypress Hotel directly. He stopped off at a toy store downtown. It was still hot out, though, and Nash, because he wanted to be formal at the meeting, wore a three-piece suit, charcoal with pinstripes and an ivory-white shirt too highly starched so it rasped against his neck all day and made him irritable. He sweated now, getting out of the car, even the downtown man-made shade seeming to collect the heat and focus it on him.

He prowled the toy store quickly. It was impossible to be sad or worried there. Children and their mothers tugged each other along cluttered, bright aisles of dolls, models, huge stuffed animals, displays of different-sized model trains. For the first time in months, Nash didn't feel a pang when he saw a woman with a child, usually a boy. He still thought of Kim and Ben instantly when he saw a young woman, her son dragging her fiercely forward, as if she were a reluctant pack animal. But the ice-pick pain was gone.

He quickly picked out a large model jet fighter, shown on its box trailing a great swath of exhaust. He was disappointed to find out it would take ten days to reach L.A., but it would give him another excuse to call Ben, to tell him a surprise was coming.

He came out of the toy store, standing a moment in the midst of the rush-hour frenzy, immobile and watchful. Why had he bought the model for his son? Was it to appease my conscience? he thought, feeling the sweat like little wet buttons on his skin.

The Cypress Hotel was about a ten-minute drive from the toy store in slow, thick traffic. Santa Maria was darker and older along this route, several turn-of-the-century brick fire stations solidly surrounded by elms and oaks, streets of late nineteenth-century homes, high roofed and ornamented with wooden trelliswork, arches and circles around their spacious porches. The city's wealthy used to live here, not the very richest, but the families who owned the stores and factories, the rice and flour mills. As Nash passed down the cracked sidewalks, the rough streets, he saw the boards along the broken windows, mottled grass, people in T-shirts sitting on the sagging wood stairs.

The Cypress Hotel was in a better part of the city, about the same age as the old courthouse, a skyscraper in those days, casting its own implacable shadow on the stores crowded around its glass and granite facade, brass doors and maroon awnings. Nash parked in the garage, following a press of laughing men in variously fitting tuxedos and women in long, rustling dresses into the lobby.

His high school prom had been held at the hotel. He'd gone with Francine Mayhew, who was a cheerleader, and it had been a very good night.

The lobby of the Cypress, unlike the Hilton's, was low ceilinged, dark paneled, with heavy blue-red carpets and immovable sofas and thick chairs stuck between large pots of fresh flowers. Memory and that indefinable mix of emotions came over him again. Nash went to the men's room off the lobby, as he remembered he had upon arriving on that prom evening to comb his hair for Francine, check his cummerbund, squirm against the metal clasps at his throat and his suspenders, and make sure again he had brought a couple of rubbers in his wallet, with the fifty dollars to cover the evening. He combed his hair now and realized he was ready for whatever was going to happen.

He found Janice Dillon sitting on one of the stuffed chairs, a newspaper folded neatly into quarters in her hand.

"I'm surprised you picked this hotel." Nash sat down. "It's old and out of the way."

"Well, it's a luxury hotel."

"Why is that important?"

Janice smiled. He liked her smile, easy and open. "It seemed like the kind of hotel you'd pick for doing business."

"Meaning I'm a snob or I have good taste?"

"Oh, good taste definitely." She put the paper down on a marble inlaid table. "And Neil wanted the FBI agents to have a comfortable place to sleep."

"They're staying here?"

She nodded and got up. "When we're not using the suite upstairs, anybody in the operation can live here. We always have agents sleeping in monitored rooms."

Nash laughed. "I have to admit this place has memories."

"Good ones?"

"Mostly. Do you want a drink?" He pointed at the bar off to the left.

She looked at her watch. "We've got about fifteen minutes. I wanted to talk to you first. Neil will be joining us, too."

They walked over to the Edwardian room called St. George's, lit by false gaslights, the bar highly buffed, the man behind it with a waxed handlebar mustache. Nash ordered for them and they sat down almost alone in the bar. He enjoyed simply sitting here with her.

"What's your connection with Roemer?" Nash asked when their drinks came to the table. It sounded innocent.

"I worked with Neil when he was based in Washington. When he transferred to Miami, I followed him."

"Wherever he went?"

"Most places," she said, and sipped her drink. "There must be a lot of places in Santa Maria with memories for you."

Nash noticed she was avoiding his inquiries like a good cross-examiner. "It sounds to me you don't have a place like that."

She nodded. "My father worked for Coca-Cola. We moved all the time, Montgomery, Dallas, Houston, up to New York. I didn't have time to put roots down anywhere."

"There are some drawbacks to living your whole life in one place."

"Because you don't see other cities, the way other people live?"

Nash shook his head, set his drink down. "No, the real vice is that everybody knows you. And you know everybody."

"This isn't exactly a small town."

"Every place is a small town for some people. I've moved among the same people all my life. You always have the sense someone's watching you."

Janice smiled. "I felt just the opposite. We did so much wandering, I never thought anybody cared where I was or who I was."

"Well, here we both are," and he raised his glass and they toasted each other. "Roemer's back from Washington?"

She nodded and checked her watch again. Nash had the impression she rarely did anything without thinking it out and then executing the plan carefully. Even the delight of spontaneity he got from her had an undertone of calculation and forethought.

112

"It's been nonstop for the last twenty-four hours." Janice finished her drink. "We'll meet Vismara in a few minutes. He's not quite an ordinary snitch."

"How?"

"Well, you'll see for yourself. He's very intense. He's very anxious to work for us."

"That's nothing new. I did a lot of cases with snitches who wanted to work off things. They were very intense."

"He's different. He's almost a volunteer."

"He's not working off some beef?"

"Yes. He is. But I think he'd do this anyway."

"At least he'll be enthusiastic."

She got up. "That's the problem. You'll have to keep an eye on him. Vismara might get too enthusiastic."

"He'd blow the whole sting. You're talking about entrapment, aren't you? Vismara might step over the line?"

They walked to the gentle whirring and the bells of the elevators. "You have to watch him, Tim. Make sure he stays on our side of the line."

On the twentieth floor of the Cypress Hotel, in suite 537, Nash was introduced to several people. Roemer made the introductions with hearty exuberance, as if they were all friends, and not people who worked for him.

"Judge, this is Larry Jacobs and Ed Sanchez. They'll both be with you most of the time here."

Nash shook hands with the two men. Jacobs and Sanchez were in their thirties, Jacobs fairly tall with crew-cut dark hair. Sanchez was square, impassive, his hands behind his back. "You're both with the FBI?" Nash asked.

Jacobs nodded and winked. "We're lifers, Judge. We like doing this stuff."

"He likes it. I love it," Sanchez said.

"We'll be tagging along with you," Jacobs said, "making sure everything's okay. We're your shadows."

"Good guys. They do good work. We've done a lot of good work together," Roemer said. He moved to a third man. "Tom Testa's our maintenance man." He slapped a short, dour young man.

"I run the equipment," Testa said.

"He'll make sure whatever is said in this suite or wherever you are is recorded. So everybody can hear it."

"I'll get it on video, too."

"Pleased to meet you," Nash said. He did not see anyone else, particularly the mysterious Vismara.

"I can catch it on the fly if I have to, but I like to work with fixed sites better. You get much sharper audio and pictures," Testa said.

"I don't see any cameras." Nash glanced around.

"Nobody will." Roemer grinned. The two FBI agents did, too. Janice had quietly gone into a room at the far end of the suite. It was a modestly done place, from what Nash could see. Gray and salmon pink dominated, with heavy chairs and two tables to seat eight.

"What's the arrangement on the suite?" Nash asked.

"It's yours. As far as everyone's concerned, you live here. You'll have your meetings here. We needed more space than you've got at your apartment for the equipment."

Testa said, "Way too small out there. Way, way."

Nash said, "You checked my apartment? When?"

"Just the blueprints," Roemer said. "Tom knows how much room he needs, and we've pretty much filled this place. Besides, you need somewhere you can go to sleep. Get away from the operation."

"That's a good thought," Nash said, again impressed with Roemer's thoroughness. "I don't like to live too well," he said, glancing at the suite again.

Roemer frowned. "Is it too downscale? Out of character?"

"No. Just about right. What I could afford downtown."

Roemer relaxed. "Good. We had a number of discussions about what kind of place you might live in, how you'd want to set up a bribe, the atmosphere."

"Janice and I talked about that." Nash walked the large room. "What's she doing in the operation exactly?"

Roemer said, "She collects all the reports, whatever Larry and Ed generate. She makes initial evaluations about how a particular target is behaving. She's my eyes and ears."

"She's watching me?" Nash asked.

"She keeps track of everything, Judge," Roemer said.

Nash was glad he understood her position. It was commonsense that she was keeping Roemer apprised of events. It did not bother him. "Well, where is she? Where's the snitch?"

Roemer called her name. Jacobs said, "Ole Ed and me'll be downstairs sucking up a few."

"He's kidding," Sanchez said.

They left with Testa grumbling behind them as Janice and a short man, olive skinned, dressed with an odd formality, down to a green handkerchief in the breast pocket of his too dark, too shiny suit, came out of the bedroom.

"I thought just us would be better, no agents," Roemer whispered to Nash.

"Judge," Janice said, "this is Louis Vismara."

"Junior," Vismara held up a small finger. He had bright, button-sized eyes and slick hair.

"Vismara, Jr. He's going to be your bait," Janice said.

Vismara advanced to Nash, put out a hand that looked too large for him. "I am very honored to meet you," he said.

When Nash shook his hand, he noticed it was sweaty. "How do you do, Mr. Vismara?"

"Okay, thank you, Your Honor. I'm very good today." He smiled nervously, gamely, without much point. "I've never met a judge except in court."

"Come on back here," Roemer interrupted. "I want you to see the control room," and he waved them to the bedroom.

Nash and Janice walked together, Vismara following. Nash had the uneasy feeling the smaller man was measuring the distance between them, making certain he did not tread too closely. He seemed unduly uncomfortable, and Nash did not think he'd present a credible picture as a felon who could bribe his way out of court.

Roemer pointed around the bedroom. "What we've got here is a complete capability of taping everything that happens anywhere in the suite."

The beds, Nash saw, had been pushed against one wall. The rest of the large room was crowded with VCRs and TV monitors, four showing the entry doorway, the short hallway, the living room, the two dining tables, and then a lower-level view of the length of the whole suite, as if seen from a mousehole.

Vismara peered down at the TV screens flickering in color, digital readouts in their corners relentlessly rolling off the time in seconds and the date. "I watched this while we back here. You see everybody, you hear the whole thing, like your own TV show." He grinned at Nash, showing uneven, poorly spaced teeth. "Like you famous, you on so many TVs."

Roemer grinned and Janice watched Nash closely. It was as if they were proudly showing off a railroad train set in their basement and not equipment to catch people breaking their oaths of office and destroying their lives.

"Put this on," and Roemer handed Nash a pair of headsets.

Nash put them on and heard the low hum of the air conditioner in the next room, echoing faintly. On the large audiotape recorder little needles swung slightly to the right, spools of tape rolled on, trapping every sound.

"The quality's much better than what I used to have." Nash took off the headset. "There's no distortion. I'm sure you'll get everything."

"Four cameras mounted throughout the suite, five microphones with overlapping range. Anyone in there can walk and talk, and Testa won't miss one footstep. The jury will be able to see and hear it better than you, Tim."

Janice nodded. "Nobody ever got away from this kind of evidence in court."

"DeLorean did," Nash reminded her.

"This is different," Roemer said, taking them back into the living room. "DeLorean had a very good lawyer, a very stupid jury, and a very lazy prosecutor. I know there won't be a lazy prosecutor on this case." He grinned again.

There was no offer of anything to eat or drink, Nash saw. The campaign had begun. He was pleased with how much effort had been put into it.

Vismara kept nodding and looking around the room, fussing with his lapels or the handkerchief, worried that his appearance was going.

"What have they promised you, Mr. Vismara?" Nash asked.

"I can tell you our deal," Roemer said.

"I'd like him to tell me," Nash said bluntly. Vismara cleared his throat, smiled nervously.

"I've been to the joint once."

"Where?"

"Soledad. I didn't like it. I'm not going back."

"What is the deal?" Nash asked again. "Pretend I'm just someone who's interested."

Roemer and Janice sat down at the dining table, observing and evaluating. They're checking us both out, Nash thought. Me and the snitch.

"You mind calling me Louis? Like you know me?" Vismara asked hesitantly.

"Okay. Call me Tim."

This pleased Vismara, Nash saw. A genuine, thoughtless smile broke across his face. "Thank you. That's what I'm going to call you."

"Tell him what we agreed on," Roemer broke in. He leaned his head on one hand and glanced every so often at Janice.

"Right now, like I got a charge in Alameda County, they got me, they say they got me on some heroin."

"Sale?"

Vismara nodded. "That's what they say. They say, 'He's selling shit, he's dealing big time.' So these guys"—he pointed at Roemer— "they got this federal rap on me for transportation, you know."

"That's a lot of time, Louis. All of it goes away if you help out on this deal?" Nash asked. He stood close to Vismara, watching him. It was an odd feeling to realize the lives of people he worked with and had known for years would depend on this corrupt little man. My life is tied up to a snitch now, too, Nash thought.

"I want to help. I mean, the other stuff's important"—Vismara grinned badly again—"but I want to do this."

"Why?"

"It's like a second chance," Vismara said seriously. "Maybe I do it better next time, I get to try again. I can maybe straighten everything out."

Nash looked at him skeptically. He had heard the proffered penitence before, as a prosecutor, and every day on the bench. *I will do better, Judge, if you just give me a break. I will get a job and pay back my victims. I will help with their hospital bills. I will support my kids.* His expression must have revealed how he felt.

Vismara's face fell. "You don't believe me."

"There's no other deal? You get a free ride on all state and federal charges for your part in this sting?"

"Swear to God, that's it." Vismara raised his hand. He fidgeted with his tightly knotted, glistening black tie.

"What else does he have on his rap?" Nash asked Roemer.

"It's pretty long. He's got enough to make it believable he'd do anything to get out of going back to the joint again."

"I could still go to the joint, I don't do you guys a good job."

"Do you mind if I look at a copy of your rap sheet, Louis?" Nash asked.

"Hey, no problem with me. I'm not proud of it."

"I'll get you a copy, Tim." Roemer made a note but appeared annoyed.

"You're going to follow this all the way through trial?" Nash asked Vismara roughly. "Testify before a grand jury, testify at the trial? No matter how hard it gets?"

Vismara grinned, bobbing his head. He spoke to Roemer and

Janice as much as Nash. "Swear to God. This is my second chance. It's like a great honor, I get to do this with a guy, a judge like you."

"You don't have to impress me," Nash said.

"Hey, I hope, I mean this, that when we done, you have a little bit of the respect I got for you," Vismara said, pointing to Nash, then himself. He sat down and took out his green handkerchief, rubbing his cheeks. "I sweat real easy. Like my mother."

Nash had used snitches and made deals before. He sat in court and heard the worst people could do, and it became a stream of misery that flowed on and on, so that no single act of brutality or callousness could divert it or make it pause.

I don't know, he thought, if I can still hear the sound of repentance. He hoped he had not grown so cold and empty he would ignore a hand thrust out of the whirling water for help.

"I'm going to be rotating in agents," Roemer said, getting up to adjust the room's temperature. "But Jacobs and Sanchez will be here for the duration. They're going to be your guardian angels."

"The people I talk to aren't violent," Nash said.

"People do funny things when they've got a lot at risk."

Vismara nodded. "Even a little guy, no muscle, no nothing, he still got a gun, he got a knife. You can get hurt."

"I doubt it," Nash said.

"Neil, we've got a fund-raiser," Janice said, glancing at Nash. "We ought to go through it once."

Roemer had his hands in his pockets. "I forgot you and Tim are out on the town tonight. Okay. You ready to do a rehearsal, Tim?"

"Sure. What am I supposed to say?"

"We'll do it as we run through it. Louis, you sit over there on the sofa. Tim, you sit here at the table. We'll put the judge on candid camera opposite you at the table." Roemer sat down with Nash. "I'll be the crooked judge tonight, okay?"

Nash looked at Janice, standing behind Vismara. He was excited by her cool, intent gaze. He was looking forward to the evening with her, even if it rankled Roemer. "I'll be myself."

"You be yourself." Roemer winked at Janice. She folded her arms across her chest. Vismara put his hands on his knees and squirmed slightly on the sofa. He grinned, his head ducking around, trying to spot the hidden cameras and microphones.

"Fire away," Nash said.

"So, Tim, my old buddy, my old pal, what's this wonderful offer you've got for your lifelong best friend in the whole world?" Roemer smiled, but his voice was steel.

19

I STUTTERED," NASH SAID INCREDULOUSLY. "LIKE A KID."

Janice had her head back on the seat. "We'll do it again. You'll feel perfectly at ease when you actually do it."

Nash shook his head, watching the freeway as he drove. "I haven't felt so nervous since I was in grade school. I felt like a complete fool. I looked like one."

"I testified once in a counterfeiting trial. I was the former prosecutor. The defense claimed I'd made some under-the-table deal with our chief witness." Janice sat up, and Nash glanced over at her. "I thought I'd pass out. I was being cross-examined by the same asshole I'd taken apart in other trials. But now he had me on the stand and it was completely different."

"What happened?"

"I got through it all right. I had some phone logs that proved I couldn't have talked with our witness when they said I did."

"We both do better asking the questions," Nash said with a smile.

"There's usually a lot less at stake," she answered.

He had taken the interstate north from the hotel, following what looked like the march of home developments for miles. The sun was lowering, but the heat had paradoxically risen in the colorless air so that the trees and grass, even the edge of the horizon, seemed yellow stained. Nash had the air conditioner on high.

He had not been pleased with the run-through at the hotel. His own tenseness was one reason. He did not like Janice to see him so clumsy and ill prepared. Vismara, by comparison, who had seemed so nervous earlier, acted like a trouper. He was arrogant, sly, utterly convincing.

"Vismara lies like a con. I see prison guards come in on trials and they always sound like they're lying. The cons always sound like they're telling the truth."

"Lying isn't a job for the guards," Janice answered. "Most of them still have a conscience."

"I think you're making a mistake paying Vismara."

"Didn't you ever pay a snitch?"

Nash glanced at the dry countryside crowded with small new homes. Cars and heavy-laden trucks crowded around him on the freeway. Eucalyptus trees, dusty green and ancient, bowed over the cinder-block walls protecting the new homes. "Not as much as you've paid him."

"Living expenses. He can account for everything. We're just taking care of his utilities and rented house," she said. She had been much friendlier before they met with Roemer and Vismara. He thought the undercurrent of some past with Roemer was getting in the way now. Like it's hard to throw off, Nash thought.

"It's still going to look like he's being paid for his testimony."

"Nobody's paying you. And we'll have the tapes."

Nash didn't want to argue with her, but the potential harm was immense for him, too. "If he's honest, why give him money at all?"

Janice looked at him with surprise. "He had to have a new address, new car, new credit. We'll work him. Neil's good at keeping snitches in line. But Vismara's got to live somewhere while we're running the operation."

"I always had trouble whenever a snitch got money from the DA or the cops."

"Did you ever lose a snitch when he couldn't pay his bills or feel safe because he was dumping on everything he'd done before he came over to you?"

Nash nodded. "A couple. I had a couple go sideways at trial even after they got paid and got a deal."

"We've done the cost-benefit analysis," Janice said, checking her purse, looking at her hair in a small mirror. "It balances out. We've got a pretty good win ratio."

"You and Roemer?"

She smiled at him. "Us. The government."

Nash took an off-ramp at Palisade Avenue, dropping down steeply into an interchange of long lights and long lines of cars and trucks. Santa Maria's explosive growth was most vivid here, like a focused beam of sunlight through a magnifying glass. All around were fast-food restaurants, gas stations, motels, small quick-stop markets that sold nothing more than cigarettes, liquor, and candy. Nothing stayed in place, people and businesses were in constant motion. It was, Nash thought with dislike, the antithesis of the way he had grown up, among people and houses that were unchanging and solid.

About four miles farther, Palisade Avenue veered off to the left in a slow arc, and Tyler Way straightened out into a flatland of long parking lots and carefully cultivated industrial parks complete with glass buildings that burned in the dying sunlight.

"See something?" Nash asked Janice after she had stared out the window for some time.

"It looks like a pleasant city."

Rising ahead of them were the grandstand and bleachers of the Santa Maria Race Track. The orange-tiled roof of the bleachers glowed heatedly, the empty white seats in their thousands were ghostly. Nash turned into the nearly deserted parking lot, driving down slowly.

"In the summer they used to have demo derbies here," he said, pointing at the long, eliptical path of the track.

"Did you go?"

"I loved them. It sounds dumb, but I liked watching a bunch of old clunkers tear around and crash into each other."

"They don't do it anymore?"

"The neighbors complained. You should have seen the dust cloud. Went up and covered everything. I used to come home covered with dust. It was great."

A man in a short-sleeve white shirt, white pants, dark glasses, waved them forward, pointing to a parking space. Other cars were coming in, and Nash noticed men spread throughout the lot directing them into spaces. He followed where the man pointed.

Janice, as though the thing had built up in her, said abruptly, "You don't strike me as naive, Tim."

He parked the car between a Cadillac and a Mercedes. "I was a DA for ten years. I've been a judge for five. I think I've seen about everything." The question puzzled him, like her intensity about it.

"But you are naive. Have you thought about what happens when you become a government witness?"

He had his hand on the door. With the engine off, the car was rapidly getting hot. The white-dressed man went on waving and directing incoming cars. Atchley must be getting a good turnout, Nash thought.

"I'll be a witness. That's all. Let's get out of the car." He started to open his door. Janice didn't move. She looked at him with almost the same implicit pleading Terhune had shown several nights before.

"When it's over, Neil and I go on to something else. You stay here. This is your city. You grew up here."

"That's why I agreed to do it."

"Do you really think anybody will trust you again? Even your friends? Do you think you can go on being a judge?"

"Why shouldn't I? Being a judge is completely separate. Roemer agreed with that. I've got a trial still going on."

Janice breathed deeply in the heating, confined air in the car. On the asphalt, the shimmering heat made the grandstand and bleachers waver and bend, as if dreams. "I want you to think about what will happen to you. You can stop right now. I don't have to meet these judges. We don't have to go any further."

"I don't understand." He felt the door handle warm in his hand. "I assumed you were ready to go."

"I am."

"Why the questions then?"

"I'm offering you a chance to reconsider. It's a second chance."

"Why? Is Roemer holding something? I'll stop right now if he is," Nash vowed, his door open, the air thickly coating them both as it swept into the car.

"No. He told you everything. I want to make sure you've thought it out."

"I have. I know what I'm doing. Thanks for worrying." He got out of the car.

She got out, slammed her door. "I was only discharging a promise I made to myself."

"What was it?" They started across the limitless asphalt, toward the faint music layered into the dusky air, coming from the Turf Club on the grandstand's exclusive second tier.

"I promised I'd offer the next witness a second chance. I never had one."

More men in white, with dark glasses, directed them to the Turf Club, and from the rising glassed-in elevator Nash saw the whole track and the expanse of bleachers. At the club's entrance on the second tier, he and Janice faced a white and red banner, REELECT JUDGE HAROLD ATCHLEY TO SUPERIOR COURT, like a giant bandage. Like offspring, smaller red and white signs with Atchley's name on them were posted along the club's walls between pictures of dead quarter horses. The signs were laid against the table where Nash got name tags for himself and Janice. The two middle-aged ladies at the table tittered at his name because they had known his father. The signs all said HE DOES THE JOB over and over, without further explanation.

Nash took Janice's arm and they went into the club. It felt comfortable touching her, natural. She looked around the crowd.

"Those guys outside, with the shades? They're all off-duty cops," he said.

"Are they being paid?"

He shrugged. "Sometimes they'll do it for free. Sometimes all you have to do is tell the captain or the chief you need some cops to work a campaign event."

She nodded. "That's illegal."

"Everybody knows that."

"I'll keep that in mind."

She rebuffed any attempt he made to find out what she meant by her last cryptic comment in the car. There was time enough, later, she said, to tell him. He had made his choice now.

"Hungry?" he asked.

"Actually I am. Let's point toward the food." They walked through the people knotted together, talking, laughing, holding plastic cups of red or white wine, or something stronger. A wet bar, with two chubby men in white, starched coats, did brisk business.

At the far end of the club, underneath the largest REELECT JUDGE HAROLD ATCHLEY TO SUPERIOR COURT banner, a mariachi band of four women and two men played guitars and sang raggedly through speakers. Their drum said they were Los Gorriónes Amarillos, and they all wore yellow costumes, the dark-haired women singing without vigor, their yellow dresses black dotted. The men swayed slightly and tried to smile and had on black string ties.

"Are you mad about something?" Nash asked as they got in the line winding up to the serving tables.

"No," Janice said, holding a plate. "I'm working now. So are you."

"I thought we were on a date," he tried to kid her.

"This is business."

They moved slowly. Servers, also in white shirts and string ties, dumped large pieces of overcooked pork with a pile of rice onto the plates until whoever held the plate walked on. The servers did not speak English.

"Okay," Nash said. He had annoyed her somehow, but he was

content for the moment to have her near. For an instant, her perfume triumphed over the spicy food. "I count fifteen judges, muni and super here. Everybody's out showing the flag for Harold."

"Which one's he?"

"He's the one about to grab you."

She turned slightly to see Atchley wearing a Philippine wedding shirt, his belly heavy, a plastic cup in one hand. He didn't grab Janice. He shook Nash's shoulder.

"You like this?" Atchley demanded with a high, wide smile. "This is a great bunch of people. This is when you find out who your friends are." He stared at Janice.

"This is Janice Dillon. With the U.S. Attorney in Sacramento."

She shook hands with Atchley. "I hope your campaign is going well."

"Oh, sure. Everybody came. Everybody who didn't have to be someplace. Everybody bought tickets." Atchley grinned. Several couples had come to him and were smiling, chatting with him whenever he turned to admire the people, the signs, the music and food conjured for his benefit. They walked along the table, food dropped onto their plates. Atchley insisted Janice take more. "I've got a deal with my caterer. I can get anything and pay as long in the future as I want."

"Makes campaigning easy."

"Oh, yeah. Tim and I were talking about that the other day. It's a sin to make judges run for office, go through all of this."

Janice pointed with her cup of white wine. "There's a clear space," and she led Nash. He hoped Atchley, his other guests at his side, would drop away and mingle.

But Atchley, with a growing group of couples who wanted to chat, trailed alongside to the other side of the room where it was less crowded. The band, warbling in high-pitched Spanish, made conversation hard.

The closer Atchley clung to him, bragging about property he'd just bought over on North C Street, where an old junkyard was being turned into condominiums, how much money he was raising, how all the city's unions had endorsed him, from the police to the maintenance workers, the more Nash wanted to catch him on Roemer's omnivorous tapes. Atchley was crude and corrupt and Nash hated him for trying to trade on their slight acquaintance.

When Atchley's wife called him away, Nash saw his chance. He took Janice's arm again. "I can't stand the guy. There are some good people here."

"I'm going to check his last campaign statement," she said as they headed for a small clot of judges, "see how much he takes in."

"He needs money. You always do in a campaign."

"I don't." Frank Wisot overheard them. He was with Peatling and Kalbacher and Susanna Jardine, all of whom came over with fresh drinks. "Neither did Tim's father. Or Tim. If Tim ever decides to run for something better, he can raise whatever he wants." Wisot was slightly drunk. "How about Senator Nash?"

"Fuck a doughnut, Frank," Nash said without malice, and Jardine chuckled.

"How long is it decent for us to stay at this funeral?" Peatling asked.

"Harold's going to make a speech. Walk out during that," Susanna advised. "I'm going to."

They chatted about the heat and how Janice liked working for the Eastern District's U.S. Attorney. Nash listened, watched her. He had to miss what she said every so often when people came up to him. He was getting nearly as much attention as Atchley. "How's your dad, Tim?" was the frequent question. Lawyers and civic types, all in suits with their wives, made a point of a quick word. Other judges, Croncota with his daughter, nearly as tall as him, Henshaw and Miyazumi with his wife between them, stopped over. Everyone drank, nodded solemnly at the news that Mike Sinclair's fever was up and now the quacks weren't saying when he could leave the hospital.

In an hour Nash got looser and put his arm on Janice more often and noticed how Susanna or Kalbacher watched the gesture over their cup rims.

"Escobar's pulling all kinds of crap. He told the jury there was no murder today," Nash said indignantly. The band, in full throat, banged and strummed into a lilting version of "Home on the Range."

"No murder?" Janice asked. "I've been following the trial a little."

"Tim doesn't talk about it at the end of the day?" Ruth Frenkel joined them, holding two cups, drinking alternately from them. One earring had come off.

"I don't see him every day," Janice answered.

"But what he says," Nash interjected, "is the victim was such a bad guy, he wasn't human. So no murder. I've got to watch that guy every second to make sure he doesn't slip junk in front of the jury. Benisek isn't doing anything."

125

"You ever see a situation where two lawyers get together and they don't start talking shop in five minutes?" Wisot asked Janice.

"We've all been on real good behavior tonight," Susanna said.

"Damn Escobar," Nash said. He wanted to leave, but Janice apparently wanted to stay. Getting stuff on all of us, he thought. Me, too. He looked around the club, the couples clustered more tightly, the band working to be heard over the increasingly boisterous chatter and laughter. From the walls, the jockeys and long-dead race winners dolefully looked down.

"I got an Escobar story," Wisot said. "KO told me this one."

"A local public defender," Nash said to Janice.

"Everybody's got Escobar stories, Frank." Kalbacher looked around for his wife. Nash had never thought much about how wives and judges separated at these functions. He recalled what his mother told him and thought it had probably been fairly dull, or worse, for Kim.

"Well, seems old Vince's got this boyfriend-girlfriend assault case. Just a terrible case. The gal calls the cops and they've got the tape with her screaming and him yelling, and you could hear him hitting her. With a broom handle."

He had their attention, Nash saw. Frenkel winced and drank. At the end of the room, Atchley was slowly getting onto a low stage where Los Gorriónes Amarillos swayed gently and looked straight ahead.

"Better hurry," Nash advised. "Harold's heading for the mike."

Wisot hunched his shoulders in horror. "It's a really good case, we all think. Cops saw her injuries, the hospital took pictures of this woman with bruises and a busted lip. But Escobar knows she still loves the guy. So he waits until the lunch recess one day. I had to take a long lunch. One of these back molars was hurting, so I had to see the dentist." Wisot shook his head.

"I thought you said KO told you this story," Nash said.

Wisot waved his free hand dismissively. "It was me, my trial. I felt so stupid afterward."

"I think I've heard this one," Henshaw said.

"Okay, well, over this long lunch, Escobar marries the victim and the defendant."

"He does?"

"Vince's a minister in the Church of Divine Perfection," Nash said to Janice. "You send them fifty dollars and you're a minister. I think for a hundred dollars you can be a bishop."

"But she could still testify against him," Janice said. "I don't think that kind of marriage would prevent a wife testifying against her husband."

"No, probably not. It's a question though." Wisot patted his coat for a cigarette. "What Escobar was really doing was showing the jury how crappy the case was. Christ, he's telling them, she loves this man so much, even after all he did, she married him. The jury went out and acquitted him in one hour and twenty minutes."

"Long enough to elect a foreman and sign the verdict forms," Kalbacher said. He wrinkled his nose. "Think I'll sneeze." He did into his paper napkin.

"Even with all of that physical evidence, they acquitted?" Janice looked at Nash. She was used to FBI-agent-prepared cases and never going to trial unless the evidence was both overwhelming and detailed. The much more relaxed standards of state court clearly surprised her.

"Every judge has stories about juries coming back with verdicts that make no sense legally but sound reasonable," Nash said.

"It doesn't happen very often on the federal side," Janice said.

"Look out," Frenkel warned, "Harold's telling the band to stop."

On the stage, with his wife at his side, Atchley smiled and waved his hand at the leader of the mariachi band, who went on strumming his guitar.

"You know how Scotty Shea, my bailiff, picks the jury foreman?" Nash asked them. Peatling, the newest judge, shook his head.

"He decides who would be the best foreman, the smartest or the most likely to convict," Nash explained. "When I send the jury out to deliberate, Scotty gathers up the pencils and jury forms and takes them back to the jurors and he gives them to the one he wants, making sure the others know who's been favored by the guy with a gun. This person now has all the forms and acts official. The jurors almost always pick whoever Scotty's picked."

"I hadn't heard that. I've been trying cases for years and I always thought the jurors just voted," Janice said.

"I got into trouble about a year ago," Susanna Jardine said, "when I had one of my first trials. I told the jury to go back and pick a foreperson to return with the verdicts." She grinned shyly.

"Very progressive." Wisot found his cigarette, lit it, and inhaled with pleasure. Nash kept an eye on Atchley's efforts to stop the singers in midchord. He thought they were a strange choice for a rambunctious fund-raiser. Their singing was sweet, memory laden, and sad. Atchley had probably gotten them at a discount.

"I thought I was being very nonsexist," Susanna said. "The jury came back with guilty-verdict forms signed by four people. I had to send them back to the jury room to pick one person to sign one form."

Just then a hideous electronic screech drowned out the elegiac singing, laughter, and conversation. Atchley closed his eyes tightly, shook his head, smiled, and grabbed the microphone.

"Thank you all for coming, my friends. This has been a wonderful, wonderful event for me and Lilian"—the woman beside him with unkempt hair and bulging eyes waved a little at the crowd—"and you've been a big, big help to my campaign. I want to stay on the bench with my friends, my colleagues, my companions," he went on.

"My cronies, my acquaintances, my buddies, my fellow mouth-breathers," Frenkel said not very quietly. She looked around to see who else thought it was funny.

Nash observed the people listening with new eyes, almost predatory in his survey. He did not know whom Roemer had information about, but he could make suggestions. Undercover operations grew outward like ripples, rarely confining themselves to the original targets. He wondered, as Janice had meant him to, what would happen once the operation was over. Could he realistically expect any of these people to trust him anymore? I'm different from Vismara or snitches, he thought. They all have things to work off. I don't. Everybody will realize I was only trying to make Santa Maria better.

Two women nearby went on whispering as Atchley spoke.

"I never raised goldens. Are they hard?"

"No. No. Retrievers are wonderful to raise. I've taken two of mine to the show."

"I took my collies to the dog show in San Diego. I don't know if I want to change breeds."

Nash wondered how these people, unperturbed, undisturbed, set on certain immutable pastimes such as dog breeding for show, would handle what he was about to do.

There was a certain rebellious pleasure in realizing how much he would upset this smug tide pool and its encrusted inhabitants.

"He's talking about you," Janice whispered.

"Who?"

"Your friend up there." She pointed.

Nash looked at Atchley. "So when I asked him, Tim Nash was graciously able to come, and I thank you, Tim. Your support and all that means will be a big help."

128

"I'm not supporting the son of a bitch," he snorted to the other judges.

"Tim, would you come up here?" Atchley waved to him, heads turned.

Nash waved back and shook his head. "I'm not going up there with him."

"I understand. He's tied up. But thanks, thanks again," and Atchley, beneath his giant banner, as the mariachis struck several loud chords, raised his wife's hand in victory.

Nash and Janice left soon afterward, the other judges and their wives hanging around. Most of the off-duty cops were gone, too. A genial sense of desertion settled over Atchley's event.

"That bastard," Nash said. "Using me."

"I've seen much worse." Janice looked at him steadily.

"Do you have anything on Atchley? Is he on your list?"

"Nothing definite. I'm still going to look at his campaign disclosure statements."

That would not satisfy Nash. "How about I make him a proposition?"

Janice didn't hesitate. She stood beside the table at the Turf Club's entrance, discarded name tags and brochures, bent HE DOES THE JOB signs spilled around. "Why don't you set it up for tomorrow or sometime soon? Bring him to the Cypress."

"Wait here a second," and he pushed his way back into the club. The people still talking were well soaked and either a little shaky on their feet or rock firm, so Nash had to force his way several times.

He found Atchley and his wife on the stage, talking to two judges from the muni court. "Can you give me a minute, Harold?" Nash asked, his voice steady even though he felt as apprehensive as he had about his first date.

"Tim. Yes. Tim. Sure, sure," and Atchley walked from the little group to one side with Nash. Over them rose the sorrel-colored majesty of a long-gone quarter horse memorialized in oils. The yellow-dressed men and women of the band slowly packed their instruments and spoke in low Spanish to each other.

"I need some financial help," Nash said. Atchley's grin faded.

"I thought you were going to say you'd endorse me."

"You can help me and I need it right now."

Atchley bit his lip and disapprovingly watched the band snap shut their instrument cases, pull a thick quilting over their amplifiers. "I paid them for three hours and they only gave me two hours twenty minutes. The rest was part of setting up. I just don't do this very well."

Nash pressed him. "There is a way for us both to make some money."

"I can give you a personal loan." Atchley brightened again at the idea of Nash beholden to him. "I'd have to charge some interest, but we could keep it friendly."

"I need more than you can afford, Harold."

"Then how can I help you?"

"You've got a case coming to your court. As a favor to me, I'd like you to talk to a guy. He can help me and he can help you."

It was said. Nash saw Atchley's frown grow, a puzzled inability to grasp what had been done. His wife laughed uproariously a few feet away, covered her mouth, and the band walked out in a single line.

"You want to talk to me about a case? A defendant?"

"All you have to do is listen and make up your own mind, Harold."

"I don't quite get what you're saying." Atchley blinked, looked at the emptying room. "I don't like it."

"It would be a very great favor to me, Harold," Nash bore in, "if you'd just meet me tomorrow at the Cypress, room five thirty-seven. I'm staying there now."

"If it's just a favor, all right. I'll come." Atchley patted Nash's arm. "Maybe we can straighten out your problem together."

The offer daunted Nash momentarily. Perhaps Atchley really did want to help him. "Thanks. I'll see you at seven?"

"That's what friends are for," Atchley said.

Janice did not ask him where she was being taken. His agitation as he drove was obvious. She had seen this reaction before, felt it herself. People unused to calculated deception, particularly of acquaintances, had an almost physical experience afterward.

Nash drove through a gated, brightly lit apartment complex thick with the dark bulk of willows and elms in the near night. He parked, got out jingling his keys.

"What you heard about Escobar tonight, don't even think about doing anything to him."

"I didn't think of it," she said. She walked to him, but he didn't move or look at her.

"He's off-limits. He's probably crooked. You could probably nail him big time"—she almost smiled at the lapse into police jargon—"but he's in trial with me. You'd wreck the trial."

"We'll stay clear of him." She looked around.

"I've got to talk to you," he said. "This doesn't feel right."

He led her around to the right, past glowing blue swimming pools rippling scalloped wavelets in the warm breeze that had come up since dusk. Most of the other apartments were yellow lit, the heavy smell of lighter fluid, cooking meat on barbecues over it all. Several couples still lounged on long chairs, drinking and talking. There was an indolent innocence that night, she thought.

Nash took her into his apartment. "I've been living here since my wife and I split up."

"She obviously got all the furniture." Janice took off her shoes.

Nash fumbled around finding the air conditioner, turning on lights, taking off his coat, opening the patio doors to let the breeze in until the air cooled. The turquoise drapes rose and fell slightly. "Everything here came with the place. You want something to drink?"

"I'd like something light with soda."

"Light with soda," he repeated uncertainly, and began rummaging in the kitchen, which was part of the dining room. A small chandelier scattered pearly-hard light over the basically bare room.

Janice breathed deeply, the crickets loud, a breeze carrying faint laughter and music. She realized she was a little drunk, but keyed up, almost as much as he was. Maybe because he was. As he made the drinks, rattling ice, pouring, he told her what Atchley had agreed to.

"I'll make sure we're ready," she said, taking the glass from him. "Neil can pull Vismara's chain and get him, too."

"It's ridiculous. I feel very strange about doing this," he said.

"It's natural. It's one thing to sit on the other side of the desk and tell the cops what to do, but it's very different when you're doing it."

"I'll get over it." He suddenly didn't want to talk about how he felt, but she could see from the way he moved, eyes distractedly roving the room, stopping at her, then moving on, that he was oppressed by the first act of betrayal.

"This is Ben?" she asked, picking up a photograph prominently displayed in an almost empty bookshelf, almost like a shrine.

"Taken when he was eight. See the missing front teeth? He started dropping them about one every week." Nash laughed. "I told him he looked like a Halloween pumpkin."

"I've got three older brothers. They lost most of their teeth playing hockey in college."

"You're not married?" Nash watched her put the photo back, to insure it was replaced precisely where it had been.

"No," she said. "The next question usually is, why not?"

"I wasn't going to ask it."

"I was engaged to a pediatrician." She laughed, put her drink down, and sat on the stiff couch, wincing and bouncing on it a little. "We lived together for nearly a year. He had kids swarming all around him, some very sick."

"Don't say you dislike kids."

"No. I didn't like him after a while." She stretched slowly. "This kind of assignment has funny hours. I better go home."

Nash watched her get ready to leave and said nothing. Then, as if she had done something, he began talking about his son. Not his wife, but a torrent of impressions and memories flooded out about the boy. The nest of caterpillars he had tended so diligently; a small plastic box was their cage and he'd dropped leaves in for them, added twigs, hoping one morning he'd get up to see their cocoons, then the magical butterflies. "Ben was seven and he hung around that cage all the time. Nothing ever happened. Too late in the year, wrong temperature or something."

He sat down beside her on the couch, talking on. The first camping trip, the first conference with Ben's teachers at Horace Mann Elementary School. Janice listened with interest. It was more than polite attentiveness. She enjoyed the animation Nash had, the way his face was unguarded, as if released. On paper, she regarded him as a perfect potential witness. When she'd met him, he seemed dry and vaguely unpleasant in his aloof coolness.

But that was probably how he had grown up in this city with those parents. Every action of his from childhood would be considered a reflection not only on his famous and respected father but on his own future. Everyone wants to kick over the NO TRESPASSING or NO SWIMMING sign sometime, to walk barefoot in the middle of town, or climb through your high school girlfriend's bedroom window. This was what Janice imagined Nash yearned to do.

She wondered if Neil had seen that yearning and picked Nash because he'd finally stand on his own in Operation Broken Trust.

"He had soccer practice lately," Nash said, sitting close to her, his leg pressed against her. "That was a lot of running around for me, too. Drop him off, pick up him at Valley Vista's field. He's doing very well. His team beat Markham, Hawthorne, South Clare- mont, and he was playing forward, so that was all his effort."

Nash had his arm around her and Janice leaned to him. There was a furious pounding on his door. He held her closer.

Janice was surprised. Her heart rocked suddenly and she thought he'd get up and answer the door or say something to whoever was knocking so imperiously. He simply held her and watched the door, as if the enemy were about to launch an assault on their temporary security.

The knocking stopped, and in contrast, a woman whispered, "Tim? Tim? Tim?" several times. Then the sound of bare feet slap- ping irritatedly on the concrete path outside faded.

Janice was about to make a snide remark when Nash pulled her face to his and kissed her.

He'll be all right, she thought. He'll survive what's coming. It was a prayer as much as a sober evaluation.

He kissed her again, pulling the covers over them. She was facing the window, the drapes in the bedroom translucent with faint light from around the pool. The breeze was cooler, more insistent, and she shivered a little.

"Cold?" he asked softly. He was pressed against her naked back.

"A little. I didn't think it got cold on hot days like this."

"When you're naked and you've been sweating." He chuckled into the back of her neck and she giggled.

"That tickles."

"I could do it some more."

She rolled over halfway, holding the covers, the fuzz of the blan- kets reassuring, as if they shared a cave together, safe from every- thing roaming the night outside.

The drape cord clacked against the wall in a gust. "I better close the windows. It is cold." He started to get out of bed.

"No. Leave it. I like the feeling. We can get closer to stay warm," and they drew closer.

In the exhausted late evening, she could hear the metal, thin clink of chimes and a cat's mournful howl distantly. A train whistle sounded, like a hum a thousand miles away.

Her clothes, all neatly folded, the blouse hung up, were arranged on the single chair in the bedroom. I'm always neat, she thought.

He and I are like that. We don't tear into passion, dropping clothes, bodies rushing together heedlessly. Forms and routines, habits, he and I could probably go on following them until we smother.

"What's the matter?" Nash's voice was concerned, tender.

"Nothing. I was thinking."

"You must be cold. That was a shudder." His breath was warm, his weight beside her comforting.

"You better drive me back to the hotel," she said. She had left her car at the Cypress the night before.

"Not yet. It's only four."

"I've got a lot to do. I don't want to show up like I didn't get home last night."

"You didn't. You were here," Nash said, but she detected surrender. People whose lives conform do not overturn those forms. "There's nothing wrong."

"Except we've both got a lot of work to do tomorrow. It's your first interview." She rubbed his forearm, feeling the light hairs.

"Right now, you know, I almost hope Atchley isn't as crooked as he seems. The guy's always talking about deals he's made on things, cutting corners, stiffing people. He lets everyone else pay for drinks."

"Oh, that's a real crime."

"Part of me hopes we miss him today."

"If he's dishonest, he'll go to jail. If he isn't, he's free."

"What was the second chance you never had?" Nash asked, half-sitting up in bed. "What did you mean?"

Janice lay on her back, staring up at the ceiling, the rippling shadow reflecting off the pool in the darkness, like luminous waves. Why not tell him? In the bald recital there was nothing much. It was the consequences that mattered, the feeling inside you that counted, and she wasn't ready to tell him about that. He might find out himself soon enough.

"I was working in the Orlando office," she said. "I was just out of law school. More or less. I was doing civil cases and I found out that one of my bosses, my team leader, was stealing money."

"How?"

"A case would be settled. The agreement letter signed off, and he would get a chunk of money. The people we sued, garbage-collection outfits, developers, truckers, they'd pay him to lowball the settlement and pay him a fee."

"It's a kickback. It doesn't sound sophisticated." He made her discovery seem insignificant, and it had changed her life.

"It wasn't. It was greed." She tensed a little, his arm across her. "I shouldn't even have found out about it. The case file came back to me for a dispo memo because I'd worked on it a little. My original demand letter was in it."

"And he'd settled for a lot less," Nash finished.

"I went to the U.S. Attorney because it looked very odd. They'd been worried about my boss for a while. They set surveillance cameras in an air-conditioning duct in his office, and they sent me to smoke him out."

"You did." Nash said it calmly. It was what he would be doing tomorrow. Today. Tonight.

"It all went on videotape and I was the prime witness. He didn't go to trial. They worked out an early resignation and got him to start paying the money back."

"Sounds like a happy ending."

"Not for me. I couldn't stay in the Orlando office after that. People begin to treat you differently, Tim. They guard what they say. They close drawers when you come into a room. They stop talking." She stroked his arm. "I started moving from office to office until Neil caught up with me. He took me in with him. Public Integrity. That's what I'll be doing until I retire."

"You won't be staying in the Sacramento office." He couldn't keep the disappointment from his voice.

"Maybe for a year. Maybe less. It depends on how long Neil wants to work in this part of the country. I go where he goes."

She felt Nash's leg slowly push its way between hers, scissored flesh pressed together. Another night gust blew over them, and the cat's distant, solitary howl cut off abruptly, the silence growing swiftly around its absence. Nash kissed her, his arm tightening around her. "What I've learned," she whispered, "is that no one likes to be reminded how weak we all are. They don't forgive you for reminding them."

"I'm going to be all right," he said. "I know what I'm doing. I want to do it."

She pulled from him suddenly, half-sitting up, her skin cold and gooseflesh over her arms and breasts. "How much money would you take to dump a trial?"

"What?" He grinned. It was a joke. He tried to kiss her again.

"Just answer. How much would you want to rule in favor of one side in a trial?"

"I don't know. An awful lot." He was still laughing.

"It's not funny."

"Seems like it right now." He lay on his back, staring up at the ceiling.

"How about ten thousand dollars? Or twenty? You're going to offer Atchley twenty-five thousand tonight to dump a case in his court. Would you do it for that much money?" Her voice was hard.

"No. I wouldn't."

"How much would it take?"

"I wouldn't do it."

"You're lying, Tim. You don't know how much you'd want. If I walked into your courtroom today and said I had a hundred thousand tax-free, hidden dollars to give you to make a couple of rulings in favor of my client, what would you do? Really?"

"I don't know."

"That's the right answer. Nobody knows until it happens to them."

"I hope I'd act the right way and tell you to go to hell." He let out a long, thoughtful breath. He gently pulled her down to the pillow again, drawing the cover over her, his hands rubbing away the night's invading cold. "I agreed to work for Roemer and you because it's the right thing to do. You can't talk me out of it."

"I wasn't trying to," Janice said. "I was only telling you what I did."

They made love again under the rippling, luminous wave reflections on the ceiling.

"Is the judge all tucked in?" Roemer asked. He and Janice walked slowly along the dock, past blue metal warehouses and ships just being unloaded, the forklift and crane operators shouting to each other as pallets of wooden boxes were stacked up. The sky was still ink colored, a violet wash only starting at the horizon and the stars fading like dimming lamps overhead.

"Sleeping like a baby, Neil."

"So what's the progress report?" He yawned. "Sorry. I don't like getting up much before six."

"I remember." She stopped. The long river glinted with the first lights of dawn farther down, the banks dark with clustered warehouses and cranes and the inert bulks of ships. "He's set up a meeting for tonight at the Cypress with Atchley. It's for seven."

"Atchley? The one who's campaigning?" He noticed she shivered and held her arms close to her body. She had on a heavy winter coat, blue, belted. She hadn't slept.

"I said we're all ready." She noticed he hadn't shaved and he watched her intently. A heavy pallet thudded to the concrete a few yards away. They leaned against a steel railing, heard the green-black water lapping against the dock pilings.

"I thought we'd go for one of the heavy hitters first. Frenkel or Wisot or Burgess."

"It was his idea. Can you set everything up?"

"We're all set now. I'll get Louis. I won't hang around this one." He grinned. "I don't want to make myself a witness."

One by one, starting at the horizon, the stars winked out as the dawn strengthened and the sky turned to a washed-out blue. The ships' horns sounded raucously.

"How long are you staying?" she asked.

"About a week this time. I think I've got that mother Cleary out of the picture, but he keeps working, so I've got to be there. I've got the operations in Bakersfield and San Diego to watch."

He leaned over and kissed her. She didn't move and he pulled back. "Forget it," he said, sighing.

"No more bullshit," she said.

"Jesus, it is cold out here." He rubbed his arm. "Anything else?"

She shook her head. "Let's get some coffee or something."

"You cold, too?"

She nodded.

"We could try making some fire by friction," he said.

"You'd have to try it on your own." She started walking back along the dock toward their cars. She had called Roemer as soon as she got to the hotel. He was staying at a second hotel, under a different name.

"No thanks," he said. They walked close together. He squinted disinterestedly around him. "Carla called twice last night. She says the kids want to see me."

"Go home. I can take care of things here."

"No thanks," he said. They swung a rusted steel gate closed behind them, their feet now on the crunching gravel of the parking lot beside the docks, filled with old cars and pickup trucks. Men with lunch boxes swaggered toward the dock.

Roemer met her at the riverfront docks because he was certain no one would overhear them and there was no place to put a bug. He preferred briefings in the open, away from rooms and cars, because too much could be captured within walls.

"The judge's ready?" he asked.

"He's ready."

"Maybe if he gets Atchley, we can start a daisy chain early, string a bunch of them together." He glanced around. "I saw a joint that looked decent about a mile away." He got in his car.

"I'll follow you," she said.

20

YOU WANT TO START TRAINING FOR A MARATHON?" SCOTTY SHEA breathily asked Nash. They ran side by side along a wide dirt track that looped around Juarez Park. Shea had on gloves and two sweat-shirts against the early-morning cold. Nash wore only a T-shirt, droopy and misshapen with his sweat.

"Nope," he managed to say.

"How come you're setting such a fast pace?"

"Can't keep up?"

Shea grinned. Although he was big, he moved lightly. Packs of other diligents passed them, runners tuned into radios clamped to their heads. "Hey, Tim, I'm the one's been running every day for the last six months. Not you."

"I want to get a good start," Nash said, then pulled up short. He wheezed, doubled over, and held his upper legs. Shea jogged in place beside him for a moment.

"We done?"

"I am." Nash hacked, looked up. The sky was cloudless and hard blue and would swiftly get hot. The night cold was an illusion; only the day's heat, day after day, was real.

Nash straightened up. Three men, all wearing thick glasses, jogged by like a chorus line. "Stop showing off," Nash said, watching Shea's effortless jogging.

"Man, you're on a rag. No action last night?"

"Too much. I'm all keyed up." Nash started walking. The air near them was pungent with eucalyptus oil from the tall trees hanging over the track.

"Who is she? Anybody I know?"

Nash shook his head. "Nope. I just met her."

"Goddamn. I felt sorry for you last couple days. You been looking kind of bad during the trial."

"I'm taking that one day at a time."

Shea stopped, wiped his sweating forehead. He was guileless, but he knew Nash's moods, and there was more to this frantic run than an overabundance of energy after sex. "Something's wrong. Something with Kim? Your kid?"

Nash bent over again. He had come out, desperate to move, to flee perhaps. He hadn't eaten, but the water he had drunk boiled in his stomach. The other joggers, the geese and ducks sauntering around the pond in the park's center, ignored him. "I've got a bad case of stage fright," he said finally.

Waiting for an elevator in the courthouse basement after driving in, Nash hoped he wouldn't see anyone he knew. But Henshaw, complaining of an allergy attack, and Susanna Jardine waited with him. He didn't want to talk or answer. Susanna, humming to herself, glanced at him curiously. "Oh, Tim, have you paid the indigent-criminal defense bills for this month?"

"Not yet."

Henshaw coughed, blew his nose. "Hold those bills for two months. At least. Then cut them in half. The bastards on the panel pad them anyway."

"Not all of them," Nash said.

"Most of them do."

Nash was afraid his reticence would turn to anger, which was worse. A tall black man in a baggy three-piece suit, his gray hair flying out at angles from his head, shambled to the elevator from the county law library at the other end of the corridor. His old suit pockets were stuffed with torn papers. He carried a ripped briefcase. He looked like a lawyer who had been blown up, still dazed.

"I have found the answer to my case," he announced, looking to each judge.

"Good for you," Susanna answered. Henshaw groaned and coughed.

"It was in *Cal App.*, volume forty-three, page two hundred sixty-six in a footnote," said the tattered man. He was not a lawyer. He spent days in the law library, writing, reading, then explaining his findings at endless length to whoever got too close to him. He was called the Petitioner around the courthouse. No one knew exactly what his grievance was, or if he had several. His reasoning was wild and elaborate. He seemed content this morning to stand with the three judges, like a broken mirror image of themselves.

Nash said, "Some of the attorneys are abusing the bills, but I'm not going to screw all of them."

"They'll take advantage of you," Henshaw said. "Treat them rough and they'll understand."

Susanna said, "Okay. Anybody want to go to lunch today?"

Before Nash could answer, the elevator arrived. The Petitioner was at his side, close enough to smell of onions and stale beer. "What they've been doing was cheating me," the man said. "They sensed my greatness and started to cheat me from the beginning," and he walked toward the elevator.

"Shut up," Nash said to the man. "That's a court order."

Susanna and Henshaw were in the elevator. The tattered man stopped, startled into silence. They chuckled.

"Take another elevator," Nash said, the door closing.

"I think he's harmless, but he scares me," Susanna said.

Nash wanted the anger in himself to fade. He held his own briefcase more tightly. Nothing would be the same after tonight. He knew that now. Something will happen, he thought.

"And I'm the one everybody jumps on for being insensitive," Henshaw complained, sniffing, when they got to the third floor.

Nash thought he did a fairly good job of getting through the rest of the day. Vi kept studying him at the breaks in the trial, but she wouldn't say anything.

In the afternoon, the jurors were drowsy, heavy with lunch, dopey with the heat outside, even if there was a monotone coolness in the courtroom. Mr. Sparling's head drifted down several times. Mrs. Lamar Kelso ("That's Kelso with a *k*") had the hiccups and burned with embarrassment.

Nash sat on the bench, tapping a pencil, wiggling his toes under the bench, even slipping his shoes off, pressing the toes hard against the carpeted floor, hoping to focus his mind on what was happening in the courtroom. He wanted to talk to Janice. He thought about her, how she looked the first time they made love last night, her blond hair tangled, splayed on the pillow. In a way, he did not want to see her tonight, mixed in with this Atchley setup.

Soika rattled his chains at the breaks, after the jury was out of the courtroom and the bailiffs came to shackle him up. Nash wished Soika would try to escape. Something to deflect the night's coming event, some distraction or excuse he could use for calling it off.

On the witness stand was an ID tech from the Santa Maria Police Department. Blowups of whorled fingerprints flanked him.

"On People's Exhibit Forty-eight for identification, I found eleven points of similarity with the known fingerprints of the defendant." The man held a batch of note cards, his angular face expressionless, a briefcase open on the witness stand.

"Objection. Objection. Objection," Escobar said.

Nash took a moment to respond. "Who's objecting?"

"I am, Your Honor," Escobar said. Benisek was leisurely getting to his feet.

"Why? The witness is stating an opinion. You can cross-examine him if you think he's in error," Nash said.

Escobar strolled from the counsel table. Cindy Duryea, his assistant, patted Soika's back. Soika wore his best clothes, as he had ever since the alarm several days before. Nash thought it had all been planned.

"I haven't stipulated there are any known fingerprints of Evan," Escobar said.

"So what? He just said the exhibit was for ID purposes." Benisek pointed at Nash with his pen.

"He did not."

"I didn't hear it," Nash admitted.

"I move to strike his testimony to this point, Your Honor. The witness has left the jury with the impression some connection has been made to Evan Soika with the shotgun at the scene," Escobar said.

"Oh. That is incredible. Every person who's come in here said he had the shotgun," Benisek snapped.

"Then you don't need this witness. I move to strike his testimony as cumulative," Escobar replied. Duryea stopped patting Soika, who hunched forward.

Nash looked at the ID tech, who held his cards, his briefcase open, as if frozen in midword, as if his switch had been turned. They were all looking at Nash, waiting for him to rule on the motions. His mind had wandered, worrying, thinking, plotting out everything that could happen tonight.

"I didn't hear the question," Nash said. "Please read it back," he said to the court reporter.

The jury stirred. A college girl on the panel smiled at him.

The court reporter flipped through the long paper tail from her steno machine, found the spot, and read in a flat tone. Nash was eager for something to explode the inner whirl of his mind.

"All right," Nash said, slipping his shoes on under the bench. His robe fell around his hand and he pulled it back. "The witness explained that the lifted prints were for ID purposes only. Isn't that right?" he asked the tech.

"Yes, sir. I've been testifying that way because they haven't been moved into evidence yet."

"And I never agreed that the other things, those other cards"— Escobar waved dismissively—"have anything to do with Evan Soika."

"I thought you did. I thought you agreed those are his prints."

"I didn't."

"Can you authenticate those known fingerprints as the defendant's so this man can proceed with the results of his comparison?" Nash asked Benisek.

"All of the paperwork is back in my office. Like the court, I thought this was settled."

"I'm not helping the DA put on his case." Escobar folded his arms, his bald head thrust forward. "This whole trial has been a railroad from the start."

"That's it, Mr. Escobar," Nash said. "That's all from you."

"Is the court gagging me?"

"Did I say that?"

Escobar beseeched Cindy Duryea, Evan Soika, then the jury. "The court is putting a gag on me if I can't defend my client as vigorously as my abilities permit."

Nash sensed another performance for the record and the jury coming. He was irritated that his own inattention had given Escobar an opening, however small, to exploit. But he could not chastise Escobar or truly silence him. Any conviction for murder of Soika would be unanimously reversed by the Supreme Court if he did that.

"Your point is made, Mr. Escobar. Everybody here is trying to do his job, you, Mr. Benisek, me. We don't need reminders."

"Thank you, Your Honor. So you will strike this witness?"

Nash shook his head. He had been writing in the large bound volume, his trial record. He had broken off when his mind went to the sting. Now he began writing as he spoke, the pen smooth on the pages, blue ink, black robe, white paper.

"I think this man has very significant evidence for the jury to

142

hear, Mr. Escobar. No. I will not strike his testimony or rule it cumulative. You will not stipulate that the technician has known fingerprints of Evan Soika?"

"I don't think he does. I don't know it." Escobar jutted his chin out. He sat down.

"Can you take impressions of the defendant now? Do you have your cards and ink?" Nash asked the ID tech.

"Yes, I do, Your Honor."

"All right. We'll take a fifteen-minute recess. Bailiff, take Mr. Soika to the clerk's office. I want his fingerprints taken right now, and then we can come back and just shoot straight through."

"I object to this practice." Escobar got up hastily. "You're forcing him to give evidence against himself."

"You know I'm not. If you say anything else, Mr. Escobar, I will immediately instruct the jury on nontestimonial evidence and what kind of samples anybody must provide."

Escobar took it gracefully, nodding, sitting down, doing his own patting of Soika. Vi stood up. Nash could tell the jury that blood, hair, or fingerprints were not protected by the right against self-incrimination, even if your own body damned you. Soika would have to give the fingerprints.

"Sorry," Nash whispered to Vi. She frowned at him, her small face annoyed. She obviously did not like the idea of Soika in her office.

Soika didn't like the whole notion either. As the jury was being taken out by Shea, Soika squirmed in his seat, his voice rising. Nash got off the bench, robe flapping around him. He looked at the trio, Escobar, Duryea, Soika, the bailiffs moving in with chains, the ID tech and his ink pad and fingerprint cards waiting. He really hoped, for an instant, that Soika would blow up out of his seat, the bailiffs clinging to him, alarms going off everywhere.

I could tell Janice and Roemer that there was an escape in my court. I can't do it tonight.

Then, he thought, you wanted it. You picked Atchley. You're doing the right thing.

As he went into his chambers, Soika was still complaining, but docilely being shackled.

He didn't take off his robe. He paced the room, his door closed. He wanted to call Janice, but had nothing to say. Nor did Nash have anything he could say to his father. Hey, Dad, I'm going undercover tonight. It would be a first in the family, just like Dick's going on the federal bench had been a first, but this was something Nash knew his father wouldn't like. It sounded underhanded, furtive. Having done narcotic cases for three years, Nash knew there was no other way to get some kinds of evidence against some suspects.

He unzipped his robe. Soika swore on the other side of the door as his prints were taken. Nash sat down and dialed Kim's sister in Los Angeles. When she answered, he hesitated, then spoke.

"It's me. Anybody around?"

"Oh. Hello," Nel said casually. "Yes. Everyone's here."

"Let me talk to Ben."

"I shouldn't be doing this for you, Tim." Her voice dropped. "Kim will hate me."

"He's my son, Nel. You know Kim. She's going to use him. She won't let me talk to him."

"Oh, damn. Damn. I know. I'm frantic sometimes that Ben's going to blab to her. By accident. Then you and I'll both be dog poop."

"Ben won't say anything. We've talked about it. Put him on."

Nel sighed. "I'll say you're the school counselor if Kim asks. She doesn't like talking to him."

"Is Ben having trouble?"

"He's a discipline problem, so called. School's only been going for a week now and they've decided he's some kind of delinquent."

Nash swore. He had feared his absence would upset Ben. "I've got to see him. I can't wait for October," which was his first visit scheduled by the court in the divorce decree.

"You know me, Tim. I'll help if I can. I love Ben. Kim's not as reasonable about you two as she should be. That's the only reason I'm going along with fooling her like this."

"If I came down to L.A., could we get him away for a couple of hours? You take him and bring him to me?"

He listened tautly. He could almost hear Kim's sister thinking about this newer, deeper secret to be kept. "Maybe I'm putting myself too much in the middle," Nel said. "I don't know."

"I need to see him. He needs to see me. Something's wrong now."

"Yes. All right. Call me again and we'll set it up. I'll get him now."

"You're a princess, Nel," he said. It had taken less persuasion than he'd feared to get Nel to facilitate these clandestine calls to Ben. It was another secret communications network in his life, which appeared to be sprouting underground links faster than he could manage.

Nash's heart rose when he heard Ben's voice a few moments later. His son was cheerful. He did not talk about any difficulties at this new school in L.A. He liked the biology class, looked forward to the dissection on Friday of a frog. He hated his math class. As he talked, Nash thought, I told a strange woman all about him last night, made him a part of her and me together. As if Ben could be grafted onto a new relationship like a plant sprig.

"Bear," Nash said, "I'm going to come see you soon. We can catch up better together, all right?"

"You, me, and Mom?"

"No, just you and me. Don't tell your mom. Aunt Nel's going to help us, but it'll be our secret. We'll do some stuff together. Have a good time."

"Okay, if we do it when I'm in school."

Nash chuckled. "You mean you don't want to see me on a weekend?"

"Yeah, that's okay, but it's better if I get out of school."

"We'll do it on a school day. You miss me?"

He heard the intake of breath. He thought Nel was talking in the background, in some unimaginable kitchen, in a house he had never seen, on a street in a city that was as remote as a planet. "I still want to come home," and Nash heard the bewildered question *What did I do wrong?* when Ben spoke.

"I'll come to you, bear, very soon. Just remember that it's a secret. Only Aunt Nel knows."

They made their final, trivial comments to each other. Shea knocked on his door. "We're ready, Judge," he said through the door.

As Nash was about to hang up, Ben said, "Don't forget me."

Nash put the phone down and zipped his robe with hard fingers. Time to get back to the trial, to the world of violent lies and death and justice. He suddenly did not feel so concerned about working for Roemer tonight. Not after what Ben said.

Roemer's undercover secrets seemed inconsequential by comparison to the secret life Nash and Ben shared. The public failures and betrayals proceeded from more intimate ones. Atchley's baiting and hooking would be painless beside Nash's personal undercover work.

Don't forget me, his son had said.

21

THE SUITE AT THE CYPRESS WAS CROWDED, TENSE WITH OPENING-night anticipation.

"He's late. It's past seven-thirty," Jacobs, the FBI man, said to Nash, then to Janice, then Roemer beside her.

"Harold's always late," Nash said. He was nervous, too. "He's never made a judges' meeting on time since I've been on the bench."

"No panic then," Roemer said evenly. He watched Vismara eat another hamburger, crouching over it at the dining room table. "We're still on track."

Nash had been surprised when he found Roemer at the suite since Janice had told him Neil wanted to avoid this first interview. "I changed my mind," Roemer said. "I think I better make sure everything goes all right. You think I should be here?" he asked Janice.

"Definitely," she answered. She had her legal pad out and she was dressed in jeans, as if this were some kind of class or an after-work frolic. She and Nash had talked about the night before. He wanted to see her again, but tonight she barely acknowledged him. He had, he thought, become part of the operation. She had separated the man from his utility.

The TV was on, Roemer falling down into the sofa to watch it, his arms crossed. In the equipment-packed bedroom, Testa and Sanchez worked the VCRs and audio recorders for a final check.

Everyone kept chatting with him, watching him, Nash noticed. How's the judge holding up? Is he getting jittery? Sweating? Is this whole thing going to blow up on us? The only one who sweated was Vismara, dabbing frequently at his cheeks with a silk handkerchief. He did not look much like a seasoned major drug dealer.

146

He also ate continuously. Two empty plates of food he'd gone through were on the table. The others had managed to get down sodas.

Nash checked his watch again. Janice sat beside Roemer, talking low. He felt jealous seeing them together. They had secrets from him certainly, and he didn't want her to conceal anything from him anymore.

Nash didn't stay in any spot long. He sat down at the bar, grinned emptily at Jacobs, who was humming, sat on a chair, watched the TV briefly, drank soda water, pushed aside the heavy drapes and stared out at the night city, colorfully decorated. He picked out the ruby aircraft warning lights on the dark mass of the Alhambra Towers, the long, flat roofs of Macy's and other large stores in the downtown mall, the sidewalks like white, glowing ribbons against the darkness. The river stretched west, dark and glinting with the reflected light from the three bridges that spanned it as the city went to the edge of the delta and the river broke free to run to the sea.

Nash had trouble concentrating on the Atchley meeting. He was thinking of how to arrange a chance to see Ben. He saw that it was seven forty-five. "He's on his way. He'd call if he wasn't coming," Nash said.

"How about you call him in a couple of minutes, see if he's left yet?" Roemer asked. Janice nodded.

"Okay. Couple of minutes, sure."

Jacobs, still humming, came from the bar. He alone was calm, even jaunty. He was dressed for the hot days, a light tan suit. He looked like a successful department-store floor manager. "I'll be back with Ed and Tommy," he said, going to the bedroom. Nash knew he was being seen on the TV monitors, his voice picked up by the hidden microphones. It was what he tried to do in his courtroom every day. In each trial, Nash as the judge struggled to freeze a moment in history, a mundane instant when a bullet had been fired or a lock broken, a scream overheard, a man running. Except we usually use witnesses and mute evidence, not the voices and pictures of the crime itself.

For the first time in a sting, Nash felt what it was like to be in a place, with other people, knowing a crime was going to happen. He would not preside over the collection of its pieces. He would be in at the creation. He would make it happen himself.

The waiting was hard. Nash sat down with Vismara. The little man wiped his mouth, smiled anxiously, reached for a bowl of fruit, and began chewing on grapes and a pear. "I sweat and I eat. Like they go together."

"You've done deals before."

"I got nervous before, too."

Nash hadn't been friendly to Vismara at all. He'd read his rap sheet: two armed robberies in San Francisco, assault, possession of heroin, sale of cocaine in Santa Maria. Vismara did not look violent anymore. His slicked hair was glistening and he kept dabbing at his mouth while eating the pear.

Janice and Roemer were together, talking again. Where was Atchley? Nash cursed him silently and felt clumsy even before the operation started.

Vismara kept glancing at him, obviously shy about talking. He wants me to respect him. He respects me, Nash thought. Together we're going to nail a Superior Court judge.

"You married, Louis?" he asked.

"Not so much."

"You divorced?"

Vismara smiled his nervous smile, touching the thin mustache over his thick lips. "I ain't got around to it yet."

"I just did," Nash said, surprised he was talking so openly to a man he would hardly acknowledge in his courtroom. "It's not much fun."

"I seen how they do it, so I ain't rushing," Vismara agreed. "She don't mind so much either. She just don't want to see me."

"That's too bad."

"Why? I don't like her."

Nash grinned and so did Vismara. "I've got a son. He's with his mother in L.A."

"Yeah? I got two kids, two girls. They move around so I don't see them so much either. They don't want to see me either." It was said with some sadness, but not as much as Nash expected.

The kinship with Vismara was not as deep as he imagined, Nash realized. Probably just the accident of the two of them thrown together. "I miss him a lot. I've got to figure out some way to get down to L.A. and see him."

"Yeah?" Vismara looked intrigued. He dropped the chewed-down pear core, wiped his fingers and mouth again. "Can I help? You need something down there, I could help?"

"I don't think so."

"No, no. Look, I got friends. I got favors they owe to me." He pointed to his green-shirted chest. "I could make them owe favors to you."

"I'll have to figure out something myself," Nash said.

"Okay. You tell me anytime, there's anything I can do. Whatever."

Nash got up. Roemer and Janice broke toward him. "We should find out if we've got a meeting or we don't," Roemer said.

Nash was slightly embarrassed pretending to be impersonal around Janice, but she didn't seem bothered by doing it herself. "I'll call his campaign office. They might know where he is."

Nash called the small office, in the north end of the county, that Atchley had rented for his campaign headquarters.

"He hasn't checked in tonight. They didn't even know he was meeting me," Nash said, hanging up. "Harold's not a great organizer."

"You want to give him more time?"

Nash nodded. "I'll wait."

They waited another unsettled ten minutes before the phone rang. The only incoming calls on the suite's visible telephone were from people who wanted Nash. All other calls were routed through special lines in the bedroom, with silent phones that flashed instead of ringing.

Nash picked it up. "He's in the lobby," he said aloud.

Roemer rolled his eyes and Janice shook her head. Don't announce it, Nash thought. Idiot.

Vismara was on his feet. In the bedroom, the tape reels spun with the first words.

"Come on up, Harold," Nash said.

Atchley's words didn't register on Nash at first. Janice watched him, her pad at her side. "We can go to eat later," Nash replied. "I want to talk now."

He shook his head. Roemer swore silently and darted into the bedroom, Janice waiting beside Nash. Vismara stared apprehensively, touching his mustache nervously.

"I know you're hungry. I know you didn't eat." Nash tried not to growl. "We'll go to a restaurant in a couple of minutes. Why don't you come up now and we'll take care of our business?"

He shook his head again for Janice. She made a cutting motion across her throat. Nash understood. End it. Time to make a new plan. He had heard about these abrupt changes from cops on stings he'd set up in Narcotics. Now he was living one and the surge he felt was both exhilarating and made him queasy.

"All right, Harold," he conceded. "We'll talk over dinner. I'll meet you in the lobby in a few minutes." He hung up.

Roemer and Jacobs, Sanchez trailing, trotted from the bedroom.

"What? What?" Vismara asked, but no one answered him.

"He won't come up. He says he's been out walking a neighborhood precinct and he's starving. He wants to eat."

"Okay. You'll go eat," Roemer said. "You should have specified a location."

"I can page him. He's just downstairs."

"Hey, Tommy. Get out here," Roemer commanded, and Testa came out holding a set of earphones, his face dour.

"On the fly. I figured. I set this all up nice and I'm going to do it on the fly, right?" Testa said sourly.

"Can you set something up if the judge gives us a little head start and stalls Atchley? Nothing great, one mike at the table wherever they're going?" Roemer said, his suspenders hanging down his pants.

"Sure I can. But you won't get any video. I can't guarantee great sound. I can bring the van, we can use that equipment, but someone's got to be wired."

"Judge? You want to wear a wire?"

Nash looked at Janice. He was being propelled by unpredictable circumstance. "I told you I've never worn one. I don't know if I'd act wrong."

"It's no trick," Roemer said. "But, I don't want to make you feel uncomfortable. Just be yourself, okay?"

"I done it." Vismara was already opening his shirt, showing a hairless brown chest, exposed like a child in a doctor's office. "I wear it for the judge."

Testa had gone back to the bedroom and returned with a small dime-sized microphone and a slim battery and amplifying pack like a woman's compact. It was much more elegant, simple, than the equipment Nash had used. Testa taped the microphone to Vismara's chest, at the level of his heart, looping the slim pack down his torso. Vismara giggled when it tickled.

"I'll tell Atchley we'll go to Strawn's. It's a steak house he likes. It's on East Riverview Drive, about fifteen minutes from here." Nash reached for the phone again.

"We better move out first," Jacobs said to Sanchez. "How about you tell us what kind of car he's in?"

"You can't miss it. He's got his campaign stickers all over it, a LeBaron. Four door, gray."

Vismara buttoned his shirt, adjusted his shiny black suit. Testa checked the appearance. Nothing hinted beneath the clothes. "Anybody riding with me in the van?"

"Okay, I'll go," Sanchez volunteered.

"Pick up Montgomery and Stupak," Roemer said. "Bring your briefcase, Tommy. Maybe you can get some pictures if you sit close enough."

"Yeah, sure, sure. Last-minute crap," Testa complained, and he went to get the videocamera concealed in a briefcase.

Nash got Atchley on the phone and said he was making a reservation at Strawn's for them. "Take your time. I'm having a drink," Atchley said.

"Now he wants to take his time," Nash said, hanging up. Jacobs and Sanchez helped Testa carry several cases out.

"I'll show you the van sometime," Roemer said. "We got it on loan from the IRS for this operation. It's outer space."

"These guys," Jacobs chuckled.

"I got the heavy one," Sanchez said, following him.

"Don't look so worried," Janice soothed. She patted his arm maternally. Not like last night when there was nothing secure or predictable as their bodies touched, came together, tore from each other. "You have to expect changes."

"The judge expects surprises," Roemer said, noticing the intimacy between Nash and Janice.

"I'll give the guys a chance to get to the restaurant. We'll have a drink downstairs," Nash said. Vismara had sat down, nipping at a fingernail.

"Let's go, Louis," Nash said to Vismara.

They walked along green-marbled floors spread with thick carpet, past contented men and women strolling around the lobby. Nash was very nervous, in part because he sensed Vismara's tension. The little man walked close by him, putting on a slight swagger, eyes stopping on each face that passed them.

"Are you always nervous?" Nash said quietly.

"Not so much," Vismara said. "One time, these guys in Oakland, they all sticking guns at me, yelling, how come I'm not delivering the shit on time? Then I was nervous." Vismara bobbed his head.

Nash saw Atchley first. He paced around a piano, coat over one arm, face red, his shirt stuck to his bulky back.

"I've got very low blood sugar," Atchley said, shifting his coat over his shoulder when Nash and Vismara got to him. "Let's go. I parked in the garage so it's costing two dollars every fifteen minutes."

"I thought you wanted a drink."

"I had one. I got my juices going," Atchley said. He looked at Vismara. "I'll drive."

"This is Louis Vismara, Jr.," Nash said. Vismara had undergone a transformation during the walk to the piano bar. His face was set, savagely contemplative, like that of a lord of drug dealers. He was fluid when he shook hands, grave. Only the sweating cheeks betrayed him.

They all started to the basement garage. Nash wondered what Testa and the agents were getting in the van, all of this useless chatter.

"Louis has a case coming to you, Harold. It's what I wanted to talk to you about at dinner."

Vismara nodded solemnly.

Atchley's hand froze over the car door, his voice petulantly echoing in the concrete garage, against the squeal of cars being parked. "Oh, no. Oh, no. He's not coming. Get out of here," he said, waving Vismara away.

"Don't insult him, Harold. He's going to help both of us," Nash said quickly.

Atchley got into the car, garish with his signs HE DOES THE JOB in its windows, the REELECT JUDGE ATCHLEY bumper stickers front and back. "I'm not riding with a defendant. That's it. Now I'm hungry."

He had become more arrogant since the fund-raiser. Nash whispered to Vismara, "Go back upstairs. I'll go with him."

"I should go."

"Not this time. It won't work. There'll be another meeting," Nash said.

"Come on, Tim," Atchley urged impatiently. "I don't want him in my car."

Vismara whispered fiercely, "You on your own. You got nothing."

"It's all right," Nash said, acting as though he were saying good-bye to a friend. He got in with Atchley. Vismara turned and walked toward the elevators again.

"He can do us both a lot of good, Harold. You made him upset." Nash's irritation and excitement were real.

Atchley started his car, backing out with a lurch. "You were about to get us both into a lot of trouble." He glanced at Nash. "I think this is going to be an interesting dinner."

22

DURING THE DRIVE TO STRAWN'S, NASH LOOKED AROUND TO SEE if a van was near them. He didn't see one. Either the FBI agents were very good or his ability to spot them was poor. It didn't ease his tension.

Atchley, once he'd commented on Nash's strange request to put a defendant in the car with them, talked about his campaign stops that day and what he was doing for the next week. He was full of enthusiasm. His race was going well now, his opponent unable to make any issues.

When they got to Strawn's, Nash hadn't seen any of the FBI agents.

He and Atchley got a table quickly. Strawn's major business came at lunch, bankers and lawyers from nearby office buildings who wanted a dark, old-fashioned place to eat.

Nash and Atchley sat in a rear booth. The whole place was red and black Leatherette and dim lights. The air was smoky, music thin and bleating. Nash glanced at the other tables. The closest ones were empty. He didn't see Jacobs or Sanchez. He had no mike.

They ordered, and Atchley sat back expansively, eyeing the room for voters. Perhaps this meeting should be called off, Nash worried. I could arrange everything for the next time. Then, he thought he could make the proposal to Atchley now and record him actually taking the money at a second meeting. Vismara would be there. See if Atchley's interested tonight, Nash decided.

His mind changed again. Should he wait longer for the agents? Try to have everything he said to Atchley about a bribe recorded? They hadn't gone over this refinement in the rehearsals. He didn't know what Roemer wanted.

"Nature calls," he said to Atchley, standing up.

"You drank two glasses of water in the last couple of minutes."

153

Nash grinned gamely. Atchley shrugged and chewed on a bread-stick.

Nash went to the phones, out of sight of the tables, beside the bustling kitchen, waiters in red vests hurrying in and out with large aluminum trays and plates. He called the Cypress.

"Nobody's here," he said to Janice.

"Jacobs radioed. They got lost. They're on their way."

"So nothing's set up here? There's nothing?"

"No. Try to stall a little longer."

"How about if I simply set up another meeting. He didn't want to be near Vismara. Maybe I can get him to agree to that tonight."

Janice said levelly, "Neil thinks it would be best to have this initial meeting on record, Tim. I do, too. You know what happens when the defense starts talking about promises that were made and we can't produce a tape proving there were none."

"I lost a couple of cases like that," Nash admitted. "This one was my idea. It feels very strange on this side of the fence."

Roemer broke in. He had been on the line. "It's like swimming. You'll get it. Everything's under control."

"Bullshit," Nash said quietly.

"I had to say it." Roemer sounded amused. "Have a good meal. Don't order too much. This is a taxpayer dinner."

"I'll let Harold pick it up."

"Not if he's as cheap as you say." The line went dead.

He went back to the booth and found salad had come and Atchley was eating. He sat down, wiping his damp hands on the linen napkin. They talked about courthouse gossip, who was losing a clerk, who was being laughed at by the staff, whether Frenkel could get the PJ election. Nash told some stories his father had passed on about the drudgery of being presiding judge. He ate slowly, without taste, always looking around. People came and went, trays were brought, plates removed, but the FBI agents didn't appear. His nerves grew more fragile.

"You want to hear a crazy one?" Atchley demanded. He ate and drank, sighing constantly, complaining about the campaign rounds he made, his sore feet and aching shoulders.

"Sure."

"Wisot's check for my fund-raiser? Bounced. I put it through twice. No go." He worked on a cheesecake. The smoky, meaty air was cloying around them.

"Frank probably just forgot to make a deposit."

"Sure. He's so busy with the St. Andrew children's hospital thing, all that sound and fury about starting a magnet school in the North-gate district. Do you know what the real explanation is?"

"No, I don't." He disliked Atchley's injured tone, the wheedling insinuations.

"Frank's broke. That's all."

"You're kidding."

"No. He's got nothing left in his pension account at the credit union. No savings."

"How'd you find out?"

"When I lose that much money, Tim, I find out. I have ways of checking things," Atchley said. "So poor old Frank's hollow. He's got a new house that costs about two thousand more than his salary a month. His wife's spending a lot. You and I don't have to worry about that."

"I know why I don't," Nash said. "Why don't you?"

"Lilian doesn't buy things," Atchley said simply.

"What are you going to do about the check?"

"Nothing. I threw it away. Frank didn't seem to care. He said he was sorry."

Nash was inwardly relieved. He had visions of Atchley's publicly denouncing Wisot, and that would have been grotesque. Everyone liked Frank and very few people liked Atchley, at least around the courthouse.

"I didn't realize he was so hard up."

Atchley pushed his plate away. "I needed that. One good meal a day. Juggling my trial schedule, trying to get Kalbacher to lighten up on me so I can get out and campaign"—he shook his head—"plays hell with my diet." He grinned sadly. "I'm getting fat again."

Nash nodded, went on eating. He had seen Jacobs and another man come in, carrying the videocamera briefcase. They sat at a table about ten feet away, chatting and oblivious. He wondered how much the lens in the briefcase could take in, how far its electronic ear could reach. There was no time to kill anymore. He stopped eating, folded his napkin, and laid it on the table. Atchley was as relaxed and sated as he ever would be.

"Frank's not the only one with money trouble, Harold," Nash said, the lie coming easily, like a breath. "I'm in trouble."

"Did you get stripped in the divorce?"

Nash nodded. "It's going to get worse."

"How can I help?" Atchley said flatly.

* * *

I have heard truth and lies in court, Nash thought. I dismissed a case when I thought a cop was lying about when he shot a fleeing suspect. I have endorsed lies, like Ross told Soika. Sometimes it is confusing, but the confusion ends when you understand that the end served is not truth but justice. Truth is a road, justice the destination.

The one thing we all pride ourselves on, he thought, listening to himself lie to Atchley, is knowing when we hear falsehood. It's professional pride. No judge likes to think he's sitting up there, robed in black, above everyone, being a fool.

He feared that Atchley would detect the lies.

But he didn't. It was something else, quite unexpected.

"I ran into Vismara when I was doing Narcotics," Nash said. "We had him on a possession-for-sale deal. Cocaine. He got out of it because it was a hand-to-hand sale and my snitch disappeared. I offered him the possession charge, just to get something."

"He turned it down."

"Sure did. But he kept in touch," Nash said slowly. "He had another case and I helped him with that one."

Atchley nodded as if the information was nothing. He absently smoothed the tablecloth. "What kind of help?"

"I dismissed a possession case. He had about ten grams of coke on him and I dumped it in the interest of justice. I said there was a bad bust."

"I bet the cops didn't go for that."

Nash shrugged. He nearly believed the story himself. Ending a prosecution was one of the easiest things in the world, checking a different box on a form, ordering drugs destroyed, a phone call to the narcs blabbing about some technical infraction and a promise to nail the bad guy the next time. "They went along with me."

Atchley leaned forward on his short arms, his sweaty smell nearly as strong as the broiling steaks. "Are you saying you took a bribe, Tim? That's what you're telling me?"

Jacobs and the other man went on talking, laughing. The camera and Testa's powerful microphone inexorably documenting. The pulse Nash felt was as real as if he actually were confessing to a crime.

"Vismara gave me twenty thousand, Harold. For doing nothing. Exercising my discretion the other way."

"My God," Atchley said calmly. "That's the damnedest thing I've heard. My God." He did not look perturbed.

"Vismara got arrested several nights ago on a DUI. He wasn't drunk but he had a significant amount of coke in the car. He's got that case coming through muni court for arraignment."

"Oh, no," Atchley's head shook. "I don't want to hear any more." He didn't get up.

"I've got that part of his problem taken care of, Harold," Nash said. "In the DA's office, an old friend of mine. That case won't make it. Insufficient evidence. Vismara's problem is going to be in your court."

"Mine? How?"

"The probation department's filing a violation on him for his old sale charge. They can send him back to prison if you find him in violation."

Atchley watched Nash closely. "All I'll be doing is reading the police reports of the arrest and hearing a criminalist testify." He held his tightly bunched napkin. "You'd like me to deny the violation?"

"It's completely yours," Nash said, "like rejecting a case in the DA's office. Use your discretion to say the probation guys didn't meet their burden of proof."

"For what?"

"Vismara's a fairly heavy guy, Harold. He doesn't want to go back to the joint. He's willing to pay sixty thousand dollars to have the underlying charge and the violation fold up. I'll take fifteen, you get twenty, the rest goes to the DA."

"Who's your friend in the DA's office?" Atchley frowned.

"You know I won't tell you."

Atchley nodded. "That's why everybody trusts you. You're loyal."

Nash steadied himself. He could feel Atchley nosing at the bait, hear the interest in his voice and questions.

"I don't give up friends," Nash said.

"Twenty thousand dollars?" Atchley went on. His voice was very low suddenly. "I assume in cash?"

"Yes. Use it for the campaign."

"Would this be between you and me? I don't talk to anyone else?"

"If you want."

Atchley sat back, breathing noisily, staring at Nash. Did he spot the lies? Did he disbelieve the idea that Tim Nash would take bribes and offer them? Nash pushed away his still-full plate of raspberry tart. A couple, older, got up near them, the man's arm around his wife, and Nash's eyes followed them. A short waiter bent his heavy dessert tray down to another table, trying to persuade the two large women staring at it to make a selection.

"What's it going to be, Harold? There isn't a lot of time. The new case comes up in forty-eight hours. The violation will probably be filed tomorrow, put on your calendar," Nash prodded.

But Atchley pushed his chair back. "I'm going, Tim. You want a ride?"

"That's it?"

"Yes."

"I'll get a cab." Nash couldn't hide the real bitterness in his voice. At least that was real. Atchley had gotten away.

Atchley stood by the table, then bent down, his breath thick with wine and cheesecake, his eyes dark, face flushed. "It's been a revelation. You've shown me things I didn't realize existed."

"You've been around the courthouse. You've been around the city," Nash snapped back, turning away.

"I know about the others. It's you. It's people you know who surprise me. Maybe you were trying to flatter me by making me part of this corrupt club. But I'm not flattered. It makes me sick."

Nash saw genuine disgust on Atchley's face and was startled. "I was trying to help us both, that's all."

"Is it?" Atchley straightened up, his coat loosely pulled on, his stomach over his belt.

"There's nothing you can do, Harold. There's no record anywhere."

Atchley glanced around. "It would make a great campaign issue. A judge cleans out the courthouse."

"You know what would happen to your support? The other judges? You'd be alone." It was a threat with real value in Atchley's case. Nash was frustrated and wished he could call Jacobs over to wipe the self-righteous look off Atchley's face. It's a sting, Harold, and you almost got bit.

"Maybe I would," Atchley said, shaking his head a little. "I've got one suggestion, Tim. In light of tonight, you might want to seriously reconsider endorsing me. That might solve a world of potential problems."

Atchley touched his loose tie, smeared his forehead with a limp hand, and left. Nash sat at the booth, thinking. He noticed that Atchley had left him with the check. He got up, paid it, and went out. Jacobs and the other man followed him shortly, none of them speaking to each other. Parked outside the restaurant was a light blue panel van in the shadow between two streetlights. There was little traffic at that time of night downtown. Nash stood outside. He had been prepared for anything except failure.

"Then the son of a bitch turns around and tries to blackmail me," he said angrily to Roemer and Janice at the Cypress suite.

"We heard the tapes," Roemer said.

"How about blackmail? That's good enough for a start."

Janice shook her head. "It's ambiguous the way he puts it, Tim. He simply asked you for a campaign endorsement. He specifically rejected the money."

"I'm not going to endorse the fucker." Nash got up from his chair. The FBI agents had gone back to the van to bring in their portable equipment. Roemer was nonplussed by what had happened.

"It's up to you. I'm not worried about that guy doing anything," Roemer said. "He's the kind of guy who runs."

"I would have sworn Atchley'd take a bribe," Nash said.

"Live and learn," Janice said.

"I want to get another one going right away," Nash said. He looked around the unused yet lived-in suite. "It's all a waste otherwise."

Roemer held a glass of club soda. He had never, so far, taken a drink in Nash's presence. Even when they sat in the cramped bedroom a few minutes ago watching the infrared, grainy pictures from the restaurant, taken through the blinkered camera lens in the briefcase, Roemer was at ease. He sensed a different pace to being undercover than Nash did. He wanted to feel momentum and Atchley had stopped any dead.

It was amazing to see the booth at Strawn's through that camera eye. Seconds flickered by in the right-hand corner readout, and his own voice and Atchley's slightly muffled, hushed, like looking at a twin of himself. It reminded Nash of the time, when he was eighteen, he had gone to Santa Maria Community hospital to be tested for an ulcer. The doctor put him in an X-ray machine, standing up, made him drink barium, and watched, on the green-glowing screen, as the opaque liquid slid down a gray, translucent tube, encased in gray ribs. The sight of his own innards at work repelled and fascinated Nash.

It was the realization he was seeing something otherwise hidden, protected in secrecy by his skin. Like the hidden video of the meeting tonight, it would have been lost. It was, he thought, never meant to be seen.

"Yeah, I think it's time we moved on," Roemer said. He had the chart of judges Nash had seen earlier spread on the dining table. "You know Ruth Frenkel pretty well?"

"Not socially very much. We're friendly."

"We've got significant information that she's sold out."

Nash took this hard. So it begins. Atchley was his choice, his tryout for pique. Now here was someone he knew selected by others. "Doing what? What did she do?"

Roemer looked at Janice. "Promised a reduced sentence to one defendant for five thousand dollars. It was an ADW." Assault with a deadly weapon.

"Bad injuries?"

Janice shook her head. "Not really. A broken arm. A Marine on leave, visiting his family. The defendant could pay."

"Your source is a guy in the joint?" Nash was incredulous. "That's not the most reliable."

"He bragged about a crooked judge in Santa Maria. We've found two other questionable sentencings, we've got a witness ready."

"Okay," Nash said. "I'll see what Ruth does. I don't think she'll do it."

"Then we'll have another honest judge to help us," Roemer said, carefully folding the chart. "I really will have to stay in the background. If I put these cases on, I don't want some fucking defense lawyer subpoenaing me as a witness in my own trials." He laughed.

Nash felt very tired. It was midnight and he thought he had run miles and gotten nowhere. He heard Jacobs, two other agents, and Testa coming down the hallway with their equipment suitcases. "I'll talk to Ruth tomorrow. First thing. I'll set up something here as soon as I can."

"Let's get some use out of this place besides sleeping," Roemer said to Janice.

Nash looked at her longingly. He said, "Vismara feel too badly?"

"Louis is in for the long haul. He's a realist. He knows there will be other setups," she said. She looked away.

Like a troupe of stagehands, the agents came in, grumbling good-naturedly, joking with Nash about how twitchy he appeared in the restaurant. They took their black suitcases with audio and camera equipment into the bedroom.

"Can I drop you at home?" he asked Janice. He touched her lightly. She smiled and nodded.

"I'll go home with Tim," she said to Roemer.

"Okay," Roemer said, tossing the chart onto the sofa with his carelessly crumpled coat. "Suit yourself."

23

Roger Valles disliked hospitals and Mercy Emergency in particular. It was midmorning, cooler than the last few days, but the cloud-mottled blue sky was still as hard and implacable as porcelain. He and Witwer wore dyed T-shirts and people avoided getting too close to them. "Like a couple of psycho hippies," Witwer said with pleasure as they strolled into the hospital.

Valles hated the hospital because it was the place where all lunatics were taken first when they were picked up on the street. His first tour in the department had been patrol, driving the large black-and-white wagon that could hold eight in its reinforced belly, prowling around the downtown parks and dark alleys and ancient hotels where the chronic drunks lay or growled. He wore gloves. He washed his clothes and those gloves frequently, but the smells never came off from handling the drunks. He had picked up one shaggy-haired man in the alley beside the Clarion Hotel, a day-rent, plywood-boarded haven beside the Greyhound bus terminal on Marklee Avenue. It was seven at night, in October, and Valles and his partner first thought the curled-up body, stinking in the cool night, was dead. So he bent with his gloved hands and lifted, the drunk groaned, released incoherent curses and a pool of urine. It was then that Valles noticed the maggots falling out of the drunk's clothes onto his uniform, into the cuffs of his pants, onto his shoes. He yelled, dropped the drunk, and began frantically scraping the white slugs off himself. He found them at home, burrowing into creases in his clothes. He felt them for days, even after Arlene washed everything.

That drunk had come to Mercy Emergency. So had the others, the babblers and shriekers who roamed the downtown streets, scooped up by Valles and his black-and-white van.

After them came the others, gunshot and stabbed, raped and bleeding, the whole torn, bruised collection of people a city produces in an average day. Valles would have to come to Mercy Emergency and take their statements. He took the statement from a man who had been hit in the forehead with a machete, the blade still embedded in his skull, while he talked, quite lucidly, and then died. The very worst, though, and what had turned Mercy Emergency's nondescript pile of brick and white-framed windows into a place of revulsion for him, were the children. Scalded, cut, slashed, repaired outwardly and he would coax a statement from them. It always seemed to be in the same linoleum-floored room, with a dozen wheezing, crying people in it, and doctors and nurses threading their way from one to the other, and everything stank of chemicals and fear. He remembered one little girl named Tina, six years old, who showed him how she practiced the piano, who told him how she had been hurt, and who had on her otherwise perfect white chest the black and red burn of the iron her stepfather had pressed on her.

"Who else you been to see?" Valles asked Witwer about their search for Vismara. He did not want to talk about the past in this hospital. It was too vivid, possessed too much vitality.

"Lazarus, Hokey, two mopes living where Ratman used to hang out." He pushed open the door to the hospital's jail ward. The colors were softened here, only dead green, but the smells were sharper as if to compensate.

"His place on South Manzanita?"

"No. The place he had on Starling. With the busted fridge on the front lawn?"

Valles showed his ID to the SMPD officer posted in a wire enclosure just inside the door. Witwer whisked his badge out, too. They got two small clip-on tags in return and had to check their guns in. "I thought he just crashed on Starling. I thought he only stayed in the Manzanita joint," Valles said.

"He ain't there now. He ain't on Starling, either. I ran him through CII, talked to the mopes. He's dropped out."

"Dead."

"Long's I don't have to worry about him."

They forgot about that cold trail to Vismara. The women's wing of the jail ward was a bright-lit room, somehow antique in appearance because of the old lights and high, framed windows, the few flowers set out on tables. There were ten beds, some enclosed by lime-green curtains. There were ten women in the room, a few reading, one sitting on the edge of her bed coughing. Most were thin and there was the vague trace of talcum in the air. Valles and Witwer went to the fourth bed from the door.

"Hey, Maiz. You been hard to find," Valles said genially.

The small black woman in the bed turned her head. She had a concave face and tightly curled hair. Her right ankle was secured to the bed's steel post. Valles had a quick impression of a fox caught in a trap.

"How you doing?" Witwer asked, smiling, glancing at the other women, who were all watching and listening.

The woman on the bed stirred again. Her eyes were large and bloodshot. "What you bring me?" she asked.

"I didn't bring nothing," Valles said.

"You didn't ask," Witwer said.

"You go down to the store, you bring me back some grass, some crank, they got any good shit, you bring me some of that."

"I'll make a list," Valles said. They stood close to her to speak softly. In appearance they could have been dealers or friends.

"You get busted for an eleven three fifty? That's what I heard," Valles said. He leaned against the bed. Part of her skinny leg was uncovered.

"I had this little bit left, just enough, I was going to get high once more, this fucker say he needs something, so I help him out and he bust me."

"Undercover narcs are the worst fuckers, Maiz. You got to watch them assholes," Witwer said.

"So how can you help me out here?" she asked slowly. Her tongue was thick and she had a thick layer of old sweat, almost gelatinous, on her face.

"We helped you already. We're square, Maiz," Valles said.

"Shit. I got a lot of shit for you."

"Well, what we'd like is something new. A new guy named Louis Vismara, about so high"—Valles held his hand off the chipped floor at five feet six—"dresses neat, little mustache, greasy little guy. Does coke mostly."

"You know I helped with that other shit, you got some good shit out of that," Maiz said, straightening up a little in bed. The sunlight from the high, unreachable windows hit her flat in the face and she squinted. "I'm so hot."

"I tell Jerry you are. He don't believe me," Valles said. "You seen this little mother? Heard about him?"

"Can I get some help with my court date?"

"Oh, sure. Look, I'll come in, stand up and swear you're the best," Valles said, bobbing his head, scratching his beard. He had to jolly Maizie along. She was obviously in withdrawal and had some analgesic in her.

"I think you should be doing something for me, I did some for you, I get out, I be doing more. Soon's I'm out, I work for you," she said.

A nurse, a tall, thin Hispanic man, came in with a cart of little white cups and a plastic jug of water. Some of the women made obscene jokes about him, but he wouldn't talk to them. He was at the far end of the wing, and Valles wanted to finish with Maizie before he got close enough to listen in. She did not need a snitch jacket in the hospital. And she had been helpful. He had spent nights with her, feeding her doughnuts, sugared coffee, even pointing her to small scores when necessary. She was twenty-two and wouldn't live to be thirty. The best thing he could do for her would be to let the drug possession charge drag her through court, send her to prison where she might at least stay clean for a little while. But he needed her and there were no guarantees with someone like Maizie. Someday, perhaps long before she was thirty, Valles thought her brother Monroe would bury her. If he could be found.

"Okay, Maiz. You give me Vismara, I'll get you a ride on the new beef."

Witwer sucked in his breath and kept an eye on the nurse, clattering, shuffling down the beds toward them. The women on either side of Maizie were unconscious, IVs in their arms, mouths open and snoring.

"I don't know him," she said, lying down again, the wedge of sunlight on her belly. "Maybe I heard about him."

"Come on, Maiz. No shit now. We got no time."

"No shit," she insisted, the pinched face adamant. "I hear about a little dude like that sometimes, he come in, he go, someplace off Riverrun Avenue, down south, you know?"

"He live there?"

"You go see Morris, where I used to live, he tell you. He knows all these guys. He tell you, you tell him I tell you." She lay back.

Witwer nodded. "We check with him."

Valles was about to say something bland, a farewell. The clattering male nurse and his cart were two beds away, the man in some sort of argument with a woman who wanted a different color pill. Maizie's tongue touched her dry lips. "I got to have a little something. I going to dry up in here."

"Tell your quack." Valles grinned and started to leave with Witwer.

"Can you get me something, a little shit maybe, just get me through this? I going to be out working for you, just get through this in here?"

Valles hesitated. "Once?"

"That's all, honey."

Witwer shook his head, but Jerry hadn't been as close to Maizie. "Okay, I'll come back with a little something tonight," Valles said.

She lay back, eyes closing. "I'm going to really work for you. All the time, I get out."

The nurse huffed and pushed by them with haughty disdain.

Witwer waited until they had gotten their guns back and were leaving Mercy Emergency. An ambulance broke in as he spoke, roaring up to the hospital, men and nurses fluttering around it, as if the vehicle were suffering.

"You ain't giving Maiz anything you shouldn't, are you, Rog? That's pretty fucking stupid."

Valles was grim as they got past the lobby and its crowd of anxious, weeping, moaning relatives. "She earned it. I'll get some crack, some shit for her. I'll make a small buy from one of our little dopesters."

"I don't want to hear about it," Witwer said at the car, under the porcelain-blue sky, the hospital's thin strip of green lawn butting against the three churches, floral shops, and two funeral homes that hovered around it like obsequious, rapacious relatives at a deathbed.

"You didn't hear anything from me," Valles said.

Louis Vismara sat in the car, another slim, down-to-the-ground sports car in white with racing stripes, waiting for some instinct to tell him when to get out. He sweated in his dark suit, the sun hitting the silky material and soaking into it, the heat burning into him like a flame. Like the burning flames that wait for sinners, he thought, looking again at the stucco church and its gold-painted cross across the street. The hedges were trim, the flower beds full of colors, Jesus wept in stone on the lawn, and Vismara thought of years past when he walked up that same red-brick path, up those stone stairs, his shoes tight and new, and at the doorway, looking for him, Father Salazar frowning, rubbing his hands, because his altar boy was late again for early Mass.

"I'm burning up here," said the young woman beside Vismara. "We going somewhere?"

"I'm going in." He opened his door, slid out. Her whining complaint had been the sign. He looked at her, acid-washed jeans so tight they were like slinky skin, blouse taut against her. Her eyes and mouth were distracting, outlined in too much makeup.

"You going to church on Thursday?"

"You stay here. I be out soon." He turned from her.

"I'm burning up," she protested. "I don't want to sit here."

Vismara went ahead into St. Philomene's, the doors oak, a glossy blue and green light from the small stained glass in them falling on the red tile floor. The place was so cool and dark. He made the required gestures, crossed himself, went forward as if in a dream.

The years flooded him. The oak pews, dark and rubbed shiny by the bodies of his father, mother, sisters, the whole neighborhood kneeling, crossing, murmuring. Along the walls, in their niches, the pastel stations of the cross, and the main altar, now switched around' since he'd been coming here, facing the congregation.

He looked around. Fussing with a white basket of orange blooms on the small side altar was a thin, white-haired man in a black suit.

Vismara felt the old hatred and confusion. What had to be said, had to be. This man had to know.

"Father Salazar?" he said, fearing that the old man was not whom he wanted after all.

But when the priest turned, still holding the basket of flowers, Vismara saw it was him. The face had become paper smooth and red flecked, but the hair was still groomed so carefully Vismara marveled at its appearance of artificiality. The glasses were thicker, and the gaze less intense.

"Yes? I'm busy if it's anything complicated."

"You remember me?"

Father Salazar put the basket closer to the small altar, stepped back. His footsteps were hard in the empty, waiting church. "No," he said.

"It's Louis. You know, Louie Vismara's kid. I used to be your altar boy." He felt awkward with the introduction. It was as if this priest hadn't berated him in front of this altar so many mornings ago or disapproved of him. Vismara followed the priest.

166

"Coming through the old neighborhood?"

"To see you."

"That was very kind. Yes. How is your father?"

"He died couple years ago."

Father Salazar now paused, and the face screwed up in that familiar way either in concentration or as the herald of his anger, making Vismara think no years had passed between then and now at all. "I thought so. He stopped coming for a long time. I liked him. He had daughters."

"My three sisters. Frances, Maria, Alex. For Alexandra."

"Lovely girls. Lovely names." They had reached the small door to the sacristy, Father Salazar going ahead. He still had to duck a little under the low frame. The room itself was the same, except for a mechanical box, the size of a cabinet. The priest fiddled with it and a humming came from the machine. The priest looked at his watch and counted.

"So you remember me?" Vismara asked again.

"A minute," Salazar counted. Then he made another adjustment. "I have to change the timer on our automatic bell ringer. We had a blackout the other night and we had the bells coming on at three in the morning."

Vismara nodded, touching the beaded sweat on his forehead. Even now, the priest old, forgetful, the years of being looked down on flown by, Vismara had the horrible, inescapable sense of being judged and found wanting. "I remember you used to have that guy, Johnny? Frank? The retard? He used to come in and take care of that. Now you got this machine here," he said, forcing the conversation along. Sweating.

"That was John Guerro," Father Salazar said sourly. "He was a fine man and we all liked him."

"Sure. Sure. I didn't think of him for a long time, until just now." He trailed off. Father Salazar was at the high oak cabinets that kept the vestments stiff, smelling faintly of camphor. It all came back to Vismara now, the early mornings in here, gathering up the chalice and other things, Father Salazar irritable, the early-morning congregation shuffling, snuffling in the half-empty church. There was no faith in those frightened, harried exercises. His father hit him when Father Salazar complained finally one Sunday about Louis's being late again for early Mass.

"I'm sorry. I've got four weddings this afternoon, one on top of the other, and I've got to hurry." The priest sighed, closed the vestments in. "What was I supposed to do next?"

"I been doing something, Father."

"I don't have the time right now."

"You got to. It matters because it's you."

Father Salazar peered closer at Vismara. The inspection was disconcerting. Vismara suddenly realized that until that instant the priest had not remembered him at all. The rest of the family, yes, but he had been erased as cleanly as water thrown over a soapy window.

"Louis. You were an altar boy."

"Twenty years ago," Vismara said, sweating. "Long, long time. I been in some trouble since then."

"You were in trouble then," Father Salazar's old belligerence returned. He stared at Vismara. "You were a thief. Have you come back to steal something?"

"I'm changing, Father. I got into something that's going to fix everything."

The priest walked toward the door to a small garden on the east side of the church. "I'm very pleased to hear that. I always like to hear that people are trying to better themselves."

They walked side by side along the granite pathway beside tiny patches of herbs and flowers, tended by the Sunday school children and the church's volunteer gardener. Vismara had an overpowering urge to shout at the priest. I'm trying, he wanted to shout, what else do I have to do? I'm trying to get back where you said I was supposed to be.

"So it's okay? I can make up the bad stuff, Father? I mean, like, I can go back and change my record?"

Father Salazar frowned again, the paper-thin skin faintly flushed in the afternoon heat. At the far end of the garden, near his residence, two white stretch limousines had pulled up. The first of the weddings, and people in white and black, with flowers and cameras, struggled from the cars. "I don't know," the priest said. "I don't know what you've done."

"But that's what you always said. You can wipe out the bad stuff," Vismara pleaded angrily.

"I don't know. Maybe it is possible. I don't know what God accepts or rejects. You've got to do what is right. That's all I'm sure about."

"That's not enough."

"It's all there is. From me anyway." They had gotten to the door of the residence. A phone rang inside.

Vismara felt a desperation growing inside him. What did he have to do? What should he say?

"I remember those Masses, you know? Six A.M. You didn't shave. Sometimes you been drinking, I thought. I was a kid, but I could tell," Vismara blurted out. The image of the younger Father Salazar, hot eyed and clumsy, struggling into his vestments, came flowing back inexorably. Sometimes the priest had had to lean on his shoulder as they walked into the church.

Now Father Salazar looked at Vismara. It was not with dislike, more curiosity, as if Vismara had mentioned the eccentricity of a family member. "I needed something to wake me up. I was tired."

"You're not tired now, I bet."

"Not anymore."

"See? You changed, too." Vismara had seen the routine taking over, the command of schedules and faces passing by, day after day, weddings, funerals, baptisms, dinners and luncheons. The years had worked their way into Father Salazar. He would not complain now, Vismara thought, if I was late for Mass. It wouldn't make any difference. "Life changes, you got to try yourself."

The phone stopped inside the residence, beyond the filmy, white curtain on the windows. Father Salazar nodded, looking toward the people ambling into the church from the rented limousines.

"That's very good advice, Louis. Thank you," Father Salazar said. "Thank you for coming by. Come again."

"I don't think so."

"It was just personal? Just to see me?"

Vismara nodded.

"I must have made an impression when you were younger."

"I never forgot."

The tone wasn't grateful. Father Salazar looked at his watch. "I was much more intolerant then. But I do have to get ready." He opened the door. He glanced at Vismara briefly before closing the door finally.

Vismara walked out, past the wedding party laughing on the church's wide stone entrance, grouped together for pictures. A breeze came off the delta, miles away, carrying with it coolness and a musty signature.

He got into the sports car, sinking into the embrace of soft leather seats. The girl wouldn't look at him. Then she said petulantly, "They got a wedding here. I got to sit here and watch them."

He started the car, the engine satisfyingly loud. "I been married. It ain't so great."

"We done?"

Vismara put the car in gear, blowing a cloud of black exhaust

169

toward the people on the church's steps. "I go to see this guy, like he's going to tell me I'm doing okay now. So what? I tell him *he's* doing okay. He's got nothing to say to me."

"I'm hungry again," the girl said. She never listened.

Across the street, up half a block from St. Philomene's, Witwer started the Fairlane as Valles snapped off a final picture with his wife's Leica.

"Stay right behind him, Jerry, not too close," Valles said, winding the film onto the roll in the camera.

"I done a tail before," Witwer said, keeping the sports car in sight behind four other cars on Centralia Avenue. "You get him coming out of the church?"

"Got him nine ways up and down," Valles said, carefully putting the Leica, which Arlene treasured, into the glove compartment. "I got him coming out of that new house he's got, I got him getting into the car with the girl, got him necking, got him driving here."

"So how long you want to stay on him?"

"See where he stops next."

"What do you want to do?"

"Talk to him," Valles said, watching the sports car changing lanes, changing back, always trying to get a few car lengths ahead in the swift traffic on Centralia. "We sit down with this guy and we ask him what the fuck he's doing to us."

24

THE SURVEILLANCE OF VISMARA THAT AFTERNOON WENT ON UNTIL almost five P.M. Valles and Witwer were scheduled to start their shift at six-thirty, meeting two other agents from the Yuba County Sheriff's Department at a bar on American Point Boulevard, near the west end of the port. "They got everything coming and going out, cash, crap, illegals," Witwer said. "Should be a fun night."

"First we talk to Louis," Valles said as they drove.

"Yeah. First we do him."

There would not be much time.

After he left St. Philomene's, Valles and Witwer followed him to a sporting goods store, waited, strolled up, and saw him buy a shoulder holster. It took some time for the clerk to fit a neat one on Vismara's small torso. The girl bought a pair of gloves for bow-and-arrow shooting. Witwer raised his eyebrows at Valles.

Vismara and the girl drove to a vegetarian restaurant. He picked at a large leafy salad. She ate her way through something in a hollowed-out pineapple, then finished his salad. Then they went to a Bank of America branch on Hudalgo Way where the kid in a blue guard's uniform gaped at the sports car and the girl, then pulled his cap down in embarrassment. Witwer went into the bank, stayed in the back beside the ferns because he was not dressed for surveillance in a bank, in his T-shirt and beard. The kid guard watched him suspiciously, so did two tellers. Vismara and the girl did not. They poked each other playfully, filled out slips, and went into the safety deposit vault.

Witwer went back to the car. "They're in the safety deposit vault."

"Bet you the shithead's getting a piece."

"Insure your firearms with an agency of the federal government," Witwer said.

"Because he's such a little smart guy, he ain't going to keep guns where some probation officer can find it." Valles had the Leica out, taking pictures with a new roll of film, covering shots of the bank.

"I hope he dumps the gal." Witwer worriedly looked at a watch on his hairy wrist. "We getting mighty close to checkout time."

"We'll make it."

Witwer said, "Here comes Mickey Mouse, Rog," and he nudged Valles.

The bank guard, who really only parked cars and was twenty-two years old, lived at home, and collected comic books, was at the Fairlane's driver's side.

"Hey," he said.

"Hey, hey," Witwer responded jovially.

"You got banking business?"

"That's why we're here."

"How come you're taking pictures?"

"Testing new film," Valles said tartly.

"Well, you go test it someplace else," the kid guard said.

"Make me," Valles said, lowering the Leica.

"You're going to get it, you don't get your ass out of here," the guard said warningly. He had a baton on his waist and he reached for it.

"Make me," Valles repeated.

Witwer recognized the growing truculence in his partner's voice. Valles successfully impersonated a mean biker because, at times, he was as mean as one. The bank's kid guard was too thick to see what he was prodding with a stick, and Valles, who had been complaining about things going stale and nasty at home, was ready to strike.

"We won't put any of our money in this bank. We'll tell all our friends." Witwer started the car.

"I'm taking your license number." The kid fumbled for a piece of paper, a pen, screwed his face up, looking at the plate on the front of the car. Valles nimbly bounced from the car, reached for the paper, and shoved the kid backward. "Hey!" the kid shouted, and fell down.

Valles got back into the car. "I didn't want him writing it down," he said. "Let's go."

"Are we going to have more trouble?" Witwer said, driving onto Hudalgo, the guard scrambling to his feet, shouting. "I don't want trouble, Rog. I don't want B of A filing a complaint with Shiffley on a surveillance we ain't even supposed to be on. Okay?"

"You think I wanted him writing down the license? You think I'm getting a kick out of it?"

"You got to calm down." Witwer pulled off the street, parking under a tall palm, sprinklers watering the small lawns with watery sizzle, in front of tiny homes.

"Yeah. I do," Valles said with half sincerity. He tucked the Leica between his legs. "It was kind of like I was getting some mouth from Harry again. Every fucking day now."

"That dork ain't your kid, Rog. Don't keep running it all together on me, okay? I don't need that."

"I'll take it easy," Valles said. He looked straight ahead. The bank was visible between the interstices of a hedge bounding two of the small houses on the street. He admitted that Vismara was a real problem, not an imaginary carryover from home. But that made it more important to treat him as serious, not an extension of Harry or Arlene and the brooding evenings they spent together, when he was home, when they were even together anymore.

172

He screwed on the telephoto lens. "For his package, when he goes back to the joint," Valles said, focusing on the bank's entrance. "A shot of Louis, his car, his hubba whore, his gun. There he is. Arm around her. Very cute. Smile, Louis."

Both Valles and Witwer were well back in a deep doorway across the street from the Cypress Hotel. They could see the doorman, in his green and gold-piped uniform, rocking on his heels under the maroon awning at the entrance.

"He's got good taste," Witwer said. "I had dinner there once. They got this great restaurant downstairs, a buffet thing, you just pile your plate, steak, all kinds of chicken, stuff in sauce. I took Maggie there for our eighth anniversary. It's a great place."

"Shit. Six. I hope the little fucker isn't going to dinner."

Vismara had dropped the girl off back at the new house, on Magnolia Drive, an address Maizie's friend Morris had been persuaded to reveal when Valles pushed him against a wall and stepped very hard on his toes. The heavy construction boots made a considerable dent, and Valles had no reason to use Morris as a snitch for anything else. He was a one-shot source in a personal case.

"I wish we could go in," Witwer said. "I bet we don't eat tonight until late."

"We can't go in."

"I said I wish."

"What is that little fuck doing in that hotel? He don't live there. Doorman chats with him like they're old buds. He moving shit there?"

"Maybe he's dealing out of the place."

"He's doing okay."

"So how's he tie in with Shiffley? That hotshot sheriff?" Witwer scratched his back with a grimace. They had been standing in the doorway of the boarded and closed Apricot Afghan Pet Groomers for nearly thirty minutes.

"What if he's a big fucking dealer? What if he's bought a couple of guys?" Valles said.

"Our guys?"

"You can buy anybody with that shit, kind of money they got," Valles said, holding the Leica ready to catch Vismara when he came out of the hotel. "Maybe Shiffley's doing something for him and we get to hold the shit."

"I don't think so."

"Wouldn't be the first time, Jerry. It happens. Guys do it."

"Oh, man," Witwer said unhappily.

Valles poked him sharply. "See that?"

They both looked at the hotel's entrance. The same doorman was nodding at an indifferently dressed man with thinning blond hair, hands in his pockets, who took the red-carpeted stairs to the hotel two at a time.

Valles snapped off several pictures, swearing each time. At his side, Witwer mumbled and cursed. When the glass door of the Cypress was closed by the doorman, Valles stopped taking pictures. He held the Leica as if it contained a bomb.

"I got it," he said to Witwer. "Can't lie about a fucking picture."

"I bet it's coincidence," Witwer said. But he did not believe that himself. "Nash's okay. Good judge. Good guy, right?"

"He's in the same hotel with Vismara."

"They got to have a couple hundred people in there."

"That's Judge Nash," Valles said. "Same guy Shiffley's always bragging about being in so tight with his old man."

"I think we should just walk away," Witwer said slowly. "We got a date in twenty minutes out at the port. Let's get over there, figure it out later."

Valles shook his head. "I'm waiting for Louis."

"Come on, Rog. Later, okay? Nothing's happening tonight. We're okay tonight."

"You go. I'm waiting for Vismara to come out."

"I'm not going alone."

Valles smirked. "It ain't a fucking dance, Jerry. You can go by yourself."

"I'll hang around if you're going to," Witwer said stubbornly.

"That's what I'm going to do. I'm going to wait until that little fucker comes out and gets in his car. Then I'm going to let him feel nice and safe and pull him over."

"Where do you want to take him?" Witwer watched the fading sun splash over the old face of the hotel, salmon pink. It would have to be at the Cypress. He liked the place. He wished whatever bad was happening had taken place somewhere he disliked. The luxurious old hotel didn't seem so treacherous somehow.

"I don't care. Maybe out to Miller's Point? Nice and quiet. I worked on a homicide out there. You got a lot of trees, a lot of riverfront, and nobody around."

"Okay." Witwer always felt better when there was a plan. He did not often come up with any suggestions himself and felt much at a loss tonight. "I'll check in, tell the Yuba guys we got something up and can't make it."

"Don't take long. I don't want to be sitting here if Louis comes out," Valles warned. He had not taken his eyes off the hotel across the street, appearing to pierce it by force of concentration.

Witwer strolled from the doorway. The Fairlane, with its radio, was parked a few feet away. He did not want to think of his partner, coiled in the abandoned doorway, waiting to take out his personal demons on the sporty little man with the mustache in the hotel. He did not want to consider what sort of convolutions had caught them up unawares, simply because they'd followed a superior's orders.

But most of all, as he sat down in the car, feeling that empty, quivering feeling of fear in his stomach, Witwer did not want to think about why a respected judge like Nash was dogging a dope dealer like Vismara.

25

EMPTY YOUR POCKETS," JANICE SAID TO NASH. SHE STOOD BESIDE him at the dining table in the Cypress suite. Vismara chatted quietly with Jacobs and Sanchez and another FBI agent Roemer had brought in from Albany.

Nash put everything in his pants and suit coat on the table: wallet, comb, change, keys, checkbook. Janice noted each item on her report form. Testa was running the video in the bedroom, recording whatever was in Nash's pockets.

"That's all I have," he said, surveying the small pile. It was embarrassing, in a way, to go through this ritual. He picked up his wallet, opened it for the camera, handed it to Janice. She took out the money. "There should be twenty-eight bucks," he told her.

Vismara watched from the corner of his eye. Jacobs was telling an obscene joke about four fat ladies in a circus, his voice low so it wouldn't be overheard. "Hey, lighten up, Louie. You listening?"

"Sure, I heard it before," Vismara said. He did not think anybody would search him. The gun, in its custom-fitted shoulder holster, rode reassuringly on him.

Nash picked up his belongings. Janice, when she was around the others or talking to Roemer or even in bed with him, after they had made love, had a cool facade. She seemed to be looking out at everything from behind a thick pane of glass. She was the most controlled person he had ever met.

Jacobs strolled over. "Hands up, all right?"

Nash raised his arms for a patdown and Jacobs ran a quick brush up and down him. Vismara touched his damp cheeks. Maybe they wouldn't search him, it might just be the judge.

The suite was lemon scented from being cleaned, the furniture buffed glossy, the carpets thick. A few old newspapers were laid decoratively around, as if Nash had been reading. Nash watched Janice and winked at her. She smiled slightly.

"Let's do a quick voice and picture check," she said to Nash. "Say something."

"The rain in Spain falls mainly in the plain."

"Louis?"

"My name is Louis Vismara, Jr."

There was a slight pause. "All right, I think Tommy's got it all. Louis, would you empty your pockets?"

Vismara thought he would start trembling. It had been foolish to put the gun on, taking it from its hiding place in his safety deposit box. But he felt protected with it, even if was a violation of his parole conditions. He couldn't tell Mindy, the girl he had been with lately, what he was doing, impress her with his status as an undercover agent, but she had been suitably impressed with the gun. Now he regretted it. If they found the gun, they would dump him, and he had a lot to atone for, as he had tried to tell Father Salazar. He glanced at the judge. Nash was always calm, even when he said he was nervous. The judge was looking out the window, hands in his pockets.

As Vismara put his money, wallet, and small religious medals on the table, so the camera in the lighting fixture overhead could plainly see them, Janice took out a tan envelope.

"I'm handing you ten thousand dollars in marked government funds," she said to Nash.

He took it, put the envelope in his suit coat. Nash was impatient this time for Ruth Frenkel to sit down at the table with him, listen to the act he and Vismara would put on. He wanted to know if she would take the bribe. It was like the game you played as a child, picking which closed fist held the surprise. He wanted to know what she would choose. Perhaps it would disprove Roemer's informant and she could join the ranks of the certifiedly upright and honorable.

Janice had on a light blue outfit, her hair loose and arranged as if she were a sterile nurse, not a prosecutor or his new lover.

Jacobs handed the various items on the table back to Vismara. "Okay. Quick patdown, Louie, and we're done."

Vismara sweated heavily. "Okay. Okay. First, like I got to tell you something, like why I decided to do it, it ain't no thing about you guys, it's for me." He sprayed the words out rapidly.

Jacobs looked quizzically at him, and Nash had walked to him. Someone knocked on the door several times.

"Open up in the name of the law, Nash," Judge Frenkel said fiercely.

They all jumped slightly, Jacobs and the other agent hurrying into the bedroom with Janice. Vismara wiped his trembling lips again. Janice, as she closed the door, gave Nash a high sign. He returned it and went to the door.

She had been drinking awhile before arriving. Ruth rocked a little on the sofa, slowly working her way through a second vodka martini while Vismara sat, legs crossed evenly, eyes on her coldly, at the dining table. Nash stood, then sat. It all came easily the second time.

"I am amazed," she said. Her gaze was steady but dulled.

"What about?"

"Here we are, you and me, and Mr. Vismara. I wouldn't have thought it yesterday." She finished the drink and put the glass down carefully on the marble inlaid table.

"I thought you'd understand, Ruthie." Nash leaned forward. He recalled Frenkel's early days on the bench, coming from a partnership downtown, her brother in Sacramento pushing her appointment. She had two dogs at home when she ended work every day. Several times, doing the calendar when she first got on the bench, she'd brought Ambrose the Pekinese to work with her, kept him in her lap during court, petting him. Nash gently suggested she leave him at home. Her dark hair was tightly done, always showing white scalp. She usually took up the collections for ailing judges or spouses or clerks, bringing jingling envelopes into his chambers about once a week, it seemed. With each charity, good deed, she made some ribald comment. Three years ago she had tried to adopt a child, enlisted Nash's help with the state agencies involved, and failed. On Nash's fortieth birthday party—all the judges, their wives, friends, and a large heap of the private bar drinking and eating at the Century Club—Ruth hired a singing dancer to give Nash balloons and wind a long paper strip around him. Everyone clapped.

"You sure you can afford this?" she asked Vismara. It was so direct, Nash cringed. He knew which hand she'd chosen.

"I have enough. For friends." He smiled. He really did slip into the character neatly, all hesitation and fear gone.

"That's one thing about this business, you never know who you're going to wake up next to." She laughed. "Where is the damn case?"

"It'll be assigned to you for arraignment on the violation of probation in a few days."

"Who says?"

"A friend in Master Calendar," Nash said.

"Well, I'll tell you how we're going to work it." She put both hands on her knees. "Cheryl's been making the actual arrangements for me."

"Your clerk," Nash said for the benefit of the cameras and mikes.

"So I'll have to talk to her and figure out how we'll handle the whole thing. Is that all right?" she asked Vismara.

"As long as the matter disappears."

"Nobody'll ever hear about it again," she said. She held out her glass. "Is the bar still open?"

"Sure, Ruth. For good customers." Nash got up, taking the glass, thinking he could put it down, tell her it was all a setup, and let her walk out. Instead, he paused.

"I've got ten thousand." He took out the envelope. Frenkel watched him blandly and Vismara coughed. Why am I the one with the butterflies and ache in the head? Nash wondered.

"Like a TV show," Ruth Frenkel said, reaching for the envelope. "No. Better not. I don't want to wander around downtown after dark with that much money."

"Okay," Nash said evenly, going to the bar and making her another drink.

"The streets are dangerous. Very bad when you can't even walk alone, somebody's going to come up behind you," Vismara said to Frenkel.

"Isn't it?" she answered boredly. To Nash, who came back with her glass, another for Vismara, she asked, "You're voting for me, aren't you, Tim? I promise you won't get any dog-bite or divorce cases sent to you."

"Sure I'm voting for you," he said.

"Okay. I think I'm over the top." She glanced at Vismara. "It's office business."

Vismara gravely nodded.

Nash and Frenkel chatted amiably for another twenty minutes about her dogs and how he liked living at the Cypress. It had an unreal atmosphere for him. He had just destroyed her.

At the end, she got up a little shakily. "Having lunch with Gary Lewis from Lewis, McCann and Hitchcock on Tuesday. You want to come?"

"I don't know him."

"I'm going to find out if he wants a good old lawyer in the firm."

"You're going to quit? How come you're running for PJ if you aren't staying?"

Frenkel shook her head and grinned. A large woman, dressed heavily, uncertain and unaware under the bluster and good manners. "Maybe nobody wants to hire me. I made some enemies. If I can't get any action outside the courthouse, well, at least I get Kalbacher's chambers to park myself in."

They were at the door. "You're really serious?"

"Shit, yes. Aren't you tired of all this sometimes?" She breathed blearily on him. Her dark hair had become a little tangled, a wisp falling over one eye theatrically. "Just a pile of cases moving in, moving out. I can't keep my eyes open during a lot of the testimony anymore. I've heard it. Haven't you? Every cop. I heard him. Same voice. Same reports. Every victim. Same nonsense. The only difference is when one starts bawling on the stand. Have to take a recess or say something really sincere, like, 'Would you like a glass of water or a tissue?' " Her voice was rough, but Nash knew the strain of listening on the bench to suffering, mental, physical, always spiritual, ground down like a stone bore. In the midst of every field of pain, there was truth, and from it, the judge had to fashion justice. Every ugly trail had to be followed to its end.

And she was right. They all knew, without a doubt, how each trail ended. It was, he thought, hardest for the solitary, lonely ones such as Ruth Frenkel, with her dogs and stony, empty house reflecting back every stab taken during the day. At least I had a family to absorb some of it, the night's partial amnesia until I went back in the morning.

"I just did an auto theft case," she said, blinking her eyes, "and the bum on the stand sat there and said he honestly did not know the name of the man who came to his door and sold him this late-model, gold Cadillac Coupe de Ville for eight hundred dollars."

"They all have stories," he said with a grin.

"Yes, they do. So, I had to lean over and ask this man, 'Are you saying that you are in the habit of buying automobiles from door-to-door salesmen?' The jury broke up, but I couldn't help it. I mean, Tim, come on. How much do we have to sit and listen to?"

Nash glanced back. Vismara hadn't moved, legs still crossed, arms in his lap, grave and serene. Nash thought he must be worried that any motion would shatter the illusion he had created.

"It's not as bad as my Cattera trials last year, Ruthie," Nash said. "First trial, Cattera said he wasn't a rapist, he was a burglar. That's how his fingerprints got on the victim's bathroom window. Jury hung on that. Next trial, new jury we got in three days, Cattera says he isn't a burglar, he's a Peeping Tom. That's how his finger-prints got on the victim's porch window. Hung up on that one, too. I had to sit there and listen to this guy lie to both juries and I couldn't move a muscle. I could not say anything."

"I remember that one. You made a lot of whining noise about it. Did he ever get nailed?"

"Yeah, about six months ago. For marijuana sales. Miyazumi gave him three years in the joint."

"Justice triumphs," she said. "Well, see you back at the salt mine tomorrow. I'm glad we've got a little secret, just the two of us."

Nash pecked her perfunctorily on the cheek. It was flushed, like an apple left in the sun. "Take care, Ruthie. You'll call me when Cheryl's set?"

"Soon as she's got the paperwork and can get it squirreled away, you can give me"—her voice dropped—"that little shitburger's money."

Then she smiled dreamily, and Nash closed the door. Vismara instantly lowered his head and let out a long breath, jumped up. Nash met Janice and Jacobs, another FBI agent with them, coming from the bedroom. They started applauding and he felt uneasy.

"That was neat," Jacobs said, clapping Nash's shoulder.

Vismara anxiously bounced from one foot to the other. "Okay? I did, okay? She liked it? You like the sound, you know?"

"You did a wonderful job, Louis. You, too, Tim," Janice said, watching his unease carefully.

"She didn't take the money."

"Reeled her right in, neat, neat, neat," Jacobs said again, and the FBI agent nodded.

They watched the TV monitors in the bedroom, clustering around Testa at the console's controls. On four monitors Nash saw himself, Vismara, and Frenkel from different angles, and it was somehow easy to watch. It was as though the multiplicity of images made the event historically distant, as though he were looking at something very old. His voice sounded tinny, fraudulent. The glow of the images bounced off the faces around the screens. Testa talked to himself.

"Her voice got real low here, so I did some stuff with the audio levels," and Frenkel's throaty laughter, the background hiss and hum, rose against Nash's voice. She agreed to the bribe. It was highlighted in sound.

The FBI agents complimented him again and Vismara beamed. Testa rewound the tape and they played the important part once again. Vismara complained that he looked too stiff, and short. He wanted a higher chair next time. The people around the TV monitors laughed and he took it good-naturedly.

"I'll arrange the actual hand-to-hand transfer of the money," Nash said. He had been searched again and the money reinventoried. Vismara had never come near Nash or Frenkel, so he simply watched, a sly grin on his face.

"Let's see if we can't do some meetings with whoever else on Frenkel's staff is getting paid," Janice said as Testa rewound the videotape and placed it in a labeled box, with the date and participants, and gave it to her. "We can widen the operation into the rest of the courthouse."

"Or wherever else it goes," Nash said. He took the videotape from Janice, holding it, weighing its single purpose and the things it would do to people who did not even realize it yet.

He handed it back to Janice. The FBI agents and Testa were arguing with Vismara about a betting pool they had started, trying to guess how long into an interview it would take before the subject accepted the bribe. Jacobs and Sanchez didn't want to pay Vismara. "It's like shaving points," Sanchez complained. "You got control of the ball."

Nash wasn't listening. Janice and he were alone. She put the videotape on a metal shelf, where others would go after each session. He whispered to her.

"Our firstborn," he said.

26

UNDER A HALF-MOON LIKE A BITTEN WHITE PILL, THREE MEN moved from the narrow road that dead-ended on Miller's Point, onto the short, stiff grass, down to the steep embankment that dropped off twelve feet into the Tuolumne River. At that time of year, the river flowing by the point was slower, but its unseen currents were hazardous, and NO SWIMMING signs were posted irregularly on the grass. Two abandoned picnic tables lay upended.

Vismara was in the lead, talking constantly. Valles pushed him every so often, and Witwer followed. Beyond the point was the river, its banks lined with restaurants and houses. But they were about a mile distant. Around the men rose huge trees, black, dusty, and dolorous under the moon. It was still warm outside.

Vismara rattled off names of people. Dealers he knew. People who would vouch for him. They halted at the apex of Miller's Point, where the land ended and the river went on and on until it vanished into the sea a hundred and twenty-six miles away.

Valles had held Vismara by the scruff of his neck with one large hand, the other pulling Vismara's small arm behind his back. Every so often, Vismara had squeaked during the forced march. His arm hurt.

"We used to get petters out here," Witwer said, his eyes used to the darkness, the distant, beguiling lights. "City still keeps the grass neat."

"You get four dopesters dumped out here in the last couple months, nobody wants to park and fuck around," Valles said. He shook Vismara. "You ever come out here with a girlfriend?"

"You guys are messing with the wrong guy, I don't know you. I don't know anybody you know."

"You sure?" Witwer asked softly.

"Sure. I know a lot of the guys around town. You don't know anybody I say."

"You don't remember us, Louis?" Valles asked sharply.

Vismara shook his head. "Dudes with beards, man."

"We busted you about a week ago," Witwer said. He stood a few feet away, glancing wistfully toward the water. "We're cops."

"Cops?"

"With Shiffley."

Vismara nodded. He had started wiping his face with his coat sleeve, which was a little torn from when Valles had yanked him out of his car just outside the Cypress Hotel and thumped him into their car on the floor, Valles on the back seat pushing him into a tight, uncomfortable ball with his heavy shoes resting on Vismara's back. "Cops. The guys at the club, right?" He sounded calm, but his arms trembled and he was glad they could not see how he sweated. His horror at this kind of scene, late night, deserted place, guys bigger and nastier, ready to rip him up, had led him away from dealing as much as an inner need to renounce his past. He knew where the horror came from, a simple physical fear of injury or death. But the need to change himself, better himself in Father Salazar's bland phrase, was a mystery to Vismara.

Yet, for all that, here he was anyway.

"You been fucking with us, Louis," Valles said. His voice quivered with rage. "Playing with our cases, leaving us cleaning up your shit."

"We don't like it," Witwer said quietly.

"I want to know what you're doing. I want to know who you're dealing with. Are you paying Shiffley? Some asshole in the Sheriff's Department?" Valles snapped. His words floated away, lost in the still, warm night. Vismara smelled the bitter grass and river muck.

"Ask Shiffley. It's his business, man. You dudes and me, we just soldiers. That's it. I ain't doing nothing myself."

"Bullshit. You got some guys on your payroll."

"Swear to God, man. Nothing. I ain't got nothing."

"So what are you and Shiffley doing?" Witwer prodded him gently.

"Man, I can't talk about it. It's real secret."

Valles kicked one of Vismara's feet out from under him and he sprawled onto the grass, thinking lucidly that they were going to hit him. He would not hit back. When he was a teenager, Vismara discovered his own vulnerability to physical attack, and how his meager efforts to fight only roused his enemies to hit him more, harder. If he was small and quiet, they got quickly bored. He sat up on the grass, the half-moon making dim shadows of the trees and the two men over him.

"You heard about the four dopesters who got left out here, Louis? Did you?" Valles said. His fists were tight. He looked like a real biker.

"Sure."

"You ever wonder how they got here?"

"Nope."

"We put them here." Valles pointed to Witwer. "Me and him. We got fucking tired of these dope dealers messing up on us and causing us trouble and getting bailed out, and dealing before they even got to trial, so we figured it's time to just take some street justice. You understand me, Louis?"

"You wasted four guys?"

"Four useless motherfuckers. I'll waste four more. I'll waste you tonight." Valles had his gun out, pointing it at Vismara.

Vismara thought he might cry. He did not know if the man would shoot him, but the rage in his voice was unmistakable. He had not recited a prayer for years, had forgotten the words partly, but the cadence rose in his mind in the second after the short-barreled gun pointed at his head.

If I tell them, then it's all nothing, he thought. He had recognized them as soon as they grabbed him. He had regretted, very deeply, blurting out his knowledge of the operation that first night when they arrested him, but he was foolish. He thought they knew all about it. He had not fully realized how serious the feds were about secrecy either. This Roemer had impressed him since then with his relentless pursuit of secrecy. Vismara had silently cursed his bragging to the cops. It was a weakness, he knew. He boasted to signify his own importance. His vanity had a life all its own.

If he told these cops, who obviously did not know much if anything about the operation, the feds would charge him and send him back to prison. The operation would end tonight because of his foolish, foolish weakness. Worse even, he would be a snitch forever and any hope of redemption would be lost to him. He thought of Nash, the judge, so cool and smart. Nash would not give in. He would risk it. Vismara prayed over his own incoherent thoughts.

"He'll do it," Witwer said, but he had a hard time not laughing. Here was Rog, with a gun, standing over the little drug dealer, who held his legs tightly, and it was so much like a fraternity prank at college. So play along. Maybe Vismara would start talking.

"I'm going to do it. I'm going to do it, you don't tell me who's jerking us around." Valles's voice was tighter, the gun pressed close to Vismara's head.

It was the adamantine quality, the furious lunge in Valles's stance that instantly frightened Witwer. He realized abruptly that Rog was not saying this for effect.

"Hey, he'll talk, I know he will. He's smart."

Valles didn't move.

"Jesus, Rog, you can't shoot him," Witwer said sincerely.

Valles looked at his partner, the gun unwavering on Vismara. "Why not? Why the fuck not, Jerry? Anybody sees us, sees anything back in town, it's a couple of bikers grabbing a dope dealer. Anybody checks out here, a couple of bikers did their supplier. It ain't us," Valles said harshly. "It ain't cops."

Vismara listened to them going back and forth. He was aware of the dry grass beneath his hands, his head turned slightly away, toward the lights flickering, shimmering off the shiny black water that would go on flowing to the sea no matter what happened to him in the next few seconds.

"The hard part," Nash said, "is staying in character. I'm thinking of every gesture, how I sound. It's exhausting."

He had put his underwear on again after they moved from Janice's bedroom into the kitchen. It was three in the morning, the blackness outside her fourteenth-floor apartment windows impenetrable, all of the city's anxious noises gone, only the sound of their own low voices brightening the space.

She had put on a sleeveless T-shirt, her body mature and rounded, and she wore the little clothing without concern.

"Stings are like hothouses," she said, holding up a bottle of brandy, Nash shaking his head. "This one especially. We stay in it a lot of the time."

"It's tough."

"That's why you need to get out of it for a while. No more pretending."

He lightly touched her shoulder; she turned, smiled, and poured a small brandy. "You sure?"

"No. I'd just fall asleep."

"That's the idea."

"Not yet. I've got some other ideas."

They grinned at each other and she sipped. There was an air of celebration about being together tonight, making being together more pleasurable than it had been so far. Nash felt as if he was being rewarded.

"Can you get a wiretap on the phones in the courthouse?"

"Which ones?"

"My chambers. Ruth's. A couple of the other judges. We do most of our talking to each other by phone."

"Based on what happened tonight, I can get a warrant authorizing a few taps," she said. "Sounds lonely for you."

"It can be. If you want to be a judge—" he began.

"I don't."

"I was going to say," he went on gently, "forget about dealing with people normally anymore. It just won't happen. My dad didn't quite explain that part to me."

"It's a little like my job. We don't approach people the way others do."

He put his arms around her. "Nope." He bent to her face and whispered urgently.

"Just let me finish this." She held out the brandy.

He held her a moment more, released her. He looked at her.

"That's an appraising glance," she said.

"Sorry. This'll sound terrible. I was thinking of my wife."

"My God."

"No," he said hastily. "How she looked. She's a bike racer. Sometimes anyway. Sometimes she got very hard, kind of really lean."

"I don't think I like this."

"It's a compliment. You're perfect." He touched her breasts under the thin T-shirt. "We don't have secrets either."

Janice drank the last of her brandy and took his hand. "I do have secrets."

"You know what I mean. We can talk. I can't talk to anyone else anymore. At the courthouse, maybe it'll be someone we target. My friends are mostly lawyers, so I can't talk to them. My family, Christ, it's split all over the place now."

Nash had initially been startled at his openness with Janice. He spoke to her with utter candor, almost as though he were talking to one of Testa's hidden mikes, to one of his remorselessly recording tape machines.

"Your mother and father are still here," Janice said. They got back into bed, secure in the tented intimacy of the covers, the locked apartment, the high, remote apartment. She put her leg, warm, hairless, between his. "You've got more of your family around you than I have."

"This isn't something I could tell my dad. Or my mother," Nash said. "Bad for security, right?"

"Neil would say so."

"Even if it weren't, they know too many of the people we're going after. They couldn't be detached about it."

"You're not."

Nash felt her warmth seeping untidily into him. "I'm trying. Did you ever meet my dad?"

Janice shook her head, kissed him slowly, and he felt her breath against his face. "No."

"I'll introduce you when we're done." Nash rolled closer to her. "Maybe when it's all over, we can go back to being normal people."

She trembled against him, a short laugh or shiver. Outside, the apartment building's soft-lit halls were nearly deserted, the random, rare elevator bell dimly breaking the silence, tensely making him wait for another sound. "You'll hear some funny things on those wiretaps," he said. "When I was doing Narcotics, we could run taps on any inmates at the county jail. Not like today. It was pretty primitive, we just had an old board, like a telephone switchboard behind a panel. It was in the lineup room. You just plugged in the inmate's visitor's room you wanted bugged and turned on a tape. The junk we got," he chuckled.

"Like what?"

"You know. Boyfriend-girlfriend junk. Mother-son junk. People in jail for serious beefs arguing about who's going to feed the dog or pay the car payment."

"People are amazing." She kissed him again, but he wanted to say something more.

"Sometimes you got a guy who was smart enough to know anything he said, anybody who came to see him, was being recorded. Somebody who'd been in before."

Janice whispered, "Did anybody ever confess?"

"A couple of idiots said incriminating things. In all those years, just a couple."

"Sometimes I think they want to be heard. They don't care who hears it," she said. Below the building, on a cooling city street, a car screeched faintly.

"The one I liked was a guy named Hill. He was in on selling heroin, not a big dealer. Anyway, Hill had visitors all the time. On

187

Fridays and Saturdays we taped him. That's the big visitors days. On Monday I listened to the tapes." Nash rolled a little onto his back and chuckled. "Every Monday, Hill would say on the tape, 'Hi, Mr. Nash, I got one for you,' and tell a joke. Then he'd talk to whoever came to see him. Every Monday for four months, I got a joke to start the week."

"Funny ones?"

Nash wiggled his toes under the blankets, shadowy and upthrust in the lamplight drifting from the living room. "Usual con crap. A couple were okay. I used them at office luncheons," he said. "The best part was that he knew I was listening. I couldn't talk to Hill in court. Sent him to the joint for eight years, down to San Luis Obispo. But we both knew what was happening, what we had to do."

She kissed him again and her saliva tasted sweetly of the brandy. In their nights together, when the feelings of safety and closeness were strongest, he had found out little about her. Janice had been a brilliant student at Wesleyan in Connecticut, law school at Villanova. In the apartment she had brought a portable radio, put out several potted plants and photos of friends and family. She liked eggs scrambled, coffee weak, and closed her eyes at moments of passion. But Nash hardly ever thought he knew how she felt about things, and he did not want to know much more. It was sufficient that they broke some rules by being together and knew the inner game being played against the outside world.

He had never asked her if she had been Roemer's lover or if they were still lovers. The desire that powered Roemer and Janice, Nash knew, was to know everything and judge. He was a judge and he had learned too much about people. He did not want to know any more.

Later, he got out of bed, saw that it was still not dawn, walked around the dark apartment. Janice was asleep. He wondered about her life, moving from city to city, always listening and watching, filing charges, going to court. How could she bear to live in such an arid capsule?

Before they made love tonight, when they huddled closest together, the bedroom their own completely, Nash had made another of his impromptu confessions. Janice took them, sometimes commented, but often simply listened. But he thought she understood.

He had said to her, "You asked about my dad. I admire him a

lot. Everybody does. You know why I started working on the sting? Because he didn't know about it. He couldn't be told."

"I don't understand. I thought you were close."

"Oh, yeah," Nash answered. "I got involved here because I had a question."

"What is it?" Her voice was soft, she had her head propped on an elbow on the pillow.

"Who am I? What part of me is me, not what my father gave me, not being my father's son. My brother and me, growing up here, we were always Jack Nash's kids, not Dick and Tim. So we always saw things from him, through him."

"In my family," she said, "you could be as independent as you liked. I'm a lawyer. My brother Nick is a doctor. My brother Ralph's a mechanic. My youngest brother lives in a hut in Peru."

They both laughed. Then Nash said, "That's not me. My dad even got me my judicial appointment."

"You could have turned it down."

"No. I couldn't. Turns out I like being a judge."

"Having a lot of choices isn't always the greatest thing in the world, Tim," she said.

"Well, this sting, whatever happens, how the chips fall, it's mine. I'm doing it."

Now Nash, naked, tired but relaxed, walked through the dark apartment's living room. He thought in a little while he would shower, dress, go to the courthouse early, and review the probation reports and sentencings coming up. He could even get a quick breakfast in the cafeteria. Then the trial started again, Soika growing more restive each day, the weight of evidence upon him as the exhibits piled up on Vi's desk. Then he would see Kalbacher or Peatling at the Cypress or in his car. A recording system had been installed in the car, too, activated when he turned the wiper switch. He suggested it to prevent another situation like Atchley.

There was no time limit or boundary on the sting. It could enmesh anyone.

Reflexively, Nash began poking through papers on Janice's desk, ghostly hued in the moonlight through open curtains. Memos from Roemer on Justice Department stationery. Photos of Nash and Vismara. Photos of the judges, on the sidewalk in front of the courthouse, Wisot with Jardine, Croncota getting his shoes shined across the street, Miyazumi scowling into a store window. Someone had written on the photo "armed" and underlined it.

Nash sat down, the chair fabric on his skin. The files smelled lightly of Janice's perfume. It was too dim to read the memos. He could just make out the pictures. It was like when he was a kid, sneaking into the kitchen after everyone was sleeping, stealing a piece of his mother's vanilla cake.

In a separate pile of photos he came on ones of his father with Roemer, with Roemer and Janice under a willow tree at Garfield Park two blocks from Jack Nash's ugly new home. It was a series of pictures, Jack sitting on a park bench, ducks at his feet, smoking his Camel, mouthing something to Janice. Directly to her, Nash saw. Then Roemer sitting beside Jack Nash on the bench, legs out, as if they were simply chatting. But it was his father's posture that struck Nash. Jack Nash sat with his hands clasped between his legs, head lowered, while Janice stood at his side, sympathetically looking down at him.

There was no doubt about the tableau. Nash had seen defendants in court like that. Evan Soika sat like that sometimes between Escobar and Duryea when he heard testimony that damned him.

Clipped to the last photo was a slip of paper. Even in the faintness between night and dawn, Nash knew his father's handwriting. It was his phone number at home.

Nash took the picture and the slip into the bedroom. He wanted to be calm. His bare feet were cold on the space between the rugs in the living room and the bedroom. He stood looking at Janice sleeping. She had both arms at her sides, her breathing slow. The covers were bunched at her feet, kicked off. Only a double sheet covered her.

Nash sat down on the side of the bed, back to her. A siren lazily spun through the silent, late-night streets below him, and he held the picture of his father and Janice and wondered what to do.

He shook her slowly until her eyes opened. He snapped on the gold-stemmed lamp beside the bed. He put the picture on her belly.

"What's this?" he asked.

She yawned, glanced at it. "You know who it is."

"You told me you'd never met my father. You've got a surveillance camera on him. You've got his home phone. What's going on?"

Janice put the picture on her side of the floor. She lay back on the pillow. "I forgot, Tim. It's been so busy the last couple of weeks."

"When did you talk to him?"

"I don't know. Three or four weeks ago. It was a courtesy call Neil and I made."

"He never mentioned it. You didn't. Neither did Roemer." Nash felt chilled and he wanted to stop asking questions. "You lied to me tonight."

"No I didn't. I forgot. It was an honest piece of forgetfulness."

"You didn't forget."

She sighed. "I can't keep repeating it, Tim."

"Tell me what you talked about."

"Nothing. Pleasantries. Introducing ourselves. Why we were in Santa Maria."

"My father knows about the sting?"

Janice nodded. "In rough outline. No details. No names."

"Did he know you were coming to me?"

She sighed again and he thought it was a silent reproof to her own untidiness, leaving things out where they could be found, not regret. "I don't think we talked about anything so specific. It was just a plain and simple courtesy call."

"My father doesn't know I'm working for Roemer? Right?"

"I don't think so."

Nash looked at her. She probably was not very good in trial. Janice had no knack for composing her face. Bad news upset her too obviously and the jury would see it. So would the defense attorney, who would come back again and again to the weak point she revealed.

"I want the truth, Janice. Tell me what you talked about. He's not happy in those pictures."

"You saw the others?"

He nodded.

"I should've put everything away. Neil hates sloppiness. He's going to hate this," she said. "He had a secretary at Justice fired because she didn't shred a menu an FBI agent brought her back from lunch. Neil doesn't want people even knowing where agents working for him eat. It's very hard to fire a civil service employee like a secretary, Tim." She smiled ruefully.

"I'll talk to my dad," Nash said, getting up, putting on his clothes.

"Don't be mad. You don't need to be. I forgot and it's nothing."

"I'll ask him." Nash bent to his shoes. Already the apartment had sullenly closed to him, the bluish dawn glazed. "He can tell me."

"I wish you'd trust me," she said quietly.

"It's hard right now." He looked for his coat. "Are there any tapes? Did you get him on tape?"

"No. Just pictures. Neil likes to memorialize everything in an operation, even casual contacts. But pictures were enough."

"Yeah, they were." Nash stood over her in the frosty lamplight, her foot partway out of the sheets, vulnerable, and he wondered whether any of the world in that dawn was left intact at all.

For a long time after he came in, Louis wouldn't stop groaning. Mindy thought he had been acting strangely all day, going to church, getting a holster and then a gun, bragging a lot. But when he came home, he was dirty, his shirt torn, and his face swollen red, the lower half meaty looking.

He wouldn't talk to her. Painfully, he took off his coat. He was so fussy about that coat, always hanging it up, smoothing it. It was now ragged in several places and filthy, like he'd been dragged over the ground. He didn't have the holster or gun either, and his right eye was so bloody he could barely see her.

She made him sit in the bathtub and wash. It was sad the way the water turned gray, then streaked with red as he washed. He groaned a lot, but he wouldn't go to the hospital. She sat with him, washing his side when he couldn't turn, and she saw the blue-green bruise already forming there, like a huge force had slammed him down. As she washed, Mindy spoke gently to Louis, and he hung his head, clasped his arms around his small shoulders, as if he were trying to hide from an implacable gaze.

She'd known him for three months. They'd met at the California Bar, down near Río Consumnes Street. They danced, he had some good coke, and he acted as if he were important. She moved in with him later. This house on Magnolia Drive surprised her. All the furniture was rented, the place so new it hardly had any cracks, and the neighborhood was cloistered almost, neat houses with neat people out watering their lawns or fixing their boats. It was not the kind of place Louis belonged in and he said so. He hinted to her it was all rented, house, car, furniture, even "my life" he joked. The only thing he did that was really strange was go to Mass every Sunday. She stayed at home after going the first time, getting bored with all the guitar playing and singing, and the phony hugs people gave her for no reason. Louis said he had a lot of time to fill in. But today was the first time he had gone to church in the middle of the week.

She dried him off, gave him some Darvocet she had left over from a tooth extraction, and put him to bed. Louis didn't drink, he didn't talk about where he sold dope or to who or anything. But he liked to hint he knew important people. In the morning at breakfast he sometimes held the newspaper up, pointed at some famous guy, and said, "Yeah. He picks his fingernails when you talk to him," or "His wife's still wearing red slippers around the house," like he knew everything about these people. But they never had guests over. Mostly Louis and she went out, dancing, she drank, dinner. She tried talking to a neighbor, Mrs. Rechammer in the house two down. But that lady was so stuck-up, she just went back into her house and closed the door, leaving her gardening stuff out.

About an hour after she put Louis to bed, Mindy got up and got him some ice wrapped in a washcloth for his face. Then she got a hot-water bottle, filled it with ice and cold water, and laid it on the bed for him to put his bruised side on. He groaned all the time and he wouldn't tell her what happened. The car was okay, so it wasn't a crash or anything. She assumed a dope deal had gone bad and he'd gotten beaten up. She tried telling him it was okay, nothing to be ashamed of.

Louis groaned again. "They took my gun. They say they going to send me back to the joint." He groaned again.

"Who says?"

"Who you think? Who sends you to the joint, fucks up you life, you plans, whatever you doing?"

Mindy nodded sympathetically. "Cops do this to you?"

Louis groaned again, his eyes closed.

"They can't do that."

Louis tried to laugh when she said that, but it hurt too much and he groaned again. He wouldn't talk to her for a long time, just sort of curled up, breathing lightly. After a while, when she got tired of sitting in the crispy clean living room watching TV turned real low so it wouldn't bother Louis, Mindy came into the bedroom. She listened. Sleeping. And groaning. Carefully she got into bed. Poor guy, she thought. Poor guy.

She must have fallen asleep herself. When she opened her eyes again, it was still night, maybe four or five. Louis was sitting, naked, on the edge of the bed. He was bent over, shaking. He was crying.

Mindy was terribly embarrassed. He had his own sense of dignity. He hated being made fun of, treated like he was something small and foolish. So she didn't want to console him or ask what was wrong. She thought it would hurt him more. So she just lay there, pretending to sleep, listening to him softly crying in the dark, sitting on the edge of the bed, the moonlight on the knobby bumps of his spine.

Mindy dozed again, jerking awake when she heard Louis on the phone in the living room. He spoke quietly, but in the dense silence before dawn, in the still house on that neat, quiet street, his voice was impossible to conceal.

She heard him say, "I know it's late. Excuse me, Mr. Roemer, all right? I apologize to you, whatever you want," but he wasn't sounding at all contrite, merely sarcastic. "Look, Mr. Roemer," she heard him say intensely, "you know I'm keeping my eyes open, I been watching out, I been listening while we working. So tonight after we take care of that lady judge, I run into something you'd like to know about."

Pause, obviously Louis listening to the other man talking. Mindy held her breath to hear better.

Louis went on. "Okay. Okay. So here's what it is, Mr. Roemer. I got some more targets we got to work on, like you say. I got a couple of fucking rotten cops, they're taking money. . . . Yeah. Local cops named Valles, Witwer. . . . Yeah. I could get them ready for you."

Mindy desperately wanted to ask Louis what was going on. But she knew he would not tell her.

27

NASH SAID AFTER THE MORNING BREAK, "THE RECORD WILL REFLECT all parties present, jury present, counsel, and Mr. Soika. You may resume your examination, Mr. Benisek."

Benisek shuffled several papers and cleared his throat laconically. Get going, Nash thought. On the witness stand, the Santa Maria cop who test-fired the shotgun cleared his throat, too. The jury was alert, several of them so comfortable about being in a courtroom, they only wore the most casual clothes now.

Nash had tried to get hold of his father twice before court. He did not want to talk to his mother yet. Whatever had been said to Jack Nash might only be ephemeral, as Janice claimed.

But the pictures, he kept thinking. Roemer went to the trouble of getting the meeting down on film. He did not believe there were no tapes, no matter what Janice told him.

Benisek said, "Officer Larkin, after you fired the shotgun, People's Number Five for identification, did you recover the spent shell?"

The cop, a young, athletic man in a suit, nodded, staring at Benisek. Nash didn't think he'd been in court before. "I got it out of the test chamber. I also saved the shell casing. I put my name and badge number on both of them."

Escobar sighed, looked to the ceiling, at the jury, at Nash. Soika, dressed in a stiffly pressed white shirt, regarded the cop sullenly. His attorney waved a languid hand. "I'll stipulate to all of this. I said so. I said we agreed the bullet from that shotgun"—he pointed at the gun on Vi's desk—"was the one that killed Mr. Prentice. All right?"

"He's got a right to put on his case, Mr. Escobar," Nash said.

"But I'm willing to save us all some time. So we can get to the real issue for the jury."

"Your Honor," Benisek said, "I don't want Mr. Escobar talking to the jury."

"You're doing it," Nash said. The jurors chuckled slightly. "Go on with your examination," he directed Benisek. It was hard to listen to this mechanical side of a trial and think about what else was happening.

Escobar sighed again. I tried, he seemed to say wistfully to the jurors. Soika shook off Cindy Duryea's soothing, patting hand. Nash had brought in two more bailiffs, at the back of the courtroom, in addition to Shea and Soika's regular deputy sheriff. There was a sense of impending trouble. Soika wouldn't talk to Escobar and he grumbled constantly, sometimes talking loudly enough for the jury to hear. Nash ordered him to be quiet. He told Escobar Soika would be removed if there was another outburst, and things quieted. But it was not calm.

Benisek finished with his witness. The shells and casings he test-fired were entered into evidence.

Escobar got up, buttoned his coat. "Tell me, when you pulled the trigger, was it hard to do?"

"Sir?"

"Was it difficult to fire that shotgun?"

The young cop shook his head. "I didn't notice."

"In your report"—Escobar held a one-page document up by its corner—"would you note down irregularities like a hard pull on a trigger?"

"Probably so."

Nash wondered what the point of this was and why Benisek was letting Escobar go on. I've got other problems, he thought. Like tonight, meeting with Ruth Frenkel's clerk, then a wild card, a newly elected member of the county Board of Supervisors. Back-to-back stings and I don't know what's going on with my own family.

"How about a hair trigger? Would you write down that such and such a weapon has a hair trigger?" Escobar asked the cop.

"If I noticed it."

"May I approach the witness, Your Honor?"

Nash nodded. "Go ahead."

Escobar slid from the counsel table and picked up the sawed-off shotgun. Vi stamped a form and frowned at him. The bailiffs and Shea tensed. They were ready to jump on Soika if the shotgun came anywhere near him.

But Escobar, walking lightly on his small feet, easy and confident, handed the shotgun to the witness. "Try the trigger now."

The young cop held the shotgun, looked at Benisek for advice, then shrugged and pulled the trigger. Nash heard the small, irrevocable, useless click. The jury was still, their faces on the gun that had killed.

"Hard to pull?" Escobar asked, taking the shotgun.

"Not really."

"Easy?"

"I didn't notice anything unusual."

"Isn't it true, Officer, that this shotgun is much, much easier to fire than other similar weapons?"

Benisek rose. "Objection. He's not here as a weapons expert."

"The prosecution's own witness, Your Honor. An experienced police officer here telling us all about test-firings," Escobar said, still holding the shotgun.

"Overruled. It's within his experience," Nash said, although the young cop didn't look experienced enough to find a parking place at the courthouse.

Escobar smiled. "It is easier to pull the trigger on this weapon, isn't it?"

"No."

"Did you test what amount of pressure was needed to pull this trigger?"

"No. I was only asked to get some test-firings for ballistic comparison."

"The police had the weapon in their sole possession," Escobar said, holding the gun aloft, "and didn't want to know if it could fire accidentally?"

"That's improper, Mr. Escobar," Nash said.

"Evan Soika says the victim shot himself when the shotgun discharged on its own. The police were shooting and the gun went off," Escobar said.

"Strike those comments," Nash directed the court reporter. "You're here to question the witness, not make a speech. Save that for your closing argument."

Soika half-stood, his deputy sheriff instantly pushing him down. But he yelled, "That's what happened. It went off. I didn't do anything. I didn't even have it. It just went off."

Nash said, "Sit down, Mr. Soika. Mr. Escobar, control your client. I'm not going to have any disruptions. I've warned you."

"I apologize to the court on behalf of Mr. Soika." Escobar sat down calmly, a tight smile on his face. He looked at Nash. "Accidents do happen, Your Honor. And that gun went off accidentally."

"Objection," Benisek said, standing up, picking up the shotgun dramatically. "This gun could not go off accidentally."

Before Nash could tell him to sit down, or quiet the still-upset Soika, the shotgun in Benisek's hand made another audible click, as it had when Escobar made the witness pull the trigger. Soika grinned, sat back, and Benisek hastily put the shotgun on Vi's desk, retreating to the counsel table.

Nash knew the jury was fastened on the shotgun. They would have a wonderful time in the jury room playing with it, making that inadvertent operation of hammer hitting into the barrel.

Benisek might have just lost his case. Luck. Arrogance, Nash thought, Escobar with a triumphant expression on his face.

Vi regarded the shotgun on her desk, beside her left arm, as if it were a serpent.

Nash heard Benisek ask frantic questions on redirect.

Like finding the photos last night or whatever had happened to involve his father, Nash thought: accidents do happen. They have great consequences.

28

THE WEEK ENDED, CLOUD DARKENED AND COOLER SUDDENLY, AND Nash hadn't been able to talk to his father. He saw Janice only twice, each time after he met with a target. The row of tapes, video and audio, in Testa's hidden control room, was growing. On tape now was Del Howard, most junior member of the Board of Supervisors. They had met, sat, talked, in Nash's car, parked outside the Way- farer Motor Inn, in a nest of gas stations and freeway intersections, under mercury lights that made the asphalt glow black. Howard was only forty, worked in his family construction business, and put up ugly single-story houses in the south end of Santa Maria.

Across the parking lot, with a clear view, sat Jacobs and Sanchez and their cameras, wide angle, telephoto, high-speed film. They even had an infrared film in case Nash and his target got into an unlit place.

Howard had heard of Nash, his father. He took the envelope with the first payment of money from Nash. "I always heard this was how it's done. Late night in a parking lot."

Vismara sat in the backseat, almost silent. He had on bandages. He would not tell Nash or Janice what had happened, but said it had nothing to do with the operation.

"Who's your friend in the DA's office?" Nash asked.

"Joe Perpich. Do you know him?"

"Used to. He's a supervisor now, I think."

"Oh, yeah. He does their special investigations. He'll take care of your problem." Young Howard glanced back at Vismara.

"How about the four of us get together soon?" Nash probed. "So nobody misunderstands. There're a couple of places we could get our signals crossed, case getting out of the DA's office, the probation violation, things like that."

"Joe wants to stay in the background. Just him and me."

"You got a routine?"

Howard smirked. In the car he reminded Nash of a kid who had gone to college, all costs paid, had a new car every year from his parents, then went with insouciant ease into his family business and used the name to run for office. Like me, Nash thought. It could be me. He thought of what Janice had said their first night together. No one knew, until it was offered, if he'd take the bribe.

"I think we can start a new pipeline here," young Howard said. "There've got to be a lot of guys who come through the court, they need some help." He looked back for agreement from Vismara.

"Every day," Nash said. "They can't make bail or something."

"See? You've got a great business opportunity here. You get the bail up high, they can't make it, we step in with our service. For a fee."

They shook hands. Nash and Vismara let Howard go to his own car, the only other one in the lot, except for the discreetly placed FBI car. He honked once on his way out, like a college kid out for a forbidden drink.

Nash sat back bitterly. The FBI car drew alongside. Vismara leaned forward. "Fucking punk. They get him inside, he going to be punking for somebody in ten minutes. I bet you."

Nash said aloud, "He doesn't know Joe Perpich. He can't have him on the line. Joe wouldn't go for it. I know him." He hoped it was so.

Vismara swore. "So what? Look, Judge, you got to be realistic. We going to nail him if we want."

Nash looked up as Jacobs leaned out of his window. "We're all set for the night, you guys. You want to get a drink before we head back to the barn?"

Nash did not know when the cameras went off or the recorders stopped turning. If he did not follow the most direct path each time after an interview, he wondered if it would be noted and used later. He shook his head. "That's it for me."

"Me, too," Vismara said curtly. "I got to get my rest for those cops tomorrow."

A name dropped carelessly tonight, one of Nash's old acquaintances in the DA's office, and something would have to be done. Perpich investigated, checked out, even a recorded meeting set up to see if he really was bought. Nash hoped the two undercover cops Vismara said tried to shake him down were clean. They were meeting tomorrow night, and Nash found it harder to trust anyone.

They drove away separately to the hotel, and Nash did not see Janice afterward that night.

On the dais set up in the Johnson High School gym, Frank Wisot spoke. He had on his half-glasses. Nash enjoyed Frank's practicing the unaffected affectation of pushing the glasses up his nose when he spoke in public, grinning boyishly. Beside him sat Lenore, his wife, who had just finished speaking. Nash stood at the back of the gym. Folding metal chairs had been set up on the floor, and the men and women in them were parents, neighbors, the kind of people Nash saw daily on his juries. They clapped politely. They listened as if everything were important, and even if it wasn't. Courtesy required their appearance of attentiveness.

Wisot was in a tweed coat because the weather had become noticeably autumnal. It was midafternoon; Benisek had run out of witnesses early and Nash had to see Wisot.

"Lenore and I did not make a great contribution," Wisot said, pushing up his glasses. "But naming the new science center after us will make my grandchildren, once my daughters get out of grad school, very happy."

Applause. Lenore smiled. Behind them and the school's staff on the crowded dais, was a banner, JOHNSON HIGH SCHOOL GROWTH FUND, and a huge $200,000 and exclamation points.

Nash went to Wisot and Lenore when the dedication ceremony broke up a few minutes later. Paper plates of home-baked cookies and fruit salad circulated in the crowd.

"Surprise," Wisot said when Nash came to him.

"Hello, Tim," Lenore said. She held a plate of brownies and offered it to him. "Are we going for cocktails after this?"

"Actually, I wanted to invite you to a picnic Saturday at Mason Park."

"I love picnics," Wisot said. He had his arm around Lenore. She was a little taller than him, with a long, lineless face. "What time? Don't ask us to bring anything."

"I was thinking of noon. We can meet at Founder's Oak."

"You bringing somebody?" Wisot asked.

"Same woman you met at Harold's deal."

"Very nice, very nice." Wisot chewed a thick brownie. Several people stopped by to thank him for all the phone calls, meetings, late nights, to raise money for the school's new buildings. "You should have stayed in town for high school," Wisot said.

"Frank and I met at the first freshman dance," Lenore said. "Now it's forty-five years later and we're still in the same high school."

"I liked going away to private school. I appreciated Santa Maria a lot more," Nash said.

"God, look at this. I must go to every alumni dinner. I help with the new building. You'd think I liked this place."

Nash and Wisot's wife laughed. The mixed voices and other laughter in the gym had a carefree, light sound. It lasted for Nash until Wisot wiped his hands, grinned again at the people, and said, "Did the telephone company show up in your chambers yesterday?"

"No."

"They came by everybody on the fourth floor. Fiddled with my phone. Went down and fooled with Henshaw's, Susanna's, Fred's. I couldn't call out for a couple of hours. The good part was nobody could call in."

"What was wrong?"

"I don't know," Wisot said. "Gremlins in the line. Upgrading the courthouse phones. So be warned. They said they're hitting everybody pretty soon."

"They haven't gotten to my floor yet," Nash said. He didn't want to stay around Frank or Lenore suddenly, as if they both had become contagious.

"I complained to Terry. But you know, he says, don't bug me, Frank. I'm not going to be PJ anymore. So bug Ruth about it."

Nash imagined the tape machines, all working hour after hour now, whenever the phones were lifted in every judge's chambers. Testa's techs would have left mikes around the chambers, too. Nothing would escape.

"I'll see you Saturday," Nash said to Frank and Lenore.

"We'll bring some bean salad, I think," she said.

The invitation had been decided upon three nights ago at the Cypress Hotel by him and Janice and Roemer on a phone call. "Time for the old guys, see how they jump," Roemer said. "This one's going to make a big splash when he goes down."

Nash, that night from his own apartment, called his father. He sat on the floor in his bedroom, the phone beside him. When he finished dialing, he turned off the light, the receiver pressed painfully to his ear.

His father's voice was sleep heavy. Nash pictured him holding the phone to avoid waking Hilary. The phone was by Jack's side of the bed.

"Tim? Something's wrong?" Jack Nash said softly, thickly.

"No, Dad. Nothing's wrong."

"For Christ sake, it's so late. It's past three."

"I'm sorry. I wanted to say hello."

"There's something wrong."

"No," Nash said a little too fast. "I couldn't sleep." What do I ask him? he wondered frantically. How do I ask him about the pictures, the way he looked? How can I ask him what he was hiding?

"Couldn't sleep?" Jack Nash repeated wearily. "Lord, Lord, Timmy, you've got to stop letting these trials get to you."

"Yeah, you're right," he said, thankful his father had seized on the wrong thing so readily. "You know, Kim's not here, first time during a major trial. Death-penalty case."

"Yeah, yeah," his father said softly. "I understand."

"You have any words of wisdom?"

"Have a beer or a glass of milk and go back to bed."

Nash held the receiver more tightly. "Couple trials kept you up, I remember."

"One or two. They weren't capital cases." His father chuckled. "I slept like a log on them. Figure that out."

Nash knew he couldn't thrust a bare accusation or even a baseless question at his father. Not in the night. It was cowardly and he was too frightened himself to ask one. He wanted to run from the knowledge. "Maybe I should try sleeping again," he said.

"That's what we both should do."

"I'll talk to you soon. Sorry I got you up."

Jack Nash coughed faintly. "You're the judge, Timmy. You're in charge. That'll help you sleep."

Nash sat on the floor, in the dark, after hanging up.

29

Lᴏᴜɪs? Gᴇᴛ ᴜs sᴏᴍᴇ ᴍᴏʀᴇ ᴘᴏᴘᴄᴏʀɴ, ᴏᴋᴀʏ?" Vᴀʟʟᴇs ʜᴇʟᴅ ᴏᴜᴛ ᴀ small wicker basket.

Vismara pushed it away. "You go get it."

"Come on, Louis. Just do it." Valles sounded peeved.

Nash and Vismara sat on one side of the wood-backed booth in the Marina Bar, Valles and Witwer on the other. It was nearly ten at night, the regulars spaced around the small room, the TV over the bar glowing colorfully, sound down, a Beatles tune thumping from speakers, and a small woman standing still except for her thrusting hips, alone on the tiny stage.

"They got a great lingerie show on Tuesdays. They do a lunch preview," Witwer said, noticing Nash watching the woman with feigned indifference. A beer sign, in neon, enclosed a clock over the bar. Outside, the agitated river lapped against the building, which sat on weathered pilings over the water.

"I'll go." Witwer took the basket to the popcorn in large bags on the bar, scooping handfuls up.

Nash caught the woman wiping her nose whenever the music allowed her a slight pause. She swung her arms ungracefully.

"What do you want?" Nash asked Valles sharply. "Louis says you made demands."

"Got you here."

The music rose abruptly. "What?"

"I said, it sure as shit got you out here late at night," Valles replied, Witwer sliding back alongside him, passing the popcorn to him.

"They want to make a deal." Vismara wasn't nervous tonight, Nash saw; he was cold and hard.

"I'm surprised it was you guys."

"Hey"—Witwer chewed on a handful of popcorn—"think how I

203

felt, Judge. You could've knocked me over, I find out you and Louis are working things together.''

"What?" Nash shook his head because he couldn't hear. He leaned forward.

"I said, Louis here's getting a boost from you in your court, right?" Witwer repeated. He had slicked his beard and hair back, tied the hair with a rubber band into a small ponytail. Nash wore a sport coat over a blue shirt, and Vismara was neatly dressed as always, his recent cuts freshly bandaged.

"I thought you'd enjoy a night out, like we talked about that day we came in with the search warrant?" Valles said. "But let's cut it."

"What do you want?" Nash asked. Parked on the levee road were Jacobs, an out-of-state FBI agent, and Testa, in the IRS-loaned blue van and its complex interior of electronic equipment. On Vismara's coat, threaded into his lapel, were two sensitive microphones. "So they don't have to talk into your belly button," Testa had cheerfully explained as he dressed Vismara for the occasion. The FBI men were sitting in the van, lit by a reddish dull glow, eating boiled crawdads with their fingers, the specialty of the bar.

"We want five thousand dollars"—Valles made a dollar sign in the air—"and you and Louis can go on doing whatever you're doing together. We don't care."

"Five thousand? For both of you? That's all?"

"That's it. We ain't coming back," Valles said. He ate more popcorn. The small woman stopped moving, bowed slightly, and left the tiny stage. Another woman, in a beige, billowy blouse, stepped up, waited for the beat, and started shuffling her feet. Two men in Peterbilt caps at the bar watched intently and clapped.

"I would like to pay them," Vismara said to Nash.

"I think it's a bad idea." Nash wanted to make Valles and his partner talk. The more involved an explanation was on tape, the better it would sound at trial. "It's open-ended."

"Hey, we're in the same business, Judge. We both been doing the same things, taking care of things," Valles said. He had a grim, almost happy look, and he kept teasing Vismara, ordering him around. "Louis probably told you we pulled a .38 off of him the other night. I still got it. We can squeeze him anytime."

"He didn't tell me." Nash looked at Vismara.

"It was my own business, nobody else, just me, what I'm doing," Vismara said. Since the fight he'd been in, he had become much less talkative, more abrasive.

"You beat him up," Nash said to Valles.

"Louis, did we beat you up? Did I ever hit you? You know, maybe a playful little tap"—Valles lightly touched Vismara's arm on the scored tabletop—"but I wouldn't hit him."

"It's not right," Witwer agreed. He kept checking his watch. He tapped Valles. "Time."

"We got to go, Judge. We got a deal with some other cops cooking. Maybe we'll be in your courtroom this week, another warrant coming through. So what're you going to do?"

Nash felt Vismara's radiating hatred. For his own reasons, he wasn't being truthful, and this concerned Nash very much. It was as disconcerting as sitting opposite cops he had worked with and being shaken down. He wondered what the FBI agents outside were saying as they listened.

"I don't want you coming back to me," Nash said. "I want this transaction to be our final one."

"Time will tell, Judge," Valles said. "You should know we got pictures of you and Louis here going into the Cypress Hotel. So we can put you both together anytime."

"Time, time, Rog. We got to move," Witwer urged. He bobbed his head to the beat. The world could end, Nash thought, and an undercover cop would maintain. His carapace had become too thick to show anything other than what he wanted.

"I want to make those pictures part of the arrangement," Nash said. He wondered why these undercover cops had been at the Cypress. Janice or Roemer had known nothing about it.

"Okay. I don't need them," Valles said. "I got the gun and that's enough. For ten thousand, you can have the pictures of you and Louis, okay? That's fair."

Vismara nodded. He had stared at Valles for the whole meeting. "Would you like a down payment?"

Valles shrugged. It bored him, he seemed to say. He glanced off at the dancer. She rolled her head and someone turned up the TV on a sitcom. Nash took out the envelope. "I brought two thousand dollars with me. We'll have to make the final payment in a few days."

"How about Monday, same time, same channel?" Witwer suggested. "You know, this's a decent place."

"All right. So we're all clear. For the remainder of the money, you two will give Mr. Vismara and me any pictures, negatives, of us. You won't make any reports or statements about possible criminal activity you believe we're engaged in."

Valles grimaced. "Christ, Judge. You make it sound like so legal."

"Is that what you agree to?"

Valles tapped the envelope on the table. "Okay. Sure."

Vismara sat back, a small smile of satisfaction on his face. "I don't want to be hassled by you guys again."

"See you, Judge. See you, Louis," Valles said. He and Witwer left the booth, calling out to the dancer. She waved at them.

For a moment, Vismara and Nash sat silently. "Cops. I hate seeing cops do that." Nash shook his head in disgust.

"They bad cops, Judge. They don't do what's right. It's right to get them," Vismara said, straightening his tie slightly. He patted his handkerchief.

Valles drove halfway down the levee road, stopped. Witwer complained, made a face, and lifted his shirt. The Fargo tape recorder and mike taped to his hairy chest made him look mechanical.

"Fuck it, Rog, the damn tape's stuck in my hair. I thought I was going nuts, I wanted to scratch it so bad. That's why I got up for the damn popcorn. I scratched like a son of a bitch when I was up."

Valles gently unhooked the tape and let Witwer gingerly pull the dull metal recorder off his chest, peeling hairs as he did so. Crickets loudly burred in the tall river grass along the road. Behind them, in a merry blaze of pearly-light globes, the Marina Bar advertised DANCING, DRINKING, DINING.

"Got him. Got a judge selling out." Valles held the tape cassette.

"You want to book it in tonight?"

"I'm keeping it tonight. I don't want Shiffley or anybody getting near our evidence again," Valles swore. He started the car while Witwer stuffed his shirt back in his pants. "Tomorrow I'm calling a pal in Sacramento in the state AG's office. Tell him I got a crooked judge and a puke on tape bribing me."

"Let me hold the money once," Witwer said. "I want to pretend Maggie and me could take a vacation to Mazatlán or pay some bills."

30

Nash picked up Janice and they drove to Mason Park. Saturday was a lingering summer day, the trees in the park changing color and looking out of place in the sunlight.

They arrived before Wisot and Lenore and staked a claim to a table and barbecue on a hillock up from the man-made lake in the park's center.

They unpacked the chicken she'd made, potato salad he'd bought, beer, and coffee, setting up on the weathered picnic table. Kids threw Frisbees around them, couples strolled, and the ducks made impetuous and querulous noises.

Under his thin wool coat, frayed cuffs reminding Nash he'd worn it since college, was a small microphone. Nash thought he owed Wisot the chance to refuse a bribe without Vismara around. It was between them. Even if the FBI agents listened in.

"I called my dad the other night," Nash said, putting down the plates.

"Any resolutions?" Janice paused. Her gray eyes were darker in the autumn light. She wouldn't say anything compromising, he thought. The agents were probably tuned in already.

"No," Nash said. "I couldn't ask him."

"Why not?"

"I couldn't," he said simply. "Maybe I'll figure out a way to do it."

"I've already explained it to you. There isn't anything more."

Nash didn't answer. He couldn't, and they were both too conscious of being overheard. He wanted to say something about their last night together.

He squinted off toward the lake, then pointed at a small outcropping of uncontoured land that dropped sharply to the sloping grass at one end of the park. He had to talk to her, bring her closer, even if he couldn't speak freely. "That's where Arkansas Avenue ends. The summer I was fourteen, my brother, Dick, was about eight. I wanted to show off. So I jumped off, figured I'd land on the grass."

"You're joking." Janice looked at the height of the hill.

"Broke my right arm. I had a swell cast for a couple of months."

"You learned a lesson about showing off, I hope."

"Would you have stopped me?" He looked at her seriously.

Janice put her hand on his. Too far probably for the agents to see, and this expedition was strictly audio anyway. "It depends on how much it meant to you."

He saw Frank Wisot and Lenore waving, unloading a picnic hamper from their old station wagon. Wisot grunted and swung the picnic hamper onto the table when they walked up. He had on a red warm-up jacket and Lenore a blue one. Pretend it's only a picnic, make it feel more natural for us all, Nash thought.

The introductions were brief, hearty, beer passed around, the fire started with the Wisots' charcoal. It was warm enough to take off the jackets, and while the food cooked, the smell rich, languid, and invigorating, they laughed and joked. Nash sat next to Janice.

Wisot put his hands up. "I had a doc on the stand yesterday. You'll appreciate this, Janice. On the federal side you don't hear these kind of motions so often."

"But I do. I get instant replay every night," Lenore said with a smile.

"And it's always witty, pithy, full of insight," Wisot said.

"What about the doctor?" Nash asked.

"Well, it was one of these motions to suppress. We had a couple of cons from Folsom prison, and the powers that be got wind they were planning an escape, they had knives. The powers that be made the cons go through the X ray to see if they'd stashed the knives up the old kazoo." Wisot drank his beer.

"What about the doctor, Frank?" Nash persisted.

"Hold on. The essence of this motion yesterday was that the X ray was a Fourth Amendment violation of these gentlemen, seizing images inside their bodies."

Janice chuckled. "Novel."

"Stupid. I had to listen to these experts on nuclear this and that tell me how less dangerous other methods of checking for concealed weapons in body cavities are." Wisot inhaled the aroma of the chicken. "Wonderful. I'm on a low-fat, no-taste diet at home. This doc gets on the stand and he starts telling me how you can use a proctoscope to check for hidden objects. No discomfort. Then he says you could also use a sigmoidoscope and it'll cause some discomfort. I leaned over to him. I said, 'Doctor, don't you mean it would hurt?' He looked up at me. 'It would cause some discomfort, but I don't know if I'd call it pain.' This burned me. 'Doctor, don't you mean this device will hurt like hell?' He finally got my message. 'I think I hear the voice of experience.' I said, 'Damn right. I'd rather have an X ray any day. Motion denied.' "

Justice was sometimes that simple.

They ate fully, and then Nash and Janice rinsed off some of the cooking utensils at a faucet near a hiking trail. Wisot and Lenore strolled off toward the lake, hand in hand.

"I'm not going after Frank," Nash said.

"The information is good, Tim. It's got to be done."

"Not today then."

"All you have to do is set it up. We can do the actual transaction later." Janice shook the spatulas and knives, wiped her hands on her jeans.

"Look at him. He can't be dirty. I've known him a long time."

"Two lawyers say he proposed bribes in return for lesser sentences for their clients. You read the reports."

"I don't know who accused him. I'm not going to rely on anonymous informants."

Janice walked back to the table. "All you have to do is test him," she said. Nash thought she meant their relationship, too. She challenged him to let her prove herself.

"Very nice, Tim. Nice girl. Yes." Wisot watched his wife and Janice bending by the lake to feed the ducks, talking to the kids clustered on the lake's edge. "How'd you meet her again?"

"Last year's judges' conference in Monterey. I found her number again and I called her."

Wisot nodded. He had another beer, his lined face easing. They walked by a small baseball diamond and the pickup game going on, a dust cloud raised faintly, the shouting and booing good-natured. Men and women in shorts and T-shirts strove to compress summer into a final game.

"I'm sorry about this thing with you and Kim," Wisot said.

"I'm going to L.A. next week to see Ben. Clandestine meeting." Nash drank his own beer, the can sweating and warm. "Kim doesn't know."

"Oh, damn, the things that happen to us."

"It's not my choice."

"Are you going to the conference this month? Kalbacher letting you out for a field trip?" Wisot grinned. The annual judges' conference, which was held at the same location and date as the State Bar Convention, usually depleted the courthouse of judges, and the PJ was reluctant to let more than the bare minimum attend. Even so, the week when the others were gone was a frantic one for the judges who stayed in Santa Maria. There were many postponements of trials, endless delays, much cursing.

"I am going. You want to drive over together?"

"No. Lenore and me are taking a day early. Drive, sightsee, take it easy."

They paused to see a home run hit, the fat-thighed man chugging purposefully around the bases while the people standing around the diamond yelled.

"Janice and I are going together," Nash decided.

"Make it a vacation. There's nothing worth listening to."

They both laughed. About all any judge came back from the conference with were more scripts for pleas and sentencings, reflecting changes in the law since the last conference, a wicked hangover, and perhaps the lingering memory of a strenuous evening or two in a strange hotel with a strange woman.

"Atchley's gotten to be a real pain," Nash said. "He's got the election in the bag. I wish Terry or Ruth would stick him back in Traffic Court."

Wisot nodded, finished his beer. "Lenore and Janice are getting along okay. Good. Most of our friends these days seem to be people on committees. God."

Janice and Lenore Wisot were talking intently, tossing bits of bread into the greenish water.

Then Wisot said to Nash, "Speaking of old Harold. He told me a strange tale. About you."

"Me?" Nash knew what it was. He wanted to be impassive enough to shrug away whatever Frank said next, but the beer, food, being close and distant from Janice, had unsettled him.

"Yeah. Strange thing. How about you stop by my house when we're done here?"

"All right. Now you've got me in suspense. What could that asshole have said?" Nash asked lightly.

He was in confusion, wondering what Wisot was going to confront him with. Now was the moment to test Frank, but Nash hoped

Wisot would give him a way out. Maybe Frank wants to warn me. Maybe he wants to help me, Nash thought.

They got hold of a discarded Frisbee, the four of them tossing it on the grass, the warm breeze over them and the afternoon sentimental, fleeting. He felt the mike rub ticklingly on his chest when he moved. I'm a fraud, he thought, playing around with old friends. I hope to God you let me off the hook, Frank, Nash thought.

Wisot and Lenore left first, and Nash and Janice loaded their car alone.

"He wants to see me. I'll have to go alone," Nash said.

"Don't make assumptions, Tim. Make the approach, listen to him, see what happens."

"I don't assume anything anymore."

She touched his arm, warm hand on sun-heated skin where he'd pushed the sleeves up. "You can't get everyone under oath. You may not be able to tell if people are lying. Even people you respect."

Even people you love, she said with her expression. The yellowing afternoon had the mixed pleasure of a fading picture, grasped and elusive all at once. He touched her lips gently. "I'll see you tonight."

"You can give me a complete report," Janice said. He could see she wouldn't risk saying more.

"Looks like you got a little burn out there today." Frank sat back and lit a cigarette.

Nash glanced at the pink color of his arm. "Not much, Frank." Lenore had gone to change and Nash hoped she wouldn't return until he and Wisot were through. They sat in Wisot's study, a mounted bluetail on the wall, arcing as though still fighting a hook, photos of Wisot over the years and diplomas scattered all over each wall. Frank kept no such mementos or honors in his chambers at the courthouse. They were all here, to admire, but not to gloat over publicly. Nash's immediate neighbor at the courthouse, Allen Burgess, had so many plaques and certificates of award in his chambers he had stacked them against one wall.

The study was simple, book filled, dark, a few white-shaded lamps. Outside, Nash could see the backyard and Lenore's stone birdbath. They had two children, grown, living on the East Coast.

A small gold-plated clock spun its flywheel silently in the late, smoky afternoon.

Frank sat in a large, slick-covered chair, his feet up, arms folded.

"Lenore'll probably bring us something to drink. Unless you stop her," Wisot said.

"No, I'll take anything you're offering."

Wisot nodded. "You've got an interesting thing here from Atchley, Tim. He told me because he thinks I'm the oldest guy in the building, nobody cares so much what I do."

"Not true, Frank."

"Well, then I'm not a threat. I'm not running for anything. I'll be gone in a few years at the most."

"Ruth told me she's thinking of retiring. She's tired."

Wisot looked at his cigarette, got up, and stood near Nash. The shadow thrown by the blinds in the door leading to the backyard crossed his face slantwise. "So am I, Tim. Very, very tired."

A light tap, and Lenore, now in a heavy bathrobe, came in. She and Nash had known each other for so long, the informality was taken for granted. He got up, took a glass of white wine, ice-cold, from her, handed the other to Wisot. He made a face. "This is it?"

"To increase the appetite, not kill it," she said. She sat down on a chair to the right of Wisot's. He sat down again, too. Nash was dismayed. He would not be able to talk about Atchley's mischief freely now.

He took a drink of the icy wine. "We were just talking some office nonsense, Lenore," Nash explained.

She sipped her wine. "I thought you'd be talking about Harold's story by now."

Nash paused. She had not changed from the woman he had known since he was a child, played with when he was a child, sat next to at dinners and parties, comparing notes about the city and whoever was around. Kim and Lenore were fast friends. "Frank was starting to. What's Atchley saying, Frank?"

Wisot ground out the cigarette. He looked as brisk as he did during morning calendar. "You offered him a bribe. A big one."

"Why did he tell you?"

"Bragging. It showed how important he is. Who knows."

Lenore said, "Did you, Tim? Want to pay him on a case?"

"It's not important. It's between Atchley and me," Nash said tersely. The two people in front of him seemed to be melting, shifting, re-forming into something close to what had been there an hour ago, but different. He felt his gut contract.

"Well, if it's a matter of fixing a case," Wisot said, "you know, making some adjustment"—he grinned—"we can get the things transferred to my court, can't we? I mean, I can help you if Harold won't."

"Just send the whole thing to Frank," Lenore said, pulling the robe around her feet a little. "Keep it between us."

"Why? Why should you?" Nash tried to keep calm. They were different people. The clock tinkled five times, fading, sad and unnoticed.

Wisot's eyes were hard, his creased face tight. "I'm broke. I've been doing this for a lot of years and I haven't made any money and I've got to quit very soon and I don't want to work anymore. It's fairly simple."

"It's a retirement fund." Lenore smiled.

"All right, Frank." Nash finished his wine, put it down on a dog-eared *Field and Stream* magazine. Wisot had two rifles and guns locked in a cedar cabinet in the study. He went hunting in the Sierras every winter and brought back venison steaks for friends. "I'll call on Monday"—he stood up—"and we can set the thing up."

"Harold said the offer was twenty thousand from this character." Wisot frowned, forgetting the name.

"Vismara. He'll pay twenty thousand to dismiss a violation of probation."

"And you've got it covered in muni court? Or the DA's office?"

"DA's office."

"And you're all set yourself? You're provided for?"

Nash nodded. He thought of Wisot's daughters playing out in the backyard on a late-summer afternoon, or Frank and Lenore dancing a slow dance together at the high school, thinking and dreaming and then ending up here. "Vismara's got a lot of dirty money."

Lenore stood up. "Well, I think we all had a very productive afternoon."

"Drugs. My calendar's about sixty percent drug cases now," Wisot said, lighting another cigarette, staring at Nash. "The problem's right there, Tim. So much money washing through the system, so many cases, we're all going under."

"You're retiring."

Wisot grinned. "Len and I'll think of you and the dealers and their bastard lawyers every morning on our own little lake in Florida."

"Come and visit. It's a beautiful little town. No crime. No drugs.

213

Everybody talks nicely and they're nice to you," Lenore said. "We'll be right on the lake. They have beautiful sunrises."

"It does sound nice," was all Nash could think to say. His mind had become empty trying to avoid the two people sitting with him.

"I have to tell you, Tim." Wisot opened the back door, his voice fading, the mingling bird cries and close-by lawn mowers reminding Nash of when he and Dick had first come to this study. Years ago, sitting on that same old sofa, while Frank Wisot and Jack Nash swapped stories and the two sons alternately wrestled or looked through yellowing copies of *American Heritage*.

"Tell me what?" Nash asked.

"Atchley didn't surprise me." Wisot turned from the door. "You're Jack's boy."

"What does that mean, Frank?" Nash asked harshly. He wanted to hit old Frank Wisot.

Lenore strolled out leisurely. "The bird feeder looks empty," she said, heading for the stone birdbath.

"We never do things on our own," Wisot said. "Your dad made the same decision a long time ago. I'm sure he didn't tell you."

"No. He didn't. You could tell me."

"I didn't mean to upset you, Tim," and Frank Wisot looked sorrowful. "Stupid remark. I'm tired, it's late, and I haven't had dinner."

"Tell me, Frank."

Wisot's mouth turned down. "He took a chance when it came to him. It turned out badly. That's why he left Terhune and Nash."

Nash thought of the surveillance pictures Janice had taken, the way his father slumped between her and Roemer. "But what did he do, Frank? What are you talking about?"

"Christ Almighty, Tim, I don't know the details. It was a big offer and he thought he could get in on it and he lost a lot of money. Ask Dennis Terhune. He'd know the whole thing."

Nash paced the smoky, electric study, memory heavy and unfamiliar, too. "What can I ask him? What can I say?"

"No, I guess you can't just go up to Terhune," Wisot said. "God, I'm sorry I let my mouth run like that."

Lenore Wisot stood outside, green robed, her back to the house, as if she had no part in the plot they had all joined in a few minutes ago. Nash had the giddy sensation of strangers entering familiar homes, skins, clothes, choosing the moments to reveal themselves.

"Who knows about it? Not the crap floating around the courthouse, Frank. I want something concrete now."

"They had an office manager who got fired about the same time your dad left the firm. She might know how to put it together for you."

"It can't be much of anything," Nash snapped. Roemer wouldn't tell him anything more than Janice, he was certain of it. He had to look for himself. "My dad's been a judge, he's been out in public for years. You shouldn't have said anything now, Frank."

"I know. I know. I know. I'm new at this bribe business and I don't have my sea legs," Wisot said. Lenore came back, closing the door. "I don't watch my mouth," he said irritatedly.

She glanced at Frank, saw the tension. "I was going to ask you to stay for dinner," she said.

"Not tonight, thanks," Nash said sadly.

"We're just having potluck. You won't miss anything," she said. "It was good seeing you again." She leaned to him for the obligatory courtesy kiss on the cheek, which she had gotten for nearly thirty years. Her cheek was cool, redolent of talc. He would never have anticipated this nonchalance from her.

"Do you remember the name of the office manager at my dad's firm, the one who got fired about the same time he left?" Nash drew his face from Lenore Wisot.

She frowned slightly. Brightening, she said, "Lynn Holiday. Halliday. Holloway. Something like that."

Frank Wisot smiled and shook his head. "In twenty-five years plus, this woman's never forgotten any name or anybody in this city."

Nash and Janice ate an early dinner on the small balcony of her apartment. More paper plates, chicken bones, paper cups of wine, scraps of lettuce, potato. The metal-ribbed chairs were hard.

"You were right about Wisot," Nash said. He pulled his chair near hers.

"Did you make a date?"

"Monday. I'll make it all neat and clear for the camera."

"It has to be done, Tim. You knew things like this would happen from the beginning."

"It still hurts."

"I'm sorry for that."

They cleaned up, threw the remnants of dinner away. It was a long time before either of them touched. Then the embrace seemed to go on for hours, as if neither felt able to release the other. "If I didn't leave after the operation was over . . . ," Janice said, the question unfinished, unanswered. They went to bed early, too, and she didn't talk about it again, but he knew what she wanted to hear. Would they stay together? Could they remain untouched by the winds that were going to blow after the arrests and trials of so many people Nash knew, who knew him, trusted him?

His head was heavy on the pillow. Janice whispered to him. He wasn't going to ask her again for the meaning of the pictures, his father, her. It was no longer a matter of words or stories. She could say anything, good or bad, a lie or truth, but Nash needed to hold some paper in his hand, see some note or hear some testimony. Like a trial, he thought.

We judges turn the world into a trial. We want to hand out justice.

So we yearn for truth.

31

VALLES AND WITWER TOLD THEIR SUPERVISOR SHIFFLEY THEY WOULD be out of touch most of the day working on a deal with the Misfit bikers. "They're dealing crank out of this house on Mesa Boulevard," Witwer explained. "It's under the freeway. Got to work our way in with these guys."

Then the two men drove for an hour and a half to Sacramento and went downtown to the mustard-colored, six-story building on K Street where the California attorney general had some of his offices. Witwer had trouble finding a place to park. They were twenty minutes late for their appointment with an assistant attorney general.

When they did get into the building, past the security station, up the elevator, escorted down a thin-red-carpeted hall, the assistant attorney general listened to them quietly. He was a tall, carefully dressed man. His office was gray-blue and neat. He had a clear desk and hanging ferns. He listened to the tape Valles had made, grimacing at the hissing, distorted quality.

"I heard it," the assistant attorney general finally said. "I heard him say it."

"We're going back for the second installment." Valles squirmed a little excitedly in his chair. "Two days from now."

"I'd like that taped, too."

"No problem."

"I could get some shots maybe," Witwer said. "We could do it outside."

The assistant attorney general was a middle-aged, thoughtful man. He tapped his lip. "Yes. I would like photos. Color if you can."

"Sure. I can do that."

"And you haven't involved anyone else in your department?"

Valles shook his head. "Like I told you, sir, I'm afraid my supervisor's in on it. I think the Sheriff's Department may be in it."

"It's possible. Can you forward the arrest reports and any documentation you've got on this Vismara asshole?"

Valles and Witwer nodded. They both liked the assistant attorney general. He wasted no time. He did not talk pointlessly or boastfully.

"The Attorney General's Office is going to pick this investigation up, guys," the assistant attorney general said. "You both will be under my supervision from now until the end of the investigation."

"All right." Valles glanced at Witwer. "We want to straighten it all out, sir. Jerry and I've been cops for a while, we've done good work, and we don't want to get screwed by some bad guys."

"I know your records," the assistant attorney general said. "I know you're good cops."

"Thank you, sir." Witwer had worn a suit and he looked—bearded, small eyed, his hair long—like a refugee from another age going to church.

"Since you are good cops, you don't have anything you want to tell me, do you?"

"About what?" Valles asked.

"I don't want to find out anything you could have told me about this situation, guys. I do not enjoy surprises from people who work for me."

"You've gotten a complete and straight report."

The assistant attorney general nodded. "Good. Good for you for coming forward." He spoke into his telephone.

Valles and Witwer both, silently, thought of the night at Miller's

217

Point and reached the conclusion it did not count, not in the great scheme of corruption they were handing over to the higher authority of the state AG.

The assistant attorney general stood up. "Come with me. I want you to meet our chief investigator. He'll see if we can't get you some better equipment. I want you to meet our specialist in judicial quality." He grinned.

They walked down the hall, which smelled of the popcorn and french fries from the cafeteria two floors down. "What does this specialist do, sir? I didn't understand," Valles said.

"He takes judges to trial," the assistant attorney general said.

BY MONDAY, NASH SAW HIS NEW LIFE HAD SETTLED INTO A ROU-tine of its own. Janice had stayed the weekend at his apartment, and when she left, clothes, toothbrush, shoes, stayed as tokens or hostages of her affection.

She agreed to come with him to the judges' conference. "We both need to get outside for a while," she said. Away from the hothouse of Santa Maria.

Nash talked to Vismara on the phone regularly. They set up the two exchanges, Wisot at six at the Cypress, the two cops at seven. Valles tried to make the meeting at the Claremont Grill, but Nash and Janice wanted to keep as many meetings at the hotel as possible where the control of equipment was better. Valles agreed reluctantly to meet at the Cypress suite.

In chambers before starting the Soika trial, Nash went through the Santa Maria phone directory. There were two dozen people listed with the names Lenore Wisot had told him, Holiday, Halliday, or Holloway, and no assurance the woman was even listed. He felt like a blind man nervously tapping his cane down the solid pavement, always unsure if the pavement would give out over a precipice. Nobody will call out a warning, he thought.

"The jury's outside," Vi said, giving him a new cup of coffee.

"How about the lawyers?"

"Yes. Only the defendant isn't here."

"Where's he?"

"They're short on officers this morning," Scotty said. Vi put her hands out, showing it was none of her doing. "It will be another couple of minutes."

"Okay, tell the jury," Nash muttered.

She was startled by his indifference, the judge who insisted on timely starts for his court. "I'm sorry," she said automatically. The old routine had changed, she realized, but how or to what, she did not know.

Nash looked at the list of names. He couldn't ask Terhune or his father directly. If there was nothing, he did not want them thinking he had even been suspicious. He called an old law school friend, senior partner in another big firm, and started asking about office managers. The court was looking for some seasoned administrators. He threw out the names Lenore Wisot mentioned. In a while, after two more calls to other partners in other firms, he found out that the office manager at Terhune and Nash had been Lynn Holloway. He tried to recollect her at all, but could not. She must have been one of the persistent ghosts of those days, the people who flitted around his father without leaving an impression on him.

There was no address for Lynn Holloway in the phone book. He tried information. Then he called a detective in the Santa Maria Sheriff's Department. "Can you run me something through DMV or CII?" Nash asked.

"You're thinking of hiring this woman?"

"Her name's floating around," Nash answered.

"Background checks on employees, that's out even for our little outfit." The detective chuckled.

"I just don't want somebody with a problem having access to every courtroom over here," Nash said. "Just run it for me, get rid of it after we talk, okay?"

"I can do that. You can pick up lunch."

Scotty Shea strolled into chambers. "Got Soika dressed and in his chair, Tim. Sorry it took so long, but we got some blue flu downstairs and at the jail."

The sheriffs, which included the bailiffs, were thinking of a strike against Santa Maria County to increase a health plan to match the city's. Moving prisoners and paper, even security around the courthouse, had slowed in the last day. In-custody defendants got to their courtrooms late.

Nash impatiently looked at the wall clock opposite his desk. The jury had been standing around for forty-five minutes while he searched for Lynn Holloway and the sheriffs dragged themselves around in the guts of the courthouse. "All right, bring the jury in. I'll be right out." He put on his robe. The phone had not rung. It would take a few minutes to telex a request to DMV for a license on the woman, a few minutes to find it, telex it back.

Escobar, in a cream-colored, three-piece suit with a yellow handkerchief, outlandish, pink tanned, and smiling, knocked on the door and walked in.

"I'm coming out. I'm taking the bench, Vince," Nash said.

"You know an old friend," Escobar said. "An old client of mine."

"We can talk at the break." Nash walked toward the side door, the bench, the poised courtroom where the sounds of the jury shuffling, stumbling, chatting into the box came to him.

"I represented Lou Vismara on his possession charges years ago," Escobar said. Nash turned, saw the smile, the poker player with a good hand staring back. "Now I hear the two of you are friends."

Benisek rested his case a little after eleven that morning. Idly, to distract himself, Nash counted the witnesses he'd listed in his trial notes. Twenty-three, and forty-seven exhibits, now all moved into evidence, all the fingerprints and the shotgun, photos, and clothing from the unambiguous shooting at the gas station.

As he had the right to do, Escobar had reserved an opening statement until the completion of the People's case. He stood up, white, confident, Soika staring up at him. Soika no longer cared if the jurors saw the shackles on his wrists. He rested them on the counsel table, beside the pile of files and legal pads. Nash had ordered him shackled in court when Soika shoved one of his guards on the way out. Since there was now one less guard because of the work slowdown, the shackles were a prudent precaution. Escobar protested. "Tell him to keep his hands under the table," Nash had said. Soika didn't bother. He grumbled, slouched in his chair, snapped at Cindy Duryea, her bland, gray young face never changing expression.

"Your Honor"—Escobar spoke in public with deference, not the threats he had used in private—"on behalf of Evan Soika, I move to dismiss the charges on the basis the People have not presented sufficient evidence to present to the jury."

A formality motion. Nash said instantly, "Denied. You can make your opening, Mr. Escobar." He saw his fingers twitch around the fountain pen writing in the trial notebook. The jurors couldn't see, nor could Vi or Soika. I know, Nash thought. I'm the only one who needs to.

Escobar stepped carefully around the counsel table, a fraternal pat on Soika's shoulder. A difficult client and Nash did not think the jury had any sympathy for him.

But Escobar isn't after a jury verdict.

He's after me. I'll end the trial for him.

"Ladies and gentlemen," Escobar said gently, hands open to them, "I won't have many chances to talk directly to you. Our system gives the prosecutor most of them because he has to prove a case to you. I do not have to prove anything. Evan Soika, as he sits there today, can sit there and sit there and wait and wait." Nash broke in.

"Make a statement. Don't argue to the jury."

"A simple reference to the presumption of innocence, Your Honor."

"I'll instruct the jury on the applicable law," Nash said. At least I can order Escobar out here, for now. The phone rang in Vi's office. She usually let it go four or five times before leaving the courtroom.

"Please answer the phone, Madame Clerk," Nash ordered. He wanted to know what the telex from DMV said. It had to be that call. Vi answered it and hung up. Escobar went on with his opening, and Nash sat back, fingers flat on the papers before him. It hadn't been his call.

"The evidence you will hear," Escobar said firmly to the jury, "is quite simple. Yes, Evan Soika went to hold up the Best Buy gas station. Yes, he had a shotgun. Yes, he threatened the victim, Mr. Prentice. This is all so. He is guilty of these crimes. But"—Escobar glanced at Soika, head thrust forward, mouth down, listening as though hearing some foreign, fascinating tale—"when the Santa Maria police surrounded the gas station, a new situation developed. Evan wanted to give up. He wanted to get out. He negotiated with the police, with Sergeant Ross, for hours. And when he agreed, and Mr. Prentice and he were going to give up, Mr. Prentice took the weapon"—Escobar pantomimed a yanking motion—"the police broke their word, fired repeatedly into the cashier's booth, the shotgun discharged, and Mr. Prentice was struck and killed."

Soika nodded.

"But for the actions of the police and the way they lied and tried to deceive, the victim would be alive, Evan Soika would have been sentenced to prison for armed robbery, and this community would be at rest. Instead, a man faces the gas chamber, the city is aroused by the actions of its own police. Who are they protecting? People like Mr. Prentice? Or you? Or me?"

"Stop arguing," Nash said directly. "Conclude your statement and call your witness." He was not going to conduct the trial any differently because of Escobar's threats.

In chambers, Escobar had said he'd been interviewing a client out at the branch jail two nights before, a man just arrested on residential burglary and auto theft. "I said I was in trial. You know what they all want, Judge." Escobar sighed. "They want all your time. Like the whole world revolves around them. Then I said I was in trial with you. My guy's face lit up. He'd heard of you. He'd been out drinking with a pal."

The friend was Louis Vismara. They had been drinking at Joe's Table, talking about days in the old neighborhoods, bulldozed into the Sand Creek Shopping Mall, the Shadow Point Shopping Mall. Then Vismara began bragging. He was friends with a judge, a famous judge in Santa Maria, Tim Nash. Judge Nash and Lou were into some big deals, he said, little hands smoothing his mustache. Big friends, Nash was doing him a big favor.

"Is it true?" Escobar had asked Nash in chambers politely. "You and Lou are friends?"

"I've met him. We're not friends. Let's go." Nash knew what Escobar would say next.

"Well, my contacts in the jail say Lou's got another charge hanging over him. Of course, he's probably got another lawyer. We didn't part on great terms because he thought I should've gotten him a better deal. I think Lou would do a lot of rolling over to stay out of the joint again. Would you help him stay out of the joint?"

"I don't know him."

Escobar sucked in his belly, a largely futile effort. If his own poking around bore fruit, Escobar said he'd find out what Vismara and the judge were doing for each other.

"I might have to see how it would affect the outcome of this trial," Escobar said. Nash noticed that he and Vismara had the same habit of patting their handkerchiefs. He wondered if Vismara had picked it up from his old lawyer.

"I don't think you'll put yourself on the line for Soika," Nash said. "I could already misinterpret your comments."

They were alone in his chambers, one man in white, the other in black, and the sight would have been ludicrous under other circumstances. "Not for Soika," Escobar agreed. "It's my own reputation. I come out very well if he walks on a case like this. I haven't said anything, either, Judge. You know I haven't."

But we both know what you mean, Nash thought in court as Escobar called his first witness, a small woman with a brown handbag and swept-back black hair. Use Vismara to bend this trial, that was the point, Nash thought. If he probes at all, Escobar will find a connection to Vismara and me, and it will look like what it's supposed to look. I'm taking a bribe.

Vi swore in the witness. Archie Marleau in the jury box coughed. He'd gotten a cold and sneezed a great deal. Nash tried to listen. It was too early to take a break. He could not stand sitting there, looking down on Soika's bitter face or Escobar's pugnacious triumph. I've got to choose the sting or the trial, he thought. One is going to be sacrificed. Which was worth more?

"Mrs. LaSalle," Escobar said from the counsel table, "you own the beauty parlor two doors down from the Best Buy gas station?"

"Yes, I do. For eight years. I've been there for twelve. It was a rattan store. But I changed it."

"You knew Mr. Prentice who owned the gas station?"

"Well, yes. We saw each other."

"He was a man with a temper, an impetuous man, wasn't he?"

Benisek waved to get Nash's drifting attention. "Objection, Your Honor. Irrelevant. The victim isn't the issue."

The phone had been ringing in Vi's office again, and when she returned, she slipped a paper to Nash. The Lynn Holloway he wanted had a last known address on Skylark Way in the south end of the city. He folded the paper, slid it under his right hand. Years of concealing his feelings rose to his assistance. Nash said, "Sustained. There's no showing of relevance."

"I can lay a foundation, Your Honor."

"I'm not going to show you how to try your case, Mr. Escobar."

Soika stirred angrily, his shackles rattling. Nash felt the paper under his hand as if it had movement of its own. It held secrets for him, and the past and present drew together relentlessly, the past not neatly put away but clawing its way into every minute of his life now.

Frank Wisot showed up at the Cypress exactly at six. He carried a green-tissue bunch of white roses, crinkling as he shifted them to his left hand to take the envelope Nash handed him into his right.

"I saw Vismara's file today, Tim. I had Charlie in Master Calendar express it to me. It's coming to me anyway, so why wait."

"We're always asking for files. Nobody cares."

"I don't see any problem with it. I've dumped probation violations with better proof than this one."

"We all have, Frank. That's why it's okay."

"The one thing that bothers me, Tim." Wisot sucked in air and Nash tensed. "Well, it's this guy himself."

"Vismara's okay. Believe me. He just wants to get away from this case and go on his merry way."

Wisot shrugged, and Nash feared he wasn't quite believable. "I don't want him coming back someday. I don't want to worry about him."

"Down there in Florida?" Nash grinned convincingly. "There's no trail. You denied the violation based on insufficient evidence. It's a pure judgment call."

Wisot sighed, nodding. "I guess I wanted to hear you say it."

"The second installment"—Nash pointed at the envelope in Wisot's hand—"comes when the violation's dumped."

"Sure. I put it on my calendar for next Wednesday. Then we all get out of town to the conference and lie around Monterey." Wisot glanced at Nash, holding a drink, preoccupied. "Can I do anything for you, Tim?"

Nash shook his head. "I'm all set. Roses for who?"

Wisot sniffed the white roses. "Len. Our anniversary's in a month, so I've been warming her up. Roses, dinner."

"That's thoughtful."

"Marriage is hard work," Wisot said. The flowers rustled against his tweed suit. "Take care of yourself."

Nash quickly disposed of Valles, who came without his partner, at seven. He thought the cop might have been trying to stand close to him as they spoke, but he wasn't certain. Vismara stayed in the bedroom while Wisot had been there. He came out and sat on the sofa, reading, while Valles and Nash made their deal. Valles talked to him, but Vismara didn't answer. When the money was passed and Valles left, Vismara got up and spat on the brushed carpet. Janice and three FBI agents ran through the tape again. This was the usual ritual. Every eye focused on the shimmering figures as they all listened to the words. When the legally sufficient moment arrived, as it did on most of the tapes, Janice or Nash would say, "Okay. He said the magic words." The crime of bribery had been completed and memorialized.

"What's the problem, Louis?" Nash asked after the video was put on the shelf, labeled, indexed, Testa shut down his equipment, the glowing lights turned off, the agents ambling into the suite again, joking, getting snacks. A hard night at the office.

"I hate that motherfucker," Vismara said.

Janice opened the drapes. "Why him particularly?"

"Just because he's a motherfucker and I'm going to like getting up in court and burning him."

The FBI agents, Sanchez especially, stared at Vismara. Sanchez made a point of needling little Louis when he could. "You're going to make a lot of guys scared," he said.

Vismara twisted on the sofa. "You watch yourself. Maybe you'll get scared."

Sanchez chuckled, and Jacobs and he gathered up reports and anything else Janice wanted moved to her office in Sacramento. Nash had to tell her about Escobar's threat. He had passed the point of thinking too much about individual riddles such as Vismara's hatred of Valles or even Valles's corruption. I'm thick-skinned now, Nash thought. The foreground issue was Escobar. And whatever, for me personally, the old days with my father have in store.

Everyone had some kind of drink; the FBI agents were working on beers from the bottle. Jacobs made notes as Janice talked to him.

"Janice, the defense lawyer in the trial I'm doing, he's put Louis and me together," Nash said.

She turned. Vismara jumped up from the sofa as if shocked. "How much?" she asked.

Vismara broke in, "I don't talk to lawyers about this deal. I ain't said anything, except this motherfucker cop, he's saying I'm doing shit with the judge, but I didn't say anything. The guy beats the shit out of me"—Vismara breathed huskily, running his words out rapidly—"you know, Judge, I ain't told him nothing."

Nash nodded. He knew now why Valles was on videotape, would

be dismissed from the police force, might go to prison. "You went after him," Nash said to Vismara.

"That's trouble," Jacobs said from behind the bar. He had taken off his tie, held it in his hand, a drink in the other.

"It's a side issue," Janice said. "What about this lawyer, Tim? What kind of connection has he made?"

He told her, and as he repeated Escobar's story, Vismara paced back and forth before the wide window, his own reflection faint and milky translucent against the darkness and the city lights spread out below and beyond. In fact, Nash saw all of them in the comfortably expensive room, standing as suspended in the night, like ghosts contemplating the state of human affairs in Santa Maria.

"We can't set up any kind of sting with Escobar," Nash said.

"Why not?" Janice sat down. She remained two people for him, cool and distant in public, open and even apologetic in their intimate moments. She was the embodiment of everything he'd encountered since the night with her and Roemer, worlds that moved beside each other, parallel and paradoxically touching decisively sometimes.

"If we nail Escobar taking money or threatening me, he's got to be charged," Nash said. He put his hands in his pockets. "The whole Soika trial goes down with him."

"Immediately?"

"If he's arrested with the others. Whenever the sting ends."

"We could hold off on him until after your trial is over."

Nash looked at Vismara, still pacing, muttering to himself. "Then Escobar says Soika was prejudiced by having me as trial judge. Conviction and sentence overturned on appeal. I don't like the idea of Soika being out again in the near future."

Vismara turned. "I ain't done anything to anybody here."

"You're not being accused," Janice said calmly.

"Not yet," Vismara replied.

Nash thought Vismara's anguish was a compound of fear he might still face his old drug charges and a deeper worry the investigation he'd given himself to heart and soul might crumble. Because of a drunken boast, the kind of self-inflation Vismara needed. "The problem is this lawyer, Louis. It isn't you."

"You're a prince," Sanchez said, and Vismara threw a murderous glare at him. The other agents clustered between the two men and Nash felt the hostility rise in the room. Great, Nash thought, now we fight each other.

"Vince Escobar's the kind of guy who'll check around until he finds out what's going on. We've been very good. He'll find out I'm a judge on the take," Nash said, trying to bring it all back to earth.

"I'd have to consult with Neil"—Janice glanced at the agents—"and get his approval, but maybe we'll have to bring Escobar in."

"Arrest him? I just told you that will kill this trial."

"No, no, tell him about Broken Trust."

Nash snorted. "He'll try to use the whole sting to blackmail you, too."

"It is a crime," Janice said.

"So what? He's gambling we place a higher value on the sting than the trial."

"Would he risk that kind of legal exposure?"

Nash nodded. Vismara had sat down, picking at his fingernails. He seemed to be talking to himself. "He won't think of it as a risk," Nash said. "I think he's right. I think Roemer would sacrifice this trial before he'd let the sting go down."

The FBI agents, who had watched with mocking appraisal, held briefcases and files. It was a marvel how much paper the sting generated; how enormous the filing space it must fill in the U.S. Attorney's office in Sacramento. "You need us anymore tonight, Janice?" Jacobs asked, snapping gum he was chewing. "This is going to be you guys sorting everything out, right?"

"We've got to make some decisions," she said. "You guys are off."

"Okay. See you all tomorrow," Jacobs said, the three men leaving. Only Sanchez paused long enough to glance at Vismara.

"Do you want to ask Neil yourself?" she said to Nash when the door to the suite closed loudly.

"Why? There are things you haven't told me, either of you. I don't know that we can even be straight."

Vismara suddenly sprawled out on the sofa, one arm over his eyes. He barely filled the sofa, like a kid in for a rest after mowing the lawn or a late date. "It ain't going to happen. Everything's okay," he said. He lowered his arm. "I can make everything okay, Judge. You trust me. I'll fix it."

"It's not just you now, Lou," Nash said. "I'm looking at the whole situation."

Janice finished her notes, closed the accordion file. He wondered where the investigation reports were at night. She no longer kept anything at her apartment since he found the photos. "Do you have a proposal, Tim? You don't want to go after this guy. You don't want to tell him."

Nash sat near the weary, ashamed Vismara. "Lou and I'll have to be very convincing for the next while. I think we can keep Escobar interested if he believes in our greed."

Vismara looked at him, childlike, almost worshipful.

"What's the point?" Janice asked. "Neil's going to make the final decision."

Nash shook his head. "No. The decision's been made. Lou and I can keep the sting alive for a little while. We've got two judges, we'll try another one, some cops, some supervisors, and that's going to be it."

"It's not your choice to conclude the operation," she said. "We have a lot more to investigate. We have other targets."

"Escobar's set the timetable. Whatever we've got open now, Lou and I will close. We'll make the final first-time approach to Peatling within the week. But the sting's got to end before my trial. That's probably only a couple of weeks. Escobar has no hold on me once the sting's over. I can finish the trial." Nash spoke to Janice as if they were alone. "I said nothing was going to interfere with my being a judge. The sting isn't going to affect this trial. I won't let it."

"That's your threat?"

"It's the way things are."

Vismara sat up and rubbed his eyes with both palms as if he had been sleeping. He had been listening, taking it all in, reaching conclusions of his own based on the dismay and frustration he heard. He admired both of these people very much.

Nash said to him, "Okay, Lou? We'll tackle the last cases?"

"I'm real sorry. I fix it," Vismara promised.

"Your solution is unacceptable, Tim," Janice said. "You're proposing to rush the operation to end it."

"I'm saying we salvage the sting. I'll stall my trial."

She doesn't like it, Roemer will hate it, but the only other choice is to lose the cases built so far, Nash thought.

Janice said without warmth, "I'll make my recommendation to Neil." She flipped through her legal pad. "Your friend Perpich in the DA's office comes up with no tax problems, no out-of-the-ordinary expenditures or trips. No irregularities. Neil thinks he may be clean."

Vismara looked to see what Nash would do. Nash said, "Sure

he's clean. Some asshole dropped his name. It could've been any-body's name."

"Neil thinks it wouldn't be productive to make an approach. We don't have the time based on what you said tonight." Janice was disappointed, he saw. She really wants to run him through, see if the guy went for the bribe.

"I was there, I know the source of the accusation against Perpich," Nash said. "He's okay."

"He gets a pass on this one," Janice said.

Nash got up, knowing he should ask her now about the sources of the accusations against Frenkel and Wisot, the upcoming ones against Peatling. Who pointed them out? Who made them targets? He had just seen how simply the avenging sword was lifted, as simply as it might have descended.

The fact is, he thought, I don't want to know.

NASH DROVE AWAY FROM THE CYPRESS HOTEL AT NINE, ALONE, with nothing decided and the threat still hanging over him. He knew Janice would be talking to Roemer. Vismara would go off to lick his wounds for having caused so much trouble and risking everything.

But Nash had no hope of finding much when he got to 1176 Skylark Way, off Meadowline Avenue down at the southernmost end of the city, where only a few miles farther the sidewalks and streets ended in still-fertile cornfields and tomato plants in their indomitable rows. Only the freeways going north and south on the state broke through this farmland. The sense of the city's stopping not so far outside the diminishing line of streetlights down the long, dirty avenue made Nash chilly. At least downtown or around the courthouse, the orderly seemed in control.

Skylark was a bleak place, small houses on treeless plots and broken cars and motorcycles flopped in the driveways. Dogs barked in the cooling evening, and the TVs groaned at each other from open windows. A few kids chased each other past him, shouting obscenities. An SMPD squad car slowly, almost delicately, cruised up the street, heading for the vanishing light far away.

The lights were on at 1176, a white and green little house with a row of white stones decorating the walkway. Nash rang the doorbell. The door opened, a woman, a TV on behind her, a dog yapping in a room. She was gray haired, glasses on, but his suit reassured her.

"Is this the Holloway home?" Nash asked.

"Bonafiglio," she said. "What is it?"

"I'm looking for the Holloways. Or Lynn Holloway."

The woman turned and yelled, "Ernest. Anybody named Holloway around here?"

A man, shorter, in a T-shirt and carpenter's apron, ambled up. "Who are you?"

"I'm a judge. I'm looking for the Holloway family."

The man and woman stared at each other, shook their heads. "We been here six years. Bought the house from the Leslies."

It took a little longer for Nash to find out the Bonafiglios had no address for the former owners. He moved down the street, tried two more houses without success, crossed the street, and on the fourth house found a woman who had been friends with Mrs. Holloway and had an address when she moved eight years before. "I don't know if it's any good," she said apologetically.

Nash thanked her and drove north two miles, got lost in the twisting warren of streets that jumped erratically when they were bisected by Anderson Boulevard. The traffic was heavy, indifferent, and the streetlights burned whitely over bars and neon-framed restaurants.

The address he had was on Castaic, a small, dark street that turned into a cul-de-sac. The house was lit by one window. He parked. Years ago he had gone to crime scenes at night, and this had the same ominous feeling, a brooding density as if the whole night would collapse upon him.

The honeysuckle and gardenia in the garden around the house grew wildly, fragrantly. He knocked. He did not know what he would say to this woman. Did my father do something wrong when you worked for his firm? Why were you fired? He could not simply begin where the whole transaction of his life seemed to be ending.

The woman who answered the door was thirty, with heavy auburn hair and eyes dark-lined with makeup. He introduced himself. She was too young, it could not be her, he thought.

Then she snapped at him, "I've been waiting for you."

They were driving twenty minutes later, in her car, and she talked constantly, using one hand to gesture.

"The minute she's sick, she's not going to make it, you stop helping her," Patty Holloway said sharply.

"I haven't done anything for your mother. I didn't even know she existed." He held on to the dashboard. They rushed down the thickly traveled boulevard, the horn honking frequently.

"Your old man. He makes her lose her job, he won't lift a finger to help her. Then he's paying her monthly rent"—she spat it out—"for a hundred years. Until she gets sick. I showed you my mom's bankbooks. Every month she got a thousand bucks. Every year. It's been twenty-something years."

"I didn't pay it. My father hasn't paid her."

"Right. She just got extra money from the pension fund."

Nash had trouble taking in the stack of bankbooks, different banks, all showing the regular deposit, the first day of every month. There were no slips or notes, simply the thousand dollars paid into the savings account of Lynn Holloway, wherever her account was.

"I don't know your mother," Nash said. Another yelp from the horn to clear traffic. "I don't know anything about what happened. It's what I want to ask her."

"Anything that gets the money coming."

"What's wrong with her? What's her illness?"

The daughter waved into the air, honked the horn again. "She's dying."

He recognized the hospital. He had walked these same white-tiled corridors when he was starting in the DA's office. It was a requirement that every new deputy handle mental hearings at the hospital. Commitments made involuntarily were only good for seventy-two hours without such hearings. Sometimes the doctor would whisper to him, "Ask the guy about meat," when the patient, dressed, cleaned, smiling, sat in a chair before a judge, the deputy DA, and the assistant public defender. Nash heard the singsong replies. Yes, I will get my own apartment. I will make my own meals. I will get a job. I will keep clean. I will buy my own groceries, but I won't buy meat. Yes, I'll take my medication.

Then Nash would ask the man, picked up off the street, what the doctor whispered. "Why won't you buy meat?"

A look of sharp horror. "I'd be eating my mother." The involuntary commitment was extended another ninety days.

The visiting hours on the ward where Lynn Holloway lay were flexible. Time had taken on a greater significance, and cutting it into artificial bits for the convenience of the hospital made no sense for the people lying in beds on that ward, waiting.

He stood back while Patty Holloway bent, whispered, stroked the sticklike woman in a white hospital gown, with only a sheet thrown over her. Nash did not know where to look. He did not want to intrude. In other curtained spaces on the ward, twelve women lay, sons and daughters sitting with them. The sibilant sounds of the nurses' rubber-soled shoes and the machinery gave the place the off-kilter intensity of a helium-filled balloon about to explode.

The woman on the bed was sixty or seventy. Her gray hair was cut very short. On the bedstand beside her metal-barred bed were a plastic cup and a small carton of whole milk. Patty Holloway lifted the cup and gave some to her mother. The old woman's hand went tremulously around the plastic cup.

A nurse stopped to ask if everything was all right, went on. Someone up the ward started crying loudly.

Patty Holloway put down the cup of milk. "Okay. Your turn."

Nash stepped to the bedside. The old woman looked at him steadily with clear blue eyes. He was startled to see how the flesh had melted off her nose, leaving it sharp. She trembled constantly.

"I'm Timothy Nash, Mrs. Holloway. I'm a judge. You used to work for my father's law firm."

Lynn Holloway smiled. "I thought you'd come."

"I know it's a long time ago, you might not remember," Nash began, but the smiling old woman went on.

"You don't have to apologize. It doesn't matter. Look at me. It doesn't matter."

Nash hesitated. He bent closer to her. Her daughter folded her arms. The crying nearby was annoying. "Mrs. Holloway, why were you fired from Terhune and Nash? What was the reason?"

"You fired me. I found out and you fired me. I couldn't get a job with anybody in town for three years, but I didn't have to worry because I was taken care of."

"The money?"

"Oh, yes. I made sure. Into my account. You fired me and I couldn't work and it was only fair." She coughed several times, but her daughter made no move to help. The tiny hands, balled up like a baby's, went to her slit of a thin mouth.

Nash recalled another patient from a murder case he'd tried, a witness with an inoperable brain tumor. That man had the same rigidity of expression and memory, as if a needle were fixed in a groove, as Lynn Holloway did. She looked at him and saw Jack Nash, as he had been.

"Lynn," Nash said, "what did you find out about me?"

"I found what you took," she said, smiling at her daughter's grim face. "Four hundred twenty-six thousand dollars from the client trust account just before I was hired. I found it and it nearly drove me crazy. You were one of the senior partners. Who could I go to? Who could I trust? So much money, and my predecessor, he'd been so sloppy, you'd gotten away with it."

So much money, Nash thought. Holloway's tiny gray hands were on the metal bed bars. He could see minute blue-green veins in her hands.

"I didn't like it when you told me you'd found out, did I?" Nash asked quietly.

"I didn't tell you." She coughed again and again.

Patty Holloway bent down, wiped the involuntary spill of saliva and fluid from her mother's mouth. Around the woman's bedside were get-well cards. Another nurse paused, walked on. There was no need to linger at this bedside. All was taking its course.

Nash gripped the metal bed bars, too. Didn't tell me, my father. "You didn't come to me, Lynn? Why not?"

"I must have stayed in my office for two days smoking, looking at the records. I didn't know what to do. What to do. What to do. The senior partner, my new job. You could go to prison."

"But I didn't," Nash said.

"I told Mr. Terhune. He understood. He said he would take care of everything."

"Did he?"

"No. You fired me. Mr. Terhune didn't stop you. But I made copies of the client account records," and she began reciting the ancient names of dead, distant people and companies that had used Terhune, Nash as legal counsel. So much money. "I had those records and you agreed to pay me. Every month, every year." She smiled up at her daughter. "I have the records."

"Where are they, Mom?" Patty Holloway finally spoke roughly. Nash sat back, waiting. The old woman stirred. "I have them."

Patty Holloway looked at Nash and shrugged. "That's all she ever says. She's got them stashed someplace. I've never found them. She's forgotten. They're gone." The daughter was bitter and resigned at the same time.

Nash did not believe her. He said to the woman on the bed, "Where are my records, Mrs. Holloway? They don't belong to you."

"Yes, they do."

"Where are they?"

A smile, tremulant, the face in motion. "I'll tell you later."

Nash leaned against the ash-filled fireplace, unused for years. Patty Holloway sat tightly on the sofa, looking at the small room, its growing disorder and clutter.

"I'm sorry your mother's ill," Nash said, rubbing his head. A deep ache had begun at the back of his skull. "But this is it."

"Sure it is. Because I don't have the damn records. All my life she kept teasing me about them. My college education. My wedding present, that's what she called them. Then she has a stroke and they're gone." Patty Holloway finished a beer.

"I don't know what's been going on," Nash said. "My father wasn't paying off your mother. He was never in debt enough to need so much money."

"He could've wanted it for something else." She crushed the beer can, flung it toward the fireplace, missing Nash by a foot. "To buy something. I don't know."

He looked again at the place, untidy, falling into neglect since Lynn Holloway's illness, papers lying around, plates, clothes, the daughter who had rushed home from Los Angeles, thinking to nurse her mother and hold on to the inheritance that had eased their lives all these years. The disappointment at the finality of it all was evident in every indifferently dropped paper and unwashed plate, Nash thought.

"We never had anything worth that much," he said.

"I sure didn't."

"Your mother made a mistake."

"It was your family," Patty Holloway snapped.

"If it was, we paid long enough."

They looked away from each other. Patty Holloway folded her

arms. "I can't open the pipeline again. I thought if you saw her, you might feel you had an obligation."

Nash laughed finally. "To keep paying? To keep this blackmail thing going?"

"You saw how bad she is. It's going to get worse for me."

"There's nothing I can do about that," he said.

Outside, Nash put his head against his car. The lights in the Holloway house went out, one by one, until only the gray-white flicker of the TV from a side room glimmered against a short hedge in the darkness. He felt alone, as if a quake had slid a mountain of earth between him and those he loved.

Nash started driving, hands loose on the wheel. There was one nearly infallible, invariant rule he had learned as a prosecutor, then as a judge. When a file or police report came to him, he was certain of some wrongdoing, no matter how apparently pristine the person's life appeared at first glance. Run a deeper check. Spread the search and something would be hauled back, an old fine, an old jail term, an old arrest years ago. Rap sheets headed forty, fifty years before, otherwise blameless lives defaulted in records, a dismissed rape case in the Midwest, a forgotten robbery jail sentence right after the Second World War. Down came family, reputation, hope. Other names, other addresses used to hide, to put it all away, and yet it never went away. Someone could summon these things into the light again.

There are no exemptions. There is no immunity for anyone. There is always something.

AFTER THE WEEKLY JUDGES' MEETING THE NEXT DAY, NASH WENT with Susanna Jardine to her chambers. On a unanimous secret ballot, Ruth Frenkel had just been elected presiding judge. There was a spatter of applause. Kalbacher had bowed sardonically to her and handed over his gavel. "May you use it with great dispatch," he said. Ruth invited them to the Pioneer Club in a week for a celebration.

Nash thought, in a week you may not be here, Ruth. He looked around the room. Or you Peatling. Or you, and he lingered at Frank Wisot, smoking placidly, winking back at him.

"I'm glad I'm going to the conference," Nash said to Jardine. "I need to get out of here."

Jardine was signing court orders left by her clerk. She had a cup of tea. They chatted about who was letting lawyers get away with judge-shopping, picking easier judges over tough ones, who was going out with a clerk, the continual courthouse gossip. Jardine finished signing the orders, got up holding her robe, ready for court.

"I'll just have to say it." Jardine held her robe over one arm, then he helped her slip it on. "People are saying things about you, Tim."

He didn't flinch when he faced her. "Like what?"

"It's vague. It's a lot of nudges and joking. But it's serious. You're doing something illegal."

"Me? You're kidding."

"It's just what I'm hearing."

"From who? This place's a rumor hothouse. It's all crap."

Jardine nodded. "I think so. I just wanted you to know. It's coming from cops and some of the characters around here." She pointed around in the direction of the other chambers.

"Anything specific? I'd like to hear it. This is the first I've heard."

"Oh, it's so nebulous. The drift is you're bending for one side or the other in cases. You know. You're getting things on the side." Her young, still-summer-tanned face was solemn.

"That's all bullshit, Susie. Do I look like I'm getting anything extra?"

"Of course not. I think a lot of it was generated by having Ruth and Harold running for office. It got everyone juiced up. Rumors flourish a lot more in campaigns."

"Then they die. Ruthie got her wish. Harold's going to stay with us. Thank God." And they both laughed.

"We've got to put up with so much. I've got those courtwatchers hanging around," Jardine said. "The right-wingers? I'm so nervous."

"Ask them back into chambers," Nash suggested. "They love it. Every time I see one of them sitting in on a trial, I bring him back and chat. I never get dinged."

"I like that. That's what I'll do."

Nash looked at his watch. "Time to bring the jackasses up if the sheriffs are working."

"Give your bailiff some candy," she said, grinning. "I get my defendants on time even with the blue flu."

"They're being nice to you," Nash said. He did not want to go back to trial. He would see Escobar and know that the time to put between the end of the sting and the present was short. With the end of the sting, Nash saw the end of whatever Lynn Holloway had discovered, like a crowbar dislodging an old, great rock.

"Don't listen to anything from the ladies and gentlemen," Nash said. "None of it's true. Except the good things."

"We all take compliments." Jardine smiled at him.

The morning dragged for Nash. He had not been able to get through to Janice or Roemer, and the things he had learned plagued him. Escobar's manner in court was nimble, outrageous, and unchanged. The jurors even listened closely to his witnesses. He had started a potentially dangerous tactic, putting on guidance counselors, a niece, two neighbors of Evan Soika's, who could talk about his troubled childhood. Benisek was then permitted to show how Soika had been a little bastard.

Nash smiled inwardly when Benisek got up before Soika's niece, a plump, blue-eyed woman. "He never lied to you?" Benisek asked.

"I never heard him."

"He always told you the truth?"

"As I remember. He was a nice guy."

Escobar's eyes were half-lidded on the jury, then Nash. He, too, knew where Benisek was going.

The prosecutor said, "Would it surprise you to learn your uncle Evan Soika lied on an application for a car loan?"

She turned her head to Soika. "I didn't know that."

"Well, would it change your opinion of him to know that he lied to get money?"

Nash thought of how the trials of the judges he had on tape would sound. The same questions to the multitude of people, lawyers, businessmen, clergymen, who respected these judges. Shock and bewilderment, betrayal personally and professionally. Especially, he thought, from Wisot. That would hurt the worst.

Soika's niece shook her head stubbornly. "He was always honest with me." Escobar nodded slowly.

Benisek shuffled a page. "Did you know he served time in jail for firing a weapon at another person?"

"It was not his fault. The gun went off accidentally."

"He told you that?"

She nodded. "Yes. And it's the truth."

"Because of all the people in the whole world, you're the only one Evan Soika never lied to?"

Escobar raised his hand, barking, "Objection to that gross falsehood." Soika angrily snapped at Escobar, then at Benisek, who stayed calmly seated.

"Withdrawn, Your Honor," Benisek said.

Nash said, "Redirect, Mr. Escobar." Keep an eye on Escobar and Soika, he thought, it was going to be a close finish between the sting and the trial.

There were many things that could not be withdrawn like a question in court, he thought. Once they were revealed, they hardened forever.

For the next several days, Nash took his lunch hours in the county law library in the courthouse basement. He stayed late nights, and when he had gathered enough, he used the County Recorder's Office, a vast paper file of every transaction in Santa Maria since 1867. Clerks with laundry bins pushed before them roamed the stacks of old files and ledgers every hour, ceaselessly.

There was only a single intermission, besides the trial, in his journey through the old records.

Janice approved making the approach to Dwight Peatling in the courthouse, in Nash's chambers. He thought the new judge might be more receptive if the setting was formal. "Peatling and I aren't social acquaintances," Nash said. "He'd think it's strange if I asked him to meet me outside of court."

"That's the kind of thing that's your call, Tim," she said.

Nash was brisker this time. Vismara was kept away, too. He would be out of place in a judge's chambers. Nash wanted to hurry up and get back to the files, whatever they held.

Nothing is ever lost, he thought, not really. Files and records can get misplaced, but they remain. Memory remains.

Testa checked the equipment in Nash's chambers in the morning, and at noon, when the clerks and the courthouse were most quiet, Nash brought Peatling in and made a show of closing the doors.

Standing beside him, Nash was amazed how young Peatling

looked, more like one of the research clerks than a judge. He quickly went through the pitch, not caring how Peatling decided.

"How much?" Peatling's unlined face was impassive.

"Twenty thousand to dump the violation."

"Could he go to twenty-five?"

"I think so. He wants to stay out of the joint."

Peatling nodded, smiled. He sucked on a mint. "Okay, make it twenty-five."

Nash couldn't resist asking a risky question. "Aren't you curious, Dwight? Don't you wonder why I asked you?"

Peatling shook his head. "I assume this is the way things get done. You know your way around this place a lot better than I do."

"Maybe I don't."

"Look, Tim, when I practiced tax law, we took commissions, too. This is a kind of commission. We don't get paid enough and so some cases make up the difference. It's not like this is a gigantic crime. It's just a drug case. Nobody died."

"Everybody's coming out fine," Nash said.

"That's how I look at it," Peatling said. "I wouldn't do this if somebody had gotten hurt."

He wouldn't even have time to get the file before the sting ended, Nash thought. Your career's over, you're going to prison and you don't know it, Nash thought, wearing a bland expression. It no longer bothered him.

Peatling made arrangements to get his money in the courthouse garage. Testa would have the van there to videotape it, Nash thought. This one was a lot easier than Frenkel or Wisot, almost impersonal. Nash put Peatling out of mind almost at once when he left. The lurking past remained to be unearthed in the law library downstairs. Peatling had just become part of the relatively unimportant present.

In the law library after court, Nash found the old Martindale-Hubbell law directory listing of Terhune and Nash, and the members of the firm. He knew the year his father had left and started his own practice, and he recalled the approximate time of year—fall—when he and Dick spent the afternoons playing football together on the El Camino High school field. Those harried, hazy days were colored by upheaval at home, his father enraged, his mother trying to keep everything working normally. Staying late, playing outdoors, Nash and his brother agreed, was better than being at home.

So now, Nash searched through the old files, ledgers, sent requests for the roaming clerks to bring him yellowing pages from that time, that year and season. He knew the kind of clients Terhune and Nash had represented, business and real estate, and he knew, too, that if Lynn Holloway had in fact discovered embezzlement of that size, the business or real estate deal would have been enormous.

As he came and went in the depths of the courthouse, he often passed the Petitioner, briefcase and tattered dignity, shambling in the corridor, on his endless quest for answers to wrongs he thought had been done to him.

Nash wondered if the wrongs he looked for were real or dreams.

At night, he tried to sleep. He thought of Ben. He had already made plane reservations, worked around the sting and trial, set up the day and time with Kim's sister. He was going to see his son again, and he desperately hoped nothing had changed.

As he worked in the Recorder's Office, seated back in the busy warren of shelves and files, away from the bustling public desk, Nash knew more than Lynn Holloway.

He knew, for example, that Jack Nash had never been rich. He had never bought anything very expensive for himself or his wife or sons. His home, all those years he was a judge, was modest. He did not gamble. He made no risky investments. He had been able, on his own, to provide for the education of his two boys.

He did not, then, have a pile of stolen money, Nash thought. But there's always something. He again thought of the photo of his father, bowed. He knew.

And after a few days of looking as only a son could, with a son's eyes and knowledge, Nash found it.

He held the black, old photostatic copies like X rays, the crisping deed transfers and notations. It was noted and recorded and he felt a sterile justification.

For nearly six years, Terhune, Marks, Heifitz and Nash had represented the development firm of McKay and McKay, run by two brothers, Lanny and Nevin. Half of the downtown skyline was McKay produced, stores and apartments, and the concrete expanses of parking lots and shopping malls. The three tallest buildings in the city, going up forty stories, were McKay built and still partly owned. Lanny was dead, Nevin gone to Palm Desert.

Nash spread the documents before him on the gray-topped table in the rear of the recorder's vast offices, as if he were organizing a case to take to trial. Here's how I would sum it up for the jury, he thought, blotting the names and their implications from his emotions. The courthouse jabber nearby drifted in. In a trial, the events of seconds were examined, dissected over and over again, as days or weeks passed. A robbery of ten seconds was replayed by witnesses over two weeks. A shooting of three seconds was described and reinvented over a month.

But I'm taking the events of years and compressing them into a few moments, he thought. It's an inversion of the order of all my life.

A clerk paused at his desk, his stare downward. "Are you finding everything you want, Judge?" she asked politely.

He didn't look up. "I've found everything."

She walked on.

The biggest property sale in recent Santa Maria history came up in late 1961, when Lanny and Nevin announced a grand plan for the development of the northern corridor of the city called Lot C, covering acres of prime land downtown. It was now the congested heart of Santa Maria. In 1961 it was several old garbage dumps, a half-used rail yard, and an abandoned water-treatment plant. The McKays, both stout, in tight black suits in old photos, smiling, standing in the desolation, would construct elegant hotels, soaring banks, tree-lined sidewalks.

A great deal of money was involved, and the McKays did not have much cash. The sale and development was financed by stock issues and the formation of various limited partnerships. McKay and McKay transferred varying amounts of interest in the Lot C development, called Crown Center, bought them back, the sales bringing in more money each time, building up the cash required by the banks.

Nash flipped through one stack of photostatic copies. Terhune, Nash was listed on each of the transfers and stock issues. But the most significant limited partnership, which bought 3 percent of the interest in Crown Center, was active just before the McKays were forced to sell one of their downtown skyscrapers. After the sale, the cost of a limited partnership jumped, nearly doubled.

There it was, Nash thought, pushing the papers aside. An insider had known when the McKays were going to sell their property, had bought into a limited partnership with them just before the sale. There was no better insider than the law firm that represented the brothers, and no better member of the firm than the aggressive Jack Nash, eager to make a name for himself and his firm.

Within a week, though, of that dramatic purchase, the same limited partnership resold its interest, at the old price, to Crown Center Development. It made no profit at all.

Which is what you'd expect if someone was discovered in an insider deal, having embezzled the $400,000 to pay for a piece of the limited partnership. Give it all back without any gain and nobody might care. No one would check.

Everyone might forget, except the office manager, brand-new, who started work and found out the senior partner in Terhune, Nash had been at the client trust account. The client account had its money back, but here was evidence of a crime.

Nash closed the books, put the papers back, got up. His back was stiff, his mouth dry. The clock said it was nearly two, time to reconvene the Soika trial upstairs.

He got the first elevator. He did not know what to do, barely spoke to the people who talked to him on his way to his courtroom. He did smile once. It was here, he thought, right beneath my feet all the time, all the records, the proof. Here in the courthouse.

35

"ARE YOU LISTENING TO ME, JUDGE?" ESCOBAR ASKED AGAIN.

Nash glanced up. "Of course."

"I didn't think so." Escobar rubbed his eyes quickly. "I'm not going to put on much of my case before you leave for the judges' conference."

"Why not?"

"You weren't listening."

Nash had the door to his chambers closed, the lights blinking on his phone. Benisek had been told to wait outside because the defense attorney had some private information to discuss with the judge and to reveal it before the prosecutor would interfere with Soika's case.

Nash looked at Escobar's bland, confident expression. Go ahead, he thought. Say it all out loud, Vince. We've got a great sound level in my chambers these days since Testa had the mikes installed. It's all going into tape recorders in my desk. I give the cassettes to Testa. We'll get you disbarred. He grinned.

"I'm only going to put on a few lightweight witnesses," Escobar said. "When you get back, well, we'll set it up that you'll grant my motion for a mistrial. Some kind of prosecutorial misconduct." He chuckled.

"I will?"

"We can start talking about you and Louie Vismara, Judge. I think I've got that pretty much straight. I've talked to a lot of people."

A fraudulent crime, Nash thought. My father's was real and the fraud has smoked it out after all these years.

"Tell me, Vince, you're threatening to expose me to some kind of legal action if I don't do what you want?" Nash leaned forward.

Escobar smiled, tapping a thin gold-plated pencil on his shoe heel. "We could call it a settlement conference."

Nash made him talk for the tapes. Then he called Terhune.

It was not a big raid. Valles, Witwer, Chavez, Enfante, and two new agents from the Bureau of Narcotic Enforcement made a daytime search and seize on the small house near the outskirts of the city and the small methamphetamine lab in one bedroom.

Erin, handcuffed and held by Chavez, said sadly to Witwer, "You were just a liar, Elvis."

"My cheating heart," Witwer said.

The men wore bright-green vests with POLICE stamped on them, and lab technicians in heavy protective gloves began loading up the beakers, flasks, and chemicals in the filthy bedroom.

Shiffley, gun drawn, marched from room to room, pushing his head in. Valles watched him. The three men and two women taken from the house were in the six police cars outside. Neighbors had crowded against the wooden barricades guarded by uniformed cops.

"Good haul," Shiffley said sanguinely, watching the small packages of crank being tagged as evidence.

"You wanted to come out on a real raid," Valles said. He did not like Shiffley's holding the gun so casually.

"You got to get out from behind the desk sometimes. You lose the edge," Shiffley said.

Witwer's job was to keep Enfante and the others away from the

243

master bedroom at the rear of the house until Valles could get Shiffley into it.

The phone rang in the kitchen where Valles and Shiffley had paused.

"You answer it," Valles said.

His supervisor shrugged, still holding his gun, and picked up the phone. "Yeah? No. Harry and Erin went to the store. What do you want? Sure, we got that shit." He started smirking. He put his hand over the receiver and said to Valles, "Guy named Albert wants to buy some crank right away. What are they charging?"

"Tell him a sixteenth for twenty bucks."

Shiffley grinned and repeated it into the phone. Then, "He says he's only got eighteen bucks."

Valles was growing impatient to get Shiffley into the master bedroom. Witwer was undoubtedly waiting to give the signal by now. "Okay, tell the asshole you'll front him two bucks. That'll get him over here."

Chavez, passing by, stopped to chime in, "Hey, boss, tell him Tiffany'll sell him the shit. She's a friend of Erin."

Shiffley passed along the message, instantly putting his hand over the receiver because he was laughing. "He says, he says, how come there're so many Tiffanys in Santa Maria?"

Witwer called from the bedroom, "Boss, Rog, come on back."

"I'll go," Chavez said.

Shiffley hung up, Valles waved Chavez away. "We got it."

Walking into the bedroom, Shiffley holstered his gun, rubbing his hands gleefully. "He's bringing a couple of pals. They're just little buyers, but every one helps, right, guys?" He called out to have the barricades temporarily taken down, the cops and neighbors out of sight. "I don't want to spook our pals."

He's getting a kick, Valles thought sourly. He absentmindedly ran his hand around his blue baseball cap, the mike inside it, the recorder back in the car he and Witwer had come in. The equipment was provided by the state Department of Justice. It was much better than the stuff he'd used on the Project.

"Okay, what's up?" Shiffley asked Witwer. Valles shut the bedroom door. Three mattresses lay on the floor, tangled and dirty sheets over them, along with empty liquor bottles, hardened food, and clothes.

"I found some cash, boss," Witwer said, glancing at Valles. This was the script the assistant attorney general wanted to follow. See how far the Vismara connection went, he said. You've got a crooked judge nailed, let's try for a crooked cop. He was as excited by the idea as Shiffley just now on the phone.

"Cash? Their buy money or something?" Shiffley looked around. Valles stood close enough for the mike in his cap to get it all.

Witwer pulled back some sheets and brought out several bundles of bills, tied with white string. "It's in hundreds. Maybe about four grand here."

"Swell. Book it in." Shiffley turned and Valles blocked him.

"Do we have to, boss?" he asked.

"Sure we have to."

"All of it?"

Shiffley frowned at them. "Yeah, all of it, Valles. What else?"

Witwer held the bundles in each hand, weighing them. "How about we book in a grand and split the other three right here?"

Shiffley said nothing for a moment. The bedroom was dark, blankets tacked to the windows, the air dank, thick with the stink of unclean human beings. He put his hands on his hips. "Book all of it," he said slowly. "I don't even want to think you're thinking of doing that shit."

"It's just us, boss. A grand apiece. The pukes aren't going to say anything," Valles pressed. He very much wanted to get Shiffley recorded taking the money.

"I want you two in my office when we're done here," he snapped. He put out his hand. "Give me the money. I'll book it."

Witwer handed it to him. "Forget about it, okay, boss? We're just screwing around."

Valles didn't say anything as Shiffley marched from the bedroom. Then, "Shit. He didn't go for it."

"He's going for us."

"He can't do anything. We didn't do anything. We're yanking his chain because he hasn't been out for so long," Valles said, kicking a mattress angrily. "Goddamn, I wanted him. Okay. We'll try again sometime."

"I'm getting awfully sick of it, Rog." Witwer sighed.

"We'll check with Vismara again. Maybe he'll give up somebody."

"Hey, the guys in Sacramento are happy. We got a judge. We don't have to prove anything to them."

I want to prove something, Valles thought. He did not much care whether the state Attorney General liked stumbling on a dishonest judge. His own agenda was to make a case against the man who had put him in jeopardy in the first place and because of his link with Vismara and Nash, was crooked without a doubt.

He kicked another mattress on his way out. "I'll tell you one thing, Jerry. I'm going to count that money and make sure the asshole books four grand in."

With an athletic flourish, Terhune sent the tennis ball flying to Nash, who grunted with effort and backhanded it. Terhune reached, missed, the ball thudding onto the red clay court.

"A very good game, Timothy. You want another?"

Nash shook his head, lowering his racket. "No. I want a drink."

"A good end to a good day."

They walked up the stone pathway to the bar at the Mount Castellano Racquet Club, passing men and women in white outfits, chattering lightly because work was over, the evening approaching. Terhune, who did not sweat, pushed the webbing of his racket. "I could still sponsor you for membership. The waiting list is down to two years now."

"I couldn't afford the membership fees."

"They're not very high. They're mostly deductible."

Across from the stone patio of the bar and its bright-umbrella-shielded tables stretched the perfect acreage of the golf course and the small, multicolored figures moving slowly along it. Nash and Terhune sat down at a table next to the stone wall, a waiter took their orders. Nash laid his racquet on the low wall. Terhune exhaled as if practicing a breathing exercise. Two couples waved and he waved back.

"I saw Lynn Holloway," Nash said, hands folded. "I've been through all the records. You paid her a lot of money for a long time."

Terhune scratched his leg and put a cloth napkin on his crossed legs. "Money," he said.

"I didn't want to talk to you until I had it all in order. I wouldn't have known except for your friend Roemer."

"You're working for him?"

Nash nodded.

"I assume you haven't talked to your father."

"No. Not really."

"Your mother?"

"She thinks it's all about the two of you," Nash said. He felt the breeze on his sweaty skin. A small band had started playing sentimental tunes inside the bar, the music lethargically intertwining with the cheerful babble of drinkers and snackers on the patio.

Terhune signed for their drinks when the waiter appeared. He lifted his in a silent toast. "It wasn't about Jack," he said gently. "A lot of it was about the firm, the firm's reputation. I valued that very much, Timothy. But, a great deal of my decision was about your mother."

Nash couldn't touch his glass. "I've learned things I didn't want to know about people in Santa Maria. Friends. Family. Do I have to know any more?" he asked harshly.

"It's your choice. In my own case, it wasn't such a difficult decision. An expensive one, but not difficult."

"You loved her. She told me there wasn't anything."

Terhune sadly finished his drink, put his napkin on the table where the breeze plucked at it gently. "No, not in that sense. I don't apologize or regret any part of my own life. I've been very lucky. Part of that luck was knowing Hilary."

Nash felt a confusing mix of anger and relief, the doubts and rumors finally finished. But after them, was the truth sustaining? He no longer knew if he could live on truth. "You made payoffs to protect the firm and my mother. You got nothing back?"

"I got a great deal in return."

"What?"

"The profound pleasure of watching Hilary's happiness. Seeing how you and your brother grew up. If I'd had children, if we could've had children"—he paused, tense—"you both were the sort of sons I'd have wanted."

"But we're Jack Nash's sons," he said curtly. "He made us what we are."

"It's been one of the great mysteries of life to me that a bastard

247

like Jack could have such a decent family," Terhune said with genuine wonderment.

The waiter appeared, unasked, and they both ordered another round, sitting in silence. The late-afternoon sky was faint blue and yellow. "They're the ones with dedication," Nash said, glancing down at the golfers trudging gamely in the fading light across the darkening green of the course. "They keep playing."

"A lot of things become habit."

Nash said, "So many things have been lies. Or I wasn't told about them."

"What was anybody supposed to say?" Terhune asked in surprise. "Jack would confess he'd stolen money? I'd say I was in love with your mother?"

"He let you pay for him all those years," Nash said with surging bitterness. "He could've said something to us."

"It was blackmail. Holloway was blackmailing him and through him, the firm. I couldn't permit that. I couldn't permit her to remain in the firm, either. Jack was blackmailing me in a way, for how I felt, he knew how I felt, and what would happen to Hilary if the embezzlement became public."

"My problem now," Nash said slowly, "is I can't trust anything I ever thought about my mother or father."

The new round of drinks was left on the glass-topped table, untouched. A stiffer breeze made the umbrella shading the table tremble, and several of the couples got up, still talking and laughing, and went inside the bar. The music died languidly in a brush of soft drums.

"Jack was a good judge, I don't quarrel with that," Terhune said. "He simply isn't a perfect human being. Maybe he isn't even a very good one. But whatever he was to you, and your brother and Hilary, the way Santa Maria looks at him, well, he is that."

"I wonder if he did anything while he was a judge."

Terhune shook his head. "No. He made one mistake."

Nash smiled without humor. "You'd be surprised how many mistakes people make. They aren't forgotten."

Terhune had gotten his equilibrium back and he seemed to Nash unchanged from years past. He was always honorable. He cleared his throat and said to Nash, "You're off to the judges' conference, I hear? With the young lady from the U.S. Attorney's Office?"

"You hear everything."

"At my age, with my contacts, I'd be insulted if I didn't."

Nash didn't intend to let him change the conversation so glibly. "When I was digging around in the records, I was thinking about that first night when you took me to Roemer. I was flattered they wanted me for this job. They made it flattering."

"You should feel complimented."

Nash pressed roughly, "But I wasn't their first choice. I saw pictures of Roemer with my father, Mr. Terhune. Surveillance pictures."

Terhune nodded, sighed. "It is getting chilly."

"You want to go in?"

"No."

"My dad was their first choice for the bait, right? Roemer picked him to be the one who got judges into the sting?"

Terhune nodded. "I assume so. I never asked Roemer. He had his heart set on Santa Maria, I think. It was the right kind of city for his operation. Jack was perfect on paper."

"They found out about the McKay deal."

"During the background check. Your brother had a lot of family information on file with the Department of Justice anyway, you know, his own background check when he went on the federal bench," Terhune said gently, fingering his still-untouched second drink. Beads of water slowly fell down the glass sides. "What is it you do for a state judicial appointment? How many pages is the application?"

"Thirty, I don't remember. I had to list one hundred lawyers who'd sponsor me, give me glowing recommendations."

"Well, they did the same thing in Washington. I'm sure your brother told you."

"The FBI interviewed his third-grade teacher."

Terhune laughed. "What mentalities." He sipped his drink finally, cocked his head when the band started playing again. A shadow fell over his lean, aging face. "If anybody ever wanted to really dig around, the McKay deal was always there. It wasn't worth anybody's time. I mean, no one ever thought to give Jack a thorough backgrounder like that. His appointment to the bench"—Terhune laughed again—"he was on the governor's list. That's how it was done in the old days."

"He didn't tell me. I saw him that night."

"He called me, Timothy, probably a day before. I think that's when the pictures must have been taken. I don't think Roemer ever explicitly threatened him, he only made it clear he knew about Jack's past. You couldn't do anything criminally. Too much time. It was a question of reputation."

"My dad called you? He hates you," Nash said.

"I know. But we share a secret, Timothy. We were friends and partners. We do have a history."

"Why didn't you tell me Roemer had seen him?" Nash demanded, recalling Terhune's uneasiness that night at the Hilton, the strong sense that Terhune was working off some debt by bringing him to see Roemer. Janice, too, Nash thought, don't forget her. She's in the picture, you've shared memories and your bed together.

"I talked to Mr. Roemer," Terhune said, his head unconsciously moving a little to the bouncy rhythms from the bar. The few couples left on the stone patio were shot through with pink and orange from the sunset to their right. "He explained the situation. You were the logical candidate. In some ways you had better qualifications than Jack."

"I was a DA."

"On the team already, was what Mr. Roemer said," Terhune added wryly. "He was going to ask you."

"You should've."

"Your decision had to be voluntary, Timothy," Terhune said sternly. "I didn't want you involved in an undercover operation because you were shielding your father's reputation."

"A son owes his father that much."

"Your choice had to be on the merits of the operation. Your own sense of duty."

Nash stood up. He felt no gratitude toward Terhune, only the realization that public virtue was conditioned by private vice for all of them. His decision had not been voluntary. He had known few of the facts and he had been vulnerable that night because of Kim. You're no victim, he reprimanded himself. You can't blame any choice on anyone else.

And I have done good. Corruption will be uprooted in my city. Nash frowned at the pompous rationalization.

"Thanks for coming," he said to Terhune. He roved over the people on the patio, talking to each other over drinks. Faces he saw in the Metro section of the paper, people he'd seen at parties, some he'd met, Mr. and Mrs. Zorich, Pollard, Cristobal, Bailey, Raymond Smith, not to be confused with Roger Smith, Heldt, Mrs. Adele Vickers at her own table, Dahl, Barber, who lounged with his current girlfriend against the stone wall. They would be here tomorrow or the day after. Nash did not know if the pain he felt or was going to inflict once Broken Trust became public would matter to them at all.

"I'm going to sit here awhile longer," Terhune said. He smiled. "My wife and I have got another dinner tonight, the Kidney Foundation. This will be my only quiet."

Nash nodded. "Before I go to Monterey, Mr. Terhune, I'm seeing my son."

"I hope it's a good visit."

"I'm going to try to be more honest with him than what I've seen." He picked up his racquet and turned from the garish sunset, its explosion of silent color brushing over Terhune, motionless, contemplative, in his plastic chair on the cooling stone patio.

37

VALLES SAT WITH WITWER NEAR THE BACK OF THE CROWDED COURT-room. The bailiff, a thin man with no hips, wearing no gun because he was near in-custody defendants, loudly called out for quiet every so often.

On the bench, Frank Wisot flapped his lips, looked at the clock. "Case number 65833, Maizie Shirelle Collins." Wisot waited for the bailiff to have her buzzed out into the courtroom from the holding cell. She appeared, wan, skinny, her eyes flitting around the courtroom, over the restless, disinterested crowd of other families and defendants.

"She looks shitty," Witwer said in a husky whisper.

"Better than when she went in."

"Man, hospitals are no good when you're sick."

The bailiff, seeing the two scruffy men whispering, shouted again, "Quiet in court!"

Wisot shut his eyes. He had gone through three-quarters of his morning calendar in less than twenty minutes, the lawyers at the counsel table in front of him bouncing up and down regularly to take papers, announce pleas, set trial dates. Years of practice gave him the ability to press cases quickly, get a resolution near what it was worth if it went to trial. He could do that with half his mind, the other half pleasantly thinking about the days in Monterey and the endless summer days of his retirement.

"Okay, Case 65833. What are we doing about this? She's charged with one count of sale of a controlled substance."

The public defender, a gray-skinned, well-dressed young woman, held several files at once. "This is the one we discussed in chambers, Your Honor. We're requesting she be released on her own recognizance."

Valles held his breath for a moment. He did not want anybody hinting in open court that Maizie was working for the narcs.

The deputy DA, as well-dressed, his hair as carefully tended as the young PD, agreed quickly. "No opposition from the People, Your Honor."

Wisot frowned. OR for a drug dealer? He could see she had a record from the flimsy sheets tacked into the court file he held. He glanced at her. A tired-out young hooker, he thought, strung out, too.

"People don't oppose putting her out on the street?" he asked.

"Based on our conversation in chambers," the DA reminded him.

Valles sank lower and Witwer whistled softly through a space in his teeth.

Wisot suddenly nodded. "Yes. Slipped my mind for a minute. I was thinking of something else. Yes. Miss Collins, I'm releasing you on your own recognizance. Your next court date is . . ." He paused for his clerk.

"October thirteenth, Judge."

"The thirteenth. You have to be back here in this department for further proceedings. Do you understand?" He spoke very quickly. He wanted a smoke in the corridor before the trial Master Calendar sent him got started. It was a dog-bite insurance claim and sounded very boring. By his side on the bench, Wisot kept a thick book by Michener and another by Dickens for the hours of jury selection.

Maizie nodded, stared at him, stared out at the courtroom, trying to find a familiar face. "I be back."

"Don't get into any trouble while you're out."

"I stay out of trouble." She shook her head and the bailiff gave her a slip to pass along to the courthouse jail control so she could be released.

Wisot said, "Okay. Number 55346. This is an old one. Anthony George Larkin," and another gray-sweat-suited defendant pushed by Maizie into the holding cell pen in the courtroom.

Valles nudged Witwer. "Let's go meet her."

They waited outside the south entrance to the new courthouse until Maizie was processed through, changed into her own clothes, and she came out, blinking and yawning onto the street.

"Okay, Maiz, we're square, right? We're working just like before, okay?" Valles said not very gently. Witwer smiled at her.

"Just like before. You know you got me in there and doing stuff for you." She licked her dry lips.

"Don't get busted again. I can't talk to the DA a second time about getting you an OR."

"I said I be good. You kept you word." She smiled at Valles, bent her head lower. "I needed that shit you got me, they got me all tied up in that bed." She shook her head. "I needed what you got me."

"Okay. That was once. No more." He held his finger up.

"I don't forget. I needed something and you helped me."

Witwer said, "Me and Rog'll see you maybe tomorrow, Maiz. See if you got anything."

"Man," she squeaked indignantly. "I got to have more than a day."

"Don't worry about it," Valles said. "You be good, Maiz."

She waved and strolled slowly from them, muttering a little to herself, smiling at the people who hurried along, avoiding her stare.

Valles and Witwer headed for the police department three blocks away. "We work her right, she's going to give up something decent," Valles said as they walked. "And we keep it this time."

Witwer stroked his beard. "I don't want to give her any more dope, Rog. It's bad for us."

"I take all the responsibility if you want to walk away from it," Valles said irritatedly.

"No, no," Witwer said. Valles was very touchy lately, probably the home problems, the strain of seeing a family counselor, he said. "We work Maiz together, I'm with you."

As Maizie walked up South Grand Avenue, away from the courthouse, toward the busy intersection of Montclare and Jasper, where she could hitch some kind of ride, the blue van pulled away from the curb and slowly followed her. From the false sunroof in the van, the FBI agents had been able to use a camera mounted on a swivel to photograph her and Valles and Witwer outside the courthouse.

The van slowed more, making cars behind it honk their horns. Sanchez got out a half block behind Maizie and the van sped up ahead of her. Jacobs got out, buttoning his coat, grinning as if he were going for a walk himself. The van double-parked near the end of Grand Avenue. Maizie, now humming tunelessly, aimlessly looking at the people she passed, scuffed her feet lightly on the sidewalk, coming directly and unknowingly toward the waiting Jacobs. Sanchez closely followed her.

NASH PUT THE SOIKA TRIAL INTO RECESS WHEN THE AFTERNOON session ended with Escobar's examination of two more Santa Maria police officers. They had seen little, but their views were confused enough to add a measure of uncertainty to what Benisek's more involved officers had done at the Best Buy shoot-out.

Keep the smoke coming, Nash thought, excusing the jury.

Vi locked her desk. "I can get some work done when you're not here."

"You'll miss me," he said.

"No, I won't."

They both grinned in the empty courtroom. Nash wondered, from the always friendly, protective attitudes of his clerk and bailiff, if the courthouse rumors Susanna Jardine had told him about were that widespread. Maybe Scotty and Vi haven't heard, he thought, shutting off the lights in his chambers. Maybe the other bailiffs and clerks won't tell them they work for a crooked judge.

He didn't think so, though. Both Scotty and Vi were acting for his benefit. They must have heard the rumors, too.

He had hesitated again and again since talking to Terhune about calling his father. He had even driven to the ugly pink house after court, stopped, waited in his car, watching. He did not go in. He saw his mother drive by and was struck, when she thought no one was looking, how old she appeared.

He didn't have the courage or imagination yet to face Jack, so Nash went through the final steps of the sting.

Roemer, through Janice, had agreed to play out their targets and wrap up the others.

The night before he flew to Los Angeles, Nash and Vismara made a transfer of ten thousand dollars in marked bills to a clerk named Helen Curtis, who had helped them work Peatling.

Nash, anxious to leave, impatient with the operation itself, didn't bother to chat when she got into the car in the Pacific Bell parking lot. It was after six, empty.

"I live just around the corner," she said. She was middle-aged, with a small mouth, bracelets. "I had to loan the car to my oldest daughter."

"Here's the money," Nash said, passing the envelope to her briskly.

She took it. The tape machines in Nash's car recorded what she said, but he was sorry there were no pictures. "We don't need it on her," Janice said. "She won't go to trial. We've got a deal for her and she'll testify."

No hesitation or doubt. Janice knew how it would go, this small sideshow in the larger Broken Trust field.

"Well. Well. I didn't think it would be so much." She took the money out of the envelope. Vismara sat beside her in the back seat. Bright headlights, in what looked like a continuous stream, flashed by on the boulevard in front of them.

"Ten thousand," Vismara said. "Are you counting it?"

"I don't know. Am I supposed to?"

"It's exactly right."

She had thick wads of bills in each hand. "Well, I guess I have to put it someplace." She sighed nervously. "This will really help. If Judge Frenkel hadn't said I should talk to you . . ." She began pushing the money into the tight pockets of her slacks. "I've got expenses this year, teeth fixed, and my mortgage rate went up." She smiled, the wads of money bulging.

"How about you coat?" Vismara suggested.

Nash watched her take the money out and fish around in the beige coat, trying to get the bills into the interior pockets.

"Why don't you try putting some in the coat and some in your other pockets?" Nash suggested.

Vismara grinned at Nash.

Flustered, Helen Curtis nodded, smiling at Vismara, talking about her daughters, and he talked about his. She stuffed the money into her coat, then her slacks, smoothing the bulges. "I should've worn my camping jacket," she said. "It's got pockets everywhere for things."

"Next time," Vismara said.

"Judge," she said nervously, "would you mind dropping me off at home? I really don't want to walk around at all with so much money."

Nash drove her around the corner, and when she got out, she wished him a good vacation in Monterey.

Vismara got into the front seat as they drove to the second meeting for that night. "This is getting like a real job, Judge, you know? Regular hours and everything."

"You sound a lot better tonight, Lou."

"I feel better. I got some things off my mind, things taken care of."

"Good. You've done well. I don't get a chance to see many guys do better."

Vismara had regained his cockiness lately after the slump when he was beaten up. Jacobs and Sanchez assured Nash and Janice there was no reason to fear Vismara was dealing. The checks they'd run showed he was still clean and living quietly with one woman.

"My old priest, I see him when we first get started. That's what he says. Yeah. I'm doing better. I'm not like the other assholes, you know, they come into court, they screw around, they don't make anything of themselves." He nodded. "You glad we almost done?"

Nash changed lanes. "Yes. This was a lot harder than I thought."

"Lot easier for me."

"We're here for slightly different reasons." Nash could not, even when he wanted to, remain very friendly with Vismara.

"We both want to come out with the same thing, you know, feel better."

"With any luck." Then Nash said, "If you need my help, Lou, with Roemer or anybody, you can have it. You are different."

"You a real good example to follow, Judge. Sometimes, things are getting tough, I'm getting worried, sweating, I can't eat, which is bad, you know, I eat a lot, I don't gain any weight. So, I ask myself, you know, tough deal coming with some judge, some home thing, I go, how would Judge Nash handle this deal here? It's okay. I get it going okay."

Nash pulled to a stop in front of a small frame house. He thought, at the very edge of the darkened horizon, he detected the insidious advance of rain clouds, the first real storm of the winter coming to the city.

"You're a good example," Nash said, honking twice. "Most of the informants I used went bad on me sooner or later. They only wanted the bargain. No jail time. No joint. That's all."

"I ain't an informant," Vismara said with a touch of pique.

"It's not an insult."

They watched the man who came out of the house, up to Nash's car window, hands in his shorts. His feet were bare.

Vismara said to Nash, "If I'm an informant, I ain't the only one."

The words bore into Nash, but the man at his window bent down. "Hi, guys. Hi, Your Honor. Payday?"

Nash nodded, and Vismara brought out the second envelope from the glove compartment. "I'm handing you two thousand dollars, Ed."

"Good enough for me." He slapped the envelope casually on his palm. "Hey, I know some guys in Vice, Narcotics," the man said to Vismara. "You hear anything, let me know. I pass it along, we can split a couple things together maybe."

Vismara feigned interest. "Sure."

"Say good day to Shea," the man said to Nash. "He owes me a couple beers."

Nash nodded. The man was a bailiff in Croncota's court, but there was no communication going back to Shea or Vi or anyone he wanted to shield. He hoped the sting would end before Vi or Shea might come to him, close the door to his chambers, and begin saying, subtly suggesting, there were some arrangements they all could make. You never knew, he thought, not until the money went out.

"I think," Vismara said, "it's been good, you know, you get to talk to a guy like me. Out of court." He grinned. "You lived pretty white-bread kind of life, you learn a few things now."

"I've learned a great deal, Lou."

At the Cypress suite, Nash and Vismara made the final debriefing for Janice, adding what promised to be the last tapes to the heavy shelf. Jacobs and Sanchez and another agent were playing cards at the dining table.

Nash wearily got a drink. Vismara went from FBI agent to agent, peering over their shoulders, joking with them. They kidded him back and he ate a handful of pretzels. They were all old friends.

It was a strange sting, Nash thought. Not like the ones I worked in Narcotics with the cops. You started low, little dealers, and went up the ladder, building the daisy chain of complicity as you went. Broken Trust started at the top with judges, worked down from them to clerks such as Curtis, the bailiff tonight, the others. But it was like every sting in one way: the little losers would be turned on the judges. For lesser sentences, they would testify and send the judges to prison.

We always want the largest corruption, Nash thought, as if what Curtis or the bailiff did wasn't as bad. Roemer, me, Janice, we're greedy kids in a toy store. We want the biggest stuffed animal.

Testa came from the bedroom with one of his tape recorders packed up. He had already started taking down his equipment.

Nash sat beside Janice on the sofa. She let him lean lightly against her.

"Neil's coming in when you get back from the conference," she said.

"We're both going."

"I'm tired. I didn't mean that."

"You want to come with me?"

"Of course. I wasn't thinking."

"You're always thinking," he said, nudging her. "Why's Roemer coming?"

"To review the whole files, listen to all the tapes."

"I think it's time we take the first solid cases to the grand jury," Nash said. "We're mostly finished. You ready to start testifying, Lou?"

Vismara, mouth working as he chewed, looked up from peering at Jacobs's cards. "Anytime. You get me into court, I start doing my thing with you, tell the story."

Sanchez and Jacobs chuckled at Vismara's enthusiasm.

"Are you ready, Tim?" Janice asked. "We'll start with Wisot and Frenkel probably."

"Yeah, I'm ready."

"I'm glad we're stopping soon," she said worriedly. "You've been looking very played out. It's a strain and you've had to carry it for weeks."

Nash untied his shoes, sighing. The cardplayers roared when Sanchez put down a winning hand. "I am tired. I'm glad we're going away. I can talk to you."

Vismara bounded up, clapping his hands.

"How come he's so jolly lately?" Nash said to Janice.

"What's tickling you tonight, Louis?" Janice asked.

Jacobs frowned at his new hand, said to her, "He's all juiced because me and Sanchez got those local cops real tight today."

"They ain't getting out," Vismara said.

Nash said, "Something besides the bribe?"

"Sure," Jacobs said, putting down a card, snatched up by the FBI agent across from him, Vismara grinning, eating. "I got this snitch they been using. She gave them up, no time. They been supplying her with crack. In the hospital," Jacobs drawled.

"And still champion!" Vismara threw his arms over his head in triumph.

Nash grinned at his exuberance. There was no ambivalence for Vismara in the sting. Nash felt the momentum changing, his trial colliding with the sting, all plunging forward relentlessly toward a verdict, and him taking the witness stand before a federal grand jury.

"I'll see you in two days," he said to Janice, touching her hand. He wanted to kiss her, but could not there.

"Good luck in L.A.," she said. "Have a good visit with Ben."

Nash left the suite to the boisterous cardplayers, the gradually obsolete recording equipment, and the woman he had come to love and wonder about. He did not want to face another loss, but he didn't know whether the end of the operation would signal their end, too.

N ASH WAS ON AN EARLY-MORNING FLIGHT TO LOS ANGELES. IT bounced its way south, and at Los Angeles International Airport, he rented a car, turned onto the coiling length of Sepulveda Boulevard, and drove toward Culver City, a map beside him.

It was dim and humid in the city, his lungs unused to the air, and he coughed frequently. He put everything from his mind except seeing Ben again, someone he could never lose or be deceived by. Ben's mine, he thought. I can count on what I do next.

In Culver City, which was indivisible from the rest of Los Angeles, he used the directions Nel, Kim's sister, had whispered to him over the phone. He found the small park, sat down on a bench in the shade of oak trees, and waited. It was not quite noon.

No more Escobar or Roemer or Soika. No pain because of lies told and untold. Sitting there, Nash finally and completely put away his marriage, and Kim became indivisible herself from the crowd of people he no longer trusted or cared for.

Cars came up, parked, and he waited. Then one parked close to his bench. Nel got out, then Ben, dressed in his soccer uniform. She was talking to him. Nash stood up, dizzy suddenly.

Ben saw him and was startled. He broke from Nel and ran to Nash, throwing his weight into Nash as he had when he was much smaller and lighter. Nash staggered back, hugged his son tightly to him.

Nel, arms folded, came to them. "I haven't seen you in ages," she said with a half-grin. She looked around them nervously.

Nash didn't answer, held Ben at arm's length. "How you doing, bear?" he said cheerfully. "You look great."

"I don't like it here very much."

Nel said anxiously, "You're not going to steal him or anything, are you, Tim?"

"No," he said.

"I told Kim he had a dentist appointment. That's how I got him out of school."

"I thought I was going to the dentist," Ben said. He had changed in the last weeks, Nash thought. His face was tighter, more filled in, as if the childhood innocence was being rubbed out leaving an adult's hardness.

"How much time?" Nash asked curtly.

"For me to get him back, maybe an hour," Nel said. She had gained some weight since Nash last saw her. "I feel so guilty, you know, doing this." She shrugged futilely.

"We'll take a walk, okay? We won't go far," Nash said to reassure her. "You hungry, Ben?" he asked.

"You want to hear about everything?" his son replied.

"Yeah, I do."

He put his arm around Ben and walked from the parked cars, Nel leaning on the hood of her car, watching with some distress.

She's cheating on her sister and she's afraid I'll kidnap my own son, Nash thought. Even seeing Ben involved deception and betrayal.

The park wasn't large and he and Ben walked to its center and sat on the grass. A few joggers, some with dogs on leashes, huffed past them. A solitary reader sat on a blanket.

Nash let his son talk. Ben pulled at grass, fooled with his high-topped sneakers, and talked about life at the new school, in the new house, with nearly every face strange, and even the familiar face, his mother's, changed by worry and uncertainty. Kim and her sister had fights every night, Ben said. "They don't like each other."

Kim was still looking for a job. When he got home from school at four, she was usually already there, sleeping, so he had to be quiet, or sitting distractedly in front of the TV.

"I don't think she likes you two being separated," Ben said, "she always says she's going to get on her feet, talk to you."

"I haven't talked to her."

"Am I staying here?"

"For the time being. You and me'll spend Thanksgiving up north."

"With Grandpa and Grandma?" Jack and Hilary were Ben's favorites because of the attention he got. He was their nearest grandchild and had benefited by that accident of geography.

"Probably. We'll have dinner over there."

Ben nodded. He coughed, too. Nash coughed and they both laughed. "It's not like home."

"We both have to make the best of it. For now." Nash thought about his father and Ben's undiminished adoration of him. This year would be unlike any before it, when it came to Thanksgiving Day. My dad isn't the same man this year that I thought he was a year ago.

They talked about school. Ben explained that he tried to be good, but the kids were different.

"It'll change, the longer you're here. People are the same everyplace," Nash said, the sun high and warm over them. It was one of the finest October days, smog or not, he could recall.

Ben nodded, without acceptance. Nash was relieved that Kim didn't seem to be telling Ben warped stories about him. It was too late to think about getting back together with her, though. Broken Trust and Janice had made that apparent.

"You know, bear, I may be famous pretty soon," Nash said, getting up. Nel had started waving.

Ben frowned. "How come?"

"I can't tell you now. But you'll be hearing about me at school probably."

Ben smiled. "I will? You?"

"Sure. You can tell the kids about coming to my courtroom, meeting Vi and Scotty, when he let you hold his gun."

"I told them that already," Ben said as they strolled back to Nel, her arms still folded. "But you'll be on TV?"

"Yeah. I'll be on TV and in the newspapers."

"That'll be great. Nobody else's dad is on TV." Ben was so pleased his father would stand out that Nash did not regret the small breach of security. Who could Ben hurt or save?

"My dad's going to be famous," Ben said to Nel.

"What's happening, Tim?" She opened the car door for Ben.

"It's a case."

"Oh. I'm sorry to rush. I can't keep him away for much longer."

"I understand," Nash said. He closed the door as his son sat alone in the car. Nel got in the driver's side. "It's not right to lie to your mom, bear, but we've got to keep this secret about coming here, okay?"

"I'm not going to tell her," Ben said in surprise.

"No."

"She wouldn't let me come to see you for Thanksgiving," he said.

Nel started the car. Nash wanted to hold Ben once more, but the moment passed as Nel backed out, and he and his son waved quickly before the car was lost in traffic.

He felt a terrific heaviness in his chest. It could be the strain or the bad air. He had trouble taking a full breath. He tried several times, then got into his rented car. I'm okay, he said over and over. I'll see him in a few weeks.

Nash drove back to Los Angeles International Airport, and since he had four hours before his flight north, he read a little, but mostly sat in the chrome-decorated bar nearest his airline. He had enough to drink that he saw the bar, the rushing ebb of people, and the airplane finally, from a tiny point far away. The pressure in his chest slackened.

At five-thirty, he laid his head back in the jet's seat and flew north.

40

HE SLEPT MOST OF THE FOLLOWING MORNING AND MISSED THE opening address at the California Judges' Association Annual Conference. A justice of the Fourth District Court of Appeals welcomed the three hundred judges and wives or husbands, told them there would be more speeches, bland food, and a lot to drink.

Nash had reserved a double room at the La Playa Hotel, about a mile from the site of the conference and the even larger gathering of lawyers at the State Bar Annual Convention. It was impossible, as he glanced out of his window, eating a small breakfast in his room, to see anything beyond lawyers and judges ambling along the streets, cameras in hand, tourists clogging every doorway.

Janice arrived in the early afternoon. She brought two large briefcases of transcripts and FBI reports for him to review. "Have you ever testified in front of a federal grand jury?" she asked, immediately settling into the room.

"Are you kidding? I took cases to the county grand jury, but that was a long time ago."

"Then we'll do this homework between your meetings and wherever else you've got to be at this conference."

"What meetings?" he asked.

Meetings were scheduled for the next three days, topics covering recent changes in California law, new procedures, practical seminars on running efficient courtrooms, and speeches all day. But Nash and Janice, as if they had just met, spent the days around the peninsula. At the west end of Cannery Row, they visited the Monterey Bay Aquarium and watched the sea otters playing. Other judges and their wives, playing hooky, crowded the place.

Nash ran into judges he'd met at earlier conferences or the college held to train new judges. Janice met several old friends from the U.S. Attorney's office who had been appointed to the bench. They went drinking or had dinner with some couples. The days were hazy with the persistent mist floating in from the sea. At night the mist thickened to fog, hung deeply over the whole peninsula, swaddling the hotel. In their bed, late, Nash and Janice heard the distant rough barking of sea lions. "They sound like dogs," she said wonderingly.

"That's our mistake," he said.

One day they spent walking the sea-spray-misted rocky beach at Point Lobos State Reserve. The review of meetings with Frank Wisot and Ruth Frenkel depressed Nash very much.

He and Janice ran into Frank and Lenore at the banquet in the conference hotel's main ballroom. "You want to keep us company during this thing?" Frank asked brightly. He had been working the no-host bar and mingling determinedly.

"I'd like to," Janice answered.

"Sure, Frank," Nash said. The featured speaker was the chief justice of the California Supreme Court. Nash saw him, white haired, tall, deep voiced like Jack Nash, standing in a circle of admiring judges and lawyers, drinks in hand.

"Nice part about these deals," Wisot said, "is everybody's nobody."

"He means all the judges act like it doesn't matter if they're on the municipal court or court of appeals or even the Supreme Court," Lenore said. She had been drinking, too, and hung on Wisot's arm.

The banquet went on, waiters moving swiftly between the closely packed tables, the lights dimming in the large ballroom around the great decorations of the scales of justice and the seal of California behind the blue-cloth-draped main table.

"Tomorrow they got a dinner at Sea World," Wisot said after the main-course plates were removed. "Fish'll put on a show."

"We're going to pass," Nash said, and Janice nodded.

Wisot squinted, looking around at the other busily eating and laughing judges. "God, I'm glad I'm getting out of it."

"Retiring?" Janice asked.

"Get Tim to tell you our plans." Wisot winked.

I know your plans, Nash thought, pushing aside the tasteless chicken breast in white sauce he had been picking at while the others ate.

Janice was caught up in conversation with a small judge from Shasta County on her right. "It's chaos if you don't expedite multiple-defendant cases in a calendar court like mine," he said.

Before the chief justice rose to speak, a single spotlight shining on him, the chatter at Nash's table had turned to gossip about which judges had come with new "traveling companions." Lenore Wisot pointed out various men and women and provided a commentary.

Wisot ground out a cigarette. He had ignored the bald San Bernardino County muni judge beside him, who kept waving the smoke away. "There's Fred. Let's go bug him, Tim."

Reluctantly, Nash went with Wisot half across the darkening room, and they joked with Fred Miyazumi and his wife. "He's getting playful," Miyazumi said, pointing to Wisot.

"What do you mean?" Nash asked.

"A snitch in my court told me this guy came in over lunch two days ago," said the little judge, "and he screwed my chair down all the way."

Wisot giggled. "You went right down to your ass when you took the bench."

"I'm going to get even."

The chief justice had started speaking and several people irritatedly hushed them. "We're not wanted," Nash said. Wisot pulled him out of the banquet, to the men's room just off the lobby.

The chief justice's stentorian voice came through the walls.

"I hate to ask you, Tim," Wisot said, lighting up again. "I wouldn't if it was you, Christ no. But since it's some dope dealer, I don't care."

"You want more, Frank?"

Wisot nodded. "I sure do."

"I don't think he'll do it."

"I know his case's moved on. I know the probation violation's killed. But he doesn't want anybody resurrecting the thing, does he?"

"No, I'm sure he doesn't."

Wisot smiled, sat back against the marble row of sinks. "I think he could stand a fair-sized payment. I think that would wrap it up for me."

"I don't have to be in it, Frank," Nash snapped. "You can talk to Vismara yourself."

"I didn't want to do it all for me, Tim. I thought we could arrange some kind of split."

Nash listened to the unavoidable, oblivious sound of the chief justice, the constant applause. "Goddamn it, Frank," he said with sudden vehemence.

The men's room door opened, a man in a tuxedo marched stiffly to the urinal. Wisot tossed his cigarette into the sink. "What's the matter?"

"Okay, okay. We'll split the money. He's just a dope dealer," Nash said savagely.

"Christ." Wisot looked in horror at the man at the urinal.

"Let's get out of here."

They walked out. "I need to put away a little more money for my retirement, Tim," Wisot said almost pleadingly. "I wasn't like your dad. I didn't go out and make a lot of money private judging."

Nash didn't answer. When they got near the table, he apologized. Then Wisot, now puckishly grinning, grabbed him and patted his shoulders and torso. "What are you doing?" Nash demanded.

"You're clean. Just checking if you're wired." Wisot smiled.

"Fuck off, Frank," Nash said harshly. He began sweating. Did Wisot truly believe he had on a mike? He couldn't and still make the offer he just did.

"Take it easy," Wisot whispered across the table, Lenore and Janice watching. "It's a joke. Everybody's doing it around the courthouse."

"I haven't seen it."

"Probably because of the rumors about you."

"They didn't want to embarrass me," Nash concluded. Jesting about bribes and informing wasn't funny if everyone believed I'm dishonest, he thought.

At the head table, dwarfed by the great scales of justice behind him, the chief justice said, "I have already obtained from the key committees in the legislature assurances of funds for an additional fifty judges." The applause was sustained and vigorous.

Nash drove along Lighthouse Avenue, the ocean to Janice's right, passing into Pacific Grove and the fog-embraced weathered Victorian houses that looked like the spirits of a New England whaling village.

He turned them to the shoreline. They got out and walked, the air salty, cold and dark.

"I don't want to talk about the grand jury or testifying or anybody who's going to get nailed," he said. "I want to forget it."

The few house and street lights visible near them glowed vaporously yellow in the fog. Janice put her arm through his. "This is very near the end, Tim."

"For everything?"

"After you testify, there won't be much excitement until any trials get started."

He pulled her closer. "I don't want to talk about that."

She waited. "There's nobody around. We're alone out here."

"I don't want you to leave Santa Maria," he said. It sounded more awkward than he wanted.

"There won't be much for me to do."

"I want us to stay together."

Janice faced him, her features indistinct, blurred in the fog, but her hand in his was warm. "I care very much for you. I care what happens to you."

"It's more than that for me," Nash said. "I love you. I guess I didn't put it exactly into those words until I saw my son."

"How does he make it clearer, Tim?"

Nash and Janice paused on the sidewalk. The fog muffled their words and the earth around them. There were houses and streets, but she had been right, the night's illusion was of loneliness held at bay because they were together. "I suddenly realized when I was with Ben," Nash said, "I don't care about anyone else really except you and him. You go through your mind, you see people, you think about them, but I kept coming back to that, Janice. It's you two I love and want to keep close."

Janice said, "The last couple of weeks, I've been trying to put some professional distance between us. When we're working together."

"I noticed."

"I haven't been completely successful."

"I'm very glad." He smiled.

"For a long time, what Neil and I did together was enough."

Nash had to ask finally, "Were you lovers?"

"Not for a long time."

"I'm glad about that, too."

They walked a little farther to a white-wood-fenced small house. It looked smudged in the dim streetlight and gray fog. "After I met you, I got very tired of being uprooted all the time," she said, looking at him. "I like the feeling of being someplace and knowing I'll stay there."

"What about the two of us?"

"That's what I'm talking about," she said. "You, the city, it's what I want."

Nash felt the sourness from talking to Wisot dissolve. He and Janice held each other and kissed, their lips faintly salty. They walked back to the car, getting a little lost, idly but comfortably talking about what she could do if she left the U.S. Attorney's office. "I know everybody in town," Nash said. "With your qualifications, you can pick any firm probably."

"We'll see."

"What does that mean?"

"Tim, once it's public that you were undercover, things are going to be different."

"I know. It won't mean I still can't help you get a job."

Janice pulled her coat belt, tightening it around her waist. A car, dark and almost invisible, swished by too fast in the night, and the fog pulled after it in tendrils. "You're going to find you have friends you didn't know. You're going to lose friends you had."

"It's not going to be that bad."

"If we stay together, if you hold on to how I feel about you, it won't."

She had raised the one unapproachable issue, and Nash knew it could not be put aside. If they were going to start fresh from that night, the question of trust was close to both of them.

They drove back slowly, the fog thicker in places, and had coffee in Monterey, in a small, brightly lit diner on Pacific Street. He was pleased there were no other judges loitering in the place.

"I've still got to get up my courage and talk to my dad," Nash said just before they left.

"I didn't want to keep that from you, Tim."

"But you did."

"I'm sorry. It was a bad decision. Dumb idea."

"I don't know how to do it, Janice," he said truthfully. "I can't ignore him."

"The right moment will come," she said. "I am sorry."

"We're starting new. Tonight," he said.

When they got back to the La Playa, they made love surrounded by transcripts and files, the mute witnesses of the future. For the first time, physically close, emotionally linked, Nash felt complete again. There had been too many sunderings since his marriage died and Ben was taken away, and his tentativeness with Janice only rubbed the sores. But they were together as of tonight.

In the first struggling light of the dawn, he sat wrapped in a sheet beside Janice, still sleeping, and luxuriated in the sight of her.

This is it today, he thought, shivering a little in the sheet, this is it tomorrow. He was happy.

41

Nash stood behind his desk. At his right, pushing his glasses, Benisek looked startled. Escobar stared back at Nash. It was a little before ten, the jury seated out in the courtroom, the chains faintly rattling meaning Soika was in place, too.

"Mr. Escobar thinks he's going to get a mistrial," Nash said. After coming back from Monterey, with Janice's love assured, he felt reckless.

"I never said anything like that," Escobar answered.

"I don't understand, Judge," Benisek said.

"Mr. Escobar threatened me last week. He said he would use information to force me to give him a mistrial."

"I think I'm entitled to one, based on this demonstration of your prejudice," Escobar said hotly, stepping back as if shocked.

"I'm not giving you one, Vince. I'm going to report you to the State Bar disciplinary board. I'm going to get your ticket pulled."

Benisek cleared his throat. "Judge, is the trial in trouble? I've got to know."

"No trouble now. We're going out and proceed." Nash got his robe, slipped it on. "Vince said he was only going to put on nothing witnesses until I gave him his mistrial. Go out and do that, Vince. It will prove you don't think you've got to make a serious effort."

Escobar fumed, his face reddening, and he demanded Nash excuse himself from the trial. But Nash had decided the trial would go forward, without Escobar's threat hanging over it. I'm bolder, he thought, after a couple days' rest.

When nothing changed, Escobar banged his way out of chambers, making Vi come in worriedly. Nash and Benisek stood quietly.

"I don't know what you're doing, Judge, but I don't like it at all," Benisek said.

269

"I don't like people trying to run my courtroom, that's all there is," Nash said. "Let's go see what Vince comes up with."

Shea announced him, the court coming to its feet. He nodded to the jurors. At the counsel table, Escobar glared up at him, and Soika, chained in, was being soothed and cajoled by Cindy Duryea.

It is my courtroom, Nash thought. Roemer's sting isn't going to change anything.

Escobar futilely tried to keep his voice low. "You can't testify," he said to Soika.

"Shit. You said you had it fixed. You said he's fixed."

"He's doing something, Ev. Let me handle it."

"Shit. I got to testify. He's going to get me, I don't," and Escobar saw the jurors staring at the maddened, determined look on Soika's face. He's losing my case, Escobar thought. In front of me, he's ruining all my work.

"I have witnesses for this morning. The ballistic guy, the criminalist I hired," Escobar said.

"I got to go on."

"We can figure out a plan at the lunch break, Ev. I can hold everything until then."

"I'm going on," Soika said tersely. "Okay?"

"You're going to destroy the whole case."

"It's my fucking trial, Vince."

"All right." Escobar stood up, feeling the sweat under his arms, in his shirt, the anger he couldn't still. Nash was coldly looking at him from the bench. Like he's some kind of avenging angel, Escobar thought. I am going to use everything I've got against him, every jailhouse snitch who can talk about Vismara and the respected judge.

But what really hurt Escobar was not Soika's intransigence so much or even Nash's unexpected behavior. It was that suddenly Escobar felt lost in the courtroom, in front of the jury he had shaped to be sympathetic to Evan Soika. He did not know what was happening and had no idea how to control things. At his side, Soika twisted in the restraints that bolted his chair to the floor and him to it. The guards were standing, poised to grab him.

"The defense calls Evan Soika," Escobar said.

The briefest flicker of surprise showed on Nash's face.

* * *

It took several minutes, the jury waiting in the corridor, to move Soika from the counsel table to the witness stand. He had a guard beside him. The shackles on his legs stayed on, but his hands were left free. Nash brought the jury back.

With exquisite care, Escobar apparently recovered from his anger. He guided an agitated Soika through the events at the Best Buy gas station with a series of very short questions. Nash saw the jurors watching closely. They always want to hear the other side. It was a black-letter rule of law that the defendant had no obligation to present any evidence, but everyone knew how unfinished juries regarded a case without hearing from the defendant.

Benisek objected—was sustained—to the rambling answers Soika gave. Escobar's tight smile never changed. He moved smoothly on his little feet from the counsel table to the exhibits before Vi to Soika. Nash's opinion was grudging but merited. Escobar was a good lawyer.

By eleven-thirty, he finished, Soika repeating his innocence time after time. Nobody's innocent, Nash thought, remembering Atchley's observation.

"Do you want to break for lunch now, Your Honor, and start my cross-examination this afternoon?" Benisek asked, still mild.

"I want you to start now."

"All right, Your Honor."

Nash sat back. Benisek stood up, hands on his legal pad. He looked at Soika, ostentatiously relaxed on the witness stand.

"You went to Best Buy with a loaded shotgun to rob whoever was there, didn't you?"

Soika waited. "I needed some money. My brother was sick."

Nash broke in. "Answer the question yes or no. Your lawyer can ask more questions of you."

"Not the way you're jamming me," Soika said, twisting in his chair.

"I warned you, Mr. Soika, about disrespect for the court." Nash was calm.

"You keep trying to jam me into prison, you been riding my lawyer," Soika said, chin out.

"Do you want to stay in the courtroom, Mr. Soika? I can have you removed."

"Sure. Sure." Soika momentarily subsided. Escobar, hands pyramided on the counsel table, said nothing. He frowned at either the judge or his client. Cindy Duryea had one hand on her forehead.

"Go ahead, Mr. Benisek," Nash ordered. He felt in absolute

charge of Department 14 and the trial again. He commanded it as he exerted control over his life once more. Janice had brought him that.

"When you put your loaded shotgun to the head of Mr. Prentice, you would have shot him, wouldn't you?" Benisek said.

"I only wanted the money. I didn't want to hurt him. The cops killed him."

"Answer yes or no," Nash directed again.

Soika stared at him. "The answer's no."

Benisek went on, "You could have turned yourself over to the police when they arrived, couldn't you?"

"No."

"Because you wanted to get away, isn't that correct?"

Soika nodded, derisive. "What do you think?"

"You were using Mr. Prentice as a human shield, right?"

"I was trying to do what was best for him and me."

Nash could not tell what was going through the minds of the jurors, sitting in their chairs with folded newspapers, paperbacks, or sewing beside them. They watched Soika.

"Putting a gun to his head was best for him?"

"I wasn't going to shoot anybody."

"It was loaded. It could have gone off."

"It did go off."

"And killed Mr. Prentice," Benisek snapped.

"It wasn't my fault," and Soika's leg shackles shook as he tried to move on the witness stand. His guard stepped closer, hand out to push him down. Soika looked at Escobar, who turned away.

Did Soika's inward intentions matter as much or more than his outward actions? Nash wondered. The law said they might, but justice was stricter. We don't have to will every action to be liable for its consequences. He had come to see that in the last few weeks of Broken Trust.

He let Benisek go on until after noon, then realized the jurors were getting anxious for a break and excused them. Soika stayed on the witness stand, and they all watched Shea hold the courtroom doors open until the jury was mingling outside with the other people streaming from the other courtrooms along the floor.

He closed the door, Soika was helped off the witness stand. Nash stood up, starting off the bench. Vi also stood up, moving to her office when the phone rang.

It happened so fast, Nash did not quite grasp the thing until the bodies were struggling on the floor, the shouts and raging voices echoing in the courtroom. He heard Vi scream twice.

He jumped back onto the bench, his fumbling fingers finding the goody button, jamming it back, and the gongs banged through the courthouse. Shea had run up, seizing the yelling Soika, who held Vi by the throat, and the other guards flung themselves forward, grabbing him. Nash thought: Soika is so much bigger than Vi, she's so tiny in his hands.

He ran down, taking her arm, pulling, the guards and Shea butting Soika, turning him, flinging him to the floor, his still-shackled legs thrashing. Nash had Vi, half-dragging her to safety at the other side of the bench.

The courtroom doors bounced open and twelve more uniformed men ran in, yelling, batons raised, falling. Shea clung to Soika's throat, and Nash heard Cindy Duryea screaming he was strangling.

The mass of yelling, pulling men bore Soika out. Nash bent to Vi, gagging, holding her throat.

"I wasn't thinking," she said. "I never walk in front of a defendant. In custody." She was more annoyed than anything else.

The sounds of Soika crying out and the cursing bailiffs came from the rear corridor. "You're okay? You're not hurt?" Nash asked her quickly.

"No. I think I'm all right. I feel so stupid."

He told her it was nothing, only her safety mattered. He felt giddy himself, clumsy in his robe as he helped her to a chair. There hadn't been any kind of violence in a courtroom for three years, not since the metal detectors and guards went on duty on the first floor.

"That scared the hell out of me," he said. "I thought he hurt you." Nash got Vi water from the carafe on the counsel table. He abruptly realized they were alone in the courtroom except for Escobar. Cindy Duryea had gone running after the roiling mass holding Soika. People were running toward the courtroom.

Escobar said to Nash, "This is your fault. You goaded him. You're railroading this case."

"Shut up," Nash said, giving the water to Vi.

"I've got it all documented," Escobar said, strolling toward the rear corridor, in no hurry. "I'm going to break this fucked-up trial and you, Judge."

42

THE JURY WAS OUTSIDE SO THEY DIDN'T SEE ANYTHING," NASH SAID to Roemer.

"Lucky."

"So I can salvage the trial. I don't have to declare a mistrial." He rubbed his eyes tiredly. Opposite him at the bar in the Cypress Hotel suite, Vismara sipped a plain soda water thoughtfully. They had been listening to early audio tapes of Ruth Frenkel and comparing their accuracy with the FBI-prepared transcripts. Nash was exhausted.

"He still going to cause you trouble, this guy?" Vismara asked.

Nash shrugged. "I don't know, Lou. He's threatening to go to the PJ. He won't. I've got too much owed upstairs."

"We'll be finished before this jerkoff can do you any damage," Roemer promised. "The grand jury's convening in Sacramento in less than two days. We'll take your testimony at night, you can be back in time to start court in the morning."

"Thanks," Nash said sarcastically. Janice came out of the bedroom. It was nearly cleared of Testa's equipment now, only two tape recorders and a VCR remaining to view the evidence Roemer would use at the grand jury. Nash had numbed to the realization he would be providing the foundation for indictments against Frank Wisot, Dwight Peatling, Ruth Frenkel, and two corrupt cops. The other cases would be handled next. "I want to get these out of the way, make some headlines, and get some attention for the investigation," Roemer had said when they all first got together that evening. He had a forced cheeriness when he spoke, his eyes hard. He ran a finger down his suspenders.

"But you still going to have trouble with this guy, Judge." Vismara came from behind the bar. "He still going to try to fuck you over."

"I can handle him."

274

"He's playing dirty."

Roemer got up and brought over another file folder. He didn't look at Janice. She's told him, Nash thought. The old romance obviously still hadn't died. Roemer was not a man who lost well.

"Once the arrests are made," Nash said, "Escobar loses any leverage. I'm not a crooked judge."

"He still going to come after you. I know him. I know guys like him in the joint," Vismara said, dabbing at his forehead with a handkerchief. "They keep coming. You turn you back, he shanks you." He made a thrusting motion as if holding a knife.

"How about your clerk?" Janice asked. She took a transcript Roemer coldly handed her.

"Vi's at home. I made her go home," Nash said, yawning. "She wanted to stay, but a little rest made more sense."

"Not hurt?" Roemer asked, reading down the transcript.

"Shocked. Like me. It's a shock when someone attacks you."

Vismara nodded to himself. He sat down at the dining table where one of the tape recorders had been set up with speakers. "You got to be a street fighter, watch you back."

"I'm no street fighter." Nash smiled.

Vismara nodded again, neatly folding his handkerchief. "Okay. We get another deal here? Night's getting old."

They returned to the tapes. Toward the end of the session, Roemer told Nash and Vismara how he intended to present the cases to the grand jury. First came the FBI witnesses, Jacobs and Sanchez primarily, a technician, probably Testa, to describe how the tapes were made, what the jury would hear. Vismara would follow Nash. Using Vismara now would defuse any dislike or distrust the jurors might have for a witness being paid and given a deal. Vismara grinned. "I make them love me," he said merrily.

"But you're at the top, Tim," Roemer said. "I'll take you through the meetings with Frenkel, the couple with Wisot and Peatling. We'll do the setup and the payoffs. I'll introduce the tapes. I'll introduce Wisot's bank records."

"Are you going into a lot of detail?"

Roemer shook his head, hands in his pockets, the truculent look back, as though he faced unfriendly reporters or critics. "Highlights only. Right to the point. Save the detail for the trials."

Janice looked at Vismara. "Remember the basic rules, Louis. Only answer what Neil asks you. Don't add to the question. Stop and think if you need to. And tell him if you don't understand."

Nash enjoyed listening to her. He smiled at her and she lowered her head slightly. She said, "There won't be any defense attorneys in the grand jury room, but the jurors may ask you some questions."

"Not the way I do a presentation," Roemer snapped. "They only hear what I let them."

"Short and sweet," Vismara said.

"We'll get the sealed indictments, we'll go arrest these assholes all at once."

Nash looked at Roemer in surprise. "Can't Ruth and Frank turn themselves in? They'll surrender. Jesus, a public arrest would be devastating." He didn't care about Peatling or the cops.

"Sure. I hope so."

"The TV publicity isn't worth the pain you're going to cause, Neil," Nash said angrily.

"It's not your decision," Roemer answered.

Nash felt heartsick at the image of Frank Wisot or Ruth being led, in handcuffs undoubtedly, from their homes, the shouting reporters crowding remorselessly around them. But, the public humiliation was part of the operation. Bringing shame on the heads of corrupt officials cleansed the disgrace. It was, he realized, the only way he could think of what would happen and live with himself.

He could not change anything. Roemer was set. The only escape would be a refusal to appear before the grand jury. But Frank and Ruth, the others, too, weren't innocent. They had willed the consequences upon themselves, however brutal.

Near eleven, Vismara stood up, stretched, put aside his copy of the meeting with Wisot, in Frank's chambers, Nash recalled with embarrassment, Frank taking the envelope of money and putting it in his desk like a pack of gum.

"We back tomorrow night, too?" Vismara asked.

"Yeah, Lou. Same time. I'll do a dress rehearsal of the grand jury with you." Roemer saw him out.

Vismara straightened his coat. "I'm going to bed," he said loudly, good-naturedly.

Roemer came back. "I just want to say it." Roemer flipped a page on a file. "I don't like ending a good partnership," he said to Janice.

"Everything ends, Neil."

Nash poured a soda water from Vismara's bottle, added ice. "We wouldn't have met at all probably except for you," he said.

"One of my smarter moves," Roemer said.

"You've got your family," Janice added. "Lovely children."

"Everybody comes out a winner."

Nash yawned again. He was past mundane fatigue into a dreamy listlessness. He wanted to call Vi once, if it wasn't too late, to make sure she was feeling better. He saw another reason why Roemer wouldn't bend on Wisot's or Frenkel's public arrests. Janice and me, he thought. Personal irritation has a public face.

"Well, I hope you find everything works out," Roemer said, looking around for his coat, carelessly flung to the sofa when he arrived hours before. "People like you always seem to find the right answers, Tim. The right moves through life."

Nash heard the bitter undercurrent, but Roemer smiled.

Janice said coolly, "You've got a generous nature, Neil."

The phone's ringing startled both Nash and Janice awake. The wavelets from the pool outside were reflected on the ceiling; otherwise there was darkness, silence, no movement.

Nash hung up, sitting still, stricken in the darkness. Then he said to her, "Get dressed. Call Roemer."

"What's the matter, Tim? I couldn't tell."

"Remember this address," and he repeated one on South Augusta Avenue, got jerkily out of bed. "Tell Roemer to meet us there."

It was nearly four in the morning and the police lines had been up for two hours. The night was cold, nearly as chilling as Monterey. Six Santa Maria squad cars were parked around the lower half of the block, and Nash counted, numbly, twelve cops moving around the scene.

Benisek met Nash and Janice. "Carriger in Homicide called me when he found out. I thought I should call you, Judge."

"Where is he?"

Benisek led them toward the alley between the Seoul Man massage parlor and a venetian-blind-fronted real estate office. Two tiny Korean women, arms folded, shivering, stamping feet in high heels, talked to police detectives in suits. Nash noticed that Benisek, in a winter overcoat, had his badge on.

Janice stayed a little apart as they entered the alley. The crime-scene van was parked against one wall, five or six men working quietly on something behind two large garbage bins. Nash stood still. The body was pressed between the bins, close by the brick wall, dark and formless, one pure-white hand lying on its hip.

"He's only number two for me," Nash said calmly. "I never went to autopsies or homicide scenes."

Two of the cops glanced up. They wore gloves and were taking blood scrapings from around the body. Janice stayed back. "Take a look," Nash said.

"All right," and she quickly peered down. She sighed.

"Escobar's a regular here," Benisek said in the same mild voice Nash had heard for so long in court. "He came in tonight and had his usual." One of the cops grinned up at them. "He left around one."

"What happened to him?" Janice asked.

"Stabbed about six, seven, eight," the cop nearest the dark mass counted. "I think nine times."

Benisek lowered his voice. "They've got a pool going on how many times he got stabbed," he said to Nash.

Nash heard another cop. "Guy could get you tickets to any game. Really. Any fucking game, you could get good seats. Shit." And the palpable sense of loss was unmistakable.

Nash, Janice, and Benisek walked out of the alley. Nash only saw three other people, standing forlornly across the street, watching curiously. Escobar's wallet was gone, so was his watch and wedding ring, the last taken off with such force his finger was cut to the bone. There were, Benisek said, no discernible defense wounds.

"He was surprised when he came out," Nash said.

"I would think so. It's a two-eleven, someone waiting for johns, and Escobar was unlucky to be the one."

Nash said, "If he doesn't have any defense wounds, he could have known who stabbed him."

Benisek shook his head. "One of the girls."

"A friend."

Roemer strolled up, waved to them, ducked under the police line unchallenged.

"I hear your defense attorney got his ashes hauled." Roemer had on a raincoat. He made no attempt to introduce himself to Benisek.

"It was a robbery, Neil," Janice said.

"Too bad. Something else?" he asked bluntly. "It's a nice night, but I'd rather be home."

"Janice's got a better theory than robbery," Nash said.

"I don't," she answered. Benisek moved away to talk to several cops. A police video crew headed into the alley. Our comings and goings all on magnetic tape, Nash thought. Janice said, "Let your police department do its job, Tim. We don't have to do anything tonight."

Roemer said, "What's going on? This isn't my jurisdiction."

"It's Vismara," Nash said. "He killed Escobar."

Roemer pushed his hands deeply into the raincoat pockets. Roemer could see someone blown to pieces in front of him, get splattered with guts, and he wouldn't show anything. Unless he wanted to, Nash thought, hating the relentless man.

"Louie?" Roemer asked. "Bullshit."

"He did it for me."

"Bullshit."

"Let's find out," Nash said.

They sat in the living room of Vismara's rented house. He wore striped pajama bottoms and his girlfriend, sitting on the hassock by the unused fireplace, had on a cloth robe. Their faces were sleep lined.

"He's been in bed with you all night?" Nash demanded.

"Since he came home. What? Midnight or something?" She shrugged, shook her head to wake up. Nash, Janice, and Roemer stood in a semicircle.

"Little earlier. I left the hotel about eleven or something, right?" Vismara, his oily hair disarrayed, asked Roemer.

"Right, Louie."

"You knew Escobar and you knew his habits," Nash said. "You were his client."

Vismara scratched his chest and spoke sharply. "I ain't sorry somebody shanked the guy, Judge. No way. He should get it big time."

"I didn't ask to have him killed."

"You a lucky guy. You got a favor. Remember, I told you about favors?" Vismara asked. "Sometimes you get a favor, you don't know who does it."

"I know," Nash said, revolted with certainty. Vismara was a man of loyalty and ruthlessness. He admires me, Nash thought. So he took out the threat to me, and to the sting.

"Get some sleep, Louie," Roemer said. "More review tomorrow. Don't think about this tonight."

Janice said, "The local police are investigating. They'll find whatever evidence exists."

"Sure." Vismara yawned, got up, and put his arm protectively around the woman in the robe. "They find everything. They catch whoever did it."

"Nighty night," Roemer said as the door closed, and the three of them stood on the neat lawn of Vismara's rented house, paid for by the government in return for his work. Roemer seemed to take satisfaction in the ordinariness of the neighborhood. All the lights were out in every house.

"He's responsible, Neil," Nash said.

"I don't think so. I think he's got a solid story."

"The police will make a case," Janice said.

It was possible, Nash saw, to relieve the conscience of any taint of complicity by holding firmly to the undefined present. The future was susceptible to any wishful meaning. The past was gone. If Janice and Roemer insisted on believing in Vismara's innocence, they could do so without strain. But innocence was delusory for all of them. They had done and seen too much.

I know, he thought. I can't hide behind the unknown future.

He said, "Keep him away from me. I don't want to be anywhere near him."

Roemer looked at the tensed, anguished man. "I'll do whatever makes it easier for you to testify, Tim."

"It's murder," Nash said to Janice in their apartment. Their mutual possessions, pictures and clothes, a lamp bought together, visible reminders of new bonds together.

"If it is Vismara, then we'll take steps," she said on the bed.

"Until then, full speed ahead? Grand jury indictments from a killer?"

"You don't know he's done anything. Nobody does."

"Honestly, Janice?"

"We'll get every report. I want to know as much as you do."

Nash was silent.

"Christ Almighty, Tim. You want to jeopardize a very expensive, very sensitive undercover operation because of a suspicion?"

"I know. You know. Neil knows, too."

"No. You're the only one."

"Roemer knows and he doesn't care. He only cares if the cops can make a provable case. Maybe they can't."

"Then that settles it," she said. "He's clear."

Nash lay back on the bed. The lights were on throughout the apartment. He still wore his coat, his shoes without socks.

"You should be candid enough to admit why you're acting like this," Janice said.

"I'm seeing the truth."

Janice was impatient. "You're angry because the trial's screwed up. You need a scapegoat."

"I'm not accusing Vismara of murder because a trial's got to be redone." Nash sat up again, looking at her in wonderment.

She was tired and irritable. "Tell the truth to everybody but yourself. That's how we go through life."

"You know what he did."

She swore again and he was afraid, even in his awful knowledge, that she would stay out of bed or leave. But she only went into the bathroom and he heard the sink being noisily used. Wash it off, all of it, the stink of the alley, hope that's all there is.

When she came out, he had turned the lights out slowly and dropped his shoes at the foot of the bed. She slipped in beside him. He could smell the fresh soap on her face.

"We're right on the edge, aren't we, Tim?" she asked in the dark.

"Yes," he whispered.

VALLES THOUGHT THE FLABBY FAMILY COUNSELOR LIKED LISTENING to himself. "I hear anger. I hear resentment. I hear frustration," the man said, striding his fern-filled office, poking the air near Valles and Arlene, Harry sitting away from them on a chair. "I don't hear support."

"We love our children," Arlene said. "We've done everything you can think of."

Valles sank back in the too soft cushions. He hated his wife's defending herself to this fraud. Valles had come along under protest to the free counseling session offered by the police department. He took some slight satisfaction that he had been right. It was a waste of time.

"Love," the counselor repeated as if it were a foreign word. "You love your parents, Harry?"

"Sure," Harry said slowly. He had on his thin denim jacket and lay half sitting, half reclining. Valles wanted to go shake him. He was embarrassing him and Arlene.

"Look," Valles snapped, "we got two kids. This one's the only problem."

"What do you think of your dad, Harry?" The counselor poked the air with a pen. "You like him, sitting here right now? What do you think right now?"

Valles tensed. How could a kid change so much so fast? Harry flicked his eyes over his parents. "Hey, look at him yourself. What do you think he looks like?" The smirk was wide.

"This's how I make a living." Valles was on his feet. "It pays the bills, okay? It pays for your room, your clothes, your smart mouth."

"I hear that anger again," sighed the counselor.

"Harry started it," Arlene said.

"Right," Harry said, smirking.

Valles could stand no more. He was now supposed to be ashamed of being a cop and working undercover. He was supposed to apologize for trying to keep drugs away from kids like Harry? He wasn't going to cringe or grovel in front of this fool and his teenage son.

"Look, I'm proud of my job. I do a good job. Right now I'm doing things that'll shake this city up. Me. My partner and me. I'm doing the best I can for my family, the people I work with. You're going to hear all about this pretty soon, you're going to feel pretty stupid sitting here criticizing me." It came out in a blurted, defiant rush, and he realized he had jumped up. But at least they'd know when the judge got arrested, the sheriff's department had deputies arrested for selling dope.

Harry, Valles saw, just shook his head at the outburst. I wish, Valles thought, taking Arlene's hand, he was eight years old again.

Nash waited until the jurors were quiet. They had all read the papers or heard the news on TV by now. He could tell from their eyes, going to the empty seat beside Soika at the counsel table. How would my dad tell them? Nash wondered, looking down from the bench. The esteemed Jack Nash might be able to make it understandable.

"Ladies and gentlemen," he said, "you've all probably heard that defense counsel in this trial was killed last night."

Archie Marleau, arms still folded, nodded. Mrs. Spirlock lowered her eyes. The faces were expressionless on the other jurors. Benisek sat with hands limply at the sides of his chair. Soika, shackled tightly, bound down so he could hardly move at all, muttered to the red-eyed Cindy Duryea. Somebody cared about Vince Escobar, Nash thought.

"I want to make certain that you do not speculate now or later about there being any connection between Mr. Escobar's death and this trial. Some of you may sit as jurors again. You should treat these sad events as totally separate." I wish I could, he thought. This morning, Janice and I barely spoke, each moving around the apartment carefully. On the edge, she'd said last night, poised to go over and be lost. Neither of us wants that, he thought.

"After hearing so much evidence, I am sorry to say, you won't have a chance to deliberate on this case," Nash went on in his official voice, eyes cold, black robed, elevated on the bench. "You will all be excused. On behalf of the county, I want to thank you for your time and attention in my courtroom. You are the basis of our system of justice. When you leave here, I'll ask you to return to the jury commissioner for possible service elsewhere in the courthouse."

He glanced down at Cindy Duryea and the confused, angry Soika.

"Anything from the defense at this time?"

"No, Your Honor," Duryea said slowly.

"People?"

"Nothing, Your Honor."

Nash faced the jurors again. "Very well. At this time I declare this case a mistrial. We'll reconvene Monday at eight forty-five to set a new trial date."

"Will the court hear a bail motion for Mr. Soika?" Cindy Duryea blew her nose on a paper tissue.

"No," Nash said. "Bail will remain."

Escobar, he thought, would have appreciated her attempt to take advantage of even his death if it would benefit their client.

When only Benisek remained, Nash said from the bench, in the empty courtroom, "Anything new on last night, Craig?"

Benisek gathered himself slowly from his seat. Weeks of testimony wasted, witnesses frightened or irritated about coming back weighed on him. "Nothing, Judge. The cops say it doesn't look too good."

"It's early. Things change."

"This is going to be unsolved homicide number twenty-six for this year," Benisek said. A wry grin appeared. "So far."

* * *

283

The drive to Sacramento was longer than Nash anticipated, and he thought frequently of how he would confront his father. No right moment had yet appeared to him. He hesitated again and again because he couldn't turn to his brother or mother or anyone. It was first and foremost between him and Jack.

The federal courthouse at night was a gray block with shafts of light driven up its cold sides from the lawn. Retired cops worked as security guards, wearing ill-fitting blue blazers, and they helped him upstairs to the grand jury. Roemer and Janice waited in the corridor. Nash's mind was a welter of facts and words, the half-heard, half-recalled things Frenkel or Frank had said. He was nervous at the threshold of testifying.

"Relax," Roemer said jovially. He wore a blue pinstripe suit and carried a long rolled-up chart of the charges and incidents he would present to the federal grand jury. "They want to hear you. They're very interested. I gave them a terrific opening statement and they're ready to sink their teeth into this case."

Janice looked sallow in the night lights burning high throughout this floor of the federal courthouse. She had to stay later with Roemer when other witnesses appeared, so Nash and she didn't drive to Sacramento together. "The jury's taking a ten-minute break," she said. "You look fine."

"Let's go in now," Nash said.

The courtroom was larger, the ceiling fading upward into elegant scrollwork, the carpet thick and rich, and Nash felt uneasy as he sat on the witness stand. There was no judge. In the jury box sat eighteen men and women, interchangeable with the unfinished Soika jury he had excused. On the special boards Roemer had wheeled in were large color and black-and-white photos of Nash with Frank Wisot at the Santa Maria courthouse or Ruth Frenkel holding the envelope at the Cypress Hotel suite. The blowups were grainy, but the faces distinct. Roemer had tacked the list of charges opposite the photos so the jury could read them. Nash saw bribery, misuse of office, tax evasion, all the offenses Janice had told him that first night. They had come to pass.

Roemer was a methodical, surprisingly colorless prosecutor with only the audience of the grand jury. Nash sat on the witness stand, trying to think only about the questions, how he would frame a clear answer. He kept losing track. Escobar or Vismara would come to mind, or his father, and the nagging feeling he was betraying Frank Wisot. He brutally tamped down this emotion.

"Did Judge Wisot accept this money from you, Judge Nash?" Roemer asked, standing a few feet away, holding a legal pad.

"Yes, he did."

"What did he say?"

"He said it would help his retirement."

"Were you searched by FBI agents when Judge Wisot left the hotel suite?"

"Yes, I was."

"Did you have any of the marked government funds still in your possession?"

"No. All of it was given to Judge Wisot."

Roemer said to the grand jury, "This concludes the incident of October twelfth. We'll now consider evidence about the incident of October fifteenth involving Judge Ruth Frenkel."

Nash, soon after he began testifying, felt sweaty, then clammy. It was a terrific strain to speak concisely, emotionlessly, about the meetings. After he was finished, Roemer would play the audio and video tapes for the jury. He saw them making notes on steno pads. He wondered, in passing judgment on Frank, Ruth, and the others, if they were passing silent judgment on him as well.

He ended his testimony before midnight and ran into Vismara sitting outside the courtroom on a bench with Janice. A security guard, with glasses and lined face, smiled benignly, like an old tailor pleased with a fit.

Nash passed them. It was the last time he saw Vismara. "You're going to get away with it, Lou," he said.

Vismara, dressed with sober care, had a more sorrowful expression than Nash expected. "I don't get away with anything, Judge. I wanted to be friends."

"That was a major mistake," Nash said. Janice glanced over at the courtroom doors opening, Roemer beckoning. She tapped Vismara and they stood up.

"I make a lot of mistakes," Vismara said, smoothing his suit, walking toward the open courtroom where Roemer impatiently waited.

* * *

Janice didn't get back until very late. She found Nash, bundled in a coat, his sweatpants sticking out, sitting by the pool, alone.

"Thinking of a swim?" she asked, sitting beside him.

"Just thinking."

"You did very well. Very well. The jury returned five sealed indictments tonight."

"When are they going to be arrested?"

Janice moved closer to him, but he didn't change position. The blue-lit water, lying in a cold rectangle under the star-filled sky, shimmered over them and the apartments nearby. "Neil's making the arrangements. It'll be soon."

"Do you know?"

"No."

"I don't really want to know."

"Don't you want to go in?"

"I don't have to be in court so punctually right now."

"You feel let down? It's natural after testifying so long, this operation's been very intense."

"I do feel let down, I guess," he admitted. "All my life here doing the right thing was simple. It wasn't confusing. It wasn't painful."

"I told you it wasn't easy, Tim. Not this kind of operation."

"I thought good motives counted for more," he said. Then he looked at her. "I'm going to try to get Vismara, Janice. I've got to do that."

She pulled away and spoke sharply. "You're being paranoid about him."

"If I ignore it, I'm part of it." He did not want to fight with her, and from the pause, he could tell she, too, had stepped back from a decisive argument. They stared at the pool. "We could go for a swim."

"It's got to be sixty degrees. It's freezing."

"A cold swim toughens you up." They had shifted to banter again as an escape valve. He did not know how long it would work.

"I'm not that tough," Janice said.

Their legs crossed on the pool chair. "Frank Wisot wants to meet me tomorrow. He's got something, some deal, something to show me."

"You don't have to go. The indictment's ready."

"He's still a friend."

"The arrests are so close, it'd be bad to spoil things with a security problem now, Tim."

"I'll be careful. I don't need to be wired, do I?" The chill crowded in again.

"Not anymore."

"I don't need Jacobs following in the van, either."

"You're on your own. I think you should put him off."

"No," Nash said resignedly, "I can't do that. It'll just be two old pals getting together like always."

NASH AND FRANK WISOT WALKED DEEPER INTO THE EMPTY machine-tool warehouse. Water dripped from a broken pipe onto the concrete floor.

"We didn't have to come out so far," Nash said. "This is in the middle of no place, Frank." They stood about four feet apart. Both wore overcoats because it was cold, the last week of October. Wisot had on sunglasses as black as his thick coat. He had his hands in his pockets.

"Place belongs to my son-in-law. Some kind of tax write-off. I wanted to come someplace without distractions."

"Distractions?"

"Every place we've met, you picked. I wasn't thinking." Wisot glanced out one of the gray windows at the orange-tinted twilight.

"You picked the banquet in Monterey," Nash said. He didn't understand Wisot's odd manner, the choice of this place. Was Frank trying to sell him an old warehouse? As they came in, Nash had seen a shuttered Chinese restaurant and a weedy, cracked asphalt lot as the closest neighbors. "I'm hungry. I've got dinner waiting," he said.

Wisot smiled faintly.

"You're not playing around, Tim? The same one? Same one you brought to Harold's fund-raiser, the picnic, the banquet?"

"Yeah. She's waiting for me."

"The U.S. Attorney's office," Wisot said to himself, acting as if Nash had vanished entirely. "Federal jurisdiction."

"She told you. She's been with them for a while." Nash didn't know where Wisot's mind was wandering. He did not like the scattered comments about Janice and her job. Wisot's behavior made him uneasy.

"I've been thinking about it all," Wisot said, looking finally at Nash.

"Vismara won't go for any more money."

"No more money." Wisot shivered. "I'm sorry I got any."

"What is it? What else do you want?"

Wisot took a gun from his heavy-overcoat pocket and pointed it at Nash. "No jokes anymore. What's going on, Tim? What are you doing to me?"

"Don't point a gun," Nash said tensely, startled. "You don't need it, for God's sake. It's me."

"Why did you offer me the money, Tim? What's going on?"

"Jesus, I just wanted to help you out. I've known you since I was a kid. You and my Father, you're old friends. I thought you needed some help, like I did."

"Crap," Wisot said loudly, his voice echoing against the tin walls of the empty warehouse. "More crap. That's all you've been giving me. I can see that now."

"I swear, Frank, Vismara came to me and wanted help and I thought I'd let you have some of it, too. Put the gun away."

Wisot had a sick smile. "Everybody's got bad luck around you. Vince Escobar. That's the damnedest thing. I just approved a bill he sent for a manslaughter trial he did in my court."

"Please put the gun away, Frank. Come on."

"My bad luck. This Vismara's a phony. I ran through all his court files, the old ones. There's Escobar's name." Wisot frowned. "My God. What is going on? I should've checked those records right off. But I trusted you."

"I swear to God, I didn't know. Vismara set me up," Nash said hastily. He would say anything to get Wisot to put the black metal gun away. He had no mike on, no van nearby, no agents listening ready to help. He was alone. The twilight deepened, the silences thickened.

"What's the setup?" Wisot demanded.

"I told you, he came to me," Nash said. The gun stayed on him.

"Not the crap. It doesn't matter to me now. What's the real setup?"

"Okay. It's an undercover operation," Nash said quickly, telling Wisot a bare-bones version of the sting. "But you aren't alone, Frank. There are others."

"Who? Anybody else on the bench? You've got other judges?"

"Yeah. Cops, too. Some court clerks, the Board of Supervisors."

Wisot's voice broke. "Oh, Jesus. Oh, Jesus."

"You can help yourself," Nash said. "You can tell Roemer names. You can offer to cooperate, make a deal. I'll help."

"Deals. My God. What did you do to me?"

"It's all taped, Frank. Video, audio, reports. The phone in your chambers, your house's tapped. You're in the files. So there's no going back."

"I want to make it like it was before any of this. I'll give back the money," Wisot said sharply.

"That's not possible. So we need to walk out of here, walk out to our cars and come to some understanding."

"Did you stop to think of my reputation? My family?" Wisot wasn't listening again, and that scared Nash very much. The gun hadn't moved. It was so close he could touch the black metal barrel. He could grab it. And Wisot would pull the trigger. Like Soika and his hostage, Nash thought. He knew how Prentice must have felt in those final despairing moments.

"Put the gun away. I've known you all my life, Frank. We can make a deal for you with Roemer."

Wisot's face sagged. "I remember when you first came to my courtroom, in the old courthouse. Remember that day? Your dad brought you and you ate all the cough drops I kept in my desk."

"Sure I remember. I liked visiting your courtroom."

Nash didn't want to indulge in recollection. He was scared and Wisot had taken bribes. As Nash started to edge backward, Wisot went on speaking, as if to himself.

"After all these years," Wisot said, "the things they'll say about me. My family. My years on the bench. Everything I've done, charities, fund-raising, school building. All ashes . . ." He trailed off.

Nash saw his chance. "Frank, come on. I can help you. I promise."

The gun shook slightly, then slowly lowered, and Wisot shivered, weeping in the bitter twilight. "Nobody else can help me," he said and jammed the gun to his head and fired.

45

Nᴀꜱʜ ʀᴇᴛᴜʀɴᴇᴅ ᴛᴏ ᴛʜᴇ Sᴀɴᴛᴀ Mᴀʀɪᴀ Cᴏᴜɴᴛʏ ᴄᴏᴜʀᴛʜᴏᴜꜱᴇ ᴛᴡᴏ days after Frank Wisot's death. He did not recognize the place in many ways. The people milling on the courthouse plaza were still there, sunshine washing over them. Inside the building, a sense of chaos prevailed. He and Janice went up to Department 14, seeing the bailiffs in clusters on each floor, hearing the subdued, funereal murmur from the lawyers, and observing the nervous glances that fastened on him all the time. He did not return any of the stares.

It was as unreal, in a way, as the night he had spent comforting Lenore, in the living room of that house. She alternated between crying and walking around. Other judges and their wives dropped by, food was brought out, a weird party sprang up. Lenore, face tear reddened, asked him over and over, "Tim, he was talking about you all that day. About you. The two of you. Something was wrong and he wouldn't tell me. I asked him. But it wouldn't come out. You know Frank, that smile he puts on when he knows something and won't talk."

"I know."

"He smiled at me. He said he'd talk to you and it would all be fine, but he was worried. I didn't know he was so worried. What was it, Tim? Was it that money?"

"I can't talk about it, Lenore." He took her hand and she laid a heavy head on him.

"You know so much about what happened to him and you won't tell me, Tim. You won't tell me."

It was at that moment, in her home, surrounded by the other judges, Janice as grave as the others, that Nash made his decision. He could not undo anything thus far, either Escobar's death or Frank's suicide. He could not even think of Frank's final seconds without the explosive horror of it wiping away his thoughts. So he put it aside, away, down deep, and tried to analyze where he was as a legal problem absolved of any moral dimension.

He had brought Janice to the courthouse to witness his decision.

It beat inside him unmercifully that Lenore Wisot would hear about Frank when the others were arrested. Janice said Roemer was delaying the arrests briefly, but the rumors in the courthouse were like fireflies. Shea told him over the phone the day before, "Hey, Tim, there's some strange shit going around this place. Judges are like closing their doors, getting together. The guys in courthouse control are saying there's some arrests coming. Judges are getting busted."

"What else?" Nash asked. He was struggling with the image of Frank's dead body falling, toppling like a collapsing building, at his feet.

"Shit. They're talking about an undercover deal. And you're the informant."

"You know me, Scotty."

"Yeah, that's what I tell them."

"You know me," Nash repeated. "I'll probably be in tomorrow."

"Hey, take it easy, man. It sounded rough for you."

Not quite as rough as it must have been for poor Frank in the last hours of his life or for Vince Escobar when he saw the knife pulled out in that alley. There must be a way, Nash thought calmly, to rectify those wrongs, some way he could think again without fearing they would shout down everything else in his mind.

He dialed the phone, Janice standing on the other side of his desk. Vi brought in coffee and looked worriedly at him. He smiled for her. "I'm fine, Vi. Thanks," he said to her unspoken concern.

Janice said, "What's going on, Tim?"

"I'm calling Neil."

"Why?"

"I'm quitting," he said. Then he heard Roemer's gruff voice on the other end of the line in the federal courthouse, the U.S. Attorney's office behind its security guards and cameras. There had been threats over the years. "Hello, Neil," Nash said. He felt at home in his chambers. Janice watched with perplexity. She would have to make her own decision soon, he thought.

"What's up, Tim? It's a busy day. I've got a lot of things to coordinate."

"The arrests are coming."

"Tomorrow. I'm going to be rock hard about it. I can't talk unless you've got something important."

Nash gripped the phone. There was, after this moment, no going back. "I'm not going to testify any more, Neil. I won't appear before the grand jury. I won't come to any trial. I'm resigning from the operation."

Janice shook her head, motioned for the phone.

"Are you kidding me?" Roemer asked.

"No. I'm done. I quit."

"Tim, I understand exactly how you feel after that thing happened."

"Wisot's suicide, Neil."

"So I won't press you on this now. You're upset. But, you've got to be crystal clear." Roemer enjoyed his pressure. "You're a crucial witness in these cases. I can make a lot of them with just Vismara and the FBI guys, but you've got to testify."

"No," Nash said.

"I'll talk to you in a day or so. I've got the next round of cases scheduled already."

"It doesn't matter," Nash said, his mind settled and his weight heavy in the chair. "I won't come in again."

"Look, Tim, I can subpoena you."

"I'll ignore it."

"If you aren't in front of the grand jury," Roemer said sharply, "I'll give you use immunity. You've got to appear."

"I won't."

"You know my next move, right? You know what I'll have to do?"

"The only way you'll get me back to the grand jury is to arrest me, Neil," Nash said. He looked at Janice's solemn face.

"Is that absolute?"

"But I still won't testify."

"You can tell me why. Maybe I might be able to jigger things if I know your thinking."

Like hell, Nash thought. But he wanted to tell Roemer anyway, if for no other reason than that Janice would hear it, too. It might help her decide. "It's not complicated," Nash said. "I think Frank would've retired, left the bench, nothing would've happened if we hadn't gone after him. I don't know what information you had on these people. It wasn't good enough for warrants or arrests. We had to push it, push them to make it work, Neil. Without us, me and Vismara and you, I don't think Wisot would've taken any money. I don't think those cops would've gone sour. I know most

292

of these people. I don't know if we actually created these crimes, but we sure as hell made it easier for them to happen."

"They were corrupt," Roemer said. "They were already corrupt."

"We pushed them over the line with the money."

"I'm going to give you a chance to reconsider," Roemer said.

Nash hung up. He thought of all the pleas for leniency he'd heard in these chambers over the years. *My guy isn't so bad, Judge. Look at his rap. He's got nothing heavy and he's been clean for three years.* Nash thought of his own lofty pronouncements in reply, the sentences he'd handed out. There was, he thought, temptation enough in the world without enlarging on it.

Janice said, "I don't understand."

"Roemer doesn't either. He says he'll arrest me."

"You haven't left him any choice, Tim. You're defying the government."

Nash got up and took her hands. "No. Just him. I'm only throwing Broken Trust back at him."

"Neil doesn't bluff. He'll do whatever he has to."

"I'm sure of it." A moral gesture was pointless without risk, and Nash needed something for the sickness he carried. A strong medicine was the only remedy for his guilt.

"How do you think you'll change anything? We've accomplished some real, positive good in Santa Maria."

"No. We've hurt a lot of people. They didn't deserve it."

"So now you want me to choose, don't you?" She hugged him closely.

"Yeah," he said, wishing there were an equivocation possible for either of them. "It's my side or his, Janice."

"It's not that defined. Because I love you, it can't be so simple." She twisted away, and he knew she had chosen.

"I want you to stand by me."

"You're making an empty, foolish point, Tim. I won't endorse that. I can't do that," she said sadly. He said something more, but could not hear himself speaking. *She's leaving, she's taking the new joy I felt with her.* He wanted to tell her that Frank Wisot's death didn't matter and Roemer was correct, the upheavals that Broken Trust had caused were sidelines compared to the bolder truth it underlined. Maybe that's it, he thought. There's a lot of truth in this sting but very little justice.

"Stay away for a couple of hours," she said. "I'll pack up. I should be spending most of my time in Sacramento anyway."

"I won't be back for a while," he said. "I've got a few things to do."

"Tim. Stop and think."

"I have."

She walked out of his chambers, and he could hear, for some distance, the sound of her footsteps on the solid floor, then the court's thin carpet, the courtroom doors squeaking slightly, faintly, and the silence that followed. He had no court business today. Ruth Frenkel had thoughtfully shifted all of his law and motion calendar to Henshaw's court.

Her arrest was coming, and Nash, alone in his chambers, felt hollow.

In the waiting room of the law firm where his father was sitting as private judge, Nash saw the stacks of newspapers carrying Wisot's picture, the formal portrait with him in his robes. The headlines were black, too.

He went back into the conference room, still littered with papers and cups, the carafes of coffee. Jack Nash, in a sweater, smoking a Camel, looked as if he had just stepped from his own house. Both parties in the land boundary line case had decided, for a fee, to pay the esteemed retired judge to hear the evidence and decide the question for them.

The other lawyers, looking tired and irritable, had filed out muttering to themselves. The case was obviously rancorous.

Nash sat down.

"Timmy, your mother and I've been worried. You didn't answer any of our calls. We wanted to help you." Jack sat beside his son.

"I'm sorry, Dad. I had to think about a lot of things."

"Oh, Jesus, yes. Oh, yes. Old Frank. God, I can't believe it."

"I had him taking a bribe, Dad. He was going to be arrested today or tomorrow. It's this sting I've been doing."

Jack Nash put down his cigarette, frowning. His white hair was combed carefully, his fingers stained with ink because he always used a fountain pen. But Nash sensed a sudden wall come down. "He was taking money, Timmy?"

"We had it all on tape. I hope they burn the tapes now, but there he was."

"Tell me about the sting."

"You know about it, Dad. They came to you and you went to Terhune and he brought me in. I know about the McKays, too.

That's my problem now. I know about you." He slumped a little. "I know everything."

"What you know"—Jack was unforgiving and unforgiven—"is nothing, Timmy. You've got a few little pieces of my life that happened so long ago I hardly remember any of it. If I can't remember who told me about a deal or showed how to help my family or my partners, why should anybody else? Why should my son? It's gone, it's all dust. Everything I am came later, and I believe you can wash all that crap away." Jack Nash drummed his fingers hard on the conference table. "But that guy from Washington, he thought a quarter century's work didn't count. All the things I did as a judge, the way people thought of me, it didn't matter. It was the shit that mattered. Because I did something years ago, my life wasn't mine anymore."

Nash heard his father's voice from the bench, untainted and unclouded, and his own fearful pain lifted. The whole justification for criminal law was that some crimes, most in fact, were expiable. No one was condemned.

"I didn't want to find out for myself," Nash said. "It's like someone telling you you're adopted. You should have told me."

"I was ashamed. I still am."

But nothing broke Jack Nash's expression. He lit another Camel and let it burn. He put his hand out. "I am sorry, Timmy."

Nash took the hand. They had shaken hands once when he and Dick were sent to summer camp. Hilary waved as they lifted their backpacks on, but Jack put his hand out to each of his sons. It was a revelation now to Nash that his father was a shy man.

They sat together and Nash told his father everything that had happened since Terhune brought him to the hotel room.

46

DWIGHT PEATLING WAS PROPPED IN BED, A BOX OF TISSUES BESIDE him, a hot-water bottle at his feet. The TV was loudly showing him a bright game, and the humidifier his wife insisted he use sprayed moistly from the dresser. It was a little before ten and he had a terrible cold.

He sneezed painfully and rubbed his red nose with a tissue. Newspapers with the Wisot thing all over them lay around him. He was relieved not to be at the courthouse today. Death, violence, all appalled him, and he didn't like the ugly mutterings going around about Wisot or Nash.

It was the talk about Nash that bothered him. He had been trying vainly to sort it out all morning, fighting against the heaviness in his head from the cold, and an unsettling fear. He should have mentioned something to his wife. Today. When she got back from the store. She had stayed away from work, too, to nurse him.

Peatling heard car doors slamming outside, the dog barking downstairs, and he tried to watch the TV. He sneezed again and muttered distractedly, wiping his nose.

The bedroom door opened. Two men, obviously cops in their suits, similar overcoats, walked in. His wife hung back. The dog was barking frantically downstairs.

"I'm off today," Peatling said impatiently. "I won't check any warrant requests. You go to the next judge on the list."

The two cops started talking and he didn't understand them at first, with the TV loudly cackling, the dog, the humidifier. They weren't here with any warrant request. What were they saying? It was impossible. It couldn't be.

Peatling's wife pushed in, sat beside him on the bed, and grabbed his shoulders, rocking him. He heard more car doors slamming outside, many cars, and voices.

Ruth Frenkel sipped a cup of tea in her chambers and made notes for Frank Wisot's memorial service, to be held at the end of the week, in the morning. It would play havoc with the trial schedules, but everyone was giving way out of respect.

She had toy dogs on the sofa and photos of her dog behind her. Cheryl, her clerk, wouldn't stop talking about the rumors rushing back and forth through the courthouse like tides. She kept bringing in phone messages from TV stations, newspapers, radio, all wanting a comment from the new presiding judge about Frank Wisot's suicide, the strong suggestion he was involved in something dishonest. Her answers were crisp. "Frank Wisot was the most decent and honorable man I knew," she said time after time to the reporters.

The sky, through the long windows of her new chambers, was cloudy. I'll have to talk to Tim soon, she thought, jotting down a note that he might speak at the memorial. Or maybe it was too shocking for him? He hadn't answered any of her calls. She recalled a line he might use, one from a funeral she'd been to as a child: "O God, whose mercies cannot be numbered," it began. Very suitable.

Then Ruth Frenkel stirred a little uneasily at the idea that Tim's involvement with her would become known. But poor Frank, nearing retirement, had simply hated coming to the end of a very long career. That made the most sense.

Ruth Frenkel glanced up. Cheryl was shouting in her office. She came running in, face straining, eyes wide. It was hard to understand her. The phones started ringing very loudly. Behind her were two men.

"They're here to arrest you," Cheryl cried. "They're going to arrest you!"

For an instant, Ruth Frenkel thought of her college Spanish class when a frantic, tearful coed ran in and yelled, "They've shot the President in the head!" and the unimaginable thing of Kennedy's dying came true.

"Are you Ruth Carol Frenkel?" asked the first man, a tall, direct man with a paper in his hand. Like a movie, she thought.

"Yes. What's going on?" Cheryl, hands to her face in her own terror, wept loudly. Ruth Frenkel had to raise her voice.

297

"My name is Lawrence Jacobs," said the man. "I'm an agent with the Federal Bureau of Investigation, and I have a warrant for your arrest."

Ruth Frenkel sucked in a quick breath involuntarily, spilling her tea over the notes for the memorial service. She suddenly saw all of the TV news trucks and reporters flocking outside the courthouse when she had driven up that morning. They aren't here for comments about Frank Wisot, she thought.

Valles and Witwer, in their biker gear, stood outside the California-Asian Market on Exeter Avenue talking seriously with three young Vietnamese men in black jeans. They had been arguing for several minutes about the price for a kilo of tar heroin that the young men wanted to buy. Baskets of cabbage and fruit were at their feet.

Valles, immersed in the transaction, didn't notice the obvious blue government sedan that crawled to the curb and stopped until Witwer coughed and glanced over at it.

None of the Vietnamese kids saw it either. They were bickering in querulous, high tones about the outrageous price Valles had quoted them. They had ambitions of going into the heroin distribution business in southern Santa Maria.

"They're watching us, Rog," Witwer said quietly.

Valles sucked his teeth noisily. "No, just some lost bozo."

"They're coming over here."

"They're going to the market."

But Valles wasn't sure. The two men who got out of the car were feds; the bearing and casual arrogance always seemed to mark them in his experience. The lead man strolled toward them.

"They're going to fuck up this deal," Witwer whispered desperately.

"Roger Valles and Jerry Witwer?" asked the lead man. His partner gazed coldly at the Vietnamese kids. They had stopped talking and then, with hummingbird fluidity, ran off down the sidewalk.

"You screwed up our deal, man," Valles said furiously. He had balled up a fist.

"You're under arrest," the lead man said.

By his watch, Valles had been sitting in the interview room at the Santa Maria County Sheriff's Department for forty minutes. It had run for much longer in his mind. He had not realized, until he was arrested, how slowly time crept by when you were stuck alone in an interview room. He clenched and unclenched his fist for exercise.

Abruptly, the door opened and Witwer, blinking, came in. The door locked behind him.

"Take a seat, Jerry," Valles offered. There was only another metal chair and a small wooden table in the room.

"Shit. I told them I had to take a piss and they brought me here."

"You take the piss?"

"Yeah. It's a weird feeling being busted, Rog," Witwer said quietly. "Like all those cameras outside and the fucking reporters."

Valles jammed his chair against the wall as he got up. "That's what burns me. They just blew us undercover. I don't know what kind of screwup they made, but our pictures are all over now. We're public."

"Crooked cops," Witwer said quietly. He scratched his beard. "Every damn reporter said we're crooked cops and how's it feel to get bagged."

"The feds screwed it up," Valles said confidently. "Look, soon's they sit down with the state guys in Sacramento, we're okay. We're running an operation for the California attorney general, Jerry. They can't mess with us."

"I hope so," Witwer sighed dispiritedly. "I feel so lonely, man."

"You call Maggie?"

"She's out. I left a message. You talk to Arlene?"

Valles laughed sardonically. "I talked to Harry. I told him, hey, come on down and bail out your old man, kid. He's in jail."

They laughed. Then Witwer looked oddly at Valles. "You know, I been so miserable the last couple of hours, I didn't even think why these assholes are putting us together like this."

Valles suddenly grinned, too. "You been questioned yet?"

Witwer shook his head. Valles sat down next to him. "Me neither," he said.

"So they put us together like this so we'll start talking about all the shit we've been doing," Witwer said.

"Like we're a couple of dumb dopers." Valles started laughing at the idea of the sheriff's detectives and feds straining even now to hear through the county's poor-quality headphones.

They both laughed for some time.

47

NASH AND HIS MOTHER AND FATHER SAT AROUND THE LARGE TV in the living room of his parents' home. The sound was lowered. On the coffee table were half-finished drinks. They had eaten dinner, and the trees clacked and brushed against the house in the night's wind.

"I can't look at that poor woman's face again," Hilary Nash said in distress. Ruth Frenkel, handcuffed, was shown again on the screen, being led out of the county courthouse. Her face was bleached and empty, and she looked right and left as if searching for help. The mass of microphones pressing toward her waved and undulated as if in a wind, too. Next came Peatling, stumbling once as he left his home, a raincoat over what appeared to be his pajamas, put into the back of an unmarked government car, his wife, shocked, interviewed in the doorway of the violated home.

Nash wondered what his father had told his mother. She had not known, he was sure, about Terhune's payments or the threat to Jack they blocked. Her attitude toward him hadn't changed, as far as Nash could see. Perhaps it never could, he thought. Too much life lived together in a certain way weighed against any change now.

Peatling's frightened wife was replaced on the TV by the two cops, both in handcuffs, saying something to the camera. Valles was cursing. Nash picked up his half-emptied vodka tonic. Enough liquor had flowed through dinner to dull any shock. His father sat on the farthest easy chair, smoking, shaking his head.

Nash said, "Harold Atchley came up to me at the elevator this morning. He said he doesn't want my endorsement anymore."

"Give it to him anyway," Jack Nash said. "That should cost him some votes."

"At least he's talking to me," Nash said.

300

"No one else?" Hilary asked. Her slim fingers curled around the sofa's armrest tightly.

"I'm the invisible man. I walk into a courtroom, it gets quiet. I get into an elevator and everybody stops talking. Ever since the arrests, I don't exist."

"They'll change," his mother said. She looked at Jack. "It can't last. You're not doing anything wrong."

"They're scared," Jack said. "Who else gets arrested? You're not invisible, Timmy. You're radioactive."

His mother shook her head disbelievingly. "You would not think so many people would call us. Threats. Lies. Obscenities."

"I'm sorry," Nash said.

"I had the number unlisted," she went on, picking up her own drink. "Who are they? I can't believe judges would do that. I didn't recognize any of the voices."

"It could be anyone, Hills. Cops or friends of cops. Nuts."

But not one call, Nash thought, from Janice. He wouldn't have minded the other judges, Croncota, Henshaw, even Jardine, moving away when he walked by on a corridor or came into the cafeteria. They had all walked out of the judges' meeting yesterday, leaving him alone in the room.

Just hearing her would be enough.

"Hey, there's our old friend," Jack said, getting out of his chair quickly, turning up the TV. Neil Roemer, dark suited, the blue suspenders peeking out, stood behind a podium on the steps of the federal courthouse. Nash's heart sank. Behind Roemer, in the crushed disorder of people, was Janice. He could read nothing in her expression. Roemer spoke into the clumsy bundle of twenty microphones.

"The first stage of Operation Broken Trust is over. The first arrests mean the uncovering of widespread corruption in the members of the Santa Maria County bench. Indictments were returned against three judges." Nash swore at the TV.

Jack said coldly, "Won't even let Frank lie down."

Roemer went on, his fighter's broken features blunt and brutal in the glare of sunlight and camera lights. "Other arrests will be made soon. And the investigation is continuing. Operation Broken Trust has demonstrated that misuse of office for private gain will not be tolerated by the American people. It doesn't matter if you're a thief or a crooked judge." He paused. "We will get you."

The reporters, brought up close, shouted questions at him, names of possible new suspects, other judges, other cops or lawyers, who else was going to be brought in? Roemer smiled. "I can't talk about specific targets. The grand jury is still meeting and our investigation is continuing, as I said."

Hilary got up and briskly snapped off the TV. "No more. He's a posturing menace."

Nash finished his drink. The wind had risen and the trees rattled fitfully. "I refused his subpoena to testify. He sent a federal marshal to serve me."

"Told him to go to hell?" Jack asked.

Nash nodded. "I said he could tell Roemer to go to hell."

Hilary stood by him, and the older, more pained weariness was obvious to Nash. "What happens next, Tim?"

"Well, he'll get the grand jury to grant me use immunity. It means I can't refuse to testify. I'm protected from any criminal prosecution so I have no right not to answer questions."

"You'll refuse to answer?"

Nash held up his glass. "I think I'll get another. Yes. I'll refuse to show up."

"And the feds will find him in contempt and they can have him arrested," Jack said. "Let me get you a lawyer, Timmy. Let me get somebody in town working on this thing right now, before there's any contempt order."

Nash paused on his way to the kitchen. "Why?"

"To stop Roemer," Jack Nash said in surprise.

Nash put down his glass and walked back unsteadily to his mother, putting his hand on her shoulder. "I've got a lot to say about Roemer and this operation, Dad. I've got to be able to say it with some legitimacy."

Hilary looked up at him. Jack grunted in puzzlement. "I can't see how having a court hold you in contempt helps, Tim," she said.

Nash thought for a moment. There were practical reasons why his information about how Operation Broken Trust was set up and run might sound better if he, too, had been a victim of its abuses and Roemer's calculation. He was first an agent of justice before he became a victim of personal ambition.

But the basic fact was that he didn't want to go any further. He could not appear before the grand jury now no matter what the compulsion might be. Standing in his way were Frank, even Escobar, and the sad desire of a dope dealer to grab a second chance. There were friends he had baited with money and deceived.

The heart of his inability to go to the grand jury wasn't practical or coherent. He simply felt it as a small, token way of reckoning his sins against others.

He gripped his mother's shoulder. "I want to be arrested," he said.

Three thousand miles away, in his office in Washington, D.C., Paul Cleary saw the Roemer press conference by cable-TV feed. He sat at his desk, a bottle of mineral water and his blood pressure pills at hand. He poured a glass of water and counted out three pale-yellow pills, swallowing them before he picked up the phone.

The twenty-four-hour-a-day operator available to him as assistant attorney general answered on the second ring.

"I'd like to speak to Neil Roemer in Sacramento, California," he said slowly. At this hour, even the best night-duty phone operators sometimes got drowsy and missed what he said.

WITH A SATISFIED SMILE, ROEMER PUT HIS HAND OVER HIS PLATE, and the white-coated black waiter nodded and paused at Paul Cleary's side. Cleary smiled slightly and the waiter neatly added a second lamb chop. He turned and a moment later, spooned mint jelly from a small silver bowl onto both plates.

"You know, I don't think I've eaten up here more than twice, all the years I've been with the department," Roemer said, knife working away on his chops. "I always liked the atmosphere."

Cleary sat back, unwilling to tackle his late-lunch plate of food. The Department of Justice dining room was large enough for the dozen or so men and women scattered at other tables to talk without their conversations mixing at all. He was reminded of the faculty room at Boston, when he was young, before it was cut in half and redecorated in plastic. Here the dark panels shone with polish, the gilt-edged paintings glimmered, the silver tableware gleamed. It was restful. To eat here was to feel an earned privilege, sustained by tradition.

"Well, I've always found it a place where things can be talked about better," Cleary said. He pushed his fork against the braised vegetables but didn't lift it. He hardly ate anything lately. After this late lunch, he would go back to his office and have a solitary apple, perhaps some cottage cheese. This lunch was official.

"I appreciate it, Paul," Roemer said, chewing happily on his food. "It was a thoughtful gesture. Premature, though."

"How so?"

"Broken Trust isn't over yet. A celebration won't be in order for a couple of months."

Cleary nodded and lifted his fork again, then laid it with a melodic sound on the plate. "The reports I've seen show a strenuous effort, Neil."

"It's been a lot of work," Roemer said. He swallowed hard from a too large mouthful. "But it's worth it. I made a lot of solid cases."

Cleary nodded noncommittally. He motioned their waiter for a second glass of wine for Roemer, then said, "You had some trouble spots."

"Always. Every operation. But nothing too bad. It all came together nicely, even the judge turning on me."

"I didn't quite understand that, Neil."

Roemer drank deeply and studied his glass with pleasure. "He wasn't a hundred percent with the operation. He fooled me at the beginning."

"Perhaps it was that suicide?"

"I don't know. He wasn't a hundred percent. Could I get another glass? I'm thirsty," he said, and Cleary again motioned for their waiter, the red wine rushing to the top of the crystal. Cleary had an unpleasant impression of his own sluggish blood.

"Then the mixed signals with the state people about those police officers," Cleary said, biting the side of his lip. "You had your own operation chasing itself around. Like a dog after his own tail." He smiled.

Roemer twisted a little in his chair to see if he recognized anyone else in the restricted dining room. "That won't be a major difficulty. The cops are bad on giving drugs to an addict-informant."

"I'm talking about everybody taping everybody else, Neil. That looks extremely unprofessional."

Roemer's chewing slowed. "It's not a problem. I'll be able to get a good spin on it. The cops were rotten."

Cleary moved his knife and fork around the cooling lamb and was unmoved by its aroma. He said, "I'm sure you're right about that. We'll do an internal review of Broken Trust from start to finish."

"A what?"

"A review. We'll do an in-house examination of the whole operation to see where we might have made mistakes, involved innocent people, put the Justice Department and the administration out on a limb."

Roemer sat back, hard eyed. "I run the operation."

"So I know you'll be willing to provide the internal auditors with all of your daily logs, your notes, your phone records," Cleary said with the wintry smile he had used on poor students.

Roemer broke in, "You're targeting me."

"You'll be a central component."

Roemer pushed his chair back. It moved jerkily in the thick carpet and their waiter darted forward to help him up. He stared at Cleary. "You can't dump any mistakes on my head, Cleary. I've done everything with approval."

"Well, one of the mandates of this review will be to consider such personal undercover operations in the future, Neil. This comes from the general personally."

"You're taking me out of undercover corruption?"

Cleary shook his head. "We're only going to dissect the causes of a homicide and suicide in a personally directed undercover operation. It may be, after all, that detailed oversight by the Special Projects Committee is needed in the future."

Roemer stood up. His chair toppled over, the waiter grappled it upright, and the other diners paused, food frozen in the air, their faces startled. "I'm not going to be a fall guy. I can fight back."

Cleary sighed with what sounded like genuine sorrow. "I know you can. You may wish to consider the public scrutiny of your private life, Neil."

"My private life?" he snapped. He threw his bunched napkin down.

"Information has come to me about a senior department official committing adultery. With another member of the department."

"You're talking about goddamn blackmail, Cleary. I won't take it. I'm going public with everything."

Cleary said gently, "That's your prerogative."

"Goddamn her," Roemer said vehemently to himself, cursing into the air, hands on his hips. Cleary felt acute embarrassment at this display. It had been his intention to do everything with calmness and civility, a mutually observed dignity. Every story about Roemer's base early life must be true, he thought.

The waiters stood immobile, startled by this exotic event, and the other diners watched perplexedly.

Cleary tried to quiet Roemer's angry outbursts. "Neil, it might help to remember that even J. Edgar Hoover had to bend before a new administration."

"Push me aside so your old pals can run things?" Roemer waved a rough-knuckled fist at Cleary. "I'm not J. Edgar Hoover."

"No," Cleary said with the years of a classroom disciplinarian behind his cold tone, "that's exactly the point."

49

BY MIDMORNING, NASH HAD GOTTEN THROUGH MOST OF HIS LAW and motion calendar, saving the sentencings for last. Department 14 was crowded with people, lawyers sitting near the front, families bunched together, children fidgeting, one or two crying. Shea stood by the tank doorway, bringing out defendants as Nash called a name and case number. Vi worked at her desk below him. It all looked normal, he thought.

But there was no trial after this calendar. He would go back and sit in his chambers, as he had for two days, waiting. Three new judges, brought in from other counties by the Judicial Council, were dispersed throughout the courthouse to take up the slack for the missing Santa Maria judges.

Nash felt it was coming, soon. He did not know when.

"Arthur Wayne Mansfield, number 47891," he said. He passed the just sentenced auto thief's file down to Vi.

The courtroom stirred and a small gray man, hands behind his back, appeared by Shea in the tank's holding pen. Nash began the script. "Does the public defender have anything to say before I pass sentence?"

At his paper- and file-cluttered place at the counsel table, KO Conway rose slowly. "Yes, Your Honor. Mr. Mansfield is a fifty-two-year-old former plumber. His record is not so bad." KO shook his head. "And his crimes, breaking into drive-up photo stands and stealing developed photographs, isn't the crime wave of the century."

Nash couldn't hear KO for a moment. Outside Department 14, in the corridor, the voices were chaotic and loud. He saw the waving arms of boom microphones, the sudden sharpness of camera lights. Shea looked up angrily.

Scotty and Vi, they've gone on as if everything's the same, he thought gratefully.

"I can't hear you, Mr. Conway," Nash said from the bench.

The courtroom's twin high doors opened, admitting a burst of shouted voices, lights, and two men in suits, who sank down into seats near the rear, watching Nash.

Nash motioned Shea to him. "Go find out who they are and tell the jackasses outside to hold it down or I'll find them all in contempt."

Shea went back, eyes following him, the courtroom's rhythm disturbed. Nash felt his heart speed up. He controlled his fear.

"I'm sorry, Mr. Conway. What else do you want to say about this defendant in mitigation?"

Conway frowned at the commotion behind him. They've come, Nash thought, trying to listen to Conway.

"Mr. Mansfield"—Nash flipped his notebook to the prescribed speeches for determinate sentences in California, the defendant's probation report beside him—"do you have anything you want to add?"

"I won't do it again," the gray man mumbled.

"People wish to be heard?"

The deputy DA shook his head. "Submitted on the recommendation of the probation department, Your Honor."

"All right." Nash glanced up, Shea coming to the side of the bench. "Arthur Wayne Mansfield, you have previously plead guilty to two counts of violation of section four fifty-nine of the Penal Code, burglary, and you have admitted one prior conviction for the crime of public lewdness." Nash paused as Shea leaned to him, tense.

"They're federal marshals, Tim. They're here to see you."

"What's outside?"

"About twenty reporters and TV cameras," Shea said disgustedly. "What's going on?"

Nash said, "I'm going to be arrested."

Shea swore loudly enough to be heard by the lawyers in the front row. They were muttering to each other, looking back. "I can throw them out, Tim. I can get some guys up here and close the courtroom."

"They're federal marshals, Scotty."

"Fuck them," Shea said.

"Thanks for the thought," Nash said. He said to the courtroom, "Excuse me for a moment," and then to Vi, who stood just below him and had heard Shea's news, "Vi, call Dennis Terhune and tell him I need him to come over to my department right now. If he can't make it, tell him to come over to the county jail."

"Can't I do anything?" she whispered.

"The call will be fine. Please call my father, too."

She moved back to her office, glancing at the men sitting at the rear of the courtroom. She started to cry and it hurt Nash to have caused her any suffering.

Shea, still angrily resolute, stared at the marshals, as if to drive them away by sheer willpower. Nash pointed back at the tank doorway, and Shea reluctantly returned to it. Nash heard Vi's soft voice indistinctly as she spoke on the phone. He thought of Ben, who would find out on the news, at school, from Kim. He would have to explain it to Ben.

He wiped his sweating hands on his robe, sat up straighter. He had five cases to finish on this last morning calendar. As long as I sit here, on the bench, they won't do anything, he thought.

He said to the empty-faced little man still in the tank holding pen, "I'm sorry, Mr. Mansfield, the court had some personal business to take care of."

"Okay with me," Mansfield said.

Nash began reciting his sentence, hoping his voice wouldn't waver. He gave the man three years in state prison on both counts, the terms to run concurrently, and added another year for the prior conviction, also to run concurrently. He was explaining, in a tight and too stiff voice, the terms of parole when the courtroom doors opened again, the reporters pushing forward, lights focused into the audience, toward the bench. He saw Janice stand in the aisle briefly, then sit down beside a Latino family, away from the two patient marshals. She smiled at him gently.

At that instant, Nash was momentarily blinded by a white camera light and he blinked quickly, trying to see her again, to see any of them again, as he finished sentencing the little man, the tank door clanked again, and he called out another name.